"We know you are watching us," the note read. "Are you one of us? We really hope that you are, and we would like to meet you. If you are interested, we will be at the address below after seven this evening. We would love to meet you." The address was written at the bottom. There were no names on the card, or a return address, but the stationery was heavy and very expensive.

It was too good to be true! She was usually shy about meeting new people, but she was just dying to introduce herself to these two women who had turned her on so much.

PROVINCETOWN SUMMER/BAD HABITS

LINDSAY WELSH

BLUE MOON BOOKS
NEW YORK

Provincetown Summer/Bad Habits

Provincetown Summer copyright © 1992, 2005 by Lindsay Welsh
Bad Habits copyright © 1992, 2005 by Lindsay Welsh

Published by
Blue Moon Books
An Imprint of Avalon Publishing Group Incorporated
245 West 17th Street, 11th floor
New York, NY 10011-5300

First Blue Moon Books edition 2005

First published by Masquerade Books in 1992

ISBN 1-56201-452-8

9 8 7 6 5 4 3 2 1

Printed in Canada
Distributed by Publishers Group West

CONTENTS

PROVINCETOWN SUMMER

The streets of Provincetown are old and the buildings hug up to them the way I curve into Leslie's body late at night. The salt of the ocean water is the taste of her skin in the lazy, hot afternoons, with the fan revolving overhead and a glass of ice and lemon by the overstuffed sofa. The grass that grows up through the sand sways as gracefully as she does when she collects shells on the beach at low tide.

I sit on the sand and watch her with a hollow feeling in my chest. Her lovely small breasts move slightly under her thin shirt as she reaches down to pick up a shell. She comes down almost every day to collect shells at low tide, then returns to her studio where she turns them into exquisite little souvenirs for the tourists who come to Cape Cod each summer. They are extremely popular, and I can see why; they are as sensuous, as windswept, as much a part of the ocean and the beach as Leslie is. I see her moods in the bright strokes of paint she adorns the fragile shells with. In the winter, she paints stunning canvases, but it is the seashell trinkets, along with an occasional spot as a waitress or grasscutter when funds get low, that pay the rent and keep the refrigerator full.

Provincetown, Massachusetts is her year-round home, which is proudly announced on the bumper sticker that is probably the only part of her car that isn't rusty, to differentiate her from the tourists and the summer people who live on the tip of the Cape only when the weather is good. I am one of these. I come here each year in the late spring, with boxes of books and my trusty typewriter, from the small trailer park in Florida that is my home base. I love Provincetown with a passion. I love its weather-beaten gray houses, its clamshell-lined driveways, and especially the fact that I can be openly lesbian and not have to hide. My downfall is the winter here, when fierce icy storms rage across the sand dunes and the temperature drops to the point where cars—and I—won't start.

I cannot tolerate the winters, which seem to rejuvenate Leslie after a summer of heat and humidity. She thrives on the cold, and basks in the tight community spirit that fills the residents left behind when the throngs of summer people pack up and leave. So each fall we say good-bye, like college lovers, and I make my way back down the coast to the palm trees and the warm December days, when I can go outside in slippers and T-shirt to pick up my morning paper. Leslie remains behind, sending letters, painting pictures. I do not know if she has lovers when I am gone; I do not ask, and she does not ask me. But each spring, when I return to the apartment over the art gallery, which I have rented for the last seven years, we are just as if the winter had never happened, as if nothing had ever torn us apart.

I look out over the sleek sand, a sight not much different than that of my other home far away. Here, though, there is more for me. Barefoot, bent over, her creamy ass tight against her shorts, Leslie makes me want to run over the hard-packed sand and take her right there, in the salty foam and seaweed. I am on a high today; the book I have been slugging away at for almost a year is only a few days from completion.

The nights are a little cooler now, though, and the streets are not as crammed with tourists as they were in July. Leslie and I are both fiercely stubborn; she will not come to Florida, for she loves the different seasons, and I cannot remain here. Instead, we choose to fill our summers with intense, frequent lovemaking, if only for a short time, and go our separate ways when the long winter is inevitable.

Most of our friends think we are totally hopeless, and in the fall when I hold her tight and my tears spill out onto her hair, I think they are right. I wonder why I can't give in and spend the winter on the ice-bound cape. But the separation becomes a breathing space for us, and in spring when I return, feeling a little foolishly like the swallows, it is as if I have never left, and we continue our summer love just as feverishly as before.

Her bag filled with shells and stones, Leslie comes back from the water's edge. We get on our bicycles and return to town. She lives on the upper floor of an old frame house a few blocks from the commercial center of the town. The smallest room is her bedroom, the next largest a combination of living room and dining nook, with a tiny kitchen off to the side. The largest room, with one wall almost completely filled with wooden-framed windows, is her studio, which is always filled with a mishmash of completed painting, works in progress, seashells, glue, paintbrushes and a photograph of me, in a silver frame, on one wall. I am moved by the prominence of my picture, but in my orderly fashion, I can never figure out how on earth she turns out anything from the mess of materials that are cluttered on the tables and floor.

Even though we are together at some time almost daily, both of us need solitude to work, and when I write or she paints we leave each other alone. Hence the need for separate apartments, although it isn't uncommon that one of them is empty throughout the night. Sleeping with her and feeling her smooth, warm body pressed against mine is one of the joys I have with her, especially when we incorporate some sex into our morning coffee routine.

We put the bicycles on the porch and I follow her upstairs, enjoying the sight of her beautiful ass above me as she walks. She leaves the bag of shells sitting on the table and puts her arms around me. We kiss slowly, and she reaches under my shirt to run her fingers around my nipple. I push my tongue into her mouth, wanting more.

I kiss her throat, the back of her neck, the sweet spot by her earlobe, her silky eyelids and brush the tip of my tongue against her temples. I love to hold her like this. Her skin is still warm from the sun and tastes slightly salty, as if all the ocean has swept over her. I reach into the back pocket of her shorts to cup her firm ass cheeks, knowing how lovely they look naked and pressed up against me. She reaches down to hold my ass and we stand for the longest time, fingers kneading firm flesh, kisses planted on anything we can reach.

Leslie moves away, smiles at me and slowly, seductively, removes her shirt. She wears no bra, and her small, firm breasts cry out for attention. I sit her down in the overstuffed chair, then kneel before her.

My tongue finds her nipples instinctively. I love to suck them in, one at a time, then run my tongue slowly around each one while it's still between my lips. I bite them gently, pulling on them, nibbling at them, still flicking my tongue over the tender tip I hold between my teeth. I run my hands up and down her slim body, over her breasts, and down to tease the spot between her legs that feels warm and salty even through her shorts. I move back up to her lips, and she takes my fingers into her mouth, sucking at them, pushing her tongue between them. It makes me weak with desire for her.

I lean back, and she reaches down to help me pull off her shorts and panties. Her pussy is a lovely, sweet oasis between blonde-haired lips, and I could stare at it all day. I trace the designs of the folds with the tip of my tongue; she sighs, and I know so well the sweet electric tinglings that must be rising from my touch.

I probe with my tongue and hands, and my finger reaches the sweet nub of flesh at the top. Leslie groans. Quickly I replace my finger with my tongue. As always, she tastes both raspberry-sweet and salty at the same time, and I lap at the moist folds eagerly. She holds my head and pushes me deeper into her. I stick my tongue as far into her hole as I can, fucking her with it. Her hands in my hair set up a rhythm and soon my tongue is sopping with her lovely juices. My face is wet and all I can smell is the perfume of her nectar. I would love to drown in her pussy if I could.

I enjoy teasing her. I move up and lash my tongue over her clit, until I can feel her tighten up, ready to come. Then I return to her hole, lapping with long strokes, and she relaxes, moaning. I go back to her clit, kissing it, sucking at it, and again when I feel her getting close I leave it, so that she collapses in the chair, nearly at the edge of orgasm. Finally, after several long minutes of teasing her cunt, I go back to her clit and center all of my attention on it, licking, flicking, lapping.

I know Leslie's responses as well as I know my own. All of her muscles tighten, and even her toes curl up. She pushes her pussy against my face, rubbing herself on the tip of my tongue. My tongue and her sweet clit are one. When she comes, she is very vocal, crying out, pushing me into her, shaking. My own cunt is throbbing as I lick every last quiver out of her. I know exactly how good it felt.

Although she is still gasping for breath, she is on me in a moment, opening my shirt to reach my sex-swollen breasts. She knows how much I love to have them touched, and she leads me into the bedroom so that I can lie down. She takes forever on my tits. She kneads them, kisses them, licks at them, rubs them together, pushes them so that they touch and then licks the cleft in between. She knows my cunt is begging to be touched, but she refuses. Instead, she snakes her tongue down there, licks the insides of my thighs, and stops just inches away from my clit. It is my reward for teasing her, and she won't even allow me to brush my pussy with my hand for relief. Instead, she goes back to sucking my nipples and pushing her tongue into my mouth.

My skin is alive and on fire with each touch of her brilliant fingers and tongue. Leslie is an expert at lovemaking, and it is a joy just to lie back and submit to her will. She paints fanciful designs on my belly with her tongue, coming closer to my hot mound with each sweep.

When she finally touches my clit, I cry out with pleasure. She has somehow managed to focus my whole body on this point, and she shows me no mercy as she licks and sucks me. Her tongue is hot and wet between my legs, licking my clit, her hot breath playing on my aching skin. She pushes her finger into my hole as she licks me and begins moving it in and out, fucking me with her hand. It drives me wild and I cry for her to lick me harder. Her hand moves faster, her fingers deep inside me, her whole hand wet with my juice, her tongue lapping at me. My orgasm catches me by surprise. The wave of feeling moves right out to my toes and fingertips. When it is finished, I cannot bear to have her touch me. It is as if my skin is gone, and the nerves are on the edge of my flesh. Like her, I quiver and shake, and finally calm down in the loving circle of her arms.

The problem with making love in the early afternoon, of course, is that not much else gets done the rest of the day. With the cool sea breezes coming in through the window and both of us basking in our orgasms, we fall asleep in each other's arms. When I finally wake up, the shadows from the plants in the window are stretched long across the floor.

I try to get up without waking her, but it is no use; her enormous blue eyes open as soon as I sit up. I hold her tightly and kiss her beautiful lips. Our bodies are cooler now and it feels good to press against her, our breasts held tightly together, our pubic hair mingling. She brushes a lock of dark hair out of my eyes and kisses me again.

We dress and walk downstairs; I have offered to

treat for dinner. We walk along the house-lined street, hand in hand, and every now and again I stop to admire the front yards. In Provincetown, gardening seems to be a way of life, and almost every house is decorated with beautifully kept, colorful flower gardens. Their vibrant shades contrast sharply with my Florida home, where houses are more commonly landscaped with palms and shrubs. The colors remind me of Leslie, so vibrant and alive. She often paints the rich gardens and it seems as if she puts her soul into the colors too; one of her gardens hangs in my trailer where it brightens my isolated winter months.

We stop for dinner in one of the many open-air sidewalk restaurants. Over an aperitif she tells me about an idea she has for a new painting, and I feel a quick pang when I realize it will probably be finished and sold before I return in the spring. Many of her paintings are sold out of the gallery below my apartment, and when she is busy working I sometimes wander downstairs and study them. Like her seashell trinkets, I can see her in them: sensuous, earthy, firmly attached to this piece of land that juts sharply out into the bay. Her works are so unlike my writing, with its wanderlust, its ever-changing horizons.

Feeling like a tourist, I order a clambake dinner. I am still high from our afternoon sex, yet I want her again so badly my pussy throbs and I rub against the hard plastic chair. Still, I am tempered by the knowledge that our summer is coming to a close, and I know how hard it will be to say good-bye to her. I take out some of my frustration by cracking the steamed clamshells sharply in half, and breaking the lobster shell loudly with the steel crackers.

Leslie enjoys a much quieter dinner of crab cakes. Each time she lifts the fork to her lips, her tongue darts out first to meet it. I can feel myself getting wet and swollen at the sight, and I imagine that tongue in my mouth, in my pussy, against my hard, aching nipples.

She sees the look in my eyes, and reaches under the table to squeeze my knee. The tablecloth is very long and with a mischievous grin, she lightly runs her fingernails up and down my thigh, putting her finger under the edge of my shorts to tickle the skin underneath.

Gradually she moves her hand up further. My lobster is quickly forgotten. Under the cover of the tablecloth, she twists her hand to push my legs apart, then moves back and forth near my crotch in her lovely, teasing manner. I can hardly believe I'm sitting in a crowded restaurant with Leslie's hand near my cunt, and I pick up my wine glass and sip at it in a foolish attempt to look natural.

The waiter comes by and asks if everything is fine. Still with her impish grin, Leslie answers yes and at the same time, rubs her thumb over my swollen clit. The waiter glances up at my sharp intake of breath, but I smile and nod at him. I am relieved when he moves away to another table. Leslie winks at me, like a schoolgirl playing a prank, and takes a forkful of her dinner. Meanwhile, her other hand is busy teasing and stroking my throbbing pussy.

She starts rubbing my clit right through my shorts, which are very thin, and I can feel each flicker of her finger over me. I am having a hard time holding still. I want to writhe on her hand, squirm in the seat, push her hand against myself and hold it tight to me. Leslie knows this, and she is having a grand time watching me trying vainly to control my movements. I warn her that she will be teased without mercy for this. She only laughs and increases the motion on my hot button.

I can feel the heat from my belly right down to my

thighs. Leslie plays me like an instrument, knowing just when to rub hard and when to pull back and gently caress. Any attempt at sipping my wine is forgotten. I feel as if the whole restaurant must know what's going on, but I'm beyond caring. All that matters is my lover's hand touching me. I tighten up, so close, so close, and then the hot, sweet wave rises up out of my pussy and moves up my spine in a rapid, blissful sweep. I bite my tongue to keep from crying out as I come. Leslie's hand rubs every last wave out of my cunt, and I can feel that my shorts are soaked with my hot juice.

I struggle to pull myself together. Playing the saint, but with a canary-swallowing grin, Leslie is now eating her carrots, the picture of poise and manners. Orgasms always relax me and I seem to need all of my strength just to lift my hands and finish eating my dinner. Luckily for me the lobster is done, for the effort would have been far too much to handle. The potato is work enough at this stage.

When coffee comes, Leslie orders a slice of cheesecake, and is right back at it again, nibbling at it and running her tongue over the fork when she slides it out of her mouth. She is an angel to me; no woman I have ever met loves sex as much as she does, or makes me want her more. When we are together, I feel as if our only purpose on earth is to love and satisfy each other.

It is dusk by the time we finally finish. The streetlights are on and the shop windows are lit up, all of them open until very late to catch the tourist trade. The streets are alive with people walking along the sidewalks and up the middle of the narrow, one-way street. We decide it is too nice a night to let slip away, and we go for a stroll ourselves.

Provincetown was built for walking. Cars defer to

pedestrians here, and drivers will usually follow a group of walkers slowly down the road rather than honk and demand that they move. Bicycles are of course another matter, and Leslie and I check carefully for any before we cross over the street. The sidewalks are wide and couples walk arm in arm, men with men, women with women, women with men. There is an easy summer feel to the place, mixed with an almost overwhelming sexual satisfaction. On a warm night like this, it feels as if everyone in town is going to be happily fucked before dawn, no matter what their preference.

We stop off in the bookstore, where both of us buy a couple of volumes. We chat for a while with the shopkeeper, who knows us well—both of us seem to spend half our income on books. When we leave, we run into another pair of friends who invite us to a nearby bar for a drink.

The bar is cool and dark, with jazz playing quietly on the sound system. I am torn in my desire; I enjoy sitting and talking with our friends, but I am dying to get home and pay Leslie back for making me come in the restaurant. As we are sitting down, I brush against her and take advantage of the opportunity to tweak her nipple. She gives me a sultry smile across the table and I know she is just as eager to be paid back.

We order a carafe of wine. Our friends are a bit older than we are, two women who have lived together in Provincetown for years. Leslie sees them frequently over the winter, and often has dinner with them. As for me, they are two of the people I am sorry to leave when I make my trip back south.

As we talk, I can't keep my eyes off Leslie. A year younger than me, her blonde hair is bleached almost white from the hours of scouring the beaches for shells. She has the lovely outdoorsy look of people who live with hot summers, icy winters and the relentless tides. Her breasts are small and firm; I can still feel her nipple hot under my fingers. Her legs are long, her feet thrust into well-worn sandals. She still wears her thin shorts, and my eyes trace up the lines of her bare thighs to where they meet at her honey-rich, blonde pussy. I can picture how beautiful it looks, and I long to be there, rubbing my fingers, licking with my tongue....

I feel a hand on my arm, and realize that I have been spoken to but am off in my sexual dream world. All three of them laugh. I explain that I'm tired because of long nights pummeling my book into shape, but Leslie smiles knowingly at me. It's not much of a secret, what I'm actually thinking about.

It seems to take forever for the wine to be finished. I engage in conversation, but all the time, my mind is riveted on making love to my Leslie. Two women at a nearby table lean over it so close that their faces touch and they kiss gently; below the table they have their hands on each other's legs. I want desperately to touch Leslie like that. I can taste her juices in my mouthful of wine. In the midst of conversation she reaches over to take my hand, to make a point. Her warm skin is electric on mine.

Finally the wine is finished, and we beg off, explaining that I need some sleep. We kiss them good-bye and head back down the busy street to my apartment. On the way I lean over for a quick kiss, which turns passionate very quickly. Leslie is just as much in need as I am. We duck into a narrow alley-way between two stores. Her tongue is in my mouth immediately, probing and pressing against mine as hard as she can. She takes my hand and guides it between her legs. I can feel her wetness through her shorts, and her flesh seems on fire. She moans and rubs against my hand, her fingers on my breasts through my shirt. We grope like two sex-starved teenagers, kissing, feeling, grabbing each other with only one thing in mind. Reluctantly, I break away and take her hand, pulling her quickly along the crowded sidewalks. I can't get home fast enough, and Leslie keeps up with me.

There is a pleasant surprise waiting. The art gallery has rearranged its window, and one of Leslie's paintings hangs in front. It is a vibrant nude woman, her full breasts tipped with pink erect nipples, her hand gently exploring the dark triangle between her legs. The face is very abstract, but Leslie told me that she painted it while thinking of me. Seeing it out in the open, studied carefully by the people in the street who stop to look at it, makes me even hotter. I want to proudly tell them that it is my Leslie's work, that it is our wonderful sex set down in oils for everyone to admire.

I unlock the door and we go up the stairs, stopping halfway up for another long, passionate kiss. Usually I stop at my desk each time I enter the apartment, if only for a few moments, to proofread a page or add a couple of lines to the sheet that's always in the typewriter. This time, I ignore all of it.

We undress each other. Leslie comes up behind me and hugs me tightly. Her hands reach for me. Her right hand cups my breast. Her left hand moves down and her finger fits perfectly into the groove of my pussy lips. She plants delicate kisses on my neck while she fingers me. I reach behind and grab her ass cheeks, pulling her sweet mound close to my body. I can feel her heat from here.

She leads me to the bed. I make her lie face down on the comforter and kneel beside her. She loves to have her back rubbed as a prelude to sex. I start at her neck, rubbing gently, feeling her sweet skin move beneath my fingers. Gradually I work my way down her spine, kneading the soft flesh around her shoulders. Every now and again I bend down and trace the curve of her spine with my tongue, burying deep in the indentation just above her ass. She sighs and begs me to touch her pussy, but I tease her instead by just brushing the blonde hairs around it.

When I reach her ass, I spend a long time kneading her firm, creamy cheeks. Then I lean down and gently tongue the cleavage between them. She moans and lifts her hips to meet me. I brush her soft pussy hair again, this time with my tongue. As a final tease, I lick just once over her hot, wet cunt. She groans and rolls over, begging me to make her come.

It's too soon for that. Her beautiful tits are now facing me, and I waste no time in getting to them. I lick and suck at them, then push my own against them. Rubbing my nipples against hers gets both of us even hotter, and my pussy is throbbing with a will of its own.

She moans and kneads my breasts, and we deep-kiss for a long time, holding each other's nipples and rolling them between our fingers. Her touch sends hot shivers through me. I reach down and cup her steamy pussy in my hand.

Leslie pushes against my hand, trying to brush her clit against me. I touch the hot button quickly, brushing it with the tips of my fingers. She moans. She knows how to get to me, and plays with my nipples until I can't control myself any longer. I reach down and sink my tongue into her gorgeous cunt.

Immediately she bucks her hips up to push her clit against my tongue. Her pussy is as sweet as always. I take my time, using the very tip of my tongue to run under her soft folds all the way around to her lovely clit and hole.

She pulls at me, and I stop long enough to move over and straddle her lips with my own hot cunt. We both love "sixty-nine," and waste no time in feasting on each other. I like it because I am so busy concentrating on eating her, it takes a while for me to come and I can enjoy the achingly beautiful buildup even longer.

I am sure the gallery patrons below can hear us, we are moaning and lapping so loudly. For a while Leslie mirrors all of my actions. When I slow down and circle her pussy, she does the same to mine. Flicking my tongue hard across her clit brings the same hot flashes across my own. It is almost as if I am eating myself.

There is a new sensation now; Leslie's fingers are deep in my cunt, her tongue still on my clit. I love the full feeling, the way her thumb moves to brush against the folds of skin. I do the same to her. Her tight tunnel is soaked and feverishly hot. I fuck her with my fingers while I concentrate my tongue on her swollen clit.

Both of us madly enjoy our lickfest a little while longer. Then Leslie asks me to move down on the bed, which I do. Her hair dishevelled and her pussy wetly glistening, she positions herself opposite me, her legs crossed scissor-style over mine. Our two pussies touch and she begins to rub against me.

I push hard to match her frantic motions. I pull myself up on my pillow so I can see, and it's gorgeous. My own dark triangle grinds against her blonde one, clits nestled together, juices flowing. I love the scratchy feeling of her hair against me. She pushes hard and I gasp.

We start a regular rhythm. Hips bucking, soft

pussies grinding into each other, we moan and gasp at the waves of pleasure that course through our bodies. Her leg is stretched along my body and I take her foot, planting kisses on it. I push my tongue between her toes and she moans, grinding even harder. I match her movements.

We are moving so fast and hard I expect our cunts to burst into flame. Mine is already on fire, heating me, tongues of flame moving up my spine as her sweet bush crushes me. Both of us are sitting up now, taking in the beautiful sight of two cunts pressing together, dark and light hair, creamy asses, outstretched legs.

Leslie moves frantically and begins to cry out. She comes violently, her juices flooding my pussy. I have never felt so wet. She moans and shivers, enjoying every last wave, pushing against me. I get even hotter watching her come.

She waits for only a moment, then gracefully pulls away from me and kneels before my cunt, spreading my legs. Her practiced fingers begin to stroke my pussy. Her hand feels as good as her hot cunt did against my flesh.

She rubs faster and faster, her finger slipping over my soaked clit. Then she slips two fingers inside my hole, while her thumb expertly rubs the swollen button. She is a master, sliding in and out of my cunt, rubbing me, while her free hand reaches up to knead my breast.

I can't believe how intense my orgasm is. I seem to come from the very tips of my toes, and Leslie rides me out. Her thumb plays out all of it, until I am weak and gasping. Then she is in my arms, kissing my face, cupping my tender pussy with her hand.

I return her kiss. I can't believe how much I love her and how good she makes me feel. We lie together on the bed, our bodies covered in sweat and pussy juice. The smell of sex is heavy in the air.

Through the open window I can hear people talking as they walk by on the sidewalk. I wonder if anyone heard our loud lovemaking. I like to think that they did.

Gently, Leslie kisses me on the lips, then snuggles down within the curve of my arm, her head resting on my shoulder. One finger absently traces circles around my nipple. I turn my head and gently kiss her forehead.

There is no question of her staying the night; I am not about to let go of her right now. She pulls the light cover over us, since neither of us seems to have the strength to get up and close the window. We say a silent prayer to the inventor of the remote control, as I click on the small television that sits atop a bookshelf. We reject a talk show, a half-hour commercial for car wax and a police drama, and finally settle on my favorite movie, *Casablanca*, already halfway through. No matter, it's worth watching from any point. We both admit that we love Ingrid Bergman's clothes, sultry eyes and beautifully full, kissable lips, and not necessarily in that order.

Unfortunately, I miss my opportunity to see Bogie put her on the plane, for the next thing I know the early morning sunlight is streaming through the window and Leslie is clattering cups in my cramped kitchen. She kisses me good morning and deposits a cup of strong black coffee on the nightstand beside me.

Always an early riser, she is dressed with her cup of coffee half finished. She hugs me tightly and tells me she has to get home to finish a piece that the gallery is waiting for. My heart sinks when I hear the door close behind her, for the breeze coming through the open window has an end-of-season chilly touch to it.

I smooth the bed, pull on my jeans and take my coffee to the typewriter. Just after one o'clock, I am finished. Once again I am filled with the same conflicting emotions that I always feel when I start to pack a book for shipping to the publisher: elation that it's finally finished, but an emotional drain knowing that the work I've been doing for so long is over.

I call Leslie to tell her, but I get her answering machine. When she is working she turns it all the way down so that she can't hear the messages. I tell her there will be victory champagne later, then I wrap the book carefully for mailing and address it.

I walk into the downtown center with the precious parcel in my arms. The breeze is coming in over the ocean heavily, and it feels like rain, but I don't care. I mail the book inside the huge old post office building, then continue walking until I am out of town, up at the sand dunes that separate the waves from the road.

There is another couple walking along the beach, two women, arm in arm. I sit down on the soft sand and watch them. They stop to look at the sky and the waves, to pick up shells on the sand. They are an older couple, gray-haired but moving as gracefully as women half their age. They obviously know each other well, their motions complementing each other, their steps matching. I can see Leslie and myself together that way in twenty years, moving with the comfortable rhythm of people who understand each other perfectly.

Eventually the women gather their bicycles and walk back to the road, nodding a hello to me as they pass. I get up and walk down to the water's edge, catching a glimpse of a shell half-buried. I pick it up and rinse it in the ripple of water that moves up close to me. I know Leslie would like it, and I slip it into my pocket.

The air is very heavy and by the time I walk back to the road, there is a thin drizzle falling. In the way of seaside storms, it grows into heavy rain very quickly. There is no point in hurrying, and so I walk back toward the town with the rain beating down on me, my clothes soaked and sticking to my skin. When it runs down my face it feels like tears.

The rain is still falling steadily when I get back to my apartment. Leslie has obviously heard my message on her machine, for she is inside the gallery, looking through the open door and talking to the owner. She tells me to hurry up and get inside to some dry clothes.

It is difficult to peel the wet jeans off. When I do, I remember the shell, and I give it to Leslie, who is fascinated with it. She has already started to run a hot bath for me. I slip into the steaming tub, filled with richly scented bubbles; the hot water on my cold clammy skin is almost erotic.

When the bathwater starts to cool, Leslie comes back in. She holds a large fluffy bathtowel and I let her dry me off, almost purring with the luxury. Finally she wraps me in my sinfully thick terrycloth robe and we go into the kitchen.

She has brought steaks for dinner. Although the kitchen is tiny we work well together, like trained chefs. I boil rice while she washes vegetables and arranges the steaks on the broiling pan.

When dinner is on the table, I open the champagne bottle with a flourish and pour two glasses. We toast the book, then eat our dinners. Leslie tells me about her painting, which is almost finished, and I promise another bottle of champagne.

After dinner we clear the table and I run hot water into the sink. But before I can start washing dishes, I feel Leslie come up behind me and slip her arms around my waist. I turn, and meet her open-mouthed, sweet kiss.

The dishes are instantly forgotten as she unties my robe and opens it. Her hand slips down expertly to my breasts and fondles my nipples. I moan and kiss at her mouth, my hand slipping between her legs to feel her pussy through her jeans.

She breaks away and leads me into the bedroom. The familiar bed is inviting and we lie down together, kissing deeply and smoothing our hands over each other's creamy soft skin. I want to get inside her, in her mouth, in her pussy, under her skin, I love her and want her so much.

She is down and working my pussy over before I even realize it. The warmth from her wet tongue radiates through my thighs and up my spine. She licks me slowly, carefully, as if I am ice cream or a forbidden sweet treat. It is as hot and intense as the warm bathwater on my cold skin.

I can only groan and go limp with the pleasure. I let the delicious feeling of Leslie's tongue in my pussy take me over. She licks my thighs and the outer lips of my cunt, then zeros in on my clit with just the very tip of her tongue. Her touch is as light as her warm breath on me, and it tickles wonderfully, like she is stroking me with a feather.

She alternates for a while, rubbing my pussy with her fingers, then licking me slowly with her tongue. I love the motion of her hand, soft yet firm on my throbbing, wet clit, followed by the fluid movements of her swift tongue. I could lie back and take this for hours, it feels so good. She knows it, and she laps at me with long wet strokes from my hole right up to my clit. I shudder with each juicy sweep.

Leslie sits up for a moment and reaches for the glass of chilled champagne she has brought into the bedroom with her. She takes a mouthful and holds it for a moment, then swallows and returns to my aching pussy.

I gasp at the first touch of her icy tongue. Delicious little shivers course through me. I can hardly believe the sensation, her cold tongue and her hot breath mingling together on my cunt. Gradually her tongue warms up, and I cry for more. She takes another sip of the pale golden wine, and once again I am treated to her sweet cold tongue and warm breath, icy-hot between my legs.

My own mouth wants her now, to share this new feeling. Reluctantly she stops and stretches out in front of me. I take a sip from her glass, then move down to the blonde pussy that I want so very badly. Like me, she moans at the fiercely cold movement on her erect little button, and she asks for seconds when my tongue warms up again on her beautiful clit.

I sip more champagne, then bend down to her beautiful pussy. I can't get enough of her. I lick her pussy lips, nibble her clit gently. She moans and pushes against my tongue. I know from experience just what she likes best, and I give it to her, little butterfly kisses on her clit, my tongue stuck deep into her hole.

I want to make her come. I concentrate on her clit now, my tongue pressed against it. I can feel her excitement as she runs her fingers through my hair and pushes me deep into her sweet lips. Faster and faster I lick her, while she gasps and squirms on the bed. Finally she cries out with her release, her hips moving as I push my tongue into her.

Leslie begs me to kiss her, so that she can taste her

juices on my tongue. I move up on the bed and hold her close, kissing her and sharing what I have done with her. It is like sharing a beautiful intimate secret.

My own pussy is still throbbing sharply. As we kiss, Leslie's hand strays to it, and I moan at the first touch of her fingers. She plays with me, still kissing me. Our breasts are pressed tightly together and I love her hard nipples so close to mine.

She asks me to kneel over her. I do, positioning my pussy over her lips. She reaches up and grabs my ass cheeks, pulling me down to her mouth. The touch of her tongue on my swollen clit is magical.

She knows me as well as I know her. She licks the spots that excite me the most and then, when I am built up and almost overcome with the sensation, she concentrates on a less sensitive area. As always she loves to tease and on this afternoon she is doing a magnificent job.

Finally she flicks her tongue hard on my clit, the movement that she knows will make me come. It doesn't take long to build up the pressure that I feel just before orgasm. Leslie licks faster and the waves roll through my legs and belly, hot tingling flashes that are just heavenly.

I move down on the bed beside her, and we snuggle in together under the light blanket. It seems as if we have spent all of our time in bed the last few days. Leslie quickly agrees that it doesn't seem to be a bad way to pass the time.

I hold her tightly in the half-lit room. We listen to the rain beating on the roof and the thunder that crashes overhead occasionally. I remember as a child lying in bed and feeling very secure and comfortable in my warm bed with the sounds of the rain outside. Holding Leslie close to me, I feel as content as I did then.

Gently, Leslie kisses me on the lips, then burrows

down within the curve of my arm, her head resting on my shoulder. One finger absently traces circles around my nipple. I turn my head and kiss her forehead.

We hold each other very tightly, as if nothing could tear us apart. From below, we can hear the faint, muffled voices of people in the gallery, but we have no desire to join the outside world right now. For the moment, we are complete, lying together in the bed.

We talk for a long time, punctuating with tiny kisses. She tells me that she has always wanted to visit Disneyworld, and likes the idea of eating vine-ripened tomatoes in the middle of December.

I tell her I am thinking about setting my next book in a seaside town in the dead of winter. She listens carefully. We know we are both telling the truth.

BIRTHDAY GIFTS

Sylvia's birthday was the day after Valentine's Day. I always made sure that there was a little gift for both days, but I always thought she was like a child born on Christmas with her birthday overshadowed. There was always the second present to remind her, and it was impossible to find a quiet restaurant since most were filled with couples around that time. It also seemed strange to receive a Valentine gift from her so close to her birthday. I always felt that she should be the only one receiving presents.

This year, our fifth Valentine's together, I was determined to make two very special days for her to celebrate. Fortunately, they fell on Saturday and

Sunday, and I planned a retreat for both of us from work, the house, and the telephone that always seemed to be ringing off the wall.

I planned the weekend very carefully. I selected three nights at a fine, full-service hotel in the middle of the city. That way, if we didn't want to venture outside in the cold, we could enjoy the pool, the sauna, the first-class restaurant and even some quiet room service. I also made sure it was close to the lively theater strip, and I booked Friday-night tickets for a play along with late-night dinner reservations at Sylvia's favorite Italian restaurant.

Then came the problem of a gift. I didn't have a clue what to buy her, until I sat and read the daily paper. Tucked into a corner, amid all the ads for flower shops and candy stores, was a picture of a gorgeous woman with the address of a store selling sex toys. I immediately knew what Sylvia was going to be unwrapping!

The store wasn't huge, but it was crammed with goodies. I was overwhelmed by the selection—bottles of oil, vibrators in all different sizes and shapes, chrome ben-wah balls, nipple jewelry, lingerie, leather restraints, unusually-shaped candies. I hardly knew where to begin.

Fortunately, the shop owner was more than happy to help. She had several suggestions for a lesbian couple hoping to enjoy a dream weekend, and when I left, I was several dollars lighter, but I had a bag containing a bottle of flavored lotion, a vibrator and a large dildo with a harness.

I surprised Sylvia when she came home from work on Friday afternoon. I gave her a card outlining everything that was planned. I thought she would be excited, but I could never have guessed how much she loved the idea of our special weekend away for two. As excited as two schoolgirls, we packed small suitcases, then got ready to go.

As usual, it didn't work out quite the way we planned. When I came out of the shower, the towel wrapped around me, Sylvia was waiting outside the door. Ever so gently, she kissed me on the lips, then pressed her tongue inside.

The towel dropped as I met her deep kiss. Her hands were on my breasts, kneading and tugging at my erect nipples, and I moaned and reached for her under her shirt. She leaned back and took it off, exposing the beautiful, chocolate-brown tits that I just loved to suck on.

I wasted no time in doing just that. Sylvia groaned as I licked and sucked each one slowly, pulling the nipples out gently between my teeth. Then I led her into the bedroom and helped her off with her skirt and panties.

At her urging I got on top of her, my pussy over her lips, her sweet hole below mine. In seconds we were into a hot sixty-nine. I could have spent all night lapping at her sweet rich cunt, and by the sounds of it, she was certainly having fun giving me the same type of tongue-lashing on my hot, swollen clit.

Sylvia got wetter and hotter the more I drove my tongue into her pussy. I sucked in her juices, licking her from top to bottom with long strokes. She was giving my clit all she had, sending ripples of pleasure through my legs and belly. She knew how to eat pussy, and was giving a wonderful performance.

I matched her motions, sucking and licking her clit. It was tough to do because she was bucking wildly, just as I was. Both of us were in a frenzy, grinding our pussies down onto each other's tongues, trying to lick each other as hard as we could. It felt so good to have her hot tongue between my pussy lips. I knew how good my own tongue must have felt in her cunt.

Even the sounds were turning me on—the moans from both of us, and the wet licking-noises as we ate each other out. I was getting so excited. I seemed to be surrounded everywhere by pussy juice and the beautiful smell of hot sex.

I couldn't help myself. My muscles tightened up and the white-hot sparks moved from my pussy up my spine. As Sylvia pushed her tongue into my cunt, I exploded. Moaning and thrashing my clit on her tongue, I kept my own still on her hot button. Moments later she came, too, pushing up to meet my mouth. She seemed to shiver and come for the longest time.

It also seemed to take the longest time to calm down from our explosive orgasms. It felt so good lying totally relaxed in my Sylvia's arms, and I could have happily stayed that way forever. However, Sylvia was a bit more realistic than I was, and she reminded me that we risked missing the play if we didn't get moving.

We dressed quickly. Sylvia wore my favorite dress, a gorgeous gold silk one that showed off her firm breasts, with a short skirt that let me see her beautiful legs. She spent several hours at the gym each week, and her gorgeous body showed the results. I could look at her for hours. Her thighs were firm, her belly was flat, and her tight skin was flawless. I exercised as well, but I didn't have quite the resolve that Sylvia did. I was fonder of sitting with a book than of pumping iron. Still, the little bit I did kept me in decent shape, and Sylvia loved to run her hands over my slightly rounder curves and softer skin. We were well suited for each other, and loved each other dearly.

Our first stop was the hotel. The doorman held

the taxi door open for us, and it seemed as if we were stepping into another world. The brightly lit façade was all 1920s art deco, and we walked to the huge glass doors along a red carpet that stretched across the sidewalk. Inside, the glorious old building was completely refurbished, and the lobby was an enormous, thickly-carpeted room filled with overstuffed couches and wing chairs. Dark paneling was illuminated by the enormous crystal chandelier that hung from the ceiling several stories above. I felt as if I had stepped into a movie.

Once we had registered, we walked toward the elevator. Sylvia insisted on a quick detour, and soon we were peeking into a thoroughly modern pool and exercise room, much to her delight. I knew I would have at least a couple of hours poolside while she checked out the fitness equipment, and was grateful for the thick book I had tucked into my bag and the bar I saw in the corner.

We went to our room. Like the lobby, it was opulently decorated, with old-fashioned rose wallpaper, mahogany trim, and a huge king-sized bed with thick pillows. The television and tiny refrigerator were hidden inside a huge carved wooden cabinet. The room was finished with a comfortable loveseat, two huge wing chairs, and a small table.

To my delight and Sylvia's surprise, I saw that the hotel had remembered the chilled bottle of champagne I had ordered. It was sitting in a silver ice bucket on the little table, and when we had hung up our clothes, we sat down in the matching wing chairs and poured two glasses.

"A toast to us," I proposed, and Sylvia touched my glass. The champagne slipped down like silk.

"I know it's early," I continued, "but your gift this year is something you might want to open before the end of the weekend." I slipped the brightly-wrapped present out of the corner of my suitcase and placed it before her.

Sylvia smiled. "I have a Valentine's present for you, too," she admitted. "I know it isn't until tomorrow, but this is the kind of gift that you won't want to wait for."

I made her open her present first. The look on her face was worth all of the time spent shopping. She was delighted with the vibrator and the nipple lotion, but was absolutely enthralled with the dildo and harness. Promising that she would make good use of all three before the weekend was over, she urged me to open my gift. She had a knowing smile on her face.

I removed the wrapping paper. Inside, from the same store I had purchased her gifts from, was a double-headed dildo. I was fascinated. I had seen them in the store and was turned on by the idea, but I didn't know if Sylvia would be interested as well. Knowing that she was made me want to forget the play and dinner and try it out right then. I told her how excited I was.

Sylvia smiled and poured another glass of champagne for us. "We'll leave all these toys here and think about them when we're out," she said. "Just imagine how hot we're going to be when we come back."

I reluctantly agreed, and knew that my pussy was going to be throbbing all the time I was out. I did get back at her, though, by reaching over and kissing Sylvia deeply. I then put my hand under her short skirt and rubbed her soft pussy through her thin panties until she closed her eyes and sighed. I could feel her flesh getting hotter and hotter. Just when I could feel her panties start to get moist, I sat back in my chair and concentrated on my champagne. She started to protest, until I reminded her that we were even. She laughed and agreed.

We corked the half-empty bottle of champagne, freshened our makeup, and went downstairs. We decided to walk, since the night wasn't very cold, and because we were early we stopped in a Japanese restaurant for a little something to tide us over until dinner.

Sitting at the sushi bar was almost torture, and the night had only begun. Perched on the small chair, toying with a tiny cup of sake, I could feel my pussy burning as I thought of the presents that were waiting back in the room for us. It was even more difficult every time I looked at her. Her chopsticks slid smoothly between her gorgeous lips, just as my nipples did when she sucked on them. Her graceful hands holding the tiny ceramic sake cup were just as suited to making me come by rubbing on my fiery clit. Under her dress I knew the curve of her breasts, the way her nipples got hard when I touched them. Sylvia was very beautiful and she drew glances from around the sushi bar. I almost felt weak at the knowledge that she belonged to me.

The theater was just as difficult. I concentrated so hard on my throbbing pussy that I barely noticed the plot. When the waiter seated us for our late dinner, I was afraid I was going to go right over the table for Sylvia's beautiful body. She had been right; I was cooking myself into a frenzy, waiting to get back to the hotel to try out our new toys. The food was delicious as always, but I was never so glad to see the check come. Rather than spend time walking back, we hailed a taxi outside the restaurant.

We got on the hotel elevator with another couple, who got off several floors before our own. As soon as the elevator door closed again, Sylvia turned to me and whispered, "I could barely keep my hands off you all night!" Immediately we were locked in a deep kiss, her hand straying up to hold my breast. Finally we were at our floor.

Inside the room, Sylvia played a maddeningly slow game of undressing me. Each button of my dress was undone, and then Sylvia's tongue carefully traced designs on the skin underneath. When my dress was off, she spent several minutes kissing my neck and throat before moving down to unhook my bra. When that was off, she lavished all her attention on my nipples, which were as hard as rocks. I felt weak as she sucked at them and gently nibbled on them with her teeth.

When I was completely naked, it was her turn. I kissed and sucked at every inch of smooth, dark skin I uncovered. When all of her clothes were in a pile on the chair, I made her lie down on the bed and opened the bottle of flavored lotion.

It was thick and creamy on my fingers, and I rubbed it into her nipples. She moaned and told me the lotion was getting hot. I quickly found out, when I bent over to lick her beautiful tits, that indeed it was. A gorgeous warmth flooded my mouth as I took my Sylvia's nipples between my lips.

Sylvia got up and anointed my nipples with the strawberry-flavored liquid. It was a lovely warmth, and even more so when Sylvia lay on her back and instructed me to lean over her face. I could now suck and knead on her breasts while my own hung above her lips. For the longest time we stayed in this mini-sixty-nine, lavishing attention on each other's nipples. Every now and again I would reach down and run my fingers over Sylvia's hot pussy, and she would moan and suck on my nipples until I thought I would almost come.

Getting up, I poured some of the strawberry lotion on my fingers and slowly rubbed it into the lips around Sylvia's pussy, and the insides of her thighs. Soon she was basking in the warmth, and I leaned down and slowly licked the smooth skin of her legs, moving in to her inner thighs and her beautiful pussy. She groaned and begged me to lick her clit, but I kept my achingly slow pace.

I ran my tongue over her pussy lips, breathing hard on her clit and occasionally brushing my tongue lightly over it. Each time she moaned and begged to be eaten. I kept teasing her, then finally began to lick her beautiful cunt.

She let out a loud moan of delight. Her pussy was just as naturally sweet as the strawberry lotion, and I couldn't get enough. I pushed my tongue into her hole and fucked her with it, then rolled her clit between my tongue and my lips. I was so hot myself I reached between my legs and fingered my own pussy. The sight of Sylvia on her back with her legs spread for me, the honey taste of her pussy, her squeals of pleasure were too much for me. I rubbed my clit hard and licked her.

Sylvia held my head, pushing my tongue deep into her pussy. I licked harder and faster, all the time rubbing my own clit hard. My fingers were soaked with my own juices, and my face was wet from Sylvia's nectar. Both of us were moving, pushing our pussies up and down.

We came at almost the same time. It was difficult to lick Sylvia when the hot waves moved through me, but seconds later she cried out and pulled me deep into her cunt.

It was one of the most intense I'd ever had. I collapsed in Sylvia's arms on the huge bed, panting. She was just as weak from hers as I was. We held each other tightly until we both calmed down. It was late, so we slipped under the smooth cotton sheets and switched the bedside light off. The bed was very comfortable and the pillows luxuriously fluffy, and I fell asleep almost immediately.

We were awakened in the morning by a quick rap at the door. It was our breakfast, hot croissants and coffee, with a pot of preserves on the side. I had never felt so pampered before. We opened the curtains and moved the chairs close to the window, so we could watch the city streets below while enjoying our meal. Sylvia was fascinated with the view and as I looked at her profile, holding her cup of coffee while the weak winter sun played on her face, I didn't think I had ever seen her look more beautiful.

When breakfast was finished, I went into the bathroom and prepared for my shower. As with most hotels where I'd stayed, the water pressure wasn't fantastic, but at least it was good and hot. I stepped under the stream and closed my eyes to wet my face.

Suddenly I felt familiar hands on me. Sylvia was in the shower with me, running her fingers up and down my wet body. We kissed under the shower head, the water pouring down our faces and making our kiss even steamier.

The weekend away had turned us both insatiable. Within moments, our hands were in each other's pussies.

Sylvia reached around the shower curtain for the thick terry washcloth. It was a fairly large one, and she soaked it under the shower head, doubled it over, and draped it over her hand. Then she rubbed it between my legs.

Sparks went off. The rough fabric tickled my clit like I'd never felt before. I moaned, and held her tightly to me, kissing her while she rubbed with the cloth. I was so hot my tongue was almost down her throat and I wanted to go even deeper.

Deftly she turned us around so that I was under the shower head. The hot water streamed down my body as Sylvia kissed me, one hand rubbing my nipple, the other sending hot rushes through my pussy with the washcloth.

It didn't take long. I had never come standing up before, and I didn't think I could do it. But the beautiful burning in my pussy quickly spread through my whole body and I cried out. It was so intense I had to get out of the shower; between my orgasm and the hot steamy water, I thought I would faint.

I dried off while Sylvia finished her shower. When she was done, I dried her with the huge, fluffy bath towel. "Now it's your turn," I said, teasing her dark pussy by rubbing gently with the towel. I led her out of the bathroom and made her sit in one of the wing chairs. "It's time to try out your new toy," I said, taking the vibrator out of its box.

It was dildo-shaped, long and thin with a smooth head and ribs down the sides. It made a low buzzing sound when I turned it on, and it had a dial for different speeds. I set it on low, and knelt before my wonderful Sylvia, sitting in the chair with her legs apart, her pussy still moist from the shower.

I started on the insides of her thighs, moving the vibrator closer and closer to her pussy. Still on the low speed, I traced around her hairy lips with the tip. She murmured her approval.

I moved toward her clit, turning the vibrator on higher. She closed her eyes and moved lower in the chair so that I could touch all of her pussy with the humming wand. When I touched her clit she moaned.

I moved it all over her pussy, turning up the dial slowly. She was squirming on the chair, enjoying every second of it. "Put it inside me," she begged, and I spread her beautiful lips with my fingers and gently pressed the tip inside.

Deeper and deeper I pushed it in, then pulled it back. I fucked her with it, rubbing her clit with my finger at the same time. "Faster, please!" she moaned, and I rubbed hard on her hot button while pushing the vibrator deep into her tunnel.

Her orgasm exploded. Thrashing on the chair, she pushed my hand so the vibrator was right inside her. Moaning, crying out, she shivered violently for the longest time. When I finally turned the vibrator off and pulled it out, shiny with her juices, she was slumped in the chair, breathing heavily and smiling at me.

After deciding how we were going to spend our day, we got dressed and went downstairs to walk along the crowded streets and visit some of the interesting shops. We seldom went into that area, and it was like exploring a whole new city. There had been a lot of renovations since our last visit, and most of the old, run-down storefronts had been turned into brand new stores, some of them elegant and expensive, a few quirky and filled with offbeat items. It was fascinating and before we knew it, it was noon. We stopped into a small deli and enjoyed heaping corned beef sandwiches and hot, homemade soup.

Gradually we made our way back to the hotel. Sylvia was eager to try out the exercise room, and we gathered our suits and made our way down to the pool. She changed into her leotards and went off to the huge room. Its glass wall faced the pool and I could see her inside, sweating and puffing as she jogged on the treadmill. I smiled, took a sip from the cold glass of white wine on the little table beside me, and stretched out on the comfy lounge chair with my book.

Still, I couldn't help sneaking glances every now and again over the top of my book. Sylvia tried out all of the equipment, her skin glistening, her muscles taut under her leotard. She was magnificent. At one point, I noticed that a pair of businessmen walking past the pool stopped and watched her as she moved up and down on the stair-climber. I was almost overcome with pride and the knowledge that no matter how much they wanted her, she belonged to me alone. I wondered if they could even imagine everything we did together, the things we had already done in this hotel, and the toys that were waiting upstairs for us.

She stayed in the room for almost an hour and a half. When she was finished, she ducked into the changing room and came out in her bathing suit. Together we entered the empty pool, swimming several laps together. There was a whirlpool bath in the corner and we decided to try it out. Sylvia pressed the switch on the wall and the small, round pool bubbled into life.

The water was very hot, and felt delicious as it cascaded around us. Then I discovered the water jets! Situated around the pool walls were the jets where the pressurized water flowed in. We quickly discovered that if we faced them and bent our knees, the rush of water, as hard as the touch of a hand, would tickle our pussies! We stayed in the whirlpool for half an hour, enjoying the teasing rush of water on our cunts. We giggled like children when we saw hotel guests walking by the glass-walled pool—if they only knew we were turning ourselves on!

Finally the timer on the whirlpool clicked off, and the bubbling stopped. We swam a few more laps in the pool to refresh ourselves, then changed and went back upstairs, our pussies still tingling from the mad rush of steamy hot water.

We had decided that it would be too crowded in the hotel's dining room, since it was Valentine's Day, and a quick peek inside proved us right. Fortunately we had already placed our order for room service, and we had scarcely dried our hair and changed into silk lounging pajamas before we heard the knock at the door.

I could not recall a better Valentine's dinner. Again we placed our chairs before the window, but now the view was almost magical, with the lights of the city spread out before us. We enjoyed a long, romantic kiss at the window before sitting down to our meal. A perfectly-cooked chateaubriand, baby vegetables, and hot rolls were waiting for us under the silver serving bells, along with a bottle of wine.

Dinner took a long time, what with us lingering over the food and discussing our day. When it was finished, though, it was time for dessert, and Sylvia eagerly brought it over: the box containing the dildo and harness.

Neither of us had used such a device before, and were very intrigued by it. As always, we started with long, slow, deep kisses, and caressing each other's bodies, hers the firm, hard one of an athlete, mine softer and yielding to her lovely touch.

Sylvia spread out on the huge bed. I strapped the harness on. The dildo stood out, large and veined, from my mound. It looked unusual but very interesting, and we both played with it for a while.

I licked Sylvia's pussy until her flesh was hot and moist, delicious as always. Then I lightly coated the dildo with jelly, and pressed its head to the opening between her chocolate lips.

Lying over her, I pushed my hips in and the dildo slid into her. She gasped. I loved the feeling of hovering over her, pushing the rubber head in and out. It didn't take long for me to work up a regular rhythm, pumping the dildo into her.

It turned me on to pump my hips that way, to fill her up. I kissed her while I stroked the dildo inside her. She moved her hand down between us and rubbed her hard clit while I fucked her. My own pussy was throbbing and I reached back to touch myself.

Moaning, gasping, we made love, the dildo going in and out of her soaked pussy, both of us rubbing our clits as hard as we could. I slowed down and gave her long, luscious strokes, then pumped hard and fast into her. She groaned and begged for my kiss. I felt as if I could come into her right through the dildo, I was so hot.

"Let's change positions," Sylvia suggested, and I pulled the wet shaft out. It was my turn to lie flat on the bed. The dildo stuck straight up, its head shiny with pussy juice. The harness was soaked with honey from both of us.

Sylvia got over me and straddled it. Ever so slowly, she sank down on it, until her pussy was resting on me. Soon she was bouncing up and down on it, pushing me into the soft bed, her beautiful tits moving with her rhythm. I played with her nipples, pulling at them and tweaking them between my fingers while she fucked me.

She played with her clit while she moved on the dildo. I couldn't believe how gorgeous she looked, grinding her hips on me, my hands on her breasts, her fingers rubbing her hot clit. Finally it was too much and she came violently, the dildo pushed into her cunt, her hand moving hard on her pussy. I was sure the guests in the next room could hear her, she cried out so much.

In an instant she was off me, unbuckling the harness and pulling the dildo away. Then she leaned down and pressed her mouth to my pussy. Her tongue moved furiously on my clit and before I knew it, I was coming too, crying out just as she had.

Once again we found ourselves in each other's arms, quivering from the passion we had just shared. The dildo and its harness lay on the corner of the bed, and we knew that this was one toy that was not going to be thrown in the drawer and forgotten. Anything that could make us feel that good was going to get its fair share of use.

Eventually we both showered and dressed, then went down to the dining room. At that late hour it was almost deserted, and we picked a cozy table in the corner. It was time for our second dessert, and this time we enjoyed rich coffee and almost sinful chocolate cheesecake. If nothing else, this was going to be our weekend to spoil ourselves silly, and never mind the cost or the calories. On the way back to the room we found that the bar was in full swing, with a band playing on the stage, so we stopped inside for "just one drink" and ended up staying until two.

Sylvia's birthday dawned cold and rainy, and after breakfast in the dining room we got a taxi and went to the museum. Both of us enjoyed the visit, but in the back of my mind all I could see was Sylvia naked before me on the bed, her beautiful body waiting for my touch. She must have felt the same way, too, for whenever we were in an empty hall she would mischievously brush against my breasts or quickly run a hand over my pussy. I longed to be back in our room, and when we had seen everything in the museum, I happily hailed a cab and gave the driver the name of the hotel.

This time we didn't even think about dinner. We

still had one more toy to play with, the double-ended dildo that Sylvia had given to me. It was daylight when we got back to our room, but I knew it would be dark before I would be finished making love with her.

It was a fair-sized one, almost as big as the one I had fucked her with, but with a smooth head at each end. We played at coating it with lubricant, stroking its length and rubbing the crease under the head. Sylvia stretched out on the bed and I caressed her pussy with my fingers, brushing her clit and stroking the lips. Gently I inserted my finger into her hole. Her soft well walls opened for me and held my finger with its velvety muscles. Then I pushed the dildo into her.

The second head and its long shaft stuck out of her, and I wanted to be on it and as close to her as I could be. I eased it into my own pussy, until our cunts met, the dildo deep inside both of us.

I felt wonderfully full, and at the same time teased as Sylvia's hair brushed against my clit. Slowly we began to move on the dildo, to fuck both ourselves and each other. It was difficult at first, but we quickly picked up a rhythm. Soon our pussies were rubbing against each other, the dildo sunk deep in our cunts.

Sylvia reached over and grabbed the vibrator, which we had left on the bedside table. (Who knows what the maid was thinking!) She switched it on and put it between us, so that each time we moved on the dildo, our clits pushed against the humming, vibrating wand.

It felt too good. I stopped pumping on the dildo and pushed against the vibrator. This pressed it tightly against Sylvia's clit, and we squirmed against it, bodies touching, cunts filled with the dildo, clits grinding against the buzzing vibrator.

Moaning, gasping, crying out with pleasure, we rubbed on the vibrator as hard as we could. I came, my eyes closed, shouting. She exploded also, pulling the vibrator as tightly as she could into her hot flesh, trembling and wetting both the vibrator and me with her juices.

I hardly had the strength to move. Sylvia hugged me tightly, the double dildo lying beside us on the bed, the vibrator forgotten and fallen to the floor. We kissed deeply. Sylvia told me that the weekend had been a dream present, the best birthday she had ever spent.

I had planned for us to go to work directly from the hotel in the morning. Sylvia snuggled into my arms and said that she wished the weekend would never end.

I held her close, and we thought about what to have for dinner, and what excuses we would give to our bosses on Monday morning when we called in sick.

METER MAID

It sure wasn't much of a night, I thought, as I waited for the traffic light to change. No one standing on the streets, no orders on the radio. I turned the cab around the corner and slowly cruised down the street. Nothing.

The dispatcher called for a car close to an intersection a few blocks away from where I was. I grabbed the microphone quickly and told him my location. It took a few tries to get through, since a lot of other drivers were trying for it too. I was beaten by a car two blocks closer than I was. Nobody was making any money tonight, and they were fighting furiously over the few calls that came in. I might have been better off staying home.

I decided to go and sit at the nearest cab stand and hope that someone would come along. There was already another car there, but it was better than driving around burning my gas. I pulled in and parked behind it.

I turned the car off and slumped in the seat, sipping my cup of take-out coffee and listening to the cab radio. There was a small flurry of three orders, none of them even close to me, then silence. I hoped I was going to make enough to be able to fill the tank with gas when my shift was over.

I watched as a gorgeous, well-dressed woman walked along the sidewalk. She looked into the cab ahead of me, then walked toward my car. I could see her looking at me directly. Then she motioned to ask if my car was available. I nodded, and sat up straight, putting the coffee cup in its holder.

The driver up ahead had been watching her in his rearview mirror. When she reached for the door handle, he jumped out of his car. "Hey, lady!" he shouted. "I'm the first car at the stand. You have to take my car!"

My passenger didn't seem the least bit ruffled as she opened the rear door. "I'm the one paying the fare," she said. "I can take any car I want, and I want this one." He glared at her, then got back behind the wheel and slammed the door shut angrily.

She gave me an address, a condominium apartment building almost on the other side of the city. Maybe the evening wasn't going to be a total write-off after all. It would be a pretty hefty fare.

I pulled out onto the street and turned the meter on. I wondered why she had chosen my car over the one in front of me at the cab stand. They were both the same model, both in the same condition and both just as clean. For a moment I entertained the thought that maybe she preferred women, but dropped it just as quickly. I knew I couldn't be that lucky.

I stopped for a red light, and looked at her in the rearview mirror. She was the type of woman I often dreamed about. Her clothes were beautiful and expensive-looking, and her hair was carefully arranged. Her face had a model's finely-cut features and beautifully drawn lips that I could just imagine kissing.

She looked up and caught my eyes in the mirror. She smiled. I thought it looked inviting, but I couldn't be sure. The light changed and I started up again.

"You don't see a lot of women driving at night," she said. Her voice was soft and elegant, but I decided not to get my hopes up. It was too good to be true; that sort of thing only happened in stories.

"I've always preferred the night shift," I said. "I don't have to haul a lot of grocery bags, and the money's better. Except on nice nights like this. Most people walk or take the bus. They don't want to spend the money for a cab."

"I was thinking about the bus," she said. "But then I saw you sitting there and decided I really didn't want to wait for one."

"Why didn't you take the first car?"

Again I caught her eye in the mirror, and she smiled. "Your car looked much more interesting."

"Why do you say that?" I asked, curious.

"I prefer women drivers," she said.

My mind was racing, and now I felt my pussy starting to stir. A lot of people say that, but they were referring to the way I handled the car. I didn't really believe that was her intention, although it was lovely to think it was. I began to feel warm, and turned the air conditioning up a notch. Glancing in the mirror, I saw that my gorgeous passenger looked as cool and calm as could be.

"Are you married?" she asked suddenly.

"Oh, no," I replied quickly. How could I explain that my love was reserved for women? That I loved to suck on female nipples, to probe clits with my tongue and smell the beautiful aroma of a woman's soft flesh? "I—I'm not really the type to have a husband," I said, and hoped desperately that she would catch the implication.

"I know what you mean," she said. "I've never been drawn toward it either."

Now my mind was really moving. I squirmed in the seat to relieve some of the pressure on my pussy. I had to be right! Every time I looked in the rearview mirror, I seemed to catch her eye.

It didn't take long to reach her address once I was on the highway. My heart sank a little when I turned off at her exit and her building was in sight. I really didn't want her to leave my cab.

I pulled up at the front door, put the meter on hold, and turned on the interior light so I could write the address on the trip sheet that I had to fill out after every passenger. Again she looked in the mirror, and I glanced at her and admired her as she opened her purse and looked for her wallet. I could still feel the quick thrill I got when our eyes met.

"Oh, dear," she said, looking in her wallet. "I thought I had another twenty. I'm a bit short." I groaned to myself, and realized that her tone sounded as if she was reciting a practiced speech. Still, it didn't add up. Deadbeats didn't usually live in classy buildings and wear expensive clothes.

"You can park the car over there and come upstairs with me to get the money," she said, indicating the nearby visitor parking lot. "I have more upstairs. I just forgot to bring it with me."

Normally my rule was never to go into a building with a passenger, for my own safety. But this time my throbbing pussy overruled my better judgment. True, I did want the money. Even more, though, I wanted to keep this fascinating woman in my sight, if only for a few extra minutes.

I let the dispatcher know that I wouldn't be answering the radio for a short time, then parked the car and followed her to the front door of the building. As we went up in the elevator, the sensual smell of her perfume reached me and I wanted her so badly I couldn't believe it.

She opened the door to her apartment, which was large and beautifully decorated. She closed and locked it behind us, and then turned to face me. I felt like I was in a crazy dream when she reached up and stroked my cheek with her fingertips. "You told me it was a really slow night," she said. "Do you have to go back out so soon?"

My heart was racing as I realized that I was going to get exactly what I had wanted. Her touch was soft but as hot as a flame to me. She ran her fingernails down my neck and then stopped just above the top button of my shirt, tracing a tiny design back and forth on my skin.

"You want this as much as I do, don't you?" she asked.

"Yes," I whispered, and she kissed me. Her lips were warm and sweet. She grew bolder and I felt her tongue press into my mouth. My pussy was so hot I wanted desperately to touch it and control the throbbing. I pushed my own tongue against hers, and I felt her moan softly as I did.

As I kissed her, I could feel her hands unbuttoning my shirt. When it was open, she reached inside. I wasn't wearing a bra and her hands were warm and smooth on my tits. She never stopped kissing me, and her hands kept moving over my skin.

I could feel my nipples get hard and tingly. She brushed them gently, then held them between her fingers and pressed them firmly. I moaned and put my arms around her.

She broke away and took my hand. "There's plenty of time," she said. "We don't have to do everything in the hallway." She led me to her bedroom. The focal point was a large bed with the head and foot fashioned out of black wrought iron and decorated with metal vines and grape leaves. It was covered with a thick, ivory-colored duvet.

"Please undress me," she said. I was only too eager to. She was wearing a tailored suit, and I slipped the blazer off her shoulders. Then I unbuttoned her silk blouse, revealing a lacy black bra under it.

I couldn't wait another minute. Her nipples were pointing out against the fabric, and I took them into my mouth. I nibbled them right through the bra. She groaned and held my head while I sucked at them. Then I reached carefully into one cup and pulled her large tit out. Her nipple was huge, with a large brown areola studded with tiny goosebumps surrounding it. I licked and sucked it into my mouth. Her skin tasted warm and rich and I took as much of her into my mouth as I could. I could feel her quiver just a little when I pulled back and pushed my tongue against the very tip of her nipple. I blew on it to cool it, then sucked it back into my warm mouth and she moaned again.

I reached behind her and unhooked the bra, then took it off her completely. Her breasts were lovely. I pushed them together and ran my tongue over both of her nipples, back and forth. I licked in between them and pushed them against my cheeks. I wanted to bury myself in them, they were so large and warm.

"Don't stop there," she said, and I reached for the small zipper on her skirt. When it dropped to the floor I discovered that she wasn't wearing any panties, but her stockings were held up with black garters decorated with tiny red silk roses. The garters looked delicious, and framed her dark triangle superbly.

"Let me lie down," she begged. The black garters looked even better against the light duvet. "Now, come here." My shirt hanging open, my jeans still on, I climbed onto the bed. She motioned for me to kiss her, and I did gladly. She massaged my tits while my mouth was on hers. I put my hand between her legs.

Her pussy was damp and slippery, and burning hot to my fingers. I moved up and down her fleshy, hairy lips, then gently pushed them apart. Her clit was huge. She pushed her tongue passionately into my mouth when I touched it, and her hands moved even faster on my tits. I wondered how crazy she would go once my tongue was on it, and I longed to lick it.

I moved my hand back to explore her hole. It felt so good to put my finger up inside her and feel the velvet-soft muscles grab and hold me tight. I moved in and out of it slowly. I loved to pull my finger out until it was almost free, then move it with short strokes and finally bury it again right up to my hand. She liked it and when I pushed in deeply, she moved her hips to grind against me and fill herself with my probing finger.

I wanted to taste her cunt so badly. I worked my way down her body slowly, licking and kissing her as I went. I dipped my tongue into the little indentation at the base of her throat, and from there moved down to her tits, licking and kissing each one a few times. I swept down her flat belly in long sweeps of my tongue and finally found myself at her beautiful pussy.

I licked all over her pussy lips and then stabbed at her clit with my tongue. She went wild, just as I thought she would. She moaned and gasped, then told me how good it felt. I loved to hear her and it spurred me on to lick faster.

"Lick me there," she said. "Right there on my hard clit! Ooh, just to the side, now harder, faster, right where you're licking. I love having my cunt lapped like that!"

I licked my finger and rubbed the entrance to her hole while I moved my tongue all over her clit. Her pussy tasted like ruby red wine, so delicious that I wanted to lick up every drop of her juice.

"That's so warm, so good!" she moaned, and she put her hands on my head and pulled me in so that my tongue pushed hard against her clit. "Oh, you lick pussy so well. Lick me again right there. Keep your finger on my hole!"

I was going crazy on her cunt now. She squeezed me between her thighs, and the soft sheer stockings slid, whisper-smooth, against my cheeks. I couldn't move, couldn't leave her pussy, and I didn't want to. Her juice was everywhere, on my chin and lips and on her thighs. I was surrounded completely by her cunt.

I licked her every way I knew possible. I tickled her clit with just the knife-edge tip of my tongue, and lapped her whole cunt with my tongue stretched out wide and flat. I pushed her clit back and forth and sucked it between my lips, flicking over it and nibbling on it gently with my teeth. All the time I was doing this, she was murmuring to me, telling me when I was hitting sensitive spots and when I should speed up or slow down. Her voice was as smooth as oiled silk and I loved to hear her.

My tongue hit a spot that she really enjoyed and I stayed on it, using short strokes to brush against it. Her voice got louder and she moaned. I kept at it, and she came.

She almost screamed as she did, and she bounced her pussy up and down on my tongue. Her cunt was all over my face and I reveled in it. She was so wild and excited I couldn't believe it was the same cool, elegant woman who sat so straight in my cab. I had never been with anyone so enthusiastic. I was so turned on that, my own pussy was crying out for immediate attention.

"Come up here," she gasped, and she kissed me hard and licked her own pussy nectar off my face. Then she unzipped my jeans and helped me to get them off. She got up and made me sit on the edge of the bed, then slipped my shirt off my shoulders and tossed it aside.

She knelt before me on the thick carpeting and took my tits into her mouth. Her tongue was as hot as her pussy and I groaned as she licked my nipples hard.

"Feels good, doesn't it?" she asked, and I could only nod. Her hand was on my thigh, moving up and down by my steamy cunt. "Your tits are so nice, I could suck on them for hours. But I want to taste your pretty pussy too."

She moved down so that her head was between my open legs. The first touch of her hot tongue on my clit was electric. My pussy was soaked and she licked my juice away first. "You taste so good," she said. "I knew you would as soon as I saw you. I knew you would want your cunt eaten."

She was doing a beautiful job. Her experienced tongue sought the folds of my pussy and moved up and down the sides of my clit. I forced myself to calm down. I didn't want to come quickly. I wanted to keep her tongue on my clit, building me up, as long as I possibly could. It just felt so wonderful and I wanted to draw it out.

It was as if she had read my mind, for she left my clit and licked my thighs slowly. I breathed out hard and relaxed, but just as I did, she pushed her tongue against my clit again. The white-hot shivers went up and down my spine, and my whole body was once again concentrated on that small nub of flesh that she was going crazy over.

She moved down to tongue my hole and then suddenly I realized that her wet finger was probing my ass. I leaned back a bit, and she expertly pushed the tip in as smoothly and gently as I could imagine. She wiggled her finger back and forth and I almost came right then and there. I loved the feeling of being full, and the way she licked me made it even better.

I could feel the familiar tingling in my belly and my legs felt weak. My muscles tightened, and she looked up at me and smiled. She licked two fingers on her other hand and pushed them into my pussy hole, then bent forward and licked hard right on my clit.

Wow! Both my holes were filled and my clit was getting a spectacular workout. Within a few moments I was gasping and moaning uncontrollably. There was nothing but the sensation in my pussy; I was aware of nothing else. Everything was forgotten except for those fingers in my ass and my hole, and that hot, wild tongue licking my clit.

I came so hard I made as much noise as she had. My whole body jerked with the wave that went through me. Even my toes and fingertips tingled. I fell back on the bed, and felt so good that I thought all my bones had melted. I didn't have the strength left to raise my hand.

I felt her pull her finger out of my ass. I raised my head and watched as she took her fingers out of my pussy, then put them in her mouth and sucked the syrup from my hole off of them. I had never seen anyone do that before and it turned me on more than I could have imagined it would.

She got onto the bed and stretched out with her head beside me. She kissed me on the lips and pushed the hair back from my damp forehead. "Better than spending your night sitting at a cab stand?" she asked.

"Much," I gasped, and took her face in my hands to kiss her deeply. I hadn't made love like that in ages and I didn't think I'd ever had an orgasm that intense in all my life. She was very, very good and I knew I would remember this session for a long time.

She looked at her watch. "I hate to break up a party," she said, "but I have to meet someone. I have enough money now. Will you take me?"

"Anywhere," I said, and kissed her again. We held each other for a long time, and then got up. Reluctantly I pulled my jeans and shirt back on. I wished I could have slept in her arms the whole night.

We took the elevator back down to where the car was waiting. She sat in the front seat this time, and gave me the address of a restaurant. I had expected her to be chatty and maybe even talk about what we had just done, but even though she was sitting beside me this time, she wasn't any more talkative than on the trip to her apartment. I felt like I was blabbering when I spoke to her, and finally just kept quiet myself and drove.

I pulled up in front of the restaurant, and she took some money out of her purse and pressed it into my palm. I didn't look at it.

She leaned close to me and touched my cheek.

"Don't get me wrong," she said. "I just don't talk much after I'm with someone. It doesn't mean anything. I think you're really great."

She kissed me deeply and pushed the tip of her tongue into my mouth. "You were fantastic," she said. "I hope I meet up with you again soon."

She got out of the cab and disappeared into the bustling restaurant. I looked at the money. She had paid what she owed for the first ride, along with the fare for this trip and a hefty tip on top of it all.

I marked the run on my trip sheet. I sat for a long time at the curb, until the cab radio finally squawked and woke me out of my daydream. I still had five hours to go on my shift. I hoped they would pass quickly. Already I wanted to go home and think about her, and maybe let my hand stray down to my hot pussy while I did.

I put the car in gear and pulled out from the curb. The streets were still empty and I cruised slowly, my eyes checking both sides of the street for people flagging me down.

I turned the corner and headed back to the cab stand, and suddenly remembered that I didn't even know her name.

OPEN CURTAINS

S ummer hit the city particularly hard that
year. Throughout the day, the relentless sun
beat down until it was possible to feel the
heat of the pavement right through a pair of shoes.
The late afternoon improved somewhat, but the
nights were still steamy. The air was heavy enough
that you felt it on your skin when you moved
through it.

Sandra sat on her apartment balcony, enjoying her
Saturday night. Her long hair was pulled back in a
ponytail and she wore only a flimsy white cotton
dress. Normally billowy and loose, it clung to her
skin, outlining her beautiful breasts and hinting at
the dark triangle between her long legs. The can of

soda, icy-cold out of the refrigerator, was now only cool. She pressed it to her cheek.

She had only been in the city for a couple of weeks, brought out by a job transfer. Normally she would have been out exploring her new surroundings, but it was just too hot to move and she was satisfied to sit out the sultry night on her tiny balcony. Occasionally she read bits of the magazine on the table beside her. It was so hot even the insects were drowsy, and she could leave the light on without being bothered by them.

Despite the heat, there was plenty of activity both in her own apartment building and the one she faced. Several residents—Sandra not among them—were fortunate enough to have air conditioners, and their hum provided a lazy background noise. One apartment was host to a party, and the music and laughter wafted over to Sandra's balcony. The couple directly below her were also sitting outside, and she could hear their voices. Occasionally a car or a bus would drive along the road that the buildings fronted on. A couple of children, their bedtimes long past, still played on the grass several floors below her. She could even hear the faint hum of machines from the laundry room, although it was beyond her to imagine anyone sitting in the room that the superintendent told her was stifling hot even on the coldest days of winter.

She took a long drink of her soda, then leaned over the balcony railing and looked into the apartments across the way. It was easy to do, since most of them had their lights on and their curtains pulled open. One family was sitting watching television. One group was sitting around the kitchen table playing cards, beer bottles in front of them. And then, directly opposite her and one floor down, she saw something that made her stop and stare.

Two women were standing together in their living room, running their hands through each other's hair and kissing passionately. Everything else was forgotten as Sandra watched, open-mouthed.

They were both lightly dressed and their hands strayed as they kissed. One was taller, light-haired, wearing shorts and a thin T-shirt. The other was darker, and she wore a loose dress similar to Sandra's. As Sandra watched, amazed and fascinated, the blonde lifted the hem of the skirt and put her hand underneath it. By the way the brunette moved, Sandra knew that she was having her pussy felt.

Sandra couldn't believe it. One of her major problems in moving to the new city was being lesbian and not knowing any others. Now they were coming to her!

The pair seemed completely oblivious to the fact that their curtains were open and they could be seen. The brunette lifted her partner's T-shirt. The blonde was not wearing a bra and her breasts were small and firm. The brunette leaned down and took one of them into her mouth. Their apartment had an air conditioner humming in the window. Sandra could just imagine how cool her flesh would feel on this scorching night, and how hard that pink nipple would feel to the lips that held it and the tongue that was licking its tip.

The brunette lavished attention on both of her lover's nipples. Sandra's own mouth opened slightly and her tongue darted out, as if she was the one licking the nude woman. Her pussy was already starting to throb as she watched the blonde close her eyes and give herself over to her partner's caress.

Sandra watched as the tall blonde woman deftly slipped out of her blue shorts. She was not wearing any panties and the brunette's hands were between her legs immediately. Sandra could almost feel the hot blonde pussy lips that the darker woman was caressing with her fingers. Her own hand was on her pussy now through her dress. She played with herself absently as she watched the two women in the apartment. She didn't even care that she was sitting out in the open herself on the balcony.

It was the brunette's turn. She lifted the loose dress over her head and stood before her lover naked. Her breasts were much larger, and Sandra longed to hold them. She watched as the two played with each other's nipples, pausing for deep kisses.

They were all over each other now. Hands were in pussies, lips were on nipples. Sandra marveled at how gorgeous they looked. It was like watching a hot video except that these were real women making love right in front of her eyes. She was so turned on it was frightening. The heat, the noise from her neighbors, everything was forgotten as she stared into the window at the two women who were making love so openly. It almost seemed as if they were putting on a show just for her.

Suddenly the women walked out of the room. Sandra was crushed; she never thought about that happening. Then she noticed that all of the curtains in the apartment were open, and all of the lights were on. She rushed into the living room, but could see nothing. She hurried into the bedroom without turning on her own light.

Perfect! Their bedroom was almost directly across from hers, but one floor lower. She could see almost everything in the room, but especially the bed where the two lovers were now sitting.

They were facing Sandra, who sat on her own bed, close to the window in her darkened bedroom. Again they kissed slowly and sensuously, the blonde's hand rubbing the dark pussy beside her and the brunette running her fingers over her lover's small, firm breasts. They were so perfectly positioned they must have known they were putting on a show. Sandra's dress was pushed up to her hips. Her hand was once again in her hot wet pussy. Her other hand was kneading her breast, her fingers rolling over the nipple under the light cotton dress.

Gently the brunette eased her partner down on the bed until she was on her back, with her legs still over the edge. Sandra could see the blonde pussy and she longed to be near it. The brunette knelt on the carpet and pressed her lips against the waiting pussy.

Sandra gasped. She could almost feel that mouth on her own steamy cunt. She could see the dark head moving and knew the fantastic tongue-lashing that the blonde was receiving. How she longed to be on the receiving end of that attention! Her own hand was now rubbing her clit hard.

The blonde was obviously enjoying her pussy workout. Her hands were on her lover's head to push her tongue deeper in. Sandra could see her mouth open in a moan of pleasure, the same type that escaped from Sandra's lips as her fingers touched her own wet pussy.

The blonde said something, and the brunette stopped and stood up. The blonde moved so that she was lying flat on the large bed. Sandra smiled as she watched the brunette straddle her on the bed, getting ready for some sixty-nine.

They were both hungry for pussy, for they were eating each other out within seconds. Sandra still couldn't believe that she was actually sitting in her bedroom watching them. They were both licking furiously, their hips moving and their pussies grinding on each other's mouths. Sandra's hand was soaked with her own pussy juices. She wanted to be part of them.

The two were giving it everything they had. Sandra saw that the blonde woman was going wild, her hips grinding furiously. Sandra pushed her hand hard against her clit and she came just as the blonde woman did. Both of them trembled as the hot sparks moved through their bodies from their wet cunts. The brunette seemed to explode a few moments later. Sandra could see her mouth open as she cried out with the feeling.

All three of them relaxed. Sandra slumped on the bed. Her pussy felt alive and fantastic and she panted for breath in the stifling air. The two women in their air-conditioned apartment held each other tightly, the brunette moving on the bed so that she could hug her lover and kiss her gently.

They stayed together on the bed for a long time, and Sandra's eyes never left them. Their bodies were beautiful. They talked to each other, kissing every so often and running their hands up and down one another. Sandra was lonely and longed for their company, if only just to sit and talk.

Eventually they got up and dressed, still not caring that their curtains were open. They both put on light summer dresses with no underwear, then fixed their hair and turned the light off. Disappointed, Sandra watched them walk through their living room and go out the front door. The apartment went dark as the blonde hit the light switch on her way out.

Sandra sat in her dark bedroom, her mind replaying their wild, abandoned sex scene. They must have known that people in Sandra's building could see them, but they didn't seem to care. Were they turned on knowing that someone might be watching? More importantly, would they make love in front of the open window again? Sandra certainly hoped so; it was so exciting watching them. After a while, she peeled off her damp dress and dropped it on the floor, then stretched naked on top of the sheets and fell into a deep, satisfied sleep.

All day Sunday she kept an eye on the apartment. The curtains were still open, but in daylight it was impossible to see inside. She sat in her chair on the balcony for almost the entire afternoon, reading a book and glancing up regularly at the apartment windows. The weather was still oppressively hot, but Sandra kept vigil at her outside post.

She was rewarded once. As she watched, the brunette walked to the window where the air conditioner was. Sandra could see her very clearly. Her features were fine, her dark curls falling to her shoulders. After she had adjusted the machine, she stood in front of the window, leaning on the sill and looking out. For a moment she looked at Sandra, who was sitting forward with her arms on the balcony. It seemed as if she flashed a smile right at her. Sandra smiled back. The woman kept looking around, then walked back in the room where Sandra could not see her.

It seemed to take forever for the sun to go down. When it finally did, the lights in the apartment went on, and Sandra could see into their living room. The blonde woman sat in a chair with her back to the window, reading the newspaper. She lifted her head and spoke to someone Sandra couldn't see, then got up. Her heart sinking, Sandra watched her pull the curtains.

She felt terrible. Obviously they had realized what they had done, and were now protecting themselves against prying eyes. She went for a walk down to the small restaurant on the corner where she had some dinner, then came back to her apartment. It seemed even tinier and more stifling. The curtains were still drawn across the way, even the ones in the bedroom. She could see that the lights were on behind them, which made her even more depressed. She wondered just what was going on in that bedroom, on that large inviting bed.

She went to work Monday, but her mind wasn't really on her job. All throughout the day she pictured the two women making love on the bed, over and over. She managed to work herself into such a frenzy that she finally excused herself and went to the washroom. There she rubbed her pussy hard until the soft waves of orgasm rushed up her spine. The rest of the day she wondered if the curtains would ever be opened again on that beautiful couple that turned her on so much.

The curtains stayed closed that night, and the next. Perhaps they had realized their error, or had received a complaint. She had given up hope of ever seeing them again, and on Wednesday night she rode out the heat wave by sitting reading on her balcony. She finished the book late into the night and was just about to go inside when her eyes strayed to the apartment.

The curtains were open. Hardly believing her luck, Sandra sat back down and turned out the little light beside her. The blonde woman was sitting in her chair, her back to Sandra and once again reading a newspaper. Sandra watched her for quite a while. Then the brunette walked into view, took the newspaper away, and leaned down to kiss the blonde woman on the lips.

Sandra was elated, but tried not to get her hopes up too high. She was afraid they would stop and close the curtains, but they didn't. Instead, the brunette eased herself into the blonde's lap and they wrapped their arms around each other, their mouths glued together in long slow kisses.

Sandra longed to be with them in the big chair. Their kisses became more passionate and their hands moved skillfully to caress sensitive areas. It was difficult for Sandra to see all that was going on, since the chair was not facing her, but every now and again she glimpsed the blonde woman's hands massaging her lover's full, large breasts through the flimsy shirt she wore.

Eventually they became too turned on for the confines of the chair. Once again they moved into the bedroom. Sandra followed them into hers. As before, they left the lights on and, to Sandra's joy, the curtains open.

Taking a deep breath, Sandra decided on a plan of action. Normally she was almost painfully shy, but she decided to throw caution to the winds. This moment was just too important to pass up and she might never have the chance again. She turned on her own bedroom light and stood right at the window. From here she could stare down into the bedroom where the two women were now slowly undressing each other.

More importantly, if they looked up through their own window, they would be able to see her standing there watching them. They would only be able to see her from the waist up, but Sandra felt that it would be enough. If they enjoyed being watched and were only doing it to attract attention, seeing her looking at them might be enough to convince them to keep their curtains open all the time. She figured at any rate she had nothing to lose.

She wasn't sure, but she thought she saw the blonde woman glance in her direction before she settled down to licking and sucking her lover's nipples.

The brunette woman was stretched out on the bed, and the blonde licked her with long, slow strokes as if she were made of candy. She pushed the brunette's large breasts together and sucked both nipples into her mouth at once, then concentrated on each one separately as her hand strayed down to the dark pubic hair.

Sandra's hands were on her breasts. They felt soft and full under her shirt, just as the brunette's must have felt under that experienced tongue. She knew that other people would be able to see her as she stood in her brightly lit window, but she was so hot and horny she didn't care. All that mattered were the two women below her, and the pussy that was aching so badly she had to put her hand there. She was burning right through her shorts, and she could feel the wetness of her cunt soaking into the fabric.

The women on the bed were now sitting opposite each other, their legs crossed over so that they were close together. They were caressing each other's breasts slowly and gently, working themselves up. It was effective; Sandra was already close to a fever pitch herself watching them.

Eventually their hands moved down to each other's pussies. Sitting so close together, they were able to kiss each other eagerly. Meanwhile, each had her hand on the other's cunt, rubbing and stroking the hot, hard clit.

Sandra's hand was also firmly on her own clit. Rubbing herself felt so good as she watched the scene being played out in front of her. The two women were obviously enjoying themselves as well. She could see their mouths open in gasps and moans when they weren't kissing each other's mouths, necks, and shoulders.

A heavy warmth was building in Sandra's belly as

she watched the two in the apartment below fucking each other with their hands. The brunette woman came first, throwing her head back, her mouth open and crying out with the force of her orgasm. She kept massaging the blonde's hot wet pussy until the taller woman came as well. Sandra watched her tremble and push her partner's hand into herself, grinding her pussy against it. Then Sandra let herself go and her own explosive orgasm overcame her as she stood by the open window.

Once again she thought she saw the blonde woman glance up at her. The two were now lying in each other's arms on top of the sheets, talking and kissing. Sandra kept standing by the window until the brunette reached over and turned out the light. Satisfied by her orgasm and by watching the couple, she realized how very tired she was. She undressed and lay down on her bed. Although the night was still very hot, she fell asleep almost immediately.

She went off to work again with the two women on her mind. The scene of them rubbing each other kept running through her head like a movie repeated over and over, but each showing was just as hot and exciting as the last. The day seemed to drag along; when she thought she'd been working for an hour, Sandra would look up at the clock and see that only ten minutes had passed. All she wanted to do was rush home and stand by the window in the hopes of catching a glimpse of the two women. Finally it was time to leave, and she rushed out of the building and down to the bus stop. Even though the bus was packed with people and horribly hot, it was a joy for her to ride home.

As her stop came up, she inched her way toward the door through the throng of passengers and got off. After the air in the bus, the hot sun was almost refreshing. She walked to the front door of her building, fumbling for the tiny key that opened her mailbox.

She checked it every day, even though she had moved so recently there hadn't been any mail for her yet. Today was different, though. Tucked amidst the advertising flyers was a small sealed envelope with no name or address written on the front.

She wondered how it could have arrived, until she noticed that there was a crease along the top edge. Someone had folded it and slipped it through the crack at the top of the mailbox door.

She got on the elevator and opened the envelope on her way up. The contents so surprised her that she got off at her floor and just stood in the middle of the hallway so that people had to walk around her to get on the elevator. The handwriting on the blank card was small and neat.

"We know you are watching us," the note read. "Are you one of us? We really hope that you are, and we would like to meet you. If you are interested, we will be at the address below after seven this evening. We would love to meet you." The address was written at the bottom. There were no names on the card, or a return address, but the stationery was heavy and very expensive.

Sandra's heart was beating so hard her hands were trembling. She could barely fit the key into her apartment door. She rushed over to the window, but the curtains in the apartment across the way were closed. She wondered how they could have known, until she realized they must have counted the number of windows in the building to determine which apartment was hers.

It was too good to be true! She was usually shy about meeting new people, but she was just dying to introduce herself to these two women who had turned her on so much. She could hardly think straight. She stood in front of her closet for ages, going over all of her clothes. Just when she thought she had selected the perfect outfit, she would go through again and come up with something else. Finally she decided on a light, flower-print dress with a neckline that dipped low over her breasts. It was her favorite and she hoped it would be a hit with them as well.

The clock moved just as slowly as it had at work. She forced herself to sit still and eat a light dinner of cold chicken. She tried to read to pass the time, but found herself going over the same paragraph several times without comprehending any of it. When it was finally time to get ready, she enjoyed a cool shower, then tried eight different ways of arranging her hair.

At six-thirty she stood in front of the full-length mirror and assessed herself. The dress really did show off her breasts, which were full and nicely shaped. Her long legs showed the effects of frequent walks and bicycle rides; they were firm, smooth, and graceful. She gave her hair a final touch-up, dabbed on a bit of perfume, and went downstairs to wait for the taxi she had called.

When she read the address off the card to the cab driver, he took her to an area of the city she had not visited before. The street was in the heart of the city, filled with shops, restaurants, and bars.

It was a decidedly upscale area, catering to the people who worked in the tall office buildings just a few blocks away. The restaurant windows were filled with plants, and menus hung in the windows by the doors. The selection was large, and she spotted a Thai restaurant, a Japanese one, and one that specialized in Hungarian food. The bars announced their presence with neon signs, and a couple of bars boasted of brewing their own beer on the premises. Even at that early hour, the sidewalks were busy with people walking in the cooler evening air, or sitting at tables in the outdoor cafés.

The cab driver stopped at the address. It was just a door, with the number engraved on a brass plaque beside it. Wondering just what kind of place it was, Sandra paid the driver and stepped out of the cab onto the hot sidewalk.

The door was not locked, and it opened onto a flight of richly carpeted stairs leading down to a landing. Sandra could hear voices and soft music.

Downstairs she met a pleasant surprise. It was an entertainment club, and obviously private. The front part was softly lit, and she could see a well-stocked bar with stools, and several tables with comfortable chairs. There was a dance floor and a booth for a disc jockey. Toward the back, under brighter lights, were three pool tables, a shuffleboard table, and two dart boards on the wall.

There was a table beside the door, and a well-dressed woman sitting behind it. "May I help you?" she asked.

"I'm here to meet a party of two women. They're expecting me," Sandra said, and gave her name.

The woman smiled. "Of course," she said. "They're expecting you. Please go inside, they're sitting at a table by the bar."

Sandra walked in, and slowly her eyes adjusted to the low lights. To her amazement, and then delight, she noticed that there were only women inside. The bartender, the couple playing pool, the two sitting on stools at the bar were all women. Then she saw the table where the two women from the apartment were sitting.

Suddenly she found herself getting nervous this close to the women she had viewed through the window. But they smiled when they saw her, and motioned for her to come over. The seemed genuinely pleased to see her. She walked over to the table.

The tall blonde woman stood up and held out her hand. "I was sure you'd come," she said. She shook Sandra's hand. "We're glad to see you. My name is Julia, and this is Susan." The brunette woman stood up and shook hands as well.

Sandra introduced herself and at their request sat down. She noticed that they were both drinking white wine, and when the bartender came over, she ordered a glass as well.

She'd rehearsed this meeting many times in her head, but now that she was actually sitting there she felt tongue-tied. She was grateful when the wine arrived and she could fidget with the glass. "Is this a lesbian club?" she asked.

"Yes, and one of the nicest," Julia replied "Susan and I have been members for a couple of years. It's a private club."

Sandra finally got her nerve up. "I—I hope you didn't mind me looking in your window," she said. "But I couldn't help noticing."

Susan's smile put her at ease. "We were hoping someone would," she said. "We knew it was risky, since someone might have complained. But we wanted to meet someone new. When we saw you in the window we couldn't believe how lucky we were. That's why we sent the note, and we're thrilled that you came out."

All three of them relaxed as the evening went on, and they opened up and soon were talking like old friends together. Julia and Susan offered to show Sandra the city sights, and being an excellent cook,

Sandra invited them to come to dinner at her apartment some evening. Gradually the club got a little busier, and Sandra even got an application to join.

The disc jockey came on, and a few couples made their way over to the dance floor. Julia asked Sandra to dance, and the two walked to the floor while Susan ordered another round of drinks.

Sandra felt a rush of pleasure as the tall blonde woman touched her. They moved together to a romantic song. Julia held her very close and Sandra caught her subtle, musky perfume. Her pussy was starting to feel warm as she moved with the blonde woman's motions.

"Won't Susan mind?" she whispered, glancing over to the table where the darker woman was sitting.

"Not at all," Julia replied. "In fact, she's just waiting for a chance to dance with you herself. We're very interested in you," she finished, and Sandra's heart skipped a beat. Her pussy was now on fire, and she clasped Julia's hand tightly.

Between dancing and talking, the night passed all too quickly. The three got a taxi outside the club. When the car pulled up on their street, Sandra began to give directions to her building.

Julia told the driver to let all three of them off at her own front door instead. Sandra looked at her; Julia smiled and said, "We'd like you to come upstairs for a nightcap first.".

Sandra was elated with the turn of events. She rode on the elevator with the two women and waited in almost a daze while Julia unlocked the apartment door.

Everything looked so familiar. The apartment was tastefully decorated, and Sandra noticed the chair in the window where she had watched the two women begin their lovemaking. At Susan's request she sat down. The air-conditioned apartment was a welcome change from her own hot, stuffy one.

She accepted a drink. She could barely keep her eyes off the two women, who sat on the sofa facing her. Both were wearing light dresses, and their lovely bodies were shown off beautifully. Sandra longed to touch them again as she had on the dance floor.

Suddenly Julia got up and closed the curtains that had taunted Sandra all those nights. Then, before Sandra even knew what was happening, she was leaning over the chair and planting kisses on her neck.

It took Sandra a moment to realize that her fantasy was finally coming true. Her pussy burned with the knowledge, and she returned Julia's whisper-soft kisses. As she did, she could feel Susan beside her, gently stroking her throat and working her way down to the top of her dress.

"You want this, don't you?" Julia purred, and Sandra could only whisper yes. She was so excited she wanted to press her tongue right down Julia's throat. She barely knew Susan was opening the buttons on her dress until she felt the lips and tongue on her nipples. She groaned and touched Susan's full breasts through the thin dress.

"Come into the bedroom," Julia said, and the two led her to the bed she knew so well. The curtains were already closed. This performance was only going to be for the three of them.

The two undressed her as she stood before them. At Julia's insistence, she stretched out on the bed and simply enjoyed everything they were doing to her. They were as eager to give her attention as she was to receive it.

They slipped quickly out of their dresses, and Julia

admired their bodies as they bent down over hers. Susan was at her breasts, licking and sucking them and playing with her nipples. Julia was working her way down her belly to Sandra's steamy pussy, already wet with desire for the two women.

When her tongue finally reached the hard clit, Sandra almost saw stars. She moaned at the double pleasure of having both her pussy and her nipples licked at the same time. Julia was an excellent lover and she flicked over Sandra's pussy hungrily.

They kept it up fort a long time, working Sandra until she got hotter and hotter. "Do you want us?" Susan whispered huskily, and Sandra nodded. Her mouth was aching to taste them as well.

Julia stayed where she was, her tongue between Sandra's wet pussy lips. Susan got up and positioned her luscious cunt right over Sandra's waiting lips. Sandra lost no time in licking the hot clit that was above her.

It was sensational. Susan was wet and it was like licking hot syrup. Meanwhile Julia was working her pussy like crazy. Sandra had never felt anything like it before. The sounds of both of them moaning with the pleasure of their threesome turned her on even more.

Julia licked and sucked hard at Sandra's clit, and she began to tremble. Her tongue still in Susan's cunt, she groaned and shook as the hot flashes overcame her. It seemed to take forever as the orgasm exploded.

"Eat me now," Julia begged. Susan got up and the tall blonde stretched out on the bed. In an instant, Susan was crouched over her, her lover's tongue on her pussy. Sandra bent down and put her mouth to Julia's mound.

Sandra looked up as she ate Julia's sweet pussy.

Julia was busy herself in Susan's cunt, and Susan was massaging her own breasts as her pussy was being worked over.

The sight was so beautiful Sandra felt her pussy throbbing again. She reached and touched herself, rubbing her clit as she licked the blonde lips in front of her.

Susan was grinding her cunt on Julia's lips. She was very close, and Julia flicked hard at her clit until she came. At the same time, Sandra fingered herself hard and a sweet second wave rose up through her whole body. Julia was the only one left, and it didn't take long with Sandra's expert tongue in her cunt. She was very loud when she came, and Susan bent down and kissed her deeply until the last of her orgasm was over.

The three lay together on the bed, panting. "That was better than I thought it could ever be," Sandra admitted, as she ran her hand down Julia's long smooth legs.

"Fantastic!" Susan agreed, and she leaned down to kiss Sandra. Then she motioned for her to move up on the bed. Sandra wedged between them, and they calmed down from their orgasms with kisses and hugs. She felt more satisfied than she had ever been before.

Julia reached over for the light switch. Sandra started to get up, but a firm kiss from Susan held her back. "Don't leave us just yet," she begged. "You can go home in the morning."

It was just what Sandra wanted to hear, and she snuggled in between the two on the big bed. Julia whispered into her ear, "We were hoping that this wouldn't be the only time."

"It won't be," Sandra promised. They stretched out quietly for a long time, until Julia reached over and began to stroke Sandra's nipples. Happily,

Sandra reached over and put her hand between Susan's legs. Her pussy was already hot and wet, and Sandra was pleased to notice that there were still a few hours left before morning.

FOR ONE NIGHT ONLY

In Colorado, the mountains that so overwhelm visitors to the state become as natural to the residents as rain or snow. So I've been told, but even after almost eight years of living in Aspen, I still marveled at them each time I went outside. Lushly green in summer or mounded white in winter, they rose up majestically on either side of the town. Their peaks always reminded me of a woman's breasts, which could be why they held such fascination for me.

The fascination had been enough for me to arrive in Aspen for a ski trip and decide, on a moment's notice, that the flat lands back at the coast were no longer what I wanted. I moved to Aspen and eventually opened a women's clothing store in the heart of the town's shopping district. Not only did it generate enough for me to live comfortably, but it was small enough that I was able to run it myself.

Although the taller peaks were still snow-capped, the June morning was sunny and warm as I locked my front door and walked to my store. Aspen attracts tourists all year round, and I was glad to see that many of the cars parked by the sidewalk had out-of-state plates. Visitors generated most of my sales.

I stopped at the bakery near my store to pick up a coffee and muffin to take with me. "Morning, Lucy!" I called to the owner, as I poured a cup of steaming coffee.

She turned around from the oven, where she was arranging pans of bread dough. "Morning, Amy," she smiled. "You're up bright and early today."

"Figure it's the only way I can guarantee getting anything," I replied. Within the hour, Lucy's bakery would be packed with people. I had learned to get up a little earlier to beat the crowd.

It also gave me a chance to talk to Lucy, who worked long hours and didn't have a lot of time to socialize. When we discovered we were both lesbian, we naturally seemed to open up to each other, and this in turn led to a firm friendship. We had never been lovers; although we never discussed it, we both seemed to prefer a platonic relationship. It just was wonderful to have a friend who thought the same way, who shared my outlooks and concerns. On the occasional evening we got together for drinks at the bar down the street from my store.

"I just took those blueberry ones out of the oven," she said, and I picked up one of the huge muffins. It was still warm and fragrant. I put it in a bag myself, as all of Lucy's regular customers did, and left the money on the counter by the cash register.

The bread in the oven, she turned to me, wiping her floury hands on a cloth. "It's going to be pretty busy today," she said. "I've got two extra batches of bread made, and extra pies. You've got it lucky, girl. All you have to do is show people where the zipper is!"

I laughed. "I expect to be run off my feet too, today," I said. A large convention was being held in one of the resort lodges in Aspen over the next four days, and almost every hotel room in the town was booked. Aspen was a small town, with most of its stores clustered together. Tourists generally walked through all of it, stopping in each store. The merchants were quite pleased with the convention, and a lot of stores were already noticing extra sales from people who had arrived a day early.

"At least you just sell the clothes, you can't have to sew them up too!" Lucy laughed. "I've been baking since three this morning. Tell you what, though. When this crowd goes home, we'll get together and treat ourselves to a nice dinner out. What do you say?"

"You're on," I said, picking up a napkin and heading for the door. "Let me know when you're free."

It felt good to unlock the front door of my shop. It gave me great satisfaction knowing that I had done it all myself and had made a pretty good business out of it. I locked the door behind me, and went back to my little office to enjoy my coffee and muffin in peace.

By opening time everything was arranged. In the front window I had some hand-painted shirts and scarves dyed to look like Navajo blankets. Belts adorned with silver and turquoise hung near the door, with beaded moccasins below on a rack. I had long ago learned to lure tourists into the shop with clothes they couldn't buy at home, and these were my most popular items.

At nine o'clock I opened the front door and used a battered corn broom to sweep the sidewalk outside the window. Other shopkeepers up and down the street were doing the same thing, and we called good mornings to each other.

Most of the day the store enjoyed a steady stream of customers. It was obvious the convention wrapped up for the day around three, for the sidewalks were packed with people in the late afternoon and I was almost run off my feet with customers, just as I had told Lucy. As I expected, my window displays were very effective and I managed to sell a large number of the expensive hand-painted shirts and the decorated belts.

Business died down around six, and now it was time for me to take a breather while the restaurants scurried to keep up with the crowds. My store was empty for the first time and I took advantage of it to unwrap the sandwich I had bought earlier in the day.

I only got a couple of bites when a woman walked in. I could only stare. She was gorgeous. She had a model's face, or a movie star's, with fine features and enormous brown eyes. Her hair was carefully arranged and she was expensively dressed. I wanted her as soon as I laid eyes on her. She was so sensuous, so graceful.

My sandwich was forgotten. "Are you looking for anything specific?" I asked, as she looked over a rack of shirts by the window.

She turned to me. Was I imagining it, or did I catch a spark in her eyes? "I'm looking for a dress," she said. "A summery one, something light."

I led her to the back of the store where the dresses were. I could smell her perfume and I wanted to touch her hair. My pussy was stirring as I looked her over, trying to decide on which style I should show her.

"How about this?" I asked. I pulled out a rich red dress that would show off her breasts. "Or maybe something shorter?" I found a lovely purple one.

"Let me try the red one," she said, smiling at me. I showed her where the fitting room was. She disappeared inside. I wished I could have gone with her to help her undress.

She came out shortly in the bright red dress. As I expected, it hung perfectly on her. It was low in front and the tops of her creamy breasts were so inviting.

"That is gorgeous!" I said, as she moved in front of the full-length mirror. It really did suit her, and she knew it. She caught my eyes in the mirror and again smiled at me.

She turned around to face me, and tugged at the neckline. "Do you think this sits right?" she asked. "Is this how it's supposed to fit?"

I reached for the fabric. "That's the way—" I stopped. She had leaned into me, so that my hand pressed against her warm breast. "Oh—excuse me," I said.

"No need to," she smiled. She looked again in the mirror. "You're right, it's perfect. I'll take it."

She went back into the changing room. I didn't know what to think. She had obviously gone out of her way to set me up and push against me. I could still feel her body against my hand, and the sensation made my pussy tingle. I didn't dare believe that she wanted me, but I wished with all my heart that she did.

She came out, and I took the dress to the counter and began to wrap it in tissue paper.

"Are you here for the convention?" I asked.

"Only for today," she said. "I had to give a seminar, but I have to be back in New York tomorrow morning. It's a shame, really. This is a beautiful place and I wish I could stay longer and see it."

I slipped the dress inside a bag. She handed over her credit card. Sharon MacMillan. I wanted to speak her name, to whisper in her ear.

"So," she said, "what do people do in this town for excitement on a Thursday night?"

"Well, there's a lot of good restaurants, and there's live entertainment in the lounge down the street," I said.

She glanced around to be sure the store was empty, then leaned toward me. "Maybe you'd like to show me around. After all, I'm only here for one night."

My heart was beating so hard I thought she could hear it. Although I wanted her, I suddenly found myself as flustered as a schoolgirl at her boldness. "I don't close the shop until nine o'clock," I stammered.

She was cool as could be, and I envied her and wanted her both at the same time. "Then I'll be back at nine," she said. "You look like the type who could show a lady a good time—are you?"

"Yes," I said, almost in a whisper. Then to my surprise, she picked up the bag, leaned over the counter and kissed me on the lips. I was shocked at first, but in seconds I was returning it. Her lips were warm and smooth, and her tongue darted out to tease mine ever so gently. Then she stood up straight.

"Nine o'clock," she promised, and left the store.

I went limp with desire. This was the sort of thing I read in magazines! But here it was, happening to me, right in my own store. My pussy was throbbing so badly I couldn't stand it. I rushed and locked the door.

I hurried into the changing room. I just couldn't bear the unsatisfied heat any longer. I pulled up my skirt and slipped off my panties. Sitting in the chair, facing the mirror, I saw my wet pussy. My hand was on my clit in seconds. Each flick of my finger was Sharon's tongue massaging my hot cunt lips. I slipped a finger inside my wet hole, and imagined that it was her finger feeling me up. My tongue darted in my mouth. I wanted to lick her pussy so badly I could almost taste it.

I watched myself in the mirror as I rubbed my pussy. My fingers were wet with my hot juice and they looked so good against the dark hair. My hand went up to hold my breast and twist the nipple through my shirt. I could feel her hands on them. I wanted to feel her hands on my cunt.

Normally I teased myself and took a long time when I made myself come. Now I was so horny I couldn't wait. My clit was so hard and rubbing it felt so good. My nipples were erect and I could see them through my shirt. I pulled them hard, gasping at how delicious it felt.

I rubbed harder and faster. I worked myself up to an edge, then let myself fall over it into my orgasm. It was wonderful. I fingered myself until the last of it was finished. I sat for a few moments to collect myself, then I straightened my dress and went back to open the store.

I went through the rest of the day almost in a dream. I had never been approached in such a way before. Sharon's shameless advances had turned me on. And that saucy kiss! No one had ever done that before. This was a very strong woman, one who would control me, and the idea was exciting. I longed to melt in her arms and let her do with me whatever she wanted.

At eight thirty I decided to close up early, the first time I had ever done so. I then went back into the shop and went through the racks of dresses. I found one that had just come in the week before, a beautiful pale silk one. I tried it on. It fit perfectly and I thought it was stunning. I hung up my own dress in the back room, fixed my hair, and decided I would worry about accounting for the dress in the stock books tomorrow.

At nine o'clock I heard a tapping at the glass door. Sharon was right on time. She was dressed in a softly tailored suit that showed off her beautiful body to full advantage. I opened the door and she walked into the store.

"You look lovely," she said. "Are you closed for the night? Good, let's go get something to eat. I'm starving."

I suggested a restaurant on the next block, and she agreed. The night was pleasantly warm and we walked over.

The restaurant was dark and quiet. We were led to a table by the window, where we could watch people walking by and see the mountains that rose up at the edge of town.

We both ordered cocktails, and the server brought us a menu. When it arrived, Sharon lifted her glass in a toast. "I'm glad I met you today," she said. "I'm usually lost in the evenings when I have to go on business trips. This is so pleasant."

"It's a nice change for me, too," I admitted. "I usually just go home and stick some dinner in the microwave, then go to bed with a book. It's nice to have my own store, but it sure means long hours."

We ordered dinner, and Sharon asked for a bottle of wine. She sat back and looked out the window. "I've never been in Colorado before," she said. "This is a beautiful place. I can understand why you live here."

"Where are you staying?" I asked.

"At a lodge just outside of town," she said. "Have you ever been inside it?" I admitted I hadn't.

She reached over and put her hand on mine. Her soft touch sent ripples through me. "Then you must come back with me and see it," she said. "I'm only here for tonight. You may not get the chance again."

My pussy was burning. I hardly even noticed what my appetizer was. All I saw were Sharon's rich, full lips and her soft hands. I wanted them on my body, and it looked as if I was going to get my wish.

She definitely wasn't subtle. Putting down her fork, she leaned across the table and looked deep into my eyes. "I want you," she said.

"I was hoping you would," I whispered. "I think you're beautiful."

She smiled. "Then let's enjoy our dinner," she said. "Fine dining is a sensual experience too. Then we can go back to my room for dessert."

She was definitely a connoisseur. The wine she had ordered matched perfectly with our food, which the restaurant had prepared in its usual impeccable style. Sharon was impressed with the quality, and admitted that it rivaled some of the finer restaurants she frequented in New York. It filled me with pride to hear her say that.

Our evening decided, Sharon switched the conversation easily. She asked about the store and my lifestyle in Aspen, and seemed genuinely interested in my answers. She told me she was a consultant for a large New York computer firm, which not only accounted for her hectic business trips but also for the fact that she refused to let me pay anything for the expensive dinner.

I enjoyed her company immensely. The time flew by, and before I knew it, it was eleven o'clock. When our coffee was finished, she asked if I was still interested in seeing her room. What a question! My pussy had been on fire throughout the entire dinner.

We walked back to my store. Sharon's car, a rented Cadillac sedan, was parked in front. It was quite a switch from my little Chevy, and I stretched out on the comfortable seat.

Within minutes we were outside of Aspen. The lodge was a beautiful one, tucked up at the base of the mountain for skiing in winter. At the front door, the valet held the car doors open for us, then got in himself and drove it away.

The front lobby was beautifully decorated, but that wasn't what I wanted to see. We went up on the elevator, and I waited while Sharon opened the door to her room.

Sharon must have been as hot as I was. As soon as she closed the door behind us, I found myself in her arms, her mouth on mine. It felt so good to let myself go. I returned her kiss. She pressed her tongue inside my mouth, and my own rose to meet it. My pussy was already wet as she ran her hands down my neck and held my breasts through my dress.

I reached for hers. They were firm and felt heavy in my hands. She kissed me for what seemed like hours. Her mouth was sweet and her kisses were like honey. Her tongue moved so beautifully in my mouth I thought that she might be able to make me come just like that.

Finally she stepped back and began to unbutton my dress. I reached for her, but she gently pushed my hands down. "Let me," she said. "You just relax. I want to make love to you."

She pushed the dress off my shoulders and it fell

to the floor. "You are exquisite," she said, and bent down to nibble at my breasts through my bra. Once again she would not let me raise my hands. I could only stand there and enjoy everything she was doing to me.

She kissed me deeply as she reached around my back to unhook my bra. She murmured approval, and immediately bent down and licked my nipple. I moaned. Her mouth was just as I had imagined it would be. My pussy was now throbbing hard and I longed for relief.

She turned me around and lowered me onto the bed. "I love your tits!" she whispered and showed her appreciation. I had never had such attention lavished on them. She ran her hands under them and pushed them together, then sucked my nipples into her mouth and licked the tips of them. She rubbed her own nipples over them, through her clothes. She tickled them with her hair, and blew gently on them to cool them off. Then she took them into her warm mouth. That made me groan with pleasure.

"Please let me see you," I begged. She sucked my nipples for a little while longer, then stood up. She took her clothes off slowly. Her body was magnificent. She really did look like a model with her firm breasts and slim waist. Her pussy was dark and I wanted more than anything to put my tongue in between her hairy lips. She even surprised me with a tiny butterfly tattoo on her hip.

She then returned to me. It turned her on to give me pleasure and she did a beautiful job. She made me roll over, and she ran her fingernails up and down my back for a long time. Then she used her tongue, moving slowly down my body until she reached my ass. Here she used her tongue to tease me, flicking it between my cheeks while she kneaded my ass with her fingers. I could only lie on the bed and soak up her attention. It was wonderful beyond comprehension.

"Roll over," she said, and I was only too happy to. Again she used her tongue to draw long strokes on my body, from my breasts down to my belly. I was getting hotter and hotter as she moved closer to my soaked pussy.

My hands moved up to touch her, but each time she gently put them back at my sides. "Just enjoy it," she said. "You'll get your turn later."

It was easy to enjoy what she was doing. She licked down to my hair, then went right around my throbbing pussy and licked the insides of my thighs. It was heavenly. Her touch was so soft as she thrilled me with her mouth.

Her first flick across my clit made me gasp. She licked me slowly the whole length of my pussy. I shivered and moaned as she stroked my clit with just the tip of her tongue.

She licked her finger, then slowly pushed it into my hole. The lubrication wasn't necessary. I was so wet I could feel my hot juice on the insides of my thighs. She slowly fucked me with one finger, then two. It was a wonderful full feeling, and even better when she went back to licking my clit as she pushed her fingers inside.

"Tell me how good it feels," she said. "I like to hear what you're feeling." She pushed her tongue under the folds of my pussy lips and ran it around the top of my cunt.

"It feels so good!" I gasped. "Your tongue—right there! Oh yes, lick me on that spot!"

"Tell me about it," she said. She slipped her hand down to tickle at my ass. I couldn't stop my hips from moving.

"It feels so warm," I said. It really did, both the

warmth from her wet tongue and the heat that was constantly building up inside me. "It's so warm, and it's just like all of you is inside me!"

She teased me. She would suck hard at my clit for a while until I got close to coming, then back off and lap slowly. The buildup was beautiful.

"Would you like to come now?" she asked. I was so worked up I could only nod, and I felt her tongue move up my pussy to my clit.

Her tongue moved so fast I couldn't believe it. I got closer and closer and then without warning the cascade started in my cunt and flooded over me. Still I wanted more, and she didn't stop. Within a few seconds, a second wave filled me and I cried out. It was so intense! My whole body was on fire as she licked the last few shivers out of me.

She stretched out beside me, idly drawing circles around my nipple with her fingernail. "It was nice, wasn't it?" she purred. I could only whisper a yes; I was still coming down from my explosive orgasm. "I knew it would be." She bent down and kissed my lips.

In one swift move she was over me, straddling my face with her beautiful pussy. I had waited so long for this. I could smell her lovely aroma and see the glistening lips. "Bring it down to me," I begged. "Let me lick your pussy!"

She did. Her cunt was rich and sweet. I held her ass cheeks and kneaded them while my tongue danced over her clit. I pulled her down so that my tongue fitted into her hole, and fucked her with it. My whole face was wet with her honey.

She moaned as I flitted over her pussy. I tried to be as slow and teasing as she had been with me, but it was impossible. She was going wild on my tongue. She moved her hips and ground her sweet pussy on my mouth. I ate her furiously. I loved having her cunt right on my face and her clit in my mouth.

"Lick me harder!" she begged. I concentrated all of my efforts on the hard nub of flesh. She began to moan, then gasped and cried out as she came. I was buried in her pussy. She trembled for a long time and I licked slowly at her until she finally got up and lay down beside me.

"Wonderful," she gasped, and kissed me again. "That was just fantastic." I ran my hands up and down her firm body and hugged her tightly.

We held each other for a long time. She reached up and smoothed my hair back from my face and gently kissed my cheek and eyelids. "I'm so glad I ran into you today," she said. "I haven't had anything that nice for so long."

"I haven't either," I said. "No one's ever eaten me like that before."

She kissed me again. "I have to be up at five to catch my plane," she said. "I can take you back to your house and you'll have lots of time to open your store. Will you please stay the night with me?"

Would I! I felt so satisfied and content, I couldn't imagine getting up and leaving. "Of course," I said. Sharon motioned for me to move so that she could pull the covers up over ourselves. I snuggled into her arms and we spent another hour just talking.

"I wish I didn't have to go so soon," she said. "I'd really like to get to know you better."

"I'm always here," I said. "You know where my store is. I'm sure you'll be back for another meeting sometime."

She smiled. "If not, then I guess I could always learn to ski. It would be a perfect excuse for a trip."

Finally she turned the light out. I fell into such a deep sleep it seemed like only minutes before the wake-up call disturbed us. Sharon kissed me and we dressed and went downstairs to where the car was waiting at the front door.

She drove me into town and stopped in front of my house. The street was still empty at that early hour.

She leaned over and kissed me, a long, gentle kiss. "I only wish we could have had more time," she said.

"So do I," I said. "It really was wonderful."

She reached into her pocket and pulled out a business card. "I'm definitely going to try to get back here soon," she said. "In the meantime, if you come out New York way, please let me know." I promised I would.

Reluctantly I got out of the car and closed the door. There was one last look, and then she pulled away from the curb. I watched the car until she finally turned the corner out of sight.

Back to my regular routine. I went in the house, showered and dressed, and watered the plants. Then I grabbed my bag and began my familiar route to work.

Lucy was making rolls in the empty bakery. I let the wooden screen door slam, as I always did, and called out my good morning as I reached for a cup and the pot of coffee.

"Morning, Amy!" she called out. "So what's new with you?"

I put the coffee pot back on the burner, then leaned over the counter and took a sip. "Lucy," I began, "you wouldn't believe it."

NAUGHTY GIRL

It's hard for me to pinpoint exactly the moment that I knew I enjoyed being spanked. Judy had always been an aggressive lover and I was satisfied to put myself under her control. I submitted to her whims, and was always ready when she told me to get undressed or to lick her waiting pussy. We gradually discovered that spanking was an important part of sex for us, and that it excited us both. Just the thought of her hand smacking my bare ass was enough to set my pussy on fire.

It had begun with friendly pats on my ass, and light slaps when we were making love. I soon realized that these gentle smacks were turning good sex into great sex, and I begged her to apply her hand a little harder. It thrilled me when she did so eagerly. Soon she was spanking me hard, and I was loving every minute of it. When I couldn't sit down afterward, I loved it most of all.

One day she admitted that turning me over her knee and whacking my behind was just as exciting for her as it was for me. I couldn't have been happier. Since that day, we regularly sent each other into ecstasy with sex and spankings.

Judy never gave me much warning before a spanking, which made it even more exciting for me. I never knew when her hand would strike and give me the delicious punishment I longed for. Sometimes I went through the house setting little traps in the hope that she would decide I needed to be spanked. Sometimes it was letting the garbage can overfill, or not putting the cap back on the shampoo bottle. Leaving the milk carton on the counter, instead of putting it back in the refrigerator, was almost always guaranteed to set her off.

"Angela!" I heard her shout as I sat in the living room reading a book. "Angela, come here immediately!"

I knew better than to disobey Judy when she used that voice. I walked slowly into the kitchen. Already my pussy was stirring and I felt giddy with desire. I knew what I was in for.

She pointed to the counter where the offending carton stood. "After last time, I didn't think I'd have to remind you again!" she said. "What do you have to say for yourself?"

I hung my head. "I forgot," I mumbled. "I was in a hurry." I was getting so horny I could hardly stand up.

Instantly I felt Judy's strong hand on the back of my neck. "That's just not good enough," she said, steering me toward our bedroom. "I think you need another lesson so you won't forget next time."

Within seconds my shorts were down around my

ankles, followed quickly by my panties. Judy sat on the bed and pulled me across her knees. I held my breath and waited.

The first crack of her hand across my buttocks made me gasp. It stung, and tears popped into my eyes. My pussy was throbbing now.

Slap! Another crack from her firm hand. "Please!" I cried out. "I'll be good! I won't ever forget again!"

"That's why you need this," she answered firmly. "To make sure you don't forget again."

Another smack, and another. I could picture my ass cheeks, stinging and red, with the imprint of her hand on them. My face was burning and I knew it must be as bright red as my behind. The pain in my ass and the heat in my pussy were almost too much to stand.

I was crying now, as Judy continued my punishment. Then she reached under me and her finger rubbed against my clit, as her other hand continued to fall on my tender ass cheeks.

She calmly counted out the blows. Four! Her finger pushed against my hard clit and I gasped. Five! I squirmed and ground my pussy on her hand. I could feel how wet her fingers were with my juice. Six! Her thumb played with my hole.

The whipping went on. Sometimes she hit one buttock and then the other, sometimes her hand landed across both. I was crying now, and I could feel the pressure building in my pussy as her fingers moved in my cunt.

I didn't get my usual ten. As she counted to nine and her hand spanked my ass, she rubbed hard on my clit. Groaning with both the pleasure and the pain, I exploded in a beautiful orgasm.

Judy was suddenly as gentle as could be, running her hand soothingly over my bruised behind. My skin was stinging. It felt as good as my pussy did.

The spanking had turned Judy on just as much. "I think you've learned your lesson this time," she said. "Now I want you to thank me for your discipline."

I needed no encouragement. I took off my shirt while she undressed and lay on her back. I parted her legs. I could see that her beautiful pussy was already glistening with her honey.

She was delicious. She moaned as I put my tongue deep in her hole and then licked all around it. Her clit was hard and hot and I moved it back and forth with my lips. Her hands were on my head, pushing my mouth hard against her sweet, sexy pussy.

The rich taste of her juice filled my mouth like wine. My ass still burned from my spanking and it spurred me on. I licked her hard, my tongue flicking fast over her clit. She was loving her tongue-lashing, squirming and grinding herself into me.

She was so worked up it didn't take long for her to come. She cried out as she did, her hips bucking crazily and her clit rubbing hard on my tongue. The heady smell of sex hung over us in the air like musky perfume. We collapsed together on the bed, both of us totally satisfied.

"I hope this teaches you not to cross me again," she said, as I ran my hand over her body.

"Oh, yes," I said, but both of us knew that it wouldn't be long before I would find a way to earn another lesson—providing that Judy didn't find a reason first.

As it turned out, it was only a few days before Judy once again found it necessary to discipline me. Of course I took the logical course and blamed the postman. Just when it became comfortable to sit down again, too!

I got home from work before Judy did, and when I emptied the mailbox I found a parcel addressed to her. Curiosity had always been one of my downfalls, and it was working overtime on that particular day. I didn't recognize the return address, a box number in San Francisco. There was nothing printed on the box to give any clue as to its contents.

It wasn't overly heavy. I shook it, but there was only a dull rustling inside, like something wrapped in crumpled paper shifting about. I tried to peek under the flap of the box, but it was securely glued shut.

I was so busy trying to guess what was in the box I didn't hear Judy come into the house. I didn't even realize she was standing beside me until the package was roughly pulled out of my hands.

Her voice was calm but icy, and it sent a luscious chill down my spine. I knew right away I was in pretty deep trouble. "You should know better than to pry into my private mail," she said. "I guess you've forgotten everything you learned. You're going to need another lesson."

I wanted her so badly I was almost dizzy. "Do you want me to take off my pants?" I asked. I could almost feel her hand connecting with my ass. I wanted to be hauled over her knees, with my tender backside ready for her.

"Oh, no," she replied, giving me a look that was both firm and seductive at the same time. "Only animals have to be punished as soon as they're caught doing something wrong."

She reached down and gently stroked my cheek with the tips of her fingers. Her touch was so distant and cold, her fingers felt icy and bloodless, and I shivered. "I'm withholding your punishment until I feel it's the right time. That way, you can think about what you've done, and why you must be disciplined. Maybe then the lesson will sink in better."

She knew how to get to me! My pussy would probably drive me crazy waiting for my spanking. I thought it was the ultimate in discipline until she revealed another trick that I knew would leave me climbing the walls.

Slowly she opened the forbidden box that had been the source of all my woes. As I had suspected, it was filled with crumpled newspaper. Inside was an object wrapped in a heavy plastic bag.

She broke the bag open, and slowly pulled the object out. I gasped, and went almost shaky with desire.

It was a leather paddle, with a heavy wooden grip. Without flinching, she slapped her palm with it twice. The crack of the leather against her skin was like a gunshot. I shivered.

She put it down on the table and put the newspaper back in the box. "You may look at it if you like," she said, picking up the box and walking into the kitchen. "Just remember that your little transgression will not be forgotten. Sooner or later I will put that to good use."

I always knew Judy was very good at disciplining me, but as I stared at the paddle, fascinated, I realized I was in the hands of an expert. My day at work, my plans for dinner, everything was forgotten as I looked it over. My mind was concentrated on only one thing. Already I could feel a tingling on my ass cheeks, and a stir in my pussy.

How long before I would feel that black leather against my ass? I picked it up. It was heavy, with a good, solid wood handle. The leather was thick and smelled delicious. I bent the edge. It was somewhat supple, but still firm. It wouldn't deliver wimpy little taps. This device was made to see active duty.

I slapped my palm with it gently. It made a lot of noise, and it managed to deliver a pleasant sting. I slapped my hand harder. This time it really hurt, and my hand immediately turned red. There was no getting away from it: I was really going to feel the effects of my curiosity!

I must have played with it longer than I thought, for soon Judy was calling me to the dining room for supper. I put the paddle back on the coffee table and hurried in, lest she use my dawdling as another reason for a spanking.

She was pouring wine into crystal glasses. "You are so forgetful, Angela," she said. "Bring that paddle in with you."

I hurried back to get it. I sat down at my place, and Judy positioned the paddle on the far corner of the table. My eyes never left it. I ate my dinner, but hardly noticed what I was putting in my mouth. Even the expensive wine had no taste for me that night. Every fiber of my being was concentrated on that beautiful leather paddle. My pussy was throbbing so badly I had to squirm on my chair for relief.

Judy noticed all of it. "It does look quite effective, doesn't it?" she asked. "I'll bet your little ass is going to be as red as a cherry when I'm through with you."

I suffered through dessert and coffee, my eyes on the leather paddle. I was sure Judy was taking longer than usual to eat, and she sat at the table for the longest time before bringing out the dessert. She even had a third cup of coffee, which she had never done before. She was playing this out as long as she possibly could.

I didn't even get a break when I washed the dishes, for Judy made sure that the paddle sat on the corner of the kitchen counter while I worked. I left a tiny crumb of food on one of the plates by mistake, and Judy coldly promised that I would receive an extra smack for that.

I followed her as she carried the paddle into the living room. It sat on the table as she relaxed on the sofa and read a book. Occasionally she would reach over and touch it. My own book was still on the table, unopened; I couldn't think about anything else. I was amazed at how excited I was.

Finally she placed her bookmark carefully and set the book down. "Take off your clothes," she ordered.

My legs were like jelly and it was difficult to stand up and undress. Somehow I managed. Judy then took off her own clothes. I loved the sight of her beautiful body. Her nipples were so large and firm, and her luscious pussy was surrounded by thick, dark hair.

She sat on the edge of the sofa, her legs apart. "Come here," she said. "On your hands and knees."

I did. The rough carpet bit into my skin. I could feel how wet my pussy was, and also how vulnerable my ass cheeks were. In that position, I was completely at her mercy. I both dreaded and longed for that paddle.

Judy reached out and pulled my head toward her pussy. "Eat me!" she ordered.

Her pussy was already wet, and I realized she must have worked herself up over my punishment as well. I didn't need to be ordered to lick her beautiful cunt. I loved doing it. I circled her tight hole with my tongue, then pushed her clit back and forth with just the tip.

CRACK! I almost screamed. It hurt like hell, and the wide paddle covered all of my ass in a single stroke. I could picture my buttocks going bone-white right after the stroke, then flushing bright red. I went dizzy, and for a moment I thought I might faint. Then the stinging set in.

The exquisite pain flowed right to my pussy, and I moaned with desire. Through a fog I heard Judy tell me to keep on licking her.

"Please be gentle," I whispered, and put my tongue back in her cunt. I was crazy for her. My tongue whipped over her clit and lapped up her sweet juice. My own pussy was begging for the same kind of attention.

Crack! My eyes welled up with tears. This time I didn't stop licking her, and she groaned with pleasure and approval.

The paddle smashed down again and again. I was crying openly, and as the tears ran down my face, I tasted their salty warmth mingled with the sweet, rich taste of Judy's cunt.

My own pussy was throbbing so badly I finally reached back and touched my clit with my fingers. "That's it!" Judy gasped. "Make us both come!" I licked hard at her delicious pussy while I fingered myself.

Four more times the wicked leather paddle smashed down on my burning ass. My tears were streaming but I didn't stop licking Judy or fingering my own pussy for a moment. It all felt so good.

"Lick me hard!" Judy gasped, and cracked the paddle down again. I sucked as hard as I could on her clit. She began to tremble, then cried out as she came.

I was so close myself. The leather slapped my ass again and I rubbed my clit hard. It was fantastic! The combination of pleasure and pain filled my pussy and I almost screamed as I came.

I struggled to catch my breath. "Come up here," Judy said, and made me lie down on my stomach. My poor ass felt raw and blistered. The paddle certainly was effective.

Judy left the room and came back with a bottle of lotion. Gently she rubbed it into my ass cheeks. "Your skin is so red, you poor thing," she said. "Let me make it better."

The lotion felt cool and soothing on my hot skin. I

wiped my tears away and enjoyed the soft touch of her hand. She rubbed me a long time, eventually giving me a complete back rub with the scented lotion. It felt so relaxing I finally fell asleep right there on the sofa. When I woke up an hour later, my ass felt swollen and tight and I had to spend the rest of the evening either standing up or lying on my stomach. Every now and again I would reach behind and gently pat my ass. The stinging reminded me of the flogging I had received, and the memory gave me sweet little twinges in my pussy.

Fortunately I didn't have to sit down at work much the next day. Each time I did, I received a quick and painful reminder of my lesson. Judy had informed me that she expected no further problems from me, but as usual, we both knew otherwise. She had hidden the paddle somewhere in the house and I was just waiting for my bruised ass to heal so that I could get into more trouble!

Judy spent the next week just teasing me. One afternoon I went into the house and found the leather paddle on the table in the hallway. I picked it up and gently stroked my cheek with it. I sniffed deeply, enjoying the musky animal smell of the leather. I almost imagined I could smell my own scent on it, my hot pussy and my blistered cheeks. I kissed it. I put it back carefully, but an hour after Judy came home, it had disappeared.

It turned up again on my dresser, and on top of the refrigerator. Just the sight of it made me weak with desire. I loved to catch the first glimpse of it out of the corner of my eye, and I was always looking for it. Judy never mentioned it and when she walked in once as I was picking it up, she ignored me and walked out again. Each time it would be gone after a couple of hours, and I did not know where she was hiding it.

Finally I could take her teasing no longer. It wasn't enough just to catch sight of that nasty black paddle; I wanted to feel it on me. Once again I tried to figure out something that Judy would feel deserved a whipping.

I left my towel in a heap on the bathroom floor and a pair of socks on the sofa, but Judy was just as determined to continue with her teasing. I found the towel neatly hung up, with the paddle on the bathroom sink. My socks were left in a pile on the sofa, with the paddle beside them. Each time, it would be whisked away an hour or two later. I could barely think straight, my pussy was so tight and tingly. I wanted that paddle so badly I was considering just taking it to her and demanding that she use it on my behind.

I finally hit paydirt with the newspaper. Judy always read it cover to cover each evening, and it was always wedged in the door by the paperboy when I came home from work. Unfailingly, I left it undisturbed on the coffee table for her, for Judy was very adamant about the condition of her newspaper. She had to be the first one to open it, and she disliked anyone rifling through it before she got a chance to. Finding it opened or the sections out of order would easily put her in a very foul mood.

I was just too hot for a lick of that paddle across my ass. I opened the paper and scattered the sections around the living room. I even took a couple of pages out of the news section and draped them over the dining room chairs. Then I changed into a light summer dress, with no underwear beneath it, and waited for Judy to come home and witness the dismantling of the evening news.

She was smiling when she walked through the door, but it quickly turned to a bitter frown when she walked into the living room and saw her paper scattered all over. Her eyes grew as cold as gray glass and her cheeks colored. I knew I was finally going to get my wish.

"Angela," she said, "what's the meaning of this?"

"I don't know," I replied, in a little-girl voice. "I didn't do it. I came home and this is what I found. It was just all over like this, honest."

She turned to me. Her eyes were still cold but I could detect a hot spark that I knew was rapidly growing. "This is terrible," she said. "First you destroy my paper, and then you lie to me about it. What are we going to do about this?"

I looked down at the floor. "Please be gentle," I said. "Please don't hurt me. I won't do it again, I promise."

"I think you need a lesson about leaving the newspaper alone, don't you?" she continued.

"I won't do it again," I repeated in a whimper.

"That's not good enough," Judy said. She walked across the room and reached inside the cabinet where we kept our videotapes. So that's where it had been hidden!

The sight of the black paddle in her hand was delicious. I could feel my pussy getting hot and wet. She slapped it against her palm, and the sharp crack made me jump.

"Now, you naughty girl," she said, "take off your dress."

I did. My nipples were hard as rocks and stood out urgently. My pussy was burning between my legs. I watched as Judy took off her dress as well. She looked so sexy, her beautiful tits and her dark pussy, and the cruel leather device in her hand. I wanted her so badly I didn't know how long I could wait.

She led me over to the sofa and made me kneel on

it. Then she pushed me down so that I was bent over the thickly padded arm. My ass was sticking up in the air, a perfect target for her leather friend. She pushed my legs apart so that my wet pussy was accessible.

She got on the sofa behind me. With my head down I couldn't see what she was doing. I tensed my bottom, expecting the firm crash of leather on my cheeks at any moment.

To my surprise, instead of the hard leather, I felt Judy's soft, warm tongue in my pussy. I groaned as she licked my hole and sucked my clit. I was confused. It felt so good and her touch was so tender, so different from the punishment I was expecting. Then just as suddenly it stopped.

Wham! The paddle came down with a sharp crack on my ass. The familiar searing pain shot through me. I cried out.

Again the paddle struck. Judy was right over me and was able to hit me with all her strength. It knocked the breath out of me and I tasted my tears. I was not going to forget this lesson quickly.

Then she leaned back and once again I felt her soft, feathery tongue on my steamy pussy. I was so confused by the blistering leather and her sweet tongue that I didn't know which felt better.

"Your ass is so red," Judy whispered, "and your pussy is so good and wet!" She licked slowly at my clit, and reached up to tease my asshole with her tongue. Gently she spread my ass cheeks apart, but I almost screamed when I felt her hands on me. My behind was so tender it hurt for her to touch me.

Her tongue on my clit was bringing me close to orgasm, but I knew she wouldn't let me go so quickly. Just as my body began to tense up, she stopped licking me and leaned back.

This time she didn't use the paddle. Instead, I felt

her firm hand spanking me hard. It didn't make as much noise as the leather, but it hurt me almost as much. She slapped both cheeks hard, then began a steady rhythm, counting out each blow as it landed on my sore skin.

"One!" she said. Her hand smacked against my ass and I cried out. "Don't use up all your tears yet," she warned. "You've been very naughty and I'm not finished with you!"

Two! This one landed across both cheeks with a resounding crack. I whimpered. My clit felt so hard and swollen I thought it might burst.

Three! Four! Five! I knew my ass was flaming red, and the skin was burning. Six! Seven! I was almost beside myself, and I wanted her tongue back on my pussy desperately.

She obliged me after two more hard smacks. My pussy felt creamy as her tongue glided back and forth over it. I could feel my juice on my thighs. It was as hot as the burning skin on my ass.

"Your cunt tastes so good," she purred, and stuck her tongue deep in my hole. I moaned with pleasure. She stuck two fingers in my wet hole and fucked me with them, rubbing my clit at the same time with her thumb.

I squirmed and pushed my clit against her. Her voice was soft and soothing. "That feels good, doesn't it?" she cooed. "Your pussy is so wet and so warm, my fingers are just sliding in. Oh, that must feel so nice."

Crack! I cried out as the leather paddle bit into my behind. Judy never stopped moving her fingers on my cunt. The pain and pleasure mingled together and I sobbed loudly. I couldn't see for the tears in my eyes.

Smack! The paddle landed again, and again. The

pain felt like boiling liquid flowing through the muscles of my ass. Then Judy bent down and sucked hard on my swollen clit.

It was too much. My climax was shattering. She kept licking me, and I just kept coming. I was dizzy as I cried out, bent over the sofa arm, my ass burning white-hot from my spanking, my clit sizzling from my licking.

Judy was just as excited. "Suck me now!" she ordered, and I turned around. She was already on her back, her legs spread apart and her pussy waiting for me.

I didn't need to be told twice. Within seconds I was down between her legs, inhaling the gorgeous thick scent of her sex. I thought her pussy would burn my tongue. She was wet all over and my tongue slid over her smooth, buttery flesh.

Her hands were on her breasts while I ate her, her fingers pulling and twisting her nipples. I loved the sight of her doing that, and it made me lick her faster and faster. She was moaning loudly and every so often she reached down and pushed my mouth hard against her clit. I took it between my lips and sucked on it, and she lifted her hips to grind it against me.

"Lick me! Lick me harder!" she cried. We were both in a frenzy, both of us soaked with sweat and very excited by my spanking. My tongue just couldn't go any faster on her.

I plunged my tongue again and again onto her clit, flicking it from side to side. Judy tensed up and shouted, "Lick me! Lick me! Ooh!" Then she came, with my tongue still firmly against her juicy clit. I loved every minute of it.

She hugged me tightly for a moment, then got up and retrieved the bottle of lotion. Once again I stretched out on the sofa and was treated to a delicious soothing massage on my fiery buttocks. I had never been spanked that hard before.

The paddle, damp with sweat, lay on the coffee table, as menacing as ever. I almost worshiped it. I shivered, and closed my eyes to enjoy Judy's light touch. She was so gentle I could hardly believe it was the same woman who had so firmly tanned my hide earlier.

"So, you naughty girl," she asked, while pouring on more cool lotion, "did you learn your lesson this time?"

"Oh, yes," I said quickly. I reached up to wipe away the last of my tears, and I knew my eyes were red and swollen also.

She continued to rub the lotion into my skin, pausing every now and again to plant a kiss on my stinging cheeks. She also stopped frequently for a kiss on my lips, and our warm tongues mingled with love and the memory of the fantastic sex we'd just shared.

I glanced over at the paddle. Even though my ass was burning, I was looking forward to another session of being at the paddle's mercy. Perhaps I had learned my lesson about the newspaper, but I knew for sure I'd soon be looking for new reasons for Judy to take me over her knee and give me a good old-fashioned spanking.

BEAUTIFUL BONDS

"She's at the booth in the corner, if you're interested."

Anne took the drink offered to her by the bartender, then looked around the room. It was difficult, for the lesbian bar was very popular, and was always filled and very smoky on Friday nights. She finally caught sight of the woman in the booth, who was watching her very intently from across the room.

Anne couldn't see her completely, but she noticed the heavy black leather motorcycle jacket right away. It definitely piqued her interest, and she felt the quick tingles in her pussy that she always had when she thought about women in leather. It was promising. Perhaps this would be the woman who would give her what she really wanted this night. It had been so long, and she was so damn horny. She picked up the drink—a perfectly mixed Manhattan, her usual order—and made her way through the crowded room.

She stood beside the booth, until the leather-clad woman motioned for her to sit down. She slipped into the empty seat opposite her. "Thank you for the drink," she said. "My name's Anne."

"My pleasure, Anne," the woman replied. "My name's Catherine. I saw you sitting up there and you looked pretty lonely, so I figured you might like some company."

Anne looked her over and was excited by what she saw. Catherine was a tall woman, with heavy breasts. Anne could tell because she wore nothing under the motorcycle jacket.

She was dressed entirely in leather. The sight made Anne catch her breath. The tight pants she wore were black leather like her jacket, and on her feet she wore heavy motorcycle boots with silver chains wrapped around the ankles and leather straps running under the soles. Catherine shifted, and Anne heard the noise they made. She peeked under the table. The sight sent a shiver down her spine. She absolutely loved the sight of chains, especially when they were wrapped firmly around something and locked tight.

Catherine noticed her right away, and she smiled. "You like those chains, do you?" she asked. "They're nice, aren't they?"

"They sure are," Anne said, sipping at her drink. She liked the way things were turning out, and she could feel her pussy starting to get wet.

Catherine looked at her over the rim of her glass. "I have a lot more chains at home," she said.

Anne was feeling weak by now. "I'd like to see them sometime," she said quietly.

Catherine reached across the table and carefully took a lock of Anne's long brown hair between her fingers. "Let's not sit and talk all night," she said. She began to twist the hair around her hand. "I think you're lovely, and I want you. I want to take you home with me and show you my chains. I think you'd like that. I think you'd like to be tied up, and have me make love to you." She paused a moment. "I'm right, aren't I?"

Was she! Anne was almost dizzy at the thought of being chained and at this woman's mercy. She nodded, and Catherine smiled knowingly. Anne squirmed on the hard wooden seat to relieve her burning pussy.

Catherine was very satisfied with her guess. "I thought so," she said. "Your cute little pussy's just dying to be worked over, isn't it?" Anne nodded again. "Then let's go see what we can do about that."

They finished their drinks and left the bar. Anne had come by taxi, but Catherine had arrived by a much more interesting means. Her huge Harley-Davidson decker sat outside and she took Anne's hand and led her over to it.

"Pretty impressive," Anne said.

"Yeah, it is nice, isn't it?" Catherine said, with obvious pride. "I've put a lot of work into it." It was painted a rich, deep purple and the chrome had been polished until it reflected like a mirror. Catherine handed over a helmet, which Anne put on, and then indicated how to climb up behind her on the seat.

The engine roared into life. Anne had never been on a bike that big before. She could feel the throbbing through the leather seat, right into her pussy that was already damp with anticipation.

They took off down the road. Anne's long hair streamed behind her and the bike's hard seat felt so good against her cunt. She began to understand the fascination Catherine had with the huge, powerful machine between her legs. She sat close to Catherine, and the warm, musky leather smell of her jacket sent a whisper-light chill through her. She looked down and saw the chains on Catherine's boots. She could almost feel chains on her wrists, on her ankles, binding her firmly and leaving her at her lover's mercy. She was torn between the pleasure of riding the motorcycle and the desire to be at Catherine's house in her bedroom.

Catherine lived a couple of miles from the bar, in a small house in a quiet neighborhood. Anne was surprised at how ordinary and domestic the area was, and she wondered what the neighbors made of this tall woman with her leather clothes and big motorcycle. She wondered what they would think if they only knew what was going to be happening inside very shortly. The garage door was open and Catherine drove the big bike inside.

Almost reluctantly Anne climbed off. On a warm night like this she would have been happy to sit behind Catherine and ride around right into the dawn. But there was more waiting for her inside, and she followed the tall woman into the house. There was no formality, no coffee in the living room and small talk beforehand. They were both as hot as they could possibly be, and Catherine took her straight into the bedroom.

Anne was surprised. On the way to Catherine's house, she had pictured a special sexual torture room, with chains hanging off the walls and all sorts of leather and metal devices. Instead, the room looked pretty much like any other as she stood in the doorway. The bed was very large and had a heavy brass headboard and foot, with spindles. The hardwood floor was polished to a high shine and there was a small braided mat beside the bed. The only other furniture were a large dresser and a pine nightstand, piled high with books.

Catherine was behind her, and suddenly Anne felt her strong hands reaching around her and cupping her breasts. Her fingers were lovely and warm through the thin fabric of Anne's shirt. Catherine played with her nipples, brushing her fingers over them and pinching them gently. Anne sighed. Her pussy was throbbing again, and deliciously wet.

"Turn around," Catherine said. Anne did, and met the tall woman's kiss. She felt her shirt being unbuttoned as Catherine's tongue pressed between her teeth and teased her. Then Catherine pushed the shirt off her shoulders and onto the floor.

"You have beautiful tits," Catherine whispered, and ran her hands over them. She then strayed down and unbuttoned Anne's slacks, letting them drop around her ankles. Anne was wearing black lace panties, and Catherine put her hand between her legs.

"Your pussy is so wet," she said, pushing Anne's hair back and kissing her neck. "You want this, don't you?"

"Yes," Anne whispered.

"I'm going to tie you to that bed so you can't move," Catherine promised. Anne felt her knees go weak. "You won't be able to do anything except lie back and let me do whatever I want. You want to be chained up, don't you? You want to be tied and maybe even gagged, right?"

"Oh, yes!" Anne whispered, and returned Catherine's probing kiss. "Yes, yes!"

Catherine led her over to the bed and made her sit down on it. Then she opened the deep drawer in the nightstand. Anne's eyes widened with delight. The drawer was crammed full of leather straps, handcuffs, and rope. Anne realized that she had definitely underestimated Catherine's bedroom, which had looked so ordinary at first glance and which was quickly turning into the secret garden of delights she had so longed for this night.

Catherine looked through the drawer, and finally decided on two pairs of gleaming chrome handcuffs. Anne felt her pussy throb as they were snapped around her wrists. Then Catherine made her lie on the bed, and the other ends were closed around the headboard spindles. She was helpless and both of them knew it.

Slowly Catherine took off her clothes. Anne's eyes never left her body. The heavy leather motorcycle jacket was unzipped and left on the floor. Catherine's breasts were large and heavy, with hard nipples that Anne longed to suck on. The boots, with the chains that Anne admired so much, were discarded as well. Then she unzipped the black leather pants, revealing black underwear. Once they were off, Anne's mouth watered at the sight of Catherine's luscious mound. She wanted to taste it so badly.

Catherine got on the bed beside Anne and reached down to kiss her. Their tongues mingled and Catherine ran her hands slowly down her captive's body. Anne wanted to touch Catherine as well, but she was firmly shackled to the brass bed. When she pulled on the handcuffs, the steel bit into her wrists. She relaxed and returned Catherine's kiss.

The tall woman inched her way down to Anne's breasts. She was very slow and careful as she licked and sucked on the nipples and twisted them with her fingers. Anne moaned. Her pussy was already hot, and she felt each touch of Catherine's tongue on her nipples as a sweltering ripple in her cunt.

Then Catherine bent over so that her tits were in Anne's face. Anne sucked them into her mouth happily. She held the hard nub of nipple gently between her teeth and flicked her tongue over them, then sucked into her mouth as much of Catherine's breast as she could.

Then just as suddenly, Catherine pulled away. "You do that well," she said. "But we have all night." Anne tried to reach for her, to pull her back, but the cruel handcuffs wouldn't let her move.

Catherine moved down on the big bed and positioned herself between Anne's legs. "I'll bet your pussy's just waiting for me, isn't it?" she asked. Anne nodded.

Catherine licked her right through her thin panties, and Anne moaned. The first hot touch of the tall woman's tongue sent a thrill right through her whole body. She pushed her hips up for more.

Catherine's tongue traced a line up Anne's inner thigh. Then, with the very tip, she pushed the thin panties back and licked the hot hairy lips underneath. She did this on both sides, leaving Anne's steamy hole and clit untouched. Anne groaned, and bent her knees so that she could move her pussy in front of Catherine's mouth.

Catherine glared at her. "You were supposed to lie still," she admonished. "I trusted that you would, but now I know you won't. I'll have to fix that."

Slowly she pulled Anne's panties off of her, taking a moment to run her finger quickly and lightly over the exposed clit. Anne sighed. Then Catherine was back in the nightstand drawer, searching for a suitable device.

She came back with two leather straps. She buckled one around each of Anne's ankles and stretched her legs apart. Then, with two large chrome clasps she firmly secured Anne's legs to the foot of the bed. Anne was now spread-eagled on the bed, her wrists contained in handcuffs, her feet bound in leather straps, unable to move.

Satisfied with her work, Catherine went back to her position between Anne's shackled legs. She was maddeningly slow and knew how badly her captive wanted her touch. It wouldn't hurt to make her wait just a little while longer.

She licked all around Anne's wet pussy. Helpless on the bed, Anne thought she would go crazy waiting for a touch on her clit. She longed to reach down and push Catherine's head between her legs, to put that hot tongue right where she wanted it and hold it there until she came. But the strong cuffs held her back.

Catherine continued her slow torture. Then she slowly slid her finger into Anne's wet, tight hole. Anne groaned, and then almost cried out as she felt the first hot sweep of Catherine's tongue on her swollen clit.

It was like liquid fire seething up through her belly. Catherine knew exactly where to put her tongue, and she flicked over the most sensitive areas for a long time until Anne was on the edge of coming. Then she would glide away and leave Anne smoldering and drum-tight, begging for more.

She kept this up for some time, Constantly bringing Anne close and then letting her slide back before concentrating her efforts again. Then she stopped completely. Anne tried to push herself up, to be closer to her and to beg for more, but her heavy bonds wouldn't let her move.

To her joy, though, Catherine moved up beside her. "You want to taste my pussy, don't you?"

"Oh, please, yes!" Anne begged. She got her wish immediately, as Catherine knelt over her.

Catherine was just as excited as she was. Her pussy was hot and wet and Anne quickly applied her tongue to it. Her salty-sweet juice was combined with a faint, warm odor from the leather she had worn. Anne breathed deeply to savor it. She was no slouch herself at eating pussy and she flicked hard over Catherine's clit. Without thinking, she tried to touch her sweet cunt and slip a finger inside. The handcuffs immediately sent out a painful but wonderfully exciting reminder.

She obeyed Catherine's commands, lapping slowly the length of her cunt when told to, pushing hard against her clit at other times. Catherine controlled her completely, grinding her pussy down at times, moving her hips so that she slid on Anne's tongue, or even pulling away for long moments while Anne waited desperately for the hot, wet flesh to come back to her.

Finally she came back, and Anne licked her juicy cunt for all she was worth. Her face was wet with Catherine's honey, and the smell of her sex was everywhere. Anne loved it, and lapped at her hard.

Catherine came noisily, rubbing her pussy against Anne's outstretched tongue until she was finally finished. "You're very good," she said, and stroked Anne's cheek. "Your poor little pussy probably wants the same thing." Anne nodded.

Once again she felt Catherine's firm tongue on her pussy, and she moaned at how good it felt. Catherine was all business now. She pushed her tongue in Anne's hole, and then flicked it up and pushed her clit with the tip. Anne felt like she was falling into her orgasm. Catherine sucked her clit as she came. She tried to squirm but the bonds held her firm and her excitement increased even more. When it was finally over she was wet with sweat.

Catherine stretched out beside her and gently kissed her, then soothingly ran her hand up and down her body. Finally, when Anne had calmed down from her orgasm and was completely relaxed, Catherine went to the foot of the bed and took the leather straps off her ankles. Anne gratefully bent her stiff knees, then moved her cramped legs back and forth. Then the handcuffs came off, and she rubbed her tender wrists. The red marks in her skin still excited her.

Catherine led her to the kitchen, where she made mugs of hot tea for both of them. They sat at the table sipping them.

"I'd really like it if you'd stay the night," Catherine said, and Anne agreed. It was late when they finished their drinks and they went back into the bedroom. There, Catherine buckled a leather strap around one of Anne's wrists and locked it to the bed. It was a symbolic gesture only, for Anne could easily have reached up and opened it, but the thought of being chained to this stranger's bed all night excited her immensely. Both of them knew she would still be locked onto it in the morning.

Catherine fell asleep hugged up tightly to her, and within moments of hearing her steady, shallow breathing, Anne fell asleep too. When she woke up, Catherine was already moving around the house as Anne was still getting her bearings.

She came into the bedroom, fully dressed, and took the strap off Anne's wrist. "I've called a taxi for you," she said. "I have to go to work today. You'd better get dressed."

She did. Her arm was cramped from lying in one

position all night, but her pussy still felt wonderfully satisfied from the previous night's session. When she went into the kitchen, Catherine had a mug of coffee waiting for her, and she drank it while waiting for her cab.

She saw the car pull up in front of the house. Catherine asked her where she was going, then pressed money into her hand to cover the fare. "I'm usually at the bar in the evenings," she said. "You might want to come back in and see me."

She kissed her deeply, then led her out of the house and locked the door behind them. Anne got into the taxi and told the driver her destination. As the car pulled away, she looked out the back window and got a glimpse of Catherine driving off in the opposite direction on the huge purple Harley.

She didn't go home, but decided to go to the mall near her apartment and do some shopping. She stopped for breakfast in the mall restaurant first and sat by herself at the window. The early summer sun was very bright and she basked in its warmth as it streamed through the glass. When she reached for her toast, the bright light showed up the angry red marks left on her wrists by the chrome handcuffs. The whole beautiful evening came back to her vividly as she rubbed her wrists carefully.

Throughout the morning she was reminded of Catherine constantly. Her arm was still sore from being shackled to the bed all night, but she relished the pain. Her ankles felt a bit raw from the heavy leather straps. When she tried on a shirt, the sales clerk adjusted the sleeves, and Anne could see that she was looking at the marks on her wrists with a puzzled expression. It pleased her no end, and she wondered if the clerk would ever know exactly what had caused them.

Walking past a shoe store, she glanced into the window and stopped dead. Right at the back of the display was a pair of expensive snakeskin cowboy boots, and slung around the ankles were decorative silver chains. She remembered the sound that Catherine's made and the way they were wrapped so tightly.

She went back to the bar on Monday night. To her pleasure, she saw the big Harley parked outside. The place was almost empty, and Catherine spotted her right away, motioning for her to sit down in the booth.

"I thought you weren't coming back," she said, motioning for the waitress to bring Anne a drink.

"I had plans I'd made a long time ago," Anne explained. "I couldn't get out of them."

Catherine reached across the table and stroked her cheek. "I've been thinking about you," she said. "I was really hoping I'd see you again."

The Manhattan arrived and Anne sipped at it. She noticed that Catherine was wearing a heavy, chainlink gold bracelet as well as the chains on her boots. She was thrilled. Everything about the woman reminded her of being helpless and shackled on the bed. She had never met anyone this powerful before.

Even Catherine's leather clothes turned her on again. Her pussy grew very warm. The black leather reminded Anne of the strap she had worn through the night, the strap that made her Catherine's property and bound her to the bed where they had enjoyed their wild sex.

Once again, Catherine was straight to the point, all business. When they finished their drinks, she paid the bill and led Anne outside. As before, they both climbed on the big bike and rumbled onto the street.

It was still fairly early and many of Catherine's

neighbors were outside. Anne still couldn't picture Catherine living in this neighborhood, where people were cutting the grass or sitting on the porch, and children were playing or riding their bicycles. Except for the motorcycle in the garage, Catherine's house looked the same as any other, with its neatly-trimmed lawn, geraniums in the flowerbed and curtains in the window. She didn't think any of the neighbors could ever dream about the wild sex scenes that took place in Catherine's bedroom, its dresser drawer jammed with handcuffs and straps. She finally realized that this was probably the whole idea behind the small, well-kept bungalow.

Catherine parked the motorcycle, closed the garage door, and unlocked the door that led into the house. This time, though, they passed by Catherine's bedroom entirely. She led Anne down the hall to another door.

This opened onto a second bedroom, but it was considerably different from Catherine's modest sleeping area. Anne's eyes opened wide as she looked around. The room was almost empty, except for a plain daybed heaped with pillows and a chair.

The walls were what fascinated her. It seemed that Catherine had a secret torture room after all. At several spots there were heavy metal rings screwed into the white paneling, all at various heights. Some were close to the floor while others were further up on the walls than Anne could reach. There were even four of them screwed into the ceiling.

One of the pairs of rings, almost at Anne's eye level, had short chains attached to them. Dangling from the chains were a pair of leather straps similar to the ones she had worn all night. She sucked in her breath. Below them, almost at the floor, were two more rings, with the same chains. The heavy leather straps lay open and inviting on the carpet.

Catherine closed the door behind them and moved to face Anne. She kissed her hard and slipped her tongue inside her captive's mouth. Anne returned the kiss, shyly at first and then with increasing excitement. She once again felt herself slipping helplessly under Catherine's powerful spell.

The tall woman undressed her quickly and led her to the wall. She positioned her so that her back was to the wall and expertly buckled the straps on her wrists and ankles.

Anne was almost beside herself with desire. Her arms were stretched out on either side of her, and she was firmly shackled so that she could hardly move. The rings holding her ankles were far enough apart that her legs were spread and her wet pussy was exposed and waiting for Catherine's touch. The wall was hard and cool behind her. Her discomfort only added to her excitement. She wondered what Catherine had in store for her.

Catherine was meanwhile doing a slow striptease in front of her. She unzipped the heavy motorcycle jacket and tossed it on the floor. Her large breasts were held in a supple black leather bra with holes cut out so that her large nipples showed through. Just as slowly she unfastened the leather pants, and stuck her hand inside to feel her own pussy. "That's for you," she promised, and Anne's tongue pressed against her teeth, desperately wanting a taste of it. Under the leather jeans, Catherine was wearing soft leather panties that matched the bra.

She stepped over to Anne and kissed her. As she did, she reached down and took Anne's breasts into her hands, cupping and kneading them. Anne groaned and returned her kiss. Every now and again

Catherine would step back and break off the kiss, then return a few moments later. Anne was helpless and could only wait for her to return. The straps kept her firmly chained to the wall and Catherine took every opportunity to remind her of it.

"Lick my tits," Catherine said, and stood straight before her. She was tall enough that Anne had only to bend her head down to reach the breast that Catherine put in front of her.

She sucked the nipple into her mouth. The leather bra tasted musky and stale in her mouth but she loved it. Catherine's nipple was firm and she could feel it growing harder and bigger between her lips. Catherine moved back and forth, feeding her one nipple and then the other. Sometimes she would step back and Anne would be cruelly reminded of her bondage before the hot nipples were given back to her.

Catherine then knelt on the floor before her. Anne's legs were already spread wide by the unforgiving straps and she moaned as she felt Catherine's hot, wet tongue part her pussy lips and slide over her clit.

Catherine's tongue danced over her. Anne wanted to move, to push that probing tongue deeper, but she could only stand ramrod-straight against the wall, her wrists hanging in the straps.

Hot thrills went up and down Anne's spine as Catherine licked her. Anne could feel hot juice on her legs and she knew her pussy was soaked. Her legs felt weak, but there was no relief from her chains. She closed her eyes and enjoyed the attention her pussy was receiving.

Catherine then stopped and stood up. Anne moaned. She had been so close to coming! But Catherine just held her tits and kissed her, seemingly oblivious to Anne's agony. Anne could taste her own pussy on Catherine's tongue, and she kissed her hard. The hot smell of her cunt seemed to be everywhere.

Then Catherine abruptly turned and walked out of the room, closing the door behind her. Anne was completely confused and struggled in her bonds, which of course didn't budge.

She waited for several minutes. Her arms had gone numb but she barely felt her discomfort. Her eyes were glued to the door, waiting for Catherine to return.

The door finally opened, and Anne's eyes went wide in surprise. The leather underwear set was gone. Instead, Catherine wore a harness strapped firmly around her hips. At the front was a large curved dildo sticking out of it.

Catherine closed the door behind her and walked toward Anne. "It's a nice big one, isn't it?" she crooned. Her hand stroked the head as if she were masturbating. "I want to fuck you with it."

She hugged Anne's neck and kissed her hard. Anne felt the dildo between them, the head pressed against her belly. It was warm, as if it had been dipped in hot water, and was made of supple rubber that felt almost like flesh. Still with her mouth on Anne's, Catherine swung her hips so that the dildo stroked them both. Then she reached down and put the head at Anne's pussy lips.

The lips were pushed aside and Anne felt the head in her cunt. She groaned and pushed her tongue in Catherine's mouth. Slowly the dildo slid into her. She felt deliciously full.

"Do you like my dick in you?" Catherine whispered. She slowly stroked it in and out of Anne's sopping pussy. "I've got a beautiful big dick, haven't I?"

"Yes!" Anne whispered. Catherine was kissing her neck, her face, her lips. The dildo was sliding in faster and faster. Catherine was kissing her neck, her face, her lips. The dildo was sliding in faster and faster. Catherine reached down and slipped her hand between them so that her fingers were on Anne's clit. Anne moaned as she felt her hot button being massaged.

Catherine was fucking her hard now. The rubber cock banged into her again and again. With each thrust, Anne felt Catherine's fingers rub her clit. There was nothing else in the world except her pussy. She wanted Anne to push the dildo in her up to its root. "Fuck me faster!" she gasped. "Oh yes, harder! Fuck me!"

Her ass was being pounded into the wall. The dildo went deep again and again and Catherine's fingers groped hard at her clit.

She came so violently she thought she would pass out. With the dildo inside her she tensed up and felt the burning flood go through her body. She all but screamed as the final throbs tore at her and she hung from her chains limply, completely drained. She would have fallen if her shackles hadn't held her up.

Catherine stepped back, sliding the dildo out of Anne's pussy. It was wet and glistening. She unbuckled the straps holding Anne's wrists. Anne's legs were too weak to support her and Catherine held her tightly, lowering her gently to the carpet until she was stretched out on her stomach. She remained shackled to the wall by her legs.

Anne sobbed as the feeling returned to her numb arms in painful swells. The agony mingled deliciously with the sweet satisfaction in her pussy. Catherine waited until she had enough strength back in her arms to lift herself up on her elbows.

She then sat on the carpet in front of Anne, her legs stretched out on either side of her. The dildo stood up defiantly from its harness. "Suck my cock!" Catherine ordered. "Suck it hard!"

Anne took the rubber dildo into her mouth. Her sweet pussy juice was all over it. She licked the head, then sucked it in deeply. Catherine watched her with a smile on her face. She loved having a woman captive and bound in front of her as much as Anne loved the feeling of ropes and chains around her wrists.

She let Anne lick and suck the cock for quite a while. Then she leaned back and unstrapped the harness. It was tossed onto the chair and Catherine stretched out on the floor, her pussy in front of Anne's face. She was just far enough away that Anne had to stretch out, the chains on her ankles holding her back. She could feel the constant pressure on her feet, a reminder that she was still very firmly under Catherine's domination.

Catherine's pussy was as wet as Anne's had been. Anne licked it eagerly, savoring the hot, wine-rich taste. Catherine held her head firmly as she sucked at the tall woman's cunt. The shackles held Anne firmly to the wall.

She used the tip of her tongue to stroke Catherine's clit, then lapped hard up and down her whole pussy. Catherine moaned. She flicked the swollen clit back and forth, faster and faster.

Catherine groaned loudly as she came, her whole body shivering. Just as she began to calm down, Anne licked her hard several times, sending rich spasms through her and prolonging the wonderful sensations.

Catherine finally got up and unbuckled the straps holding Anne's ankles. It felt so good to move her legs and bend her knees. They hugged each other, lying on the thickly carpeted floor. It felt so good to kiss and caress.

Catherine asked her if she could stay the night again, and Anne quickly agreed. It was dark outside but still warm, and Catherine got two bottles of beer out of the refrigerator and led Anne outside to the patio in the back yard.

It felt very strange to Anne, sitting in the lawn chair talking and drinking beer as if she were visiting her family at home. The quiet domestic setting was totally at odds with the Catherine who had shackled her firmly to the wall and fucked her so completely. It was like a completely different world outside the little house.

Catherine even waved to her neighbors next door when they came out to sit on their own patio. Anne felt an odd sensation go through her. She didn't know if it was pride or the fact that she knew a forbidden secret that the neighbors on the street would never be able to guess. The neighbors saw a neat house with a manicured lawn and a nicely kept flower garden. Anne knew a drawer filled with strange devices, and a room with rings on the walls and chains that dangled from them and held women tight.

The strange feeling passed quickly enough when Catherine decided it was time for bed, and they went back into the house. She would not let Anne undress herself, but insisted on doing it as Anne stood in the hallway just outside the bedroom.

Anne looked inside and saw the familiar brass bed. Then she noticed a chain firmly locked on it, and a leather strap waiting for her on the pillow. Her pussy stirred and she returned Catherine's kiss passionately. She could hardly wait.

MISTRESS' ORDERS

I heard the familiar hiss just before the riding crop landed on my bare ass. I knew it was coming, I knew how it would burn a welt into my pale skin, but it still caught me totally by surprise. My Mistress had a way of doing that.

"Stupid slave!" she said again and again, and each time the crop punctuated her words. Within moments I was sobbing and my ass was burning hot. No matter what, I knew I would never do that again.

"That" was the horrible crime of upsetting half a bucket of soapy water on the kitchen floor. I had been ordered to scrub it on my hands and knees with a small scrub brush. Somehow I had turned around too quickly and had bumped the bucket with my elbow. That was enough to knock it over, and enough to set off my Mistress' temper.

"Now finish your job, and don't fuck up again!" she hissed. I started to get up, but the crop slammed into my back. "You don't walk again until I tell you it's permissible," she said. "If you need anything, you crawl."

It wasn't easy crawling with the bucket in front of me, and I had to go all the way to the bathroom since the faucet in the tub would be the only one I would be able to reach from my knees. But my Mistress had ordered it, and that was what I would have to do.

I had been coming to my Mistress' penthouse apartment for six months. I met her when she placed an advertisement in the personals column of a local paper. I had answered it and was given her address. When I arrived, the sweet voice on the intercom invited me to come upstairs.

It was much different once I found myself in front of her apartment door. She opened it about an inch, and ordered me to strip off all of my clothes, standing there in the hallway. I'd never done anything like that before, but there was a steely strength in her voice that told me refusal would be very foolish. I dropped my clothes right there, got on all fours as she ordered, and finally crawled inside the apartment. I had been coming back regularly ever since.

I finally made my way up the long hallway to the bathroom, and slipped the bucket under the faucet. I filled it up and then discovered that getting to the bathroom had been the easy part. Getting the heavy bucket back to the kitchen without spilling any was going to take a tremendous amount of work.

I eventually did it by sliding the bucket forward an inch at a time, praying that the suds wouldn't splash out over the top. It seemed to take forever, but I got

back to the kitchen and continued scrubbing. My
knees were killing me but there was nothing I could
do. Mistress had ordered it, and I would obey.

"Alicia!"

"Yes, Mistress?" I replied.

"Alicia, hurry up with that floor." She appeared in
the doorway. As always, she was magnificent. She
was wearing a black corset and matching panties, and
her long beautiful legs were clad in black fishnet
stocking. Her heels were impossibly high. The leather
riding crop was still in her hand. "Mistress Lorna will
be here very shortly, and I don't want you still cleaning up."

"Yes, Mistress," I said, and scrubbed faster.
Mistress Lorna was one of her lovers—just how
many she had, I didn't know. She had other slaves as
well, for I'd often seen coarse clothes and shackles
that I'd never worn. But I had never met them, and I
knew better than to ask.

I was finally finished. My Mistress gave me permission to stand up, and I did so stiffly. Everything was
ready. There was a bottle of fine champagne chilling
in the refrigerator, along with the expensive hors
d'oeuvres that the catering company had dropped off
earlier in the day. The apartment was spotless.

"Go and clean yourself up," she ordered. I did so
gratefully. The shower was hot and I could have
stood under it all day, but I knew better. I soaped
myself quickly, washed my hair and got out. Keeping
my Mistress waiting was not a good idea.

I dried myself off. My Mistress was waiting in her
bedroom for me. She combed my hair and dried it. I
was spritzed with perfume, and a tiny touch of rouge
was dabbed on my nipples to bring out their color. I was
given a pair of tiny lace panties to put on. My costume
was complete when my Mistress buckled a wide leather

dog collar around my neck. It hung a bit loosely, heavy with metal studs. I loved the feeling of it around my throat. She often put it on me and snapped a leash on, making me walk around the apartment, sometimes on my feet, sometimes on my hands and knees.

She was just finishing up when the intercom buzzer rang. "Go wait in the living room, Alicia," she said, as she went to answer it.

I knew my position from past experience. There was a corner, empty of any furniture, and I got on my knees, my back straight and my hands on my thighs.

I heard her greet Mistress Lorna at the door, and soon afterward they both came into the living room. I had been in Mistress Lorna's presence once before. She was a tall black woman, beautifully built and with an icy, cold stare that sent shivers down my spine. She was dressed in a tight leather miniskirt and a shirt that showed off her hard nipples.

They sat down on the sofa. Mistress Lorna glanced over at me, but her expression didn't change. It was as if I were just another piece of furniture in the room. She talked to my Mistress casually about the traffic outside and how warm it was. Neither of them seemed to notice that there was a woman, almost naked and wearing a dog's collar, sitting on the floor in front of them.

Finally my Mistress looked over in my direction. "Alicia, we'll have some champagne now," she said. "And bring out the tray of food."

"Yes, Mistress," I said, and hurried to fulfill her orders. The champagne was very cold and I eased the cork out of the bottle, then poured two glasses and set them on a silver tray. I took it to them. They each took a glass without even glancing at me.

I returned to the kitchen, put the bottle back in the refrigerator, and took out the box containing the hors d'oeuvres. They were exquisite. There were toast rounds with caviar, little sausage rolls, shrimp in puff pastry cases and tiny tarts filled with curried chicken and pine nuts. I was hungry, and the sight of the tray made my mouth water. I knew better than to touch one, though. My ass was still tender from my lesson over the water bucket.

I set the tray down on the table and hurried back to my corner. My Mistress stopped me. "Alicia," she said, "come back and sit at the table."

I knelt down before the table, the tray of food in front of me. They ignored me, sipping their champagne and taking the tidbits between their long, painted fingernails. I wanted a treat badly and I couldn't help staring at them.

My Mistress took a bite of her sausage roll, then held the other half out to me, like she was feeding a dog. I couldn't resist and snatched it from her fingers with my teeth.

What a mistake! Immediately my Mistress slapped my face hard. I blinked away tears and hung my head.

"You know better than that!" she hissed. My cheek was burning and I knew it was bright red. "You've been taught to take food properly!"

"I'm sorry, Mistress," I said. "I should have known better. I was hungry and I forgot what I was doing."

Her voice became a bit softer, the mockery of a concerned parent. "Of course you're hungry," she said. "You've been working all day with nothing to eat. Come here, my little slave."

I did. My Mistress gave me a curry tart and then a round of the black caviar. They were delicious, but shortly after I ate them, I realized that her kindness had been a cruel trap. The salt had parched my throat and I was dreadfully thirsty.

"Please, Mistress," I begged, "may I have a drink?"

She had been in mid-sentence, speaking with Mistress Lorna. I saw her hand raise, but she moved so quickly I didn't have time to flinch. Again her hand struck my cheek hard, knocking me over. I knew better than to get up.

"Stupid slave!" she cried. "How dare you interrupt me when I'm speaking! Not only will you get no water but you can stay on the floor like that until we're ready for you."

They both carried on just as calmly as before. Neither of them even glanced at me, lying on the floor on my side, tears streaming from my eyes. I watched them intently. Even when she was cruel to me, I couldn't take my eyes off my beautiful Mistress.

My Mistress reached across and took Mistress Lorna's champagne glass out of her hand, setting it on the table. She then leaned over and kissed Mistress Lorna's full, luscious lips. My tongue licked my own lips. I wanted to be kissed by my Mistress like that.

They didn't even acknowledge that there was a third person in the room. I was only a slave and of no more account than the table or the carpet. I watched them, but stayed down; I still hadn't been given permission to get up.

My Mistress leaned back as Mistress Lorna rubbed her tits through her black corset. They kissed again, and then Mistress Lorna licked and sucked at her nipples which stuck out just over the tops of her lace cups. Kneeling on the carpet, she removed my Mistress' panties.

I saw my Mistress' beautiful cunt as she spread her legs open and leaned back into the cushions. Mistress Lorna took the place I longed to be in, right in front of that hot, steamy mound. She began to lick my Mistress' clit. My mouth was watering, my thirst forgotten, as I watched her. I desperately wanted to do it for her instead.

She licked slowly, until my Mistress told her she wanted it faster and harder. Immediately Mistress Lorna's tongue was dancing like wildfire over my Mistress' clit. I was insanely jealous, but there was nothing I could do but lie on the floor and obey my Mistress' command to stay where her blow had sent me.

My Mistress came very quickly. She did not cry out, but I saw her muscles tense and her legs quiver in the way I knew well. She pulled her panties back up, and as Mistress Lorna returned to the sofa beside her, she picked up her champagne glass and took a sip. Her eyes fell on me.

"Oh, the slave," she said. "I had forgotten about you. You may sit up now."

I did. "Thank you, Mistress."

Daintily my Mistress took a shrimp tidbit. This time I got none. "Did you bring it?" she asked Mistress Lorna.

"Of course," the black woman replied. She looked at me over the rim of her champagne glass. I dropped my eyes. Although she wasn't my Mistress, she was a dominatrix too and commanded the same respect. Only a command from my own Mistress could override any order from her. I had learned that lesson the first time I had met her. I had failed to treat her with the proper respect. My Mistress had bound me, strapped a rubber ball gag in my mouth, and beaten me thoroughly with her riding crop, allowing Mistress Lorna the privilege of a few hard strokes of her own.

Mistress Lorna reached into her purse. My eyes opened wide as she brought out a long, dildo-shaped vibrator and handed it to my Mistress.

"Take your panties off," my Mistress ordered.

I did. Mistress Lorna looked at me and said, "Oh you found yourself a cute little one." My Mistress smiled.

My Mistress turned the dial on the bottom of the device and the vibrator hummed. She held it between her hands, then ran it over her neck. "Good," she said. "This will do just fine."

To my horror, she handed the vibrator over the table to me. It was still humming and the vibrations ran through my hands. My Mistress smiled. "Use it," she said.

I looked at her puzzled. "Mistress?"

"You heard me," she said coldly. "Use it."

Slowly I moved the vibrator between my legs. I was still kneeling on the floor.

"Not that way," my Mistress said. "Lie on your back. We want to see just what you're doing."

My face was burning with shame as I stretched out on the carpet. Certainly I had masturbated before—I did it every time I went home after visiting my Mistress. But I had never done such a thing in front of anyone else. It had always been a private act for me. Now I was being forced to submit to the pleasures of a battery-operated machine while lying on the floor before my Mistress and her guest.

"We'd appreciate it if this could be accomplished today," my Mistress said sarcastically. "Or would you prefer using it with the riding crop stuffed up your ass too?"

"No, Mistress," I whispered. I put the humming vibrator to my pussy and closed my eyes.

Despite my embarrassment, the vibrator felt good on my clit. I always enjoyed making myself come, because no one knew the sensitive spots better than I did. The humiliation of doing it solely because my mistress had commanded me to heightened my excitement more than I thought it would. She knew it, too; in fact, she knew all the right buttons to push. She had not been the first dominatrix I had known, but she was definitely the best.

"Open your eyes," my Mistress said. I did. They were still drinking their champagne and eating the hors d'oeuvres. They did not watch me all the time, but occasionally looked over during their conversation.

I couldn't help myself. The vibrator felt so good, and I began pushing it hard against my clit and moving it back and forth. I was so close to coming. My hips moved up and down, grinding the humming wand deeper. I was breathing heavily, relishing the warmth in my wet pussy.

"Alicia," my Mistress said, "Mistress Lorna's glass is empty. Bring us more champagne.

I could hardly believe it. I was so close to slipping into a huge orgasm! But there would be a terrible penalty for ignoring my Mistress' command. I turned the vibrator off and got up. I waited while my Mistress drained her glass and carried them both into the kitchen.

My breath was coming in sobs. My pussy was throbbing and my whole belly felt tight and unfulfilled. I took clean glasses from the cupboard and uncorked the bottle. It seemed to take forever for the rush of bubbles to subside so that I could finish filling the glasses. Every second I spent in that kitchen was a moment away from the delicious vibrator.

I put the glasses on the silver tray and carried them back to the two women on the sofa. They took them, and I returned the tray to the kitchen, then went back and stood before my Mistress.

"Well, what are you waiting for?" she asked. "Go back to what you were doing."

158

This time I was so hot, there was no shame. I got back on the floor and turned the dial on that wonderful little device. I didn't care that they were enjoying my humiliation. All that mattered was the liquid fire in my pussy that the vibrator was stoking.

I came so violently I thought I would push the vibrator right through my clit. My legs shook and my hips bucked wildly. I felt dizzy with the rush that flowed through me, and when I finally turned the vibrator off it was soaked with my pussy juice. My whole body was covered with sweat.

"How was that, Alicia?" my Mistress asked in a buttery-smooth voice.

"Oh, wonderful, Mistress!" I said. "Thank you, Mistress. Thank you, Mistress Lorna."

"She's worked up quite a sweat," Mistress Lorna observed.

"You're right," my Mistress said. "I'd better take care of that. I don't want her getting sick or anything. I'll let her cool off."

My Mistress told me to sit up. Then she went into the bedroom and returned with a heavy leather dog leash. She snapped one end of it to the ring in my studded collar. Then she made me get up, and led me to the door that opened onto her balcony.

My knees went weak as I realized what she was going to do. "Mistress, no!" I begged. That earned me another slap on my cheek, and I kept silent. Tears were running down my face as I prepared for one of my most basic fears.

She opened the door and brazenly led me out on the balcony. We were on the top floor, but the balcony had glass walls, and anyone looking over from another penthouse would be able to see me. She tied the leash to the metal railing just above the glass. I could not reach the door, and had to remain close to the clear glass wall.

My Mistress went back into the apartment and closed the door firmly behind her. I was trapped. I curled up into a ball. It was very warm outside, and I was not uncomfortable, but it went through my mind that the nice sunny weather might make other people think about sitting on their own balconies. I looked around. No one else was out, but I was still terrified.

I could easily have untied the leash and cringed against the door, but that was out of the question. My Mistress had tied me here, and I would have to stay here until she decided it was time to take me inside. Her word was law. If she decided to leave me out all night, then I would just have to sleep curled up against the glass.

At one point she must have remembered my thirst, for she came outside—a heavy satin robe over her corset—and brought me a glass of water. I drank gratefully while she held the glass as if for a child. I thanked her, but did not ask to be let back in. It was her decision. She closed the door behind her.

I had one close call, when a neighbor decided to come out on his own balcony. I hear the door and looked over, horrified, as a man walked to the railing and took in the view below. But he never looked over, and to my immense relief, he finally went back inside. My heart beat so hard my whole body shook.

Finally, an eternity later, my Mistress came out and calmly untied the leash, then led me back inside. "Mistress Lorna has left," she said as she unsnapped it from my collar. "You may clean up now."

"Yes, Mistress," I said, and hurried to carry the trays and glasses back to the kitchen and wash them. When I was finished, she walked into the kitchen and threw my clothes on the floor. "Leave now," she said.

I dressed quickly, then stood by the door. I knew I

had to wait, without calling for her, until she was ready for me. She took a long time before walking over and unbuckling the collar from around my neck. "Thank you, Mistress," I whispered.

"I will send for you," she said, and I walked out into the hall. The door closed behind me.

All the way home I watched the people on the bus, like a child with an enormous secret. No one would ever suspect that the small, ordinary-looking woman in their midst had spent her afternoon in a collar, her most private sexual act witnessed by two women who thought nothing of it. Would they understand why I craved the humiliation of being tied naked outside? Could they know that even now my pussy was burning with desire to be in that collar again, at the mercy of my Mistress? When I finally arrived home I was so excited that I tore off my clothes and used my own vibrator to give myself another shattering orgasm.

I received a note from my Mistress in the mail a few days later. I could tell it was from her right away, by the neat script and the crisp, heavy stationery, written with the costly fountain pen I had seen her use. Everything about her was classy and expensive.

The note was brief, consisting of a single order. Be at her apartment in two days, at two o'clock. There was no signature, no return address. I felt weak and wondered how I was going to get through those two days. I suffered through two sleepless nights and when I was finally ready to leave for her apartment, I had worked myself up into a sweet sexual frenzy.

My Mistress met me at the door to her apartment. She was dressed in a tight black bodysuit made of thin, supple leather, and she wore stiletto-heeled boots that came up over her knees. Her long dark hair curled about her face. She held her riding crop in one hand and my dog collar in another. I breathed hard. I could almost have come just at the sight of her. I wanted to fall on the floor and lick her boots, giving myself over to her completely.

She motioned for me to come inside. "Undress yourself," she said, as she closed the door behind me.

I started to strip my clothes off, but I was so eager I fumbled with the buttons on my shirt. Immediately the riding crop slammed against my ass. Tears sprang to my eyes and I could feel a welt rising up. I hurried to get the shirt off, but taking much more care this time. My Mistress seldom repeated a punishment twice; if I didn't learn the first time, I could count on a much more severe reminder to follow.

When I was completely naked, the heavy dog collar was put around my neck and buckled into place. I was instructed to follow my Mistress into the kitchen. It was quickly obvious that this was the only piece of clothing I was going to receive.

At her command, I knelt before her on the hard kitchen floor. As always, it was spotless, and I wondered if another slave had been whipped while washing it as I had been. My hands on my knees, my head bowed, I sat while my Mistress reached down and toyed with a lock of my hair.

"This is a very special day, Alicia," she said. She moved closer and I could smell her rich perfume and the warm leather smell of her boots. "As a result, I have some very special instructions for you. I want you to listen carefully, for I will not repeat them."

"Yes, Mistress," I said.

"We have a guest today," she said, "a guest who has brought an interesting playmate. You are not to speak a single word to this playmate, under any circumstances. You are not to speak any words except

'Yes, Mistress,' or 'No, Mistress,' and you are only to speak when you are spoken to. Do you understand?"

"Yes, Mistress," I said. "I—"

Another mistake! Immediately I felt her fingers grab my collar and I was pulled roughly to my feet. "You stupid slave!" she said. "You can't follow even the simplest instructions! You need a lesson in discipline."

With that, she opened a drawer and pulled out two metal objects. I felt myself go cold as I realized they were nipple clamps. Within seconds she had snapped them shut on my tender flesh.

I knew screaming wouldn't be permitted, so I bit my tongue hard. My whole chest felt like the skin was being ripped off it. The cruel clamps twisted and burned. I knew from experience that they were a double-edged sword; it hurt as much to take them off as to put them on. I would pay dearly for my mistake not once, but twice.

She reached out and tapped one of the clamps with her finger. My stomach churned with the pain, but only a tiny groan escaped my lips.

"That's much better," she smiled. "No get to work. There's a bottle of champagne in the refrigerator. We will have two glasses in the living room." She turned on one incredibly high heel and left.

I struggled to uncork the bottle. Every movement of my arms seemed to make the clamps bite harder, and I had to stop and steady myself when a wave of nausea caused by the pain flashed through me. I poured the rich, wheat-colored wine and placed the glasses on the silver tray. I carried them very carefully, taking tiny steps so that my breasts didn't move and send more pain through me.

Mistress Lorna was seated on the sofa beside my Mistress. She was dressed in a luscious tight suit with cutouts for her large breasts. They stood out firmly with the nipples hard and inviting. But I had eyes only for my Mistress, who took her offered glass of champagne with her long, graceful fingers.

"Down on the floor, Alicia," my Mistress ordered once I had served Mistress Lorna. I put the tray on the table and then knelt before her.

"We have a surprise for you," Mistress Lorna said. "Come here, Sandra."

I could hardly believe it. A woman walked in from around the corner and swiftly knelt on the floor before Mistress Lorna. I stared, open-mouthed.

She was blonde, about my age, and she looked at me with the same puzzled interest. She was naked, wearing only a heavy chain around her neck and leather straps on her wrists that could quickly be snapped together to bind her. She looked at my breasts, with the unforgiving nipple clamps secured on them, and I felt my face grow red. No one but my Mistress and three of her dominatrix friends had ever seen me as a slave. I felt almost violated.

"This is Sandra," my Mistress said. "She belongs to Mistress Lorna. I am sure you two would have plenty to talk about, but she is under the same rule of silence that you are. You may not speak to each other, and you may not speak unless spoken to. If either of you breaks this rule, you will both be punished."

They sipped their champagne, then my Mistress snapped her fingers at me. "Come here, Alicia," she said. "On your hands and knees."

I did, then knelt before her. Roughly she tore the clamps off my nipples. I fought hard to keep from fainting. My flesh was burning hot and I was in agony.

"That must really hurt," my Mistress said.

"Sandra, come over here and make Alicia's nipples feel better."

"Yes, Mistress," the blonde woman said, and she crawled over on her hands and knees to me. I could hardly believe it when she tenderly took my sore tits in her hands and began to lick my nipples. The two women on the sofa sipped their drinks and looked on approvingly. This was a novelty for all of us and for once they were not ignoring me.

Her soft tongue did make my nipples feel better. I began to experience the hot stirrings in my pussy that I knew so well. The thought of being caressed by another slave, a woman I couldn't even speak to, while my Mistress and her lover watched was turning me on immensely. I could not have refused her touch. I was only a slave in my Mistress' command.

Sandra was obviously being turned on as well. She was now circling my nipples with her tongue and sucking on them, flicking her tongue over them rapidly. A soft moan escaped me. "That's it, Alicia," my Mistress said. "Let us know how good it feels." I gasped as the blonde woman nibbled gently on my sore nipple. The pain was as exquisite as the pleasure of her tongue.

"Don't be greedy," my Mistress said. "Share with Sandra. Show her what you can do."

The blonde woman sat up straight. Her nipples were huge and I sucked them into my mouth. I felt so strange making love to a woman I couldn't even speak to. She moaned as well as I worked her nipples over with my mouth.

"Sandra," Mistress Lorna said, "lie down on the floor. Do as I told you to."

"Yes, Mistress," Sandra whispered. I could see how uncomfortable she was, performing in front of them. She stretched out on her back.

"Now, Alicia," my Mistress said, "turn around and get on top of her."

My eyes widened as I realized what they expected us to do. I didn't move fast enough and within a second, the riding crop had smashed down twice across my shoulders. "I gave you an order, slave!" my Mistress hissed. "I don't expect to have to repeat it!"

"Yes, Mistress," I said. Carefully I positioned myself over the blonde woman, who looked just as embarrassed as I felt. My pussy was over her face, and her blonde mound was right below me.

I flicked my tongue over her pussy. She was hot and wet, and in that moment, I realized that I was too. This unique brand of domination was turning both of us on. I felt her hot tongue flash over my own clit and I moaned.

I couldn't help myself. It just felt so good, and within moments I was eating her cunt as joyfully as if it had been my Mistress'. Meanwhile her tongue was doing a number on my clit as well, and by the way she was moving her hips, I knew she was enjoying it too.

Everything I had was centered on the blonde woman's steamy pussy. The rich smell of her cunt was in my nose, my skin, my hair. Her thick sweet juice was all over my tongue and chin. I sucked on her clit and pushed a finger into her tight, hot hole. I continued to slide it in and out while I licked her.

She was just as occupied with me. I could feel pressure building up in my cunt as her tongue did a swift tap-dance over my clit. I licked her harder, and she responded by grinding her tongue into me.

I came first, and she followed me a few moments later. Both of us moaned loudly, our tongues still firmly in each other's cunts, our pussies pushed into each other's faces to get the very last rush of pleasure. Finally we both stopped, exhausted and satisfied.

My Mistress' voice quickly broke the spell. Indeed, I had been so involved with Sandra that I had almost forgotten where I was. "Alicia, you may get up now," she said.

"Yes, Mistress," I replied, and moved back into a kneeling position before her. At Mistress Lorna's command, Sandra did the same thing. We looked at each other, both breathing hard, our hair mussed and our lips glistening with pussy juice.

When Mistress Lorna finished her glass of champagne, she decided it was time to leave. She slipped a loose dress over her lovely suit and threw Sandra's clothes to her. I watched them go with a strange feeling in my chest. I had just shared one of the most intimate acts with this woman; I could still taste her pussy on my lips. But I had never spoken a word with her, and knew I would probably never see her again.

My Mistress closed the door, then turned to me and smiled. "I give you permission to speak, slave," she said. "Did you enjoy your little encounter?"

"Very much, Mistress," I said.

She lifted my chin with her fingers and looked into my eyes. "It was fun to watch," she said. "But my little slave can't have all the excitement."

"Mistress?" I asked.

She stood with her legs spread apart, and motioned for me to come over. "Pleasure me, slave," she ordered. "From the ground up."

I rushed over to lie happily between her feet. I didn't often have the pleasure and I always loved to hear the order. I started slowly, the way she wanted me to, licking her shiny black leather boots. The musty taste was sugary sweet to me.

"Polish them good," my Mistress warned. I felt the

tip of her riding crop trace a design on my bare ass and I knew I would feel its sting if I didn't meet her standards. I licked all over her foot and when she raised it, I took the stiletto heel into my mouth, sucking on it. I then worked my way slowly up the boot until I finally reached her creamy thigh. I continued licking carefully on my way up to her delicious pussy.

When I was far enough up, I realized that the tight suit had a zipper which opened the crotch. I held my breath as I pulled it open, marveling at the first sight of her dark hairs and fleshy lips.

I parted them with my tongue. Kneeling before her, pushing my tongue straight into her, I touched her clit with each stroke. I knew better than to tease her with soft caresses, and I licked hard at her hot button. The crop resting lightly on my back and the heavy collar around my neck reminded me that I had to do everything just as my Mistress preferred.

Her pussy was hot and wet and I licked greedily. Her salty-sweet taste was like honey to me. "That's a good, slave," she whispered, and I was filled with pride knowing that she was enjoying it.

It didn't take long for her to come. I lashed my tongue over her clit and was rewarded with the soft moan and the tight muscles that signified her orgasm. Her cunt quivered and I kept my tongue on it until the last spasm was over. Then I sat back.

She zipped the suit closed again and walked away. I watched her every move with rapture. My Mistress just excited me so much; I would have done anything for her if she had commanded it.

She sat in a wingback chair near the dining room. "Clean that mess up," she ordered. Quickly I picked up the empty champagne glasses and took them to the kitchen. From her seat she watched me as I washed and dried them carefully and put them away.

"Now come here," she said. I did. "Lie down on the floor, on your stomach." Again I obeyed, and she got up and walked into her bedroom.

When she came back out some time later, she looked more like a businesswoman than a domineering mistress. The tight suit and leather boots were gone, replaced by a well-cut suit. The only clue to her role in the apartment was the pair of heavy chrome handcuffs she carried.

She bent down and snapped one of the cuffs on my wrist. The other was closed around the leg of the chair.

"I have to go out now," she said. "I expect that I will find you in this position when I get back. Am I right?"

"Yes, Mistress," I said. There simply was no other answer.

I watched her as she walked to the door. I heard the key turn in the lock and realized that she could be gone ten minutes, or twelve hours. I had no way of knowing.

One thing was sure, though. My arm was going to cramp up and I was going to be sore after lying on the floor. My shoulders would hurt even more where she had beaten me with the riding crop. But my eyes would not leave the door, and my position would not change all the time she was gone. My Mistress had commanded it, and no matter how long it took, that was how I would wait for her return.

THE SECRET ROOM

"A glass of red wine, please."

"Right away," the waiter said, and hurried to get it. Jennifer smiled. She didn't know if it was her voice, or her bearing, her attitude, or a combination of all three, but people always seemed very eager to carry out her wishes.

Most of them did it because she asked them to. A few did it because she told them to, in no uncertain terms, and with terrible consequences if they did not. She was sitting waiting for one of these.

It was a favorite trick of hers. She would call up one of her submissives and tell her to be at a restaurant at a specific time. Jennifer would then arrive fifteen or twenty minutes early, so that when her slave

171

arrived, she would already have a few sips of her wine gone and the submissive would know that her mistress had been sitting for a while waiting for her. All submissives knew that keeping a mistress waiting was not a very good idea, of course.

Jennifer didn't do it every time, for she liked to keep her submissives on their toes with different tricks. One woman had actually caught on to the waiting game, and had arrived at the restaurant half an hour earlier, so that she was the one sitting waiting when her mistress came in. Jennifer was secretly amused that she had figured it out, but she took her home and beat her for it anyway, to teach her that slaves should never try to outsmart the mistress.

The waiter set the glass in front of her. She picked it up and took a sip; it was very good. She looked at it thoughtfully. Burgundy always seemed like such a cruel color to her. It was the color of flesh struck repeatedly by a hand or a whip, or the shade of marks left on the skin by handcuffs.

She shivered in anticipation of her plans for the day. She was waiting for Elizabeth, a submissive who had been coming to her for several weeks. She was still very inexperienced, but eager to learn; a tiny brunette woman who was fitting into her role very rapidly. When she had first come to Jennifer, through a mutual friend, she admitted that she had never been with a dominatrix before but that she had been completely turned on by reading stories about domination. There was no doubt that the real thing completely lived up to her fantasies, for Jennifer knew that no one could fake the shattering orgasm that Elizabeth had experienced the first day, her wrist bound together and her ass burning from a spanking with a wooden hairbrush that she had earned.

She sipped her wine, and checked her watch that she kept in her pocket. It was shortly after noon. When she used this trick, she always hid her watch and made sure she wasn't seated near any clocks. That way, the submissive would never know. She also gave them very exact times, such as eighteen minutes past the hour or thirteen minutes to, and handed out punishments for being early that were just as cruel as those for being late.

Elizabeth came in at exactly the time Jennifer had given her. She watched as the tiny woman spoke to the waiter, then followed him to the table. She was surprised to see Jennifer already seated, her glass half empty, and she stood silently behind the chair. She didn't yet know the significance of the half-empty wineglass between her mistress' fingers. "Bring her a Scotch, neat," Jennifer told the waiter, who nodded and left.

She looked up at Elizabeth. "You are late," she said.

Elizabeth's face went deathly white and her eyes grew large. "No, Mistress!" she protested, quietly, so that other diners would not hear her. "I checked my watch, Mistress!"

"Sit down," Jennifer commanded, and Elizabeth slipped quickly into the chair. She looked coldly at the young woman. "Are you implying that I don't know what time it is?"

Elizabeth looked down at the table like a scolded child. "No," she said.

"No?" Jennifer's eyebrows went up.

"Oh—no, Mistress!" Elizabeth quickly added. "I'm sorry, Mistress, I honestly thought I was on time."

"I'm sure you did," Jennifer said. "But obviously you didn't check carefully enough. No matter, you will pay for it later."

"Yes, Mistress," Elizabeth said. Her cheeks were blazing. Jennifer knew it was a combination of shame and excitement.

The Scotch arrived. Elizabeth looked at it warily. "I don't like Scotch, Mistress," she said.

Jennifer leaned over the table and spoke in a low, icy voice. "I don't give a good goddamn what you like or don't like," she said. "I ordered it for you, and you will drink it. You are already to be punished for being late. Do you want to add to your suffering by being disobedient?"

"Oh, no, Mistress," Elizabeth said. She sipped the amber liquid, making a face as she did so.

Jennifer went into her bag for a cigarette, which she lit with her gold lighter. Elizabeth's eyes never left her. She smoked it until there was a long ash on the end of it.

She looked around. "There doesn't seem to be an ashtray on this table," she observed.

"I will get you one, Mistress," Elizabeth said quickly as she started to get up. She sat back down at a swift motion from her mistress.

"That won't be necessary, Elizabeth," Jennifer said. "Hold out your hand."

Elizabeth looked frightened as she did. Jennifer casually flicked the ash into her outstretched hand. By the time the cigarette was almost finished, there was a small gray pile of it in her palm.

"Now eat it," Jennifer ordered.

Elizabeth looked at her, horrified, but did not dare say a word. After a long pause, she lifted her hand slowly to her mouth and licked the ash off. She swallowed heavily and took a hefty drink of the Scotch. For a moment she looked like she was going to be sick, but finally composed herself. She stared in terror at the end of the cigarette between Jennifer's fingers. When Jennifer reached over to the empty table beside them for an ashtray and stubbed it out, she let out a huge sigh of relief. She had no doubt that Jennifer would have extinguished it in her hand just as calmly.

Jennifer motioned for the waiter and paid for the drinks. She waited until Elizabeth had finished every swallow of the hated Scotch, then walked out of the restaurant. Elizabeth meekly followed several steps behind.

They went out to the parking lot, where Jennifer's dark blue Lincoln was waiting. She opened the doors, and Elizabeth obediently got into the back seat. Within minutes they were on the highway, heading for Jennifer's house. Elizabeth lived only a short distance from her mistress, and the trip to the restaurant had taken several buses and the better part of the morning. Jennifer knew this, and basked in the knowledge that her submissive had traveled all that way just to have a drink she didn't want and a ride back to almost the same spot she had started out from.

Her pussy felt hot as she glanced in the rearview mirror at the woman sitting in the back seat. She had a whole stable of them, women who would obey her every command no matter how bizarre. The power she held over them was incredible. She enjoyed laying traps for them just so that she could punish them when they were taken in by them. No matter how cruel her discipline, they waited anxiously for her to summon them again, and showed up punctually wherever she told them to be.

There were other benefits as well. Her house was always spotless and her chores always done for her, with only a spoken order. She also remembered the old days, before she had given herself over to her role as a dominatrix. Sex had always required the age-old game of introductions, drinks and dinners, conversation and uncertain kisses, and after all that, chances were good that she'd end up frustrated anyway. Not anymore. Now if she wanted sexual satisfaction, she simply commanded a submissive to give it to her.

They arrived at the house and Jennifer drove into the garage, the automatic door closing behind her. She opened the door leading into the house, but this time, she searched her key ring for another, smaller key. This was going to be a very special afternoon for Elizabeth.

On previous occasions, Elizabeth had stayed on the main floor of the house while she learned her lessons from her mistress. The trip to the restaurant and been a final test, for Jennifer knew that if she had put up with the inconvenience of traveling that far, she would do anything. She was now ready to see the true side of her mistress. The hairbrushes and the padded shackles were upstairs. The real toys were kept elsewhere.

Instead of going into the living room, Jennifer led the way into the cellar. Elizabeth looked a bit puzzled but followed her silently. There, Jennifer used the small key to open the lock on a door. She swung it open and led her submissive inside.

Elizabeth gasped. She had never seen anything like it before. It was Jennifer's secret torture room, her masterpiece, a collection that had taken several months to assemble. It was magnificent.

The floor was cold concrete, painted black, as were the walls. One wall was almost completely covered by a huge mirror. Another wall was hung with dozens of devices—whips, handcuffs, chains, dildos, straps, gags, and bondage clothes and masks fashioned out of leather and rubber. There were heavy rings screwed into the walls at all heights, and a few were in the ceiling and floor. There was a wooden frame with various lengths of chain on it standing against one wall, and a padded sawhorse. A leather sling hung from the ceiling. There was also a comfortable-looking padded chair in one corner, and Elizabeth instinctively knew that it was the one piece of equipment in the room that had never been used by a slave. It looked almost like a throne and stood on a small platform. Jennifer let her stand in the middle of the room for a long time, looking around and taking everything in. Once again, her cheeks were flushed and her expression was a mixture of complete terror and raw, overwhelming sexual desire.

"Take your clothes off," Jennifer ordered. Still looking around her, Elizabeth quickly shed her clothing. From the wall, Jennifer took a pair of heavy chrome handcuffs. She made Elizabeth sit on the cold floor next to one of the heavy rings, and quickly shackled her to it. Then she turned off the light, throwing the windowless room into complete darkness, and left, closing the heavy door behind her.

Once upstairs, Jennifer took her time. She wanted Elizabeth to fully experience complete captivity, without knowing what would happen or even when her mistress would come back to get her. She undressed and ran a bath, fragrant with perfumed oil, and relaxed in it for half an hour. She toweled herself off, then stretched out on her bed and looked through a magazine. All the time, she imagined the woman in her secret torture room. She would still be hunched on the icy concrete floor, unless she had risen to her feet, but that would have meant standing while bent double; the handcuffs wouldn't let her lift her hand more than a few inches from the floor. She would see nothing but the velvet darkness, for there was no source of light to allow her to see shapes even vaguely. She would be able to hear the running water and the footsteps on the floor above her, but would have no idea what her mistress was doing. Perhaps she even needed to use the toilet and would have to suffer with a full, painful bladder.

She was becoming more and more excited by the suffering she had inflicted on the woman in the cellar. Her pussy was throbbing now, and she put her hand between her legs and touched her clit. Slowly her touch became a soft caress, and then suddenly she was rubbing hard, the white-hot rushes filling her belly.

Her fingers were creamy with her juice, and they glided swiftly over her hot flesh. She was squeezing her naked tits and playing with her nipples with her other hand as she thought about what she was going to do when she went back downstairs. In her mind's eye she was spanking that sweet little ass with a leather paddle, and for every blow, she tweaked her torrid clit.

She came, her whole body shivering with the tingling spasm that coursed through her. She leaned back on the pillow, but instead of feeling relaxed, she was so excited she could hardly wait to get downstairs. Her orgasm had just whetted her sexual appetite. She wanted to slip fully into her role as the cruel dominatrix with her slave chained below her.

She selected a costume from her closet and got dressed. It was one of her favorites, a laced leather cat suit that exposed her breasts and was cut so high in the legs it barely covered her pussy. She slipped on high patent leather boots with stiletto heels that were so shiny they reflected the light. She touched up her makeup, accentuating her large green eyes and painting her lips her favorite cruel burgundy color. Then she smoothed her hair and walked to the stairs.

When she snapped the switch in the dark room, Elizabeth closed her eyes quickly against the bright lights. She was still on the floor where Jennifer had left her. Jennifer noticed with satisfaction that her skin was covered with goosebumps and that her fingernails had a milky blue tinge.

She retrieved the tiny key and unlocked the handcuffs, then ordered Elizabeth to stand up. Her ass was deathly white where it had been pressed against the concrete floor. Jennifer decided that it could use some warming up.

"Come here, slave," she said, and led Elizabeth over to the padded sawhorse. She selected two leather cuffs from the wall display and buckled them around her captive's wrists. She then picked out a length of heavy chain, with snap closures at either end.

Elizabeth obediently held out her hands, as she had been taught to do, and Jennifer secured the cuffs on her wrists. They were heavy and studded, with metal rings on them. They looked huge on Elizabeth's tiny arms.

Roughly she pushed Elizabeth from behind so that the woman was bent over the length of the sawhorse, her feet on the floor. She snapped one end of the chain to one wrist, wrapped it around the sawhorse leg, and attached it to the other wrist. Elizabeth could not get up or stand straight.

Elizabeth watched her, eyes wide, as she walked over to the wall to make a selection. She stood for a long time deliberating, as if she were in front of her closet trying to decide which dress to wear for a party, or what song to play on the jukebox. Finally she selected a wide leather paddle, its face covered with rounded metal studs.

She walked back and ran her hand gently over Elizabeth's exposed ass. The skin was still uncomfortably cold. "Elizabeth," she said, "do you remember what happened in the restaurant?"

"Yes, Mistress," Elizabeth whispered.

"I don't like to be kept waiting," she said. She caressed her ass again, this time with the side of the paddle. The leather glided over her skin as soft as a kiss. "A slave shouldn't keep her mistress waiting, should she?"

"No, Mistress," Elizabeth whispered.

Once again the paddle whisked over her flesh, only this time she felt the icy metal studs. Jennifer smiled as she watched Elizabeth's ass cheek muscles tighten with the touch. She could see her pussy, and the lips were glistening with hot juice. She had given Elizabeth a "safe word," but she doubted if she would ever hear her use it. Her punishment was turning her on as much as it was exciting Jennifer.

"Look to your right, Elizabeth," Jennifer ordered, and the small woman did. They were looking into the huge mirror. "I want you to keep watching it. I want you to see what happens to slaves who disobey their Mistresses. You will see it, and you will feel it."

She watched the mirror herself and loved what she saw. A well-built woman, wearing tight leather clothes and high shiny boots, standing before her shackled slave. She lifted the studded paddle. She admired herself for a moment longer, then brought the paddle down hard on Elizabeth's ass.

Elizabeth screamed, then sobbed. Her ass went flaming red, and the imprints of the studs were clearly visible on her skin. She went limp and screwed her eyes up tightly as the pain seared through her.

Jennifer stood back. "That won't do at all," she said. "Most slaves don't yell as much as you do. I don't want to listen to that crap." She went back to the wall and returned with a rubber ball gag which she roughly stuffed in Elizabeth's mouth and buckled at the back of her head. Elizabeth almost choked on the musty rubber taste. Her eyes were brimming with tears.

Jennifer brought the paddle down again. Elizabeth's cries were effectively muffled by the rubber ball that forced her mouth open and then filled it. Jennifer smashed the paddle across her ass four more times. Elizabeth's tears were now streaming down her face. Her ass cheeks were horribly red and raw, and her legs trembled uncontrollably. But her pussy was even wetter than it had been before.

Jennifer went back to the wall and carefully hung the leather paddle on its hook. She had an assortment of them, but this was one of the nastiest of all with its biting chrome studs, and was her favorite. She stroked its wide flat surface for a moment with her hand. The studs were still warm from Elizabeth's ass.

She turned to Elizabeth, who had watched her the whole time. "Now that I think about it, slave," she said coldly, "I also recall that there was a small problem with the drink I ordered for you."

Elizabeth's face was white and her eyes looked like a rabbit's caught in a pair of car headlights. It was obvious that she had either forgotten the episode with the Scotch, or hadn't realized its significance. In any case, she certainly hadn't expected to be punished for it.

Jennifer walked over to her and softly stroked her cheek with a long, lacquered fingernail—her favorite cruel burgundy. She knew her gentle touch would be like icy fire to her captive. "Everything a mistress does for you is in your best interest," she said. "I know what is good for you and you must trust me. If I order you something to eat, then you must eat it. If I order you something to drink, then you must drink it. If you don't, then I must take that as a sign of disobedience."

She took a few steps beside the sawhorse and gently stroked the vulnerable naked back. "It seems that you didn't think your mistress knew what was best for you when she ordered your Scotch," she said. "Basically, your attitude said 'fuck you.' Well, that is exactly what I will do."

She selected a particularly large dildo from the wall, attached to a leather harness. Elizabeth watched her as she strapped the harness around herself. She looked in the mirror with satisfaction. The large rubber dick stood out straight from her mound. She picked up a tube of jelly and greased its large head thickly.

Elizabeth watched her until she positioned herself behind her captive; the tiny woman then turned to look at her in the mirror. Jennifer rubbed her ass cheeks gently, then spread them. She put the head of the dildo against the tight rosebud of Elizabeth's ass, and then pressed her hips in.

Elizabeth's cries were once again muffled by the rubber ball gag. Jennifer pushed the dildo until it was halfway in. Then she slowly fucked Elizabeth's asshole with it.

The view in the mirror was delicious. Her slave was shackled to the sawhorse, a strap around her head to hold her gag in place, and the huge dildo was up her ass.

"You like my dick in you, don't you, slave?" Jennifer whispered. Elizabeth didn't nod her head quickly enough, and Jennifer grabbed her hair and yanked it, pulling her head back. "That wasn't very enthusiastic, slave," she hissed. She let go, and Elizabeth, fresh tears on her face, nodded rapidly.

"That's better," she crooned. She was pumping faster now and the greased dildo was sliding in and out of Elizabeth's tender asshole. "I'm glad that you like my dick. I like to see it fucking you."

Despite her obvious pain, Elizabeth was evidently enjoying it very much too. She kept her eyes on the mirror, where she could see Jennifer slamming the dildo into her. She whimpered through the ball gag with every thrust, but she also couldn't deny the fact that her pussy was throbbing and incredibly hot and wet.

Deeper and deeper the dildo slid, until it was almost entirely in Elizabeth's tight ass. Jennifer loved the rocking motion of her hips as she pumped the heavy rubber dick in and out. Occasionally she slapped Elizabeth's ass cheeks hard with the palm of her hand. The skin was still mottled red from her paddling with the studded leather.

Finally the dildo was in as deep as it could go. Jennifer pumped it in and out a few times, then pulled it out entirely. Elizabeth went limp as the huge dick slipped out of her sore asshole. Jennifer kicked her ankles until she spread her feet wide apart. Then Jennifer rubbed the rubber cockhead on her exposed clit.

Elizabeth immediately lifted herself on her toes so that the dildo could press fully against her swollen love button. This time she moaned, muffled by the gag still tied in her mouth. Jennifer rubbed it hard against her.

She was so excited she came almost immediately. Jennifer walked away while she was still trembling and moaning, and unstrapped the dildo. Without even looking back at the woman who was still chained to the sawhorse, her mouth distended by the nasty gag, she switched off the light, closed the door and went back upstairs.

She called the restaurant where she had met Elizabeth earlier in the day, and made a reservation for herself for a late dinner. Stripping off the leather suit and the high boots, she enjoyed a long, hot shower, then styled her hair and dressed carefully in a tight skirt and a shirt that showed off her beautiful breasts and large nipples. She returned to the secret room more than an hour after she had left Elizabeth down there.

Again her captive screwed her eyes tightly closed as the bright lights were flicked back on. Jennifer unbuckled the ball gag, and Elizabeth worked her jaw stiffly, her tongue licking her parched lips. Once the leather cuffs were taken off, she straightened up slowly and with difficulty.

"I have an appointment, slave," Jennifer said, hanging the cuffs and the chain back up in their spot on the wall. "Pick up your clothes and come with me."

"Yes, Mistress," Elizabeth said, and gratefully followed the dominatrix up the stairs. The carpeted floor felt soothing under her feet, which were white and numb from standing on the cold concrete floor of the secret room.

Jennifer led her captive to the bathroom, where she started a shower for her using only cold water. "Get in," she said.

Elizabeth started to climb into the tub, until she felt the icy water sting her skin. "Mistress, it's cold!" she protested.

Jennifer slapped her as hard as she could on her cheek. "I'm not stupid, slave!" she cried. "I know it's cold. Do you think I can't tell the hot water tap from the cold one? Now get in there, before I chain you to the faucet and leave you in there."

Elizabeth whimpered as she closed the glass shower doors behind her. She tried to stand in the far end of the tub, as far away as possible from the cold water, but on Jennifer's orders stood under the shower head and soaped herself.

"I'm finished, Mistress," she said once the soap was rinsed away.

Jennifer was sitting in the small chair that fitted under the bathroom vanity. "I don't really care, slave," she said. "I'll decide when you're clean enough. Now soap yourself again. You're filthy." She watched as Elizabeth lathered herself a second time and stood under the freezing cascade of water to rinse herself off.

She left Elizabeth for a few more minutes under the shower, then gave her permission to turn off the tap and get out. Elizabeth slid the shower door open and looked longingly at the huge, fluffy bath towels that hung from the rack on the wall. Instead, Jennifer gave her a small, thin hand towel and she struggled to dry herself with it. She was shivering violently and her fingernails and lips were blue.

"Hurry up," Jennifer warned, as Elizabeth scrubbed at her hair with the small, damp towel. She was actually running about an hour early, but it gave her great satisfaction to see Elizabeth fumbling in her haste.

She gave Elizabeth an old comb from under the sink to fix her hair, then led her into the living room where she made her crouch on her hands and knees on the sofa.

"Is your asshole still sore, Elizabeth?" she asked.

"Yes, Mistress," the tiny woman replied.

"Very good," Jennifer smiled. "I was hoping that the dick wouldn't be too small for you." She disappeared into the bedroom and came out with an object in her hand. Elizabeth craned her head to see, but Jennifer slapped her ass hard and told her to keep her eyes straight ahead.

It was a small butt plug, made of rubber with a flared, round base. Jennifer squeezed some lubricant out of a tube onto it, and then pushed it slowly into Elizabeth's tightly puckered hole. Elizabeth's moan, a mixture of pain and pleasure, sent sweet erotic shivers through her.

"Now, slave," she said, "I am going back to the restaurant where you met me to have my dinner. I am taking you back there, and you can find your own way home. All the time you are traveling home, you will wear this butt plug. You will wear it until I send for you again. You will wear it to work, and when you are sitting at home. You will wear it when you go shopping and when you are eating your meals. You may take it out when you wash or use the toilet, but you must put it back in right away afterward. The next time I see you, this plug will be in place. Do you understand?"

"Yes, Mistress," Elizabeth groaned. Her ass was already distended and sore from the dildo, and the butt plug aggravated it, but she loved the delicious full feeling and the knowledge that her mistress would have complete control over her even when she was alone.

"If I see you and that plug isn't in you, then I have a much larger one," Jennifer continued. "I won't use lubricant on that one. You will wear the larger one until I am finished with you, and then I will take it out and stuff it in your mouth. Do you understand that I am very serious in this command?"

"Oh, yes, Mistress!" Elizabeth cried. "Yes, Mistress. I will not disobey."

"Good," Jennifer said. "Now get dressed. If I'm

late for my dinner, I might think about using the larger plug on you right now."

Elizabeth pulled on her clothes, wrinkled from lying on the floor, and Jennifer led her out to the car. She sat low in the back seat to relieve the pressure on her painful ass.

Jennifer slipped behind the wheel and headed for the highway nearby. Once on it, she pushed the gas pedal sharply, and the big engine responded immediately. Jennifer smiled. She loved taking control, even over machines. It thrilled her to know that she alone harnessed the huge car that was capable of such high speeds. It thrilled her, too, to know that she controlled the woman in the back seat, who looked out of the window with an expression of discomfort. The butt plug must hurt like hell, and she was excited by the knowledge that Elizabeth would put up with it until she heard from her mistress again—whether it was a few hours or several days—simply because she had been ordered to do so. Jennifer had no doubt that her orders would be carried out to the letter. She didn't know how long she would make her wait, and decided she would think about it later.

She got off at her exit and pulled into the parking lot of the restaurant. As she turned off the engine, she watched a bus pulling away from the stop across the street.

"That's your bus, isn't it, Elizabeth?" she asked.

"Yes, Mistress," the woman replied miserably.

"How long until the next one?"

"Forty-five minutes, Mistress," Elizabeth replied.

Jennifer turned in the seat to face her, with a kind expression, and for a moment Elizabeth thought she might be invited into the restaurant to share dinner with her mistress. Her hopes fell immediately. "At least you're lucky there's a bench there," Jennifer said. "You won't have to stand up for the whole time you're waiting."

They got out of the car, Elizabeth moving slowly and stiffly. Suddenly an old expression popped into Jennifer's head, one that her mother used to say all the time: "She walks like she's got a bun up her ass." She had to smile. How true it was!

"I will get in touch with you later," Jennifer said. "In the meantime, you won't forget my orders, will you?"

"No, Mistress," Elizabeth said. "May I have permission to speak?"

"Yes, slave," Jennifer granted.

"I love you, Mistress," Elizabeth said.

Jennifer touched her cheek. "That's good, slave," she said. Then she turned and walked into the restaurant. Elizabeth stood by the big Lincoln for a long time, then made her way through the parking lot to the bus stop. It would be two or three hours before she finally got home.

Jennifer stood in the foyer. The waiter who had served her earlier noticed her right away, and led her to a table by the window. She sat down and ordered a drink, and noted with satisfaction how quickly the young man rushed to fill her order.

She looked out the window, and saw Elizabeth sitting on the bench by the bus stop. She thought about it for a moment, and then decided to make her wait at least a week.

WEEKEND AWAY

The sun was just coming up as Louise started the car and waited for Meg to come out of the house. The air was warm already and the sky was clear; it was going to be a beautiful day. They would be at the cottage before noon, and the rest of the weekend would be theirs.

The cottage belonged to Meg's brother, and although the two women had stayed there several times as his guests, it was the first time they would be there alone. Stephen's office was going through a major restructuring and he would be putting in a lot of hours, so he wouldn't be able to get away to the cottage for quite a while. He phoned and told them to go up and enjoy themselves for the long weekend. Louise intended to. She loved the cottage, a simple structure set well back from the road on the shore of a small, lonely lake. Stephen owned a large chunk of the surrounding woods and in all the times they had visited, they had never seen another person. It was as far away from civilization as she could possibly imagine. It also had no luxuries—unless a wood stove and a manual pump in the kitchen could be considered a luxury—but Louise and Meg both enjoyed their rugged weekends away.

Finally Meg came out, the last bag of groceries in her hand. She stowed it in the back seat, then got into the front seat and leaned back. "Ready for takeoff, commander," she said, and arranged her long, honey-colored hair into a ponytail.

Louise backed out of the driveway and they were off. There was no traffic on the road this early and they were out of the city shortly, heading up the eight-lane highway that would soon merge into four, and finally into two, past fields and sleepy farms and independent little towns and hamlets.

Louise happily reached over to tweak Meg's nipple. She was wearing no bra, and the touch felt so good. Both of them enjoyed fishing and walking through the woods, but most of their anticipation was for a weekend at a cottage where no one would see them. They had plans to make love on the porch, in the grass, under the trees, maybe even out in the boat.

Around ten they stopped in their usual spot, the last town before the turnoff for the cottage. It wasn't really even a town, just a gas station and a general store, but the store sold cones filled with generous scoops of rich ice cream and it was considered a grave sin to drive by without stopping for one. They sat out on the front steps of the store eating them, and Louise's eyes stayed on Meg the whole time she ate hers. Meg licked hers slowly, with long, cool laps of her small pink tongue, and Louise couldn't help imagining her pussy in place of the strawberry ice cream and Meg's tongue licking slowly and carefully around her hungry, swollen clit.

Ten miles past the store they turned off the main road onto a dirt one, and five miles later onto a path that was just two wheel ruts cut into the forest floor. It was only used by people going to the cottage—most people drove by it without even noticing it was there—and small branches that had grown since Stephen's last pruning brushed against the sides of the car. They had to drive slowly since the path was bumpy and uneven. The trees grew together overhead and the sunlight through them dappled the hood of the car.

They finally reached the clearing where they parked the car, and that was when they regretted every extra item that they had packed away. Everything had to be carried the last half-mile to the cottage along a narrow footpath. Their complete privacy didn't come without a bit of hardship along the way.

Their loads were heavy, but they were able to take everything in one trip, the cooler shared between them. After the city, the woods were pastoral and almost silent except for bird songs and the rustle of the leaves when the breeze shook the trees. The path seemed three times as long as usual, and they were sweating by the time the woods finally opened up and the lake and the cottage were in sight.

They dropped their gear on the front porch and opened the door. The cottage was closed and stuffy and they opened the windows to let the cool breeze through. It was only two rooms, a bedroom and a combination kitchen, living room, and dining room with a convertible chesterfield bed. The bathroom was the little shack close to the trees.

They went into the bedroom, where the double bed was neatly made, with an extra blanket draped over the foot. Louise couldn't wait any longer. She reached for Meg and hugged her, then parted her lips for a kiss.

Meg was just as eager as she was, and thrust her tongue inside her lover's mouth. She touched Louise's pussy through her shorts and could feel the heat of her flesh through the fabric. Louise moaned and reached down to press Meg's hand hard against her horny cunt.

Louise reached for the tail of Meg's T-shirt and pulled it over her head, exposing her lovely tits. She eased Meg onto the bed and licked each nipple slowly, relishing the warm, salty taste of her skin. Her hot, sweaty skin, so out of place in the sanitized city, was real and natural out here in the quiet cottage with its surrounding woods. They kissed as Meg reached under Louise's shirt to feel for her warm tits.

Louise stood up and quickly pulled her clothes off. It felt so good to be out of them, since they were damp and clinging. The cool breeze coming through the open window felt delicious on her skin, and her nipples went hard. Meg begged her to bring them closer, and she sucked them into her mouth one at a time, circling them with her tongue and biting gently on them.

Louise unzipped Meg's shorts. Meg lifted her ass off the bed and Louise pulled off her shorts, along with her panties. Her blonde cunt was moist and inviting. Louise stroked her inner thighs softly, then ran her fingers over the sweet flesh between Meg's legs. Meg sighed and opened her legs wider. They were both relaxed now that the city and the long drive were behind them. In this secluded world of no telephones, newspapers or televisions, they could take as long as they wanted to do anything. It wouldn't bother either of them at all if a single orgasm took all day to achieve.

Louise crawled onto the bed and Meg moved up on the pillows to make more room for her. She stretched out with her head between Meg's thighs, and lazily licked the length of Meg's creamy pussy. Meg sighed and closed her eyes.

Louise lapped at her slowly. She poked her tongue into the tight hole, spreading it gently with her fingers so that she could reach in as far as possible. Her lips were wet with Meg's sweet juices. She moved up to Meg's clit and ringed it with her tongue several times, then pushed it back and forth with just the tip. She gave several quick butterfly flicks over it and returned to Meg's hole. Meg groaned as the soft wet tongue parted her pussy lips and pushed deep inside her.

Again the probing tongue moved up to her clit, and this time, Louise stayed there. She licked slowly but with a lot of pressure, grinding her tongue against Meg's sweet button. Meg moaned louder, and Louise licked faster and sucked the clit into her mouth. As she held it firmly between her lips she lapped her tongue quickly against the edge of it. Moaning and trembling, Meg slipped into a smooth, luscious orgasm. Louise licked her hard and fast and she cried out as hard spasms rocked her and a tingling wave coursed through her body right to the ends of her fingers.

"Mmmmm, that was so good," Meg purred. She took Louise's hand and pulled on it. "Come up here, you, it's your turn."

Meg looked so comfortable lying on the bed, her head deep in the fluffy pillow, that Louise knew there was no way she was going to get her to move. Instead, she got up on her knees and crouched over her blonde lover's face, her dark pussy right above Meg's mouth.

Meg may have looked sleepy, but that was all. Immediately she pushed her tongue into Louise's cunt and licked all over it. She held Louise's ass and pushed her back and forth over her outstretched tongue, pressing deep into Louise's hole and the glistening folds of her lips. Her tongue fitted perfectly into the cleft of Louise's pussy. She licked slowly and steadily, and Louise thrilled to the hot little torrents that coursed through her body and made her so warm.

"Oooh, that's nice!" Louise gasped, and moved her hips so that Meg's tongue touched every tender little crevice of her pussy. She loved it when Meg licked up both sides of her clit teasingly, and then moved in to rock it back and forth until she couldn't take any more. She could feel the tongue gliding up the sides and then hit the center. Her whole pussy felt tighter and tighter, the pressure building up in her belly and even in her legs. Then she gasped and cried out as Meg's tongue sent her hurtling over the edge. Her whole body followed into her stunning climax and she collapsed on the bed beside Meg, panting for breath.

Meg held her closely until she calmed down. They lay together on top of the blanket, as the cool breeze dried the sweat on their bodies and the pussy juice on their lips. Louise was so comfortable she could hardly believe it. Just yesterday she had been running around the office like a madwoman, trying to get things done, answering the phone that never stopped ringing, making decisions, giving orders. Now she was lying in her lover's arms, completely fulfilled from her orgasm. The only sounds were the droning of heat bugs and the melodic tones from the wind chimes that hung on the front porch.

She had almost dozed off when Meg shook her awake. "Come on," she said. "All that stuff's still out on the porch, and I don't want to have to find the refrigerator in the dark."

They got up and reached for their clothes, then looked at each other and smiled. They didn't even have to wear clothes up here if they didn't want to. Giggling like children, they went out on the porch naked to bring the gear inside.

Meg took the cooler and went off to put its contents away. The "refrigerator" was an invention of Stephen's, devised one day when he found an icy cold spring bubbling up out of the ground some distance uphill. He came back the following week with a heavy coil of rubber hose, which he inserted at the spring and snaked down to a shady area under the trees. There he attached the end firmly to an old enamel cream can. Foods requiring refrigeration were packed in bottles or sealed plastic containers and submerged in the cold water that constantly flowed into the cream can. Meg filled the can with milk, plastic containers of cold cuts and cheese, and a few cans of beer. She filled a water jug from the hose and headed back to the cottage, stopping for a moment to pick a large handful of the colorful wildflowers that Louise loved so much.

She got back and helped Louise with the rest of the unpacking, after setting the wildflowers in an old milk bottle on the kitchen table. Both of them were still excited at having the cottage to themselves. The novelty of doing their unpacking naked was an event in itself, and they stopped for a moment to enjoy a hug and a long kiss that promised many more encounters like the one they had just had.

Once everything was put away, they decided it was time to clean up. They walked down to the lake hand in hand with a bar of soap and bottle of shampoo. The water was cool, and at first they made a game of it, splashing each other as they stood in the shallow water. Then Louise got the bar of soap and rubbed it over Meg's body. Her soapy hand moved smoothly over Meg's skin. She took a long time soaping Meg's breasts. She cupped each one and rubbed the bar of soap over the nipple, back and forth, while Meg moaned softly and watched the ends of her tits grow hard and big.

She took forever to wash Meg's pussy. She slid the bar of soap over the curly blonde hairs and then rubbed the soap in with her fingers. She would have been happy to spend hours with her hand in Meg's cunt. She loved to run her fingertips over the lips, to tickle the clit and push gently at the entrance to her hole.

Meg took the bar of soap away and turned Louise around to soap her back. She ran her hands between the softly rounded cheeks of Louise's ass, sending warm thrills through her. She soaped Louise's pussy from behind, touching her clit and pulling her hand all the way back to tease gently at her tight ass. She reached around to soap Louise's breasts, and the two of them stood in the knee-high water for a long time, Meg's tits pressed tight against Louise's back, her hands playing with Louise's nipples, all the time kissing and sucking at the sun-warmed neck that she loved so much.

Eventually Meg felt the soap drying on her skin, and she took Louise's hand and led her farther out into the water until they could dive below the surface and swim around. The lake was crystal clear and the bottom was smooth and sandy, perfect for spending a lazy, hot afternoon. They swam out a considerable distance and then raced each other back. Louise won by a narrow margin. Laughing and panting, they got out and stretched out on the grass to let the sun dry them off. It was too much trouble to walk back to the cottage for a towel. Meg fell asleep, but Louise spent the time looking around, admiring the tall trees and the birds that flitted among them, the cloudless blue sky, and the lake that stretched almost motionless to the opposite shore. She also took a long time to admire Meg, who lay in the grass beside her, her beautiful tits boldly naked, her stomach flat and her blonde triangle warm and inviting.

Louise began to feel hungry, and she woke Meg up. The two of them walked back to the cottage. They were so rested and relaxed that neither of them felt like doing anything and were grateful for the prepared supper sitting on the ice left in the cooler. Louise remembered how she had insisted on bringing the coolers, over Meg's protests that they would enjoy cooking their first meal at the cottage by themselves. Louise rubbed it in until Meg picked up a cushion off the sofa and threatened to start a pillow fight.

It was too nice to sit inside, and they ate on the table that sat on the huge porch running the whole length of the cottage. They opened containers of salad and unwrapped their sandwiches, and afterward had slices of pie and glasses of buttermilk. In the city they preferred to cook exotic dishes and go to expensive restaurants as often as their budget permitted. Out here, their simple meal enjoyed in the warmth of the early evening tasted better than the dishes at their favorite French bistro.

After cleaning up, they got out their books and sat in the rocking chairs on the porch, and read until it got too dark to see. A light would have brought the mosquitoes, and neither of them wanted to go inside. Fortunately, one of Stephen's first additions to the cottage was an old-fashioned swing that hung on chains from the roof of the porch. They sat together like young lovers, instead of companions of almost fifteen years, and watched the full moon and the evening star rise up over the lake and cast magical reflections in the dark water. Louise snuggled into Meg's shoulder and thought that if the world ended that night she would have no regrets.

Soon the rest of the stars came out and they marveled at how the same sky that looked so bleak and gray against the city's lights could turn into a stunning light show that dwarfed everything below it here, only a few hours away from the city limits. The air was filled with the chirping of thousands of crickets.

They eventually went into the cottage, and Louise lit the lamp and put it on the table. They pulled a pack of playing cards out of a suitcase and opened two cans of beer. They played cards accompanied by the soft hiss of the lantern and the sound of moths banging against the screen windows, attracted by the light.

Meg looked up and watched Louise carefully as she waited for Louise to play her card. The soft light of the lantern lit Louise's face beautifully, making her look as soft and romantic as a painting. Meg couldn't believe how lovely she looked. Both of them were always so busy with a variety of real and imagined responsibilities that they seldom had time just to sit together for a full day and enjoy each other's company. Even their vacations were usually sightseeing expeditions with as much crammed into each day as humanly possible. But at this cottage there were just the two of them, without a care in the world and nothing that had to be done if they didn't feel like doing it.

At the moment, Meg decided that even the game they were in the middle of could wait. She put her cards on the table, took Louise's away from her, and laid them down also. Then she picked up the lantern, took Louise by the hand, and led her into the bedroom.

The moon was so bright it cast shadows in the room, and Meg extinguished the lantern. They had both put on light cotton robes before dinner, and Meg untied Louise's and let it fall open. Louise's breasts looked like rich cream in the moonlight. Meg licked them as if they were. The nipples reminded her of wrapped candy kisses and she sucked on them slowly, letting them slide through her lips as she pulled her head back. Louise sighed with the pleasure.

"That feels so nice," Louise said. "Come up here and kiss me." Meg straightened up and put her arms around her lover. They kissed slowly and deeply, with a sudden passionate longing that surprised them both. Meg felt like she was tasting Louise's mouth for the very first time. Louise responded to her touch and pushed her tongue deep into Meg's mouth, probing with an awakened urgency that their earlier, lazy lovemaking had only begun to tap.

Meg's hand was cupped over Louise's dark triangle. She could feel the heat on her fingers. She glided over Louise's clit, and her fingers came away wet and slippery. Thrilled, she returned Louise's kiss eagerly and probed the depths of the hot, hidden treasure between her legs. When she could wait no longer, she knelt down on the floor in front of Louise and kissed her belly, then moved down to where the dark hair began. She teased the cleft of Louise's pussy by blowing softly on it, and then she used her tongue to push the lips apart and skim over her clit.

She tasted warm and woodsy from their swim in the lake. Meg was no longer relaxed; she was aroused and feverish. She wanted to feel Louise tremble and hear her cry out. She wanted to sink as deeply as she could into the pussy she was licking.

Louise moaned and spread her feet apart. Meg crouched under her and pushed her tongue into Louise's hole. Louise moved up and down on it, fucking Meg's tongue as if it were a warm dildo. Meg's cheeks were wet with her pussy syrup. She wished she could climb right up inside her.

Louise rocked her hips so that her clit slid back and forth over Meg's outstretched tongue. Meg flicked it back and forth. She focused on the swollen little knob, and Louise groaned. Her spine was quickly turning to jelly as Meg lapped at her.

"You're going to make me come," Louise warned, and Meg doubled her efforts. Louise did as she had promised. Her orgasm was intense, and she gasped, then cried loudly as it overcame her. She sat down on the edge of the bed, and Meg followed her. She carefully licked her lover's dark pussy until every drop of her honey-sweet juice was gone.

Meg's pussy was throbbing so badly she could hardly stand it. "Lie down," she whispered huskily. She straddled Louise's thigh and rubbed her pussy hard against it. She hadn't done this for a long time, and had almost forgotten how raw and delicious it felt.

Her tits swung back and forth as she ground her pussy on Louise. Louise reached up with her hand

and brushed Meg's erect nipple with each stroke. It was a gentle touch but it was fiery hot to Meg. She moaned and moved harder and faster.

"Feels so good," she panted. Louise reached with both hands, holding Meg's breasts firmly and kneading them with her fingers. Meg felt almost dizzy. Her hot pussy was building up to a tremendous orgasm as she rode Louise on the bed. Her long hair hung around her shoulders, swinging with each move. Every touch of Louise's hand on Meg's nipples sent thrills through her and made her cunt even more sensitive.

She almost screamed when she came. She leaned forward onto Louise and the two of them hugged tightly, kissing passionately. At that moment, the cottage could have burned down around them but they would not have let go of each other.

"I love you so much," Meg gasped, and Louise kissed her and whispered her love too. Meg rolled over onto the bed, but they stayed in each other's arms and fell into a deep, dreamless, sleep holding each other tight.

Louise woke in the morning to the sounds of movement in the other room. The bedroom was still fairly dark. She looked at her watch and groaned; five o'clock. Getting up in the middle of the night had to be a trait of Meg's family, she decided; when they had shared the cottage on other weekends with Meg's brother, he and Meg had been up before dawn to go fishing or hiking. Louise had been much happier staying in bed until a considerably more civilized hour—ten, perhaps.

She clutched the pillow until her eyes finally stayed open by themselves, then she got up, pulled on her robe, and wandered into the other room. The bedroom was somewhat chilly, but the kitchen was warm. Meg had a fire going strong in the wood stove, and on top Louise could see a coffeepot, a skillet of eggs, and slices of bread toasting on the hot surface.

Meg was smart enough to hand Louise a cup of black coffee before she even spoke to her. "I've got breakfast under control," she said. "You go out and wait on the porch."

She did, and was instantly happy that she had gotten out of bed. The sun was just coming up over the lake, which was as smooth as a mirror. The morning mist was rising off of it in slowly moving wisps. The sun reflected brilliant red on the water, and then its light was caught by the millions of tiny dewdrops on the grass. Louise breathed deeply and caught the smell of wet earth and pine trees. She took a sip of her coffee and decided that all was right with the world.

Meg came out shortly afterward with their breakfast. She loved cooking and saw the wood stove as a special challenge. Generally her results were good, although perfect bread baked in the little compartment on the side of the stove still eluded her. She had been trying for years and had finally managed to get one side of the loaf raised and baked to a golden brown. Usually they settled for biscuits baked in a covered skillet.

Even out in the middle of nowhere, Meg's cooking retained its little touches. The eggs were fried with onions and peppers, and there was a small jar of brandy butter for the toast. The sun cleared the tall trees on the far side of the lake as they ate. The sky was cloudless; it was going to be a beautiful day.

"I want to go fishing," Meg said as they took their dishes inside and Louise pumped water to wash them.

"Sounds good to me," Louise said, and added a bit of hot water from the kettle on the stove to the dishpan. Within minutes the kitchen was clean, and they went into the bedroom to change.

The lake was so smooth they hated to disturb it. Stephen didn't want the sound of any motors disturbing the forest, so there was only a rowboat. They stowed their tackle box, rods, a small cooler, and a thermos of coffee, then pushed away from the shore. They had flipped a coin earlier, and Louise got the task of rowing out to the middle of the lake.

Once they were some distance from shore, Meg dropped the anchor overboard, and they got ready. For Meg, it meant selecting the proper lure for casting and retrieving. Louise's preparation consisted of putting a worm on her hook and dropping it over the side, the rod held between her knees, while she poured a cup of hot coffee from the thermos and adjusted the cushion she sat on. Casting was fine, but she couldn't see the point in wasting a perfectly good day with work when there was a container of coffee and a box of worms in the boat.

They enjoyed themselves so thoroughly that time just slipped by without notice. Louise even got to smirk a little when her lazy way of fishing put three bass on her stringer compared with the single one Meg had caught. Meg didn't mind; she was busy running through recipes in her head, deciding what would be the best way to prepare them for dinner.

The sun crept higher in the sky, and they began to get very warm. Her little thermos empty, Louise went into the cooler and got a cold soda for each of them.

The overhead sun beat down on them, and Meg's light shirt was sticking to her. "It's too hot just to sit out here," she said, reeling in her lure and setting her rod down in the bottom of the boat. "I'm going for a swim. Are you in or out?"

"In, of course," Louise said, and watched with interest as Meg unbuttoned her shirt. She looked around, but as usual, there wasn't another soul on their little part of the lake, which was surrounded almost entirely on three sides by heavy woods and the single cleared area where the cottage stood. She took her shirt off and draped it over the boat seat. She looked at Meg, who had her shirt off too. Her skin was hazy with a thin film of sweat and Louise thought her nipples looked delicious.

In a single, sinewy motion, Meg wriggled out of her shorts. As always, Louise loved the inviting look of her rich blonde pussy. Meg saw her staring, and she smiled and ran her fingers between her legs. "I like what you're thinking," she purred. "When we get back to the cottage, I want an instant replay of last night."

She got up and moved carefully so as not to upset the boat, and slipped into the water. She came over and held onto the side of the boat, pushing her wet hair out of her eyes. "It's a lot colder out in the middle than it is on shore!" she said. "It sure feels nice. Are you coming in or are you going to sit there all day?"

Louise pulled off her thin cotton pants, then sat on the edge of the boat and fell backward into the water. It was shockingly cold at first, then refreshing.

It was still a novelty to be in the lake without bathing suits, and they swam back and forth and treaded water, then dived below the surface. The sunlight filtered through the clear water in long shafts toward the bottom.

Louise held her breath and swam under the surface. She could see the large, dark shadow of the boat, and the movement of Meg's arms and legs as she treaded water. As she got closer, she could see Meg clearly, her pussy too sweet to be passed up. She surfaced right in front of her, running her hands over her body on the way up, and kissed her hard.

Meg returned her kiss. They were close to the boat, and they grabbed the heavy nylon rope attached to the anchor to hold themselves up. Close to each other, they kissed again and wrapped their free arms around each other's necks.

The sensation was unlike anything they had felt before. The cold water contrasted with their warm bodies, and there was no resistance at all when they touched each other. There was nothing but water below their feet, and it was easy to move up or down just by loosening their grip on the rope.

Meg slipped below the water, and Louise felt her nipple being sucked into her mouth. After the cold water, Louise's mouth felt fiery-hot and almost dry. She sighed as she felt Louise's tongue slide over her rock-hard nipple and flick it back and forth. When she finally let go and came up for a breath of air, the rush of cold water on her breast sent shivers through her.

She reached for Meg's tits. The cold water had made the nipples as hard as her own, and they felt like little marbles to her hands. She tweaked them and rolled them between her fingers, then held each breast in her hand and massaged them slowly and lovingly. All the while, they kissed, their tongues slipping into each other's mouths and mingling with one another.

The feelings were so delicious, they had to share them. Meg reached out her free hand and touched Louise's breasts under the water. She could see them just below the surface, and they looked even bigger and harder through the water. She was fascinated.

She watched her hand as if it belonged to someone else, holding Louise's tits and rubbing them, and enjoying the feeling of Louise's hands on her own nipples at the same time.

Gradually their hands strayed farther down. "Your pussy is so wet," Louise said, and Meg groaned loudly at her pun and put her hand between her lover's legs.

It felt so different from anything they had enjoyed before. Louise's pussy lips were chilled from the water. Meg ran her finger between them, onto her clit, which was a bit warmer. Then she slid her finger effortlessly into Louise's tight hole, which was deliciously warm and velvety smooth. Louise moaned and ran her fingers over Meg's clit.

They both held onto the anchor rope as they felt each other. Their pussies were cool from the water, but the rushes that went through their bodies were like liquid fire. Meg could feel Louise's clit growing larger and getting firm, and she knew that her own was doing the same thing. She could feel every movement of Louise's fingers as sharply and as clearly as if she were watching them. She moaned as Louise stroked her from her clit right back to her hole and finally up to her sweetly puckered ass.

They were both moaning as their hands explored every inch of each other's cunts under the surface of the water. The water lubricated their hands, and they slipped effortlessly over their fleshy cunts. Their bodies floated weightless in the water, adding to the sensation. It felt almost unreal to them. Imagine, swimming naked in the middle of a lake, out in the wilderness, with their hands in each other's cunts, feeling each other up—marvelous!

Louise came first. She moaned and gasped as her orgasm warmed her water-chilled body. She kept her hand in Meg's cunt, and the blonde woman came a few moments later. She was so excited by coming in the cold water that she let go of the anchor rope and slipped below the surface. She quickly came back up, gasping and panting both from the water and her explosive climax.

They hugged again and exchanged tiny kisses. Then they both took advantage of their new-found energy to swim back and forth around the boat and dive as far down as they possibly could. With some difficulty, Meg finally got back in the boat and helped Louise to climb in as well.

Both of them sat naked on the seats until they dried off enough to put their clothes back on. Indeed, if it hadn't been for the fear of sunburn they would have preferred not to put them on at all. It still felt new and exciting to sit up straight in the boat with nothing on. In the city, there was always the feeling that someone could be watching, and pulling curtains and closing blinds was a way of life. Out here, surrounded only by trees and birds, they could do whatever they wanted, in any stage of dress or undress they liked.

"I'd like some lunch," Louise said, and Meg agreed. She fitted the oars into the oarlocks while Louise pulled up the anchor and the stringer of fish. Then she rowed back to shore.

Louise sat back lazily, one hand trailing in the water, as they neared the cottage. It was almost noon, and everything seemed laid back and sleepy, even the birds. After lunch they might put up the double hammock and just nap in each other's arms, or hike up the shady path between the trees.

She looked over at Meg, rowing the boat back in, and smiled with love for her. Their weekend away, alone together, had been the best idea they could have possibly imagined, and it still wasn't even half over.

Across the calm water she could hear the heat bugs droning in the sunlight. She thought about the money they had saved, with no particular goal in sight. She decided that over lunch she would ask Meg her thoughts on looking for a lonely cottage all their own.

BAD
HABITS

Lindsay Welsh

ONE

Wendy bent down and deftly fastened the gold buckle on her shoe. The shoes had cost her a small fortune, but they certainly had been worth it. They were impossibly high and the heels ended in stiletto tips, so thin they appeared razor-sharp. The leather had been polished to a high gleam, and the shoes showed off her thin ankles and shapely calves to perfection.

She made a final adjustment to her black costume, then strode purposefully out of the bedroom and walked down the hall. The metal tips on her heels rang out on the gleaming hardwood floor. She knew the sound would be heard through the door.

She stopped for a moment to make a final check in the full-length mirror that hung in the hallway. She liked what she saw. Her long dark hair fell to her shoulders and her makeup was perfect. The black leather corset hugged her body, taut and strong from

5

regular workouts. Her full breasts peeked above the top of the corset, her nipples large and firm. Black panties covered her pussy and black stockings adorned her long legs. One manicured hand held a brown leather riding crop. She smiled with satisfaction and stepped toward the closed door at the end of the hall.

She turned the handle ever so slowly and swung the door open. She caught her breath momentarily at the sight that greeted her, then closed the door behind her and stood so that she could be admired in her stunningly cruel costume.

A young woman knelt in the center of the wooden floor on a small scrap of carpet. Her hands were bound behind her, and a cloth had been wrapped around her head and through her mouth as an effective gag. She was naked save for a pair of tiny white lace panties.

As the leather-clad woman entered the room, the young captive turned her head to look at her. Her blue eyes were wide, filled with a strange mixture of fear and raw sexual anticipation. Her long blonde hair cascaded down the smooth skin of her back.

Wendy smiled. How she loved it when they looked at her like that! She could feel a quick tightening between her legs. She had only known this one for a couple of months and was still trying out a wide range of punishments on her, watching her reactions. Today she had tied her up and left her kneeling on the floor for two hours while she enjoyed a luxurious bath and a good book.

"Well, Brenda, I guess you've been lonely all by yourself," she said. The blonde woman nodded, unable to answer because of the cloth in her mouth.

"I like my slaves to be able to sit quietly when I'm not with them," Wendy continued. She brushed the very tip of the leather crop up her captive's spine. Brenda moaned, muffled by the gag. "You did very well today."

She bent down and released the knot that held the gag in place. Brenda gasped as it dropped away, and gratefully licked her swollen, dry lips. "Thank you, Mistress," she whispered. Wendy could feel her pussy throbbing gently. How she loved to hear them speak so reverently!

She walked slowly around the room, so that Brenda could fully appreciate the stiletto heels, the tight corset, the cruel riding crop. She was slowly turning this spare room into her own private torture chamber. Always on the lookout for unusual and interesting devices, she already had a leather sling hanging from the ceiling and a padded sawhorse fitted with steel rings all over it, perfect for chaining slaves in any position. There were also heavy steel rings screwed into the walls at various heights, from the baseboard right up to the ceiling, which Wendy had installed so that a slave's chains or handcuffs could be snapped to them, forcing her to lie on the floor or stretch out fully against the smooth, hard wall.

For a moment she stopped and caressed the thick brown leather that covered the top of the sawhorse. With satisfaction, she saw Brenda's eyes widen with fear. The young blonde woman had been strapped to the horse a few times, and knew well how tightly it could hold her, and how cruel her mistress could be to her once she was firmly shackled to it. Wendy's long, blood red nails tapped against it; in the silent room, each tap was as loud as a gunshot to Brenda's ears. She visibly relaxed when Wendy moved away from it.

Finally Wendy walked over to Brenda and freed

her wrists from their cruel bonds. Stiffly, Brenda moved her arms.

"Get up," Wendy ordered. Brenda tried, but her poor legs had been cramped for too long on the small square of carpet. She fell on her side.

"Please, Mistress!" she cried out, as Wendy lifted the riding crop. "Please, I'm trying!" But it was no use. The crop left first one welt, then a second on the creamy skin of her back. She cried out as the harsh red marks lifted on her flesh.

"I don't take excuses well," Wendy said coldly, through clenched teeth. "Now, on your feet, or I'll wear this crop out on your hide."

Sobbing, Brenda shakily got to her feet. She swayed a bit, and her legs burned painfully as the cramped muscles responded. But she managed to remain standing.

"I never saw a slave as bad as you are with your excuses," Wendy said. "It seems like every time I give you a command, you find a reason why you can't carry it out. That's a very bad habit, Brenda. I hope you get over it very soon—before I wear my arm out with this crop."

"I'm sorry, Mistress," Brenda said.

Wendy walked over to the sawhorse and again Brenda trembled. But instead of selecting a ring to chain her slave to, Wendy slipped her panties off and sat on the padded top. Her dark pussy was gleaming with her excitement. "Now, slave," she said, "let's see if you can do something right today. Give me some pleasure."

This was a command that Wendy didn't have to repeat, or punctuate with a blow from the riding crop. Brenda truly enjoyed making her mistress come, as often as possible. She rushed over to the sawhorse and bent before Wendy's lovely dark triangle.

She loved the smell of her mistress' hot flesh and the way the dark hairs felt on her skin. Slowly she circled Wendy's pussy lips with her tongue, up and down and across the top, careful not to touch her swollen clit just yet. She had learned just what Wendy liked.

Wendy leaned back as the hot, probing tongue worked its way over her pussy. This was what she enjoyed most about being a dominatrice—orgasms whenever she wanted them, just as she liked them, and as many as she wanted. None of the verbal games, the dinners, the frustrated nights she had spent before she discovered her true nature.

Although Brenda wasn't a skilled slave in many other aspects, Wendy had to admit that Brenda did shine in this department. She had been enthusiastic right from the start, and it hadn't required a lot of training to make her familiar with all of the moves that Wendy liked.

The tip of Brenda's little tongue found the hot, swollen nub at the top of Wendy's pussy. Wendy shivered as she felt the waves go through her, starting from the very center of her clitoris. She brushed her own nipples lightly with the tips of her fingers as she looked down at Brenda, her face buried contentedly between her mistress' thighs.

Brenda's tongue moved a bit faster, playing around the folds of Wendy's hot, wet cunt. Every so often she would poke her tongue into Wendy's hole, pushing it in and pulling it out. Then she moved back up to concentrate on Wendy's clit.

She sucked it in between her lips and tickled it with the tip of her tongue. It was enough to send Wendy right over the edge. The sweet wave swept over her completely and she held onto the sawhorse tightly until her final trembling was over.

"That was good, slave," she said, as she stood up and pulled the small black panties back on.

"Thank you, Mistress," Brenda replied, licking her lips. She loved the taste of her mistress' cunt and would have been happy to stay between her legs for most of the day.

"I think I would like to relax with a glass of wine now," Wendy said. "I will be in the living room. You may bring me some white wine out there. There's a bottle chilling in the refrigerator."

She walked down the hall into the living room. Wendy had always loved beautiful things, and now that she had the money to buy them, she surrounded herself with them. The carpet was sinfully thick under her stiletto shoes. She settled on the sofa, a white leather four-seater, and looked around while she waited for the wine. She loved her things. A built-in bookcase by the fireplace held a collection of first editions, many of them signed. The crystal bowl on the mahogany coffee table, filled carelessly with hard candies, was genuine Baccarat. The paintings on the walls were real oils.

She knew the office tongues wagged almost every time she went into work. She arrived each day in her fully equipped Lincoln, wearing designer clothes, often Chanel suits. She had a corner office with a huge oak desk and thick carpeting, and the view from her windows was among the best the floor had to offer. Few in the company knew exactly what her job was, although it was rumored that she didn't really have much more work than many of the managers who came to work in secondhand Plymouths or on the bus.

Wendy found it difficult to keep from laughing every time she saw the glances from across the floor. It was true, she really didn't have to worry about deadlines and presentations the way they did, and many of the so-called "business meetings" she attended so frequently were actually luncheon dates with friends or afternoons at the gym. Nothing she did for the company warranted the huge paycheck she received regularly, which allowed her to live the way she so enjoyed.

Nothing, that is, that any other workers knew about. For they had never seen their company's vice-president nude, her hands bound with handcuffs, a ball gag thrust into her mouth, kneeling before Wendy, waiting for the gag to be removed so that she could beg to lick her mistress' dusty leather boots clean with her tongue.

She heard the gentle squeaky "pop" in the kitchen as Brenda opened the bottle of expensive French wine, then heard the cupboard door swing open as she reached for a glass.

She smiled in anticipation, but her lips immediately turned down into a frown as the blonde slave walked into the room.

She jumped up and was on Brenda before the blonde woman even realized what was going on. The object of Wendy's rage was the glass of wine, which Brenda was carrying by the glass rather than the stem, her hand wrapped around it. Wendy slapped her hard and the glass flew out of her hand, smashing against the wall, the precious golden liquid seeping into the thick carpet.

"Idiot!" Wendy hissed, and slapped her again. "Good wine like that, and you treat it like it was rotgut! Don't ever let me catch you carrying wine like that again!"

"Please, Mistress!" Brenda begged. "I'm so sorry, I didn't know!"

Once again, Wendy's hand slapped her cheek,

raising angry red marks on the pale skin. "Don't you talk back to me!" she said. "Now clean up that mess! and bring me another glass of wine—and do it right this time or I'll whip you until you faint!"

Sobbing, Brenda stooped to pick up the remains of the crystal wineglass while Wendy went back to the sofa. She carried the shards into the kitchen, then returned a short while later, with the wineglass on a small silver tray. Brenda presented it to her mistress, still fearful that she wasn't doing it correctly.

Wendy picked it up by the stem. "This is how you handle good wine," she said. "When you carry it by the glass your hand warms it up. Stupid slave, didn't you know that?"

"No, Mistress," Brenda whispered.

"Well, it's about time you learned," Wendy said. "Now clean up the carpet before it stains."

She sipped the chilled wine while Brenda knelt on the carpet, sponging up the spilled liquid. The wine was exquisite, well worth the horrendous price, and Wendy enjoyed it thoroughly. The orgasm and the wine had relaxed her, and she stretched out.

"Slave," she said, "I would like my feet rubbed."

"Right away, Mistress," Brenda said. She hurried to put the sponge back in the kitchen, then knelt by the sofa before her mistress' feet. Wendy admired Brenda's lovely breasts and large nipples as she unbuckled the straps on the leather shoes.

It seemed to Wendy, though, that Brenda was a little clumsy as she removed the shoes. Rather than slipping them off gracefully, she tugged at them and pulled them away from Wendy's feet. She decided to ignore it for the moment, sipping at the wine, but she didn't stay relaxed for very long.

Brenda pushed her thumbs against Wendy's feet, but rather than massaging them firmly, she poked and probed. Finally she pushed Wendy's toes in, and Wendy cried out as her feet cramped painfully.

"Foolish slave!" she hissed. She sat up and dealt Brenda a cruel blow that caught her on the side of the head. Brenda's pained expression was one of a child being punished without knowing the reason.

"Mistress?" she cried. "Mistress, what have I done?"

"You idiot, a massage isn't supposed to hurt!" Wendy hissed. "You're handling my feet like they were hunks of hamburger. Who on earth taught you how to do that?"

"No one, Mistress," she said. "No one ever taught me."

Suddenly it dawned on Wendy just what the problem was. Brenda wasn't being awkward on purpose; she honestly didn't know the proper way to do things.

"You mean to tell me that no one ever sat down with you and taught you how to serve, how to obey?" she asked.

"No, Mistress," Brenda admitted.

For a moment, Wendy almost felt a bit of sympathy for the blonde woman. "So how did you find out what to do?"

"I just picked it up, Mistress," Brenda said. "I did things the way I thought they should be done. If they weren't right, then I got punished, and I knew not to do it that way again."

"I thought you had a couple of mistresses before I met you," Wendy said.

"I did, Mistress," Brenda said. "But they didn't have the nice things you have, and they didn't make me do the things you do. They didn't make me serve them wine or rub their feet, Mistress, so I never knew how it was done."

Wendy drained the glass and put it back on the coffee table. "Well, I'm not about to allow some half-trained slave to tend to me," she said. "Normally I would just throw you out and be done with you—and find another slave who knows what she's doing."

As Wendy paused, Brenda trembled slightly, keeping her eyes on the floor as she knelt beside the sofa. She loved her mistress and the cruel words cut through her like a knife.

"But I think you have a lot of potential," Wendy continued. "You seem to learn quickly, and even if you do some things wrong, I like the fact that you learn from your punishment."

"Thank you, Mistress," Brenda whispered.

"I think you could be a superb slave if only you received the proper training," Wendy said. "I will teach you what you need to know. In return, I ask that you pay attention, watch carefully, and learn perfectly. I will not repeat any lesson twice—for any reason. If I teach you something and you later do it wrong, I *will* find myself a slave who knows what to do. Is that clear?"

"Yes, Mistress!" Brenda said. Her cheeks were flaming; she was thrilled to know that she would be allowed to stay.

Wendy got up, leaving her shoes carelessly cast aside on the leather sofa. "Then we will begin with the basics," she said. "I'm not about to buy new glasses every time I want some wine. Your first lesson will be how to serve me without me having to beat you."

"Yes, Mistress!" Brenda exclaimed, and followed her beloved mistress into the huge kitchen. She knew these lessons would be among the hardest she would ever have to learn, and she was determined to remember them perfectly.

TWO

Wendy looked at her watch, then got up from her desk and walked over to the huge window. Outside, the city was a hive of activity. In the building opposite hers, she could see floors and floors of workers rushing around their offices to get their jobs done. On the sidewalks, people milled about, businessmen with briefcases trying to avoid bicycle couriers. Wendy smiled and stretched luxuriously. The paperwork she'd had to finish for the day was already done and on its way, and she had a luncheon date.

She put on a light jacket, picked up her bag, and walked out of her office. In a smaller office just outside, her secretary was rearranging some files that had already been done earlier that day. Because her boss didn't always generate a lot of paper, quite often she found herself trying to look busy while the rest of the company struggled to make their deadlines each month.

15

"I have a very important meeting this afternoon, Karen," Wendy told her. "I don't know when I'll be back, or if I'll be back at all. If it goes on too long, I'll just go straight home from there."

"Yes, Ms. Hudson," Karen said.

"If anyone calls for me, tell them I'll call them back tomorrow morning, first thing." She stopped for a moment, and looked at the filing Karen was doing.

Karen dropped her eyes and squirmed in her seat. As much as she liked the leniency of her job, it always bothered her that she did so little to earn her pay. She was always terrified that someone higher up might notice the endless filing and refiling, typing and retyping that she used to fill the hours when there was simply nothing else to do, and fire her.

But Wendy smiled at her, and she immediately relaxed. "It's been pretty slow these last couple of days," Wendy said. "There's no point sitting there doing that."

"Everything else is done, Ms. Hudson," Karen protested.

"I know," Wendy said. She leaned down and spoke quietly lest anyone walking by the office hear her. Karen got a heady, delicious whiff of her perfume. "On my way out, I'll let them know that I need you to take some notes at the meeting. Then lock up and go on home. It's too nice a day to be sitting here, anyway."

Karen's face lit up. "Thank you, Ms. Hudson!" she said, and Wendy smiled again. If only Karen knew how much she loved to hear such words! Her tone was almost the same as that of a slave thanking her mistress for some small favor.

Karen watched as Wendy turned and left the office. Like almost every other employee of the company, she wondered just how Wendy kept her position and her obviously high salary when she appeared to do so very little.

Karen also noticed just how different Wendy was from other people. She was always on top of every situation, and could sway people with almost imperceptible ways that Karen still didn't fully understand. She seemed to take command of any room she walked into, and even when she was being gracious or humorous, there was an iron will behind it that would never bend.

Although she'd worked for Wendy for years, Karen was still in awe of her, and often thought she perceived an open, raw sexuality that was both exciting and a little dangerous. Sometimes she even wondered ... but that was ridiculous, Karen told herself, and she dropped the files into her desk, put her pens away and reached for her coat.

True to her word, Wendy left a message at the front desk in case anyone should question Karen's absence, then waited for the elevator that would take her to the ground floor of the huge office complex. Outside, she hailed a taxi and gave the driver the address of one of the city's better restaurants.

She asked for a secluded table, and received one in a quiet, dark corner. She was a bit early, and ordered a glass of wine while she waited. The service was impeccable, and she watched the waiter's graceful, fluid movements as he set the glass before her. Soon, she thought, such service will be second nature to Brenda.

Brenda! She smiled as she remembered last night. She had often read about the training undertaken by the finest chefs, how they would spend almost a year just washing vegetables and scrubbing pots before they would be allowed to pick up a knife.

She decided that such a process would work for slave training as well. That night, once the last of the spilled wine had been mopped up, Brenda spent an hour at the sink washing every glass in the kitchen, then drying them all and putting them away. She sat with silver polish and a rag until the silver serving trays shone like mirrors. She earned three hard lashes with the riding crop when Wendy discovered a tiny spot of polish left on one of the trays, and had to polish all of them over again.

She was then given the corkscrew, and made to examine it carefully. Wendy let her go through the motions on an empty bottle, explaining the finer points such as cutting the foil collar. But she would not let her work on a corked bottle yet; Wendy wanted the lessons to go slowly and sink in thoroughly. She gave Brenda a slim volume on different types of wine and sent her home, explaining that on her next visit she would be tested on her knowledge.

Wendy looked up and saw Diane being led to her table. As always, her friend looked beautiful. She was dressed in a light suit, which showed her chocolate skin to perfection, and today her hair was pulled back from her face in a sophisticated style. She kissed Wendy's cheek, then slid into the chair opposite her.

"I'm not too late, am I?" she asked, putting her bag down. "There must be some kind of a convention going on by our building—because there's not a taxi to be found!"

"You're not late at all," Wendy replied, then added mischievously, "I don't have to go back anyway."

"Great minds think alike," Diane said. "I told them I'd be out for the rest of the day, too."

They perused the menus given to them, but Wendy couldn't help sneaking glances over the top of hers. Diane was just so beautiful. She, too, was a dominatrix, but she and Wendy were often lovers as well. Wendy knew so well what was under the well-tailored linen suit. So many times she had sucked those delicious dark breasts into her mouth, and touched her hand to the ruby-rich folds of Diane's lovely cunt.

Her own pussy was beginning to throb, and she pressed herself hard into her chair, then reached over and took Diane's hand, caressing it gently before going back to her menu.

When the waiter came back, they ordered three small courses, enough to ensure at least a couple of hours in their secluded spot, plus a bottle of fine French wine.

"So how's your new one working out?" Wendy asked.

"Not too bad, considering how young she is," Diane replied. She had met Alicia through a mutual friend, and had immediately been intrigued with the slightly built, raven-haired beauty. Less than two weeks later, Alicia found herself in Diane's penthouse apartment with a collar around her neck kneeling at Diane's feet—a situation both of them found tremendously exciting.

"She surprised me, though," Diane continued. "She's not very big, you know, and I thought she'd be really frail. But she can take an awful lot. I caught her playing with her pussy one time when I had left her alone and told her to sit still. You know that new rack I bought? I handcuffed her to it and I let her have it good with the lash. She cried a lot, and I had to stuff a gag in her mouth, but she took every bit of it. I was really amazed."

The waiter came back with the bottle of wine, which he presented for their approval, then deftly uncorked it and poured a bit for Wendy to taste. At her nod, he half filled their glasses and left.

"That reminds me of a problem I'm having right now," Wendy said, gesturing to the waiter who had stopped at another table after serving the two women their wine. "I had a big blowup yesterday with Brenda, the little bitch." She recounted the events of the previous day, finishing with the story of the improperly handled wine and the painful massage.

"Doesn't sound good at all," Diane said, sipping her wine.

"You know," Wendy said, "it seems to me that I'm seeing more and more of that type of behavior all the time. I get new ones, and they're just full of bad habits. I know they're young, but they should be able to serve me a glass of wine properly, for heaven's sake. I asked this one who taught her, and she said nobody ever did. I'm not the first mistress she's ever had. Why on earth are women putting up with this kind of behavior?"

"I really don't know," Diane admitted. "I've noticed a lot of bad habits too, but I never really thought about it until you mentioned it just now. I thought maybe I was just being too picky. It seems that almost every one I've had recently has been really rough. You're right, it seems like no one's taking any time to train them properly. They just use them up and send them out to the next person."

Their appetizers arrived, tiny shrimp nestled into perfect avocado halves. The waiter was quite handsome, and Wendy noticed that his eyes never left Diane when he came by the table. Poor fool! she thought to herself. He'd never know that he didn't stand a chance.

"The ones I've met know the actual sexual moves quite well," Wendy said. "I haven't had one yet who was unable to satisfy me. But you know as well as I do that there's a lot more to it than that. I want one who will do what she's told the first time, without any whining about it. I want to be served properly, I want proper massages, I want them to act properly around other mistresses. I don't think that's too much to ask."

"Not at all," Diane agreed. "I think all slaves should be complete ones—and not just for sex. It's very important that they do everything right. How are you going about it with this one?"

"Very slowly," Wendy said. "Actually I have to teach her twice. First I have to train her to get rid of the bad habits, and then I have to teach her the proper ones. She spent the rest of the night washing glasses and polishing the silver. I had to beat her and make her do all the trays over again, but she got the message."

"Sounds good," Diane said huskily. She could picture Wendy standing over her blonde slave, her riding crop falling on the pale skin. Her pussy stirred at the thought.

"I'm going to take everything very slowly with her," Wendy continued. "I want her to learn all the basics first, before I move her onto more advanced things. It's going to take some time, but I'm planning on keeping this one for a while, so I think it'll be a good investment. At least I'll have one that's properly trained, not like the type we keep seeing over and over again."

"Sounds almost like going to school," Diane said.

"A school for slaves," Wendy mused. "Wouldn't it be nice if there was one somewhere? We could send them to be trained and have them come back to us knowing what to do."

"Wendy, you've got it!" Diane exclaimed.

"Got what?"

"A school for slaves!" Diane was very excited by the prospect. "You're doing it the right way, by the sounds of it. Why don't you take on a few pupils and train them all at the same time?"

"Oh, Diane, that sounds like a lot of work," Wendy protested.

"Well, you're not as busy as a lot of us are," Diane said teasingly; she knew exactly how Wendy kept her job. "And admit it, wouldn't you just love to have a whole classroom of slaves obeying your commands and licking your boots?"

"It does sound exciting," Wendy admitted.

"Besides, hon," Diane said, smiling broadly at her little joke, "a girl can always use a little more spending money, can't she?" She also knew how Wendy very handily paid for all of her luxuries.

Wendy still wasn't fully convinced. "But what do I know about running a school?" she asked.

"Well, your little training course that you've got your own slave doing sounds pretty effective," Diane said. "You know what a good slave should be able to do. Come on, who would be better for the job than you?"

Wendy took a deep breath. "All right, I'll do it!" she said. "Will you be my first customer?"

"Done," Diane said. "You let me know when your first class is coming up, and I'll send Alicia over to you. You have carte blanche with her. Do whatever you have to in order to teach her. I don't spare the rod with her, and neither should you."

"I won't," Wendy promised. "That's going to be my first rule: Expect punishment, and plenty of it. I won't let any customer down and return a poorly trained slave to her. Only when I consider a slave perfectly trained to my standards will she be allowed to graduate."

"You always did have pretty high standards," Diane said.

"Well, they're going to go even higher now," Wendy said, and grinned. "I have a business to run!"

The waiter brought their main courses. As Diane had suggested, the thought of a whole classroom of slaves licking her boots was turning Wendy on more and more. Her pussy was throbbing and she looked at Diane longingly.

She could picture them now, hanging onto her every word, trying desperately not to forget a single detail of any lesson. Of course, they wouldn't be able to remember everything, and Wendy would test them on the most difficult items, the most trivial lessons.

She could see two of them falter, their mouths working soundlessly as they tried so hard to find the proper words. She saw their tears and their pleading eyes, begging for mercy and a chance to try again. Of course, there was never a second chance.

She saw her hands grasp the first slave's long hair and throw her to the ground. She could feel the muscles in her arm tighten as she raised the riding crop, bringing it down on the smooth flesh. She saw the cruel welt rise and heard the cry. There was another lash for screaming out. Then she looked over and saw the bloodless cheeks of the second one.

This one, she forced to her hands and knees. Then she grabbed a stiff leather paddle and struck again and again on those tender buttocks until they burned a deep red, and the young woman's face was stained with silent tears. Throwing aside the paddle, she could see herself ordering them both to clean her boots with their tongues. As the two groveled at her feet, she glared a warning to the other students who had answered correctly. In their eyes, she could see two emotions battling for supremacy. One side of them was deathly afraid of doing wrong and undergoing the punishment their mistress so ably handed out. The other side longed for it, and she could see envy in their eyes for the two women whose tongues were gritty from licking her leather shoes. How they longed to lie before their mistress and prove their worth!

"Wendy! Wendy, are you there?" Diane was laughing as Wendy popped out of her fantasy. "You went into another world there."

"I was just thinking about it, and I went right into it," Wendy explained. She certainly had! Her pussy was now burning, and her nipples were hard, aching to be touched. She knew her cheeks were flushed and her whole body was on edge. Her shoulder still felt as tight as if she really had brought the riding crop crashing down on a poor slave's body. The sensation sent a rich thrill through her.

She reached for her wineglass, but it was empty. "Do you want to order another bottle?" she asked.

Diane reached across the table and took her hand. "I have a better idea," she said. "I have a nice bottle chilling at home. Why don't we go there and have a glass?" She had also been thinking about Wendy's school and was just as excited about it as Wendy was.

They motioned the waiter over and canceled their dessert, calling for the check immediately. He watched them as they walked away from their table. They were gorgeous and had been extremely polite to him throughout the meal, but like almost everyone else who came in contact with them, he detected their iron wills, stunning raw sexuality, and also the whiff of danger that seemed to always be around them. To his surprise, he found himself in awe of them and strangely enough, just a little bit jealous of those who understood the danger and who benefitted by it. He didn't understand it himself, but also like most people who met them, he wished he could.

The two women hailed a taxi outside the restaurant for the short trip to Diane's apartment. When they arrived, the doorman helped them out of the car and held the heavy glass door open for them as they walked into the richly furnished lobby. Like Wendy, Diane's taste ran to the expensive, and the well-known address was only part of it.

Her penthouse suite was as luxuriously appointed as Wendy's house. The thick carpet felt delicious under Wendy's feet as she took off her coat and carelessly tossed it on a chair. Then she kicked off her shoes, and sat down on the huge sofa.

Diane went into the kitchen and returned with two crystal glasses of white wine, then sat beside her dark-haired friend and held up her drink in a toast.

"To Wendy's School for Slaves," she said.

"May you be happy with the results," Wendy said, and gently clinked her glass against Diane's before taking a sip. "Even though I only have two pupils."

"I'll take care of that," Diane promised. "I know a few women who have noticed some bad habits in their slaves, too. I'll get in touch with them and see if they'd be interested in your services." She grinned. "We'll quote them an astronomical tuition fee, of course. These women aren't happy unless they're spending lots of money."

She took another sip of her wine, then put the glass down. Taking Wendy's glass from her, she set it down as well, then leaned toward her. "Hon, I can't wait any longer," she said, and put her arm around Wendy's neck, then kissed her deeply.

Wendy returned her kiss immediately, pushing her tongue into Diane's mouth and mingling with hers. Her pussy was throbbing so badly she couldn't stand it any longer. She reached for Diane's firm breasts through the beautiful linen suit.

"Come with me," Diane whispered huskily, and led her to the bedroom that Diane knew so well. The wrought iron, queen-sized bed looked so inviting that she wanted to press Diane onto it and take her right there. But she forced herself to go slowly, to make the afternoon's session last as long as possible.

She felt Diane's hands on the buttons of her shirt as they kissed again. Then her blouse was open, and her large tits were free. Diane massaged them, pinching the nipples. She reached down and took one into her mouth, and Wendy groaned loudly as she felt Diane's hot tongue lash across the hard nub of flesh.

"Let me have you too," she begged, and Diane stood up so that Wendy could unbutton the crisp linen suit. She ran her tongue down Diane's skin with each button she unfastened, until Diane's firm breasts were uncovered. She took each into her hands, sucking on first one nipple and then the other while Diane moaned and arched her back. Then they massaged each other's tits while they kissed.

Wendy reached around and ran her hands over Diane's firm ass, then slowly pulled down the zipper that held her skirt in place. It fell to the floor, revealing a white lace garter belt, black stockings and no panties. Instantly Wendy's hand was on Diane's beautiful dark cunt. She cupped it, enjoying its warmth and moisture, then she slowly slipped her finger between the swollen lips and tickled the ruby clit. Diane moaned and kissed her hard, then insisted that she shed the rest of her clothes too.

She did so happily, and within seconds she was

standing nude, her beautiful furry pussy aching for Diane's touch. Diane, meanwhile, had stretched out on the bed. Her smooth dark skin looked so delicious against the creamy white quilt spread over the bed. "Come here," she begged, and Wendy bent down and kissed her.

Then she was on top of her, her pussy over Diane's mouth, and her own face over Diane's sweet cunt. She could smell the lovely aroma as she bent down and ever so gently whisked the very tip of her tongue over Diane's clit. She felt a quick shiver go through the dark woman as she did.

Then Diane's mouth was on Wendy's clit, and Wendy bent and gave herself over to eating the pussy below her. Her tongue slid between the folds, so steamy hot, and she touched a finger to the entrance of Diane's hole.

Diane grabbed her ass and pulled her down so that she could feast on Wendy's pussy. One fingertip played around Wendy's tightly puckered asshole while her tongue pressed firmly on the wet clit and pushed it back and forth. Both women were groaning loudly, venting the passion they had held back for so long at the restaurant. Wendy wanted to bury her whole face in Diane's cunt and just stay there with her huge clit between her lips.

Diane held Wendy's clit gently between here teeth and used her tongue to snake back and forth across it. Wendy pushed her tongue into Diane's wet hole, pressing in as deeply as possible. She wished her tongue was twice as long.

She could feel Diane speed up, and her clit was on fire as the probing tongue swept back and forth over it. She concentrated on Diane's clit also, and soon they were both moaning loudly and bucking their hips wildly.

Diane came first, crying through her lips, which were closed on Wendy's pussy. She didn't stop her tongue lashing, though, and only a few seconds afterward, Wendy exploded as well. The sweet hot waves went all the way through her, right to her fingertips and toes, and she collapsed in Diane's arms.

"No slave can beat another mistress for sex," Diane gasped. "But I'll be happy if Alicia graduates from your school able to do that even half as well as you do."

"Wouldn't that be nice!" Wendy agreed, and kissed Diane slowly and lovingly. "Well, she'll have standards she'll have to pass. They'll all have to pass my tests before they graduate. Of course," she smiled, "if they don't, they'll just have to take their punishment and learn a few more lessons."

"That sounds even better," Diane said, snuggling close to her bedmate. "Just what kinds of punishment do you have in mind?"

"Well, I already have a sling and a sawhorse," Wendy said. "And a riding crop and a whip, of course. I want to get an X-frame, and some paddles. I'll look around and see what else strikes my fancy, of course."

"Sounds delicious," Diane said, and slowly and almost absently began stroking her own nipples, which quickly turned into hard nubs.

"And a cane!" Wendy exclaimed. "A long, thin cane, for bare bottoms. I've read stories about English boarding schools, and it seemed to me that those beautiful canes were just wasted on those horrible little boys who didn't appreciate them. I want to use one with all the glory it deserves."

"Oh, I love the sound of that one," Diane said. Her hand was now on Wendy's body, stroking her slowly.

"Just imagine them bent over, and their panties

down around their ankles," Wendy said. "That cane would move so fast, it would just be a little whistle in the air. But they'd hear it coming. Think what a perfect, thin little red line it would leave! And I wouldn't stop until that whole ass was crisscrossed with those beautiful red lines."

"Oh, hon, you're going to be a wonderful teacher," Diane whispered. She leaned down and took one of Wendy's hard nipples into her mouth, running her tongue all over it. She cold feel Wendy's fingers exploring her pussy and she moaned and spread her legs wider.

Wendy quickly and expertly slipped down on the bed and positioned herself between Diane's thighs until their pussies were touching. She loved the warm feeling and especially the sight of her creamy white skin and dark pussy hair against Diane's rich, chocolate-colored legs and black mound.

They had done this so many times before that they fell into a rhythm almost immediately. Both of their pussies were still wet and their clits slid over each other, tickled by the wiry pubic hair.

"Oh, hon, rub hard!" Diane begged, and Wendy ground her cunt into Diane's flesh as hard as she could. Their pussies were locked together and they moved their hips quickly, delighting in the hot ripples that went through them each time their clits were massaged.

They were both unbelievably excited at the thought of the caning, and they pressed against each other with an intensity that surprised them. Wendy's whole body seemed to be focused on her steaming pussy as she rubbed on Diane's clit. With each thrust of her hips, she could picture the cane coming down on smooth creamy buttocks. Each time her clit rubbed against Diane's skin she could hear the sharp crack as the whisper-thin, iron-strong cane bit into a slave's flesh.

She came violently, trembling and gasping. As soon as the last wave subsided she sat up and put her hand on Diane's pussy. Her hand was soaked with Diane's nectar almost immediately.

She pushed two fingers into Diane's hole. The velvety-soft muscles held her tightly as her thumb reached up to caress the hot nub of flesh at the top of the delicious ruby pussy. Diane moaned as Wendy rubbed her thumb hard, back and forth across her clit.

"Right there, hon!" Diane moaned. "Just like that, yes!" She was pushing her hips up to meet Wendy's probing fingers. "Oh, you do that so well!"

Finally Wendy kept her thumb on the very tip of Diane's clit, and was rewarded when Diane cried out with the delicious rush of her second orgasm. It was so fervent that her whole body felt it, and Wendy had to wait while she calmed down before they could once again lie in each other's arms.

They snuggled together for a while, until Wendy checked her watch. "It's still early," she said. "I have to do something shopping. Care to go with me?"

"Shopping again?" Diane asked. "Hon, you're going to own so many clothes you'll need another house just to hang them all up."

"Oh, no, no clothes today," Wendy said. "No, different kind of shopping. I need some school supplies."

Diane perked right up. "Well, why didn't you say so?" she said. "Oh course I'd love to go shopping. You'll never hear me say no to an offer like that."

"Then get dressed," Wendy said, getting up from the huge bed. "I've got to get on this right away. School starts very soon and I want to be prepared."

THREE

The doorman held the door open as they came out, then whistled for a cab. He often wondered about this most intriguing resident of the building, and he had his own ideas about what went on between the gorgeous black woman and the different guests who visited her. He knew that there was a world of difference between the women like Wendy, with her confident air and sophistication, and the ones who brushed by him with their eyes on the ground, but he made no connections between them, and couldn't explain why the distinctions were so clear-cut. Diane often thought it would be fun to see his reaction if he ever figured it out; as for Wendy, the door might have been opened by a robot, for all the notice she ever took of him.

The cab dropped them off at their favorite store, nestled between rows of expensive clothing stores in the city's well-heeled district. The windows were filled with the latest leather fashions, all sorts of jackets, dresses and suits, and the front half of the store was filled with racks of buttery-soft leather clothes.

Wendy and Diane ignored these things and walked to the back of the store, the area that made up the bulk of the company's sales. There were no trendy clothes here.

Instead, the walls were lined with an almost unbelievable array of goods. There were leather harnesses and heavy paddles, slings, leather cuffs and grotesque leather and rubber masks, some with zippers to close over the mouth. There were many types of gags, in a variety of materials, and heavy canvas jackets with rings and buckles to render a slave helpless. One wall held different types of whips and riding crops, another handcuffs and collars.

As they stood and admired the display, a woman came out of the back room. Her face brightened as soon as she saw who her customers were.

"Diane! Wendy!" She rushed over and planted a kiss on each cheek. "So good to see you again. What have you been up to?"

"This is a very special shopping trip, Julie," Diane said. "Wendy needs some pretty serious stuff. She's opening up a school."

"A school?" Julie was mystified. "What's this, you're going back to the three Rs?"

"Not quite," Wendy laughed. She explained the circumstances behind it, and Diane's suggestion that she take in students and teach them the proper way to serve their mistresses.

"Sounds like a fantastic idea," Julie said. "I'm surprised no one thought of something like that sooner. I might even know of a few people who could use your services; I'll let you know what they say."

Diane picked up a black braided leather whip, feeling its lovely heft in her hand. "Wendy, you'll need one of these," she said.

"Oh, let's do this properly," Julie said. "There's nothing like a job done right." She picked up a pad and pen. "You'll need a list so that nothing's forgotten. Now, Wendy, do you have enough handcuffs for a whole class?"

An hour and a half later, Wendy and Diane were back out on the sidewalk, each with a shopping bag in her hand. Julie had been very thorough and Wendy felt confident that she had everything she needed to set up an effective "classroom." In addition to a few choice items for her own use, most of the smaller purchases were in her shopping bag; the larger items would be sent to her house later, along with an X-frame Julie had promised to order.

"Are you coming back with me?" Diane asked.

"Oh, I'd love to, but I have to go home," Wendy said. "I want to unpack this stuff before Brenda comes over. I'm testing her on the wine book I gave her to study."

"Then I'll call you later about bringing mine over to you," Diane said, and kissed Wendy's cheek. "Just don't wear yourself out testing this one. I want Alicia to come back to me fully trained."

Diane held her hand out for a taxi, and Wendy watched as she got inside. She waited until the cab turned the corner and disappeared, then she turned and walked back into the store.

Julie was surprised to see her again. "Back so soon? Don't tell me you've tried everything already and you're back for more."

"Not quite," Wendy laughed. "I need your help, and I don't want Diane to know about it. It's going to be my little surprise once the training course is finished."

She explained her plan to Julie, who listened intently with a smile of anticipation on her face, a smile that grew wider the more she heard.

"Oh, Wendy, that's fantastic!" she exclaimed. "Wait a minute." She disappeared into the back room, then returned holding a business card.

"Call this woman," she said. "She's the very best there is. Tell her I sent you."

"I certainly appreciate it, Julie," Wendy said. "And not a word to anyone about it! I want it to be a complete surprise for everyone."

"My lips are sealed," Julie promised. "Oh, I wish I would be there when she does it. Once the word gets around, you're going to be swamped with women bringing their slaves to your school."

"Not so fast, Julie!" Wendy laughed. "I haven't even held my first class yet."

"Well, you'd better enjoy your leisure time while you can," Julie warned. "Once this news travels, you're going to be the busiest schoolteacher around."

"Red or white first?" Wendy demanded.

"A dry white wine precedes a red wine, Mistress," Brenda replied. She shivered a bit, partly because of the cold hardwood floor, mostly because she was terrified that her mistress would trip her up on the information she'd studied.

Once again, she was in the middle of the room, nude but for a cruel device Wendy had purchased that afternoon. The leather restraint held her ankles together, and her wrists were shackled into cuffs attached to it. Her spine was bent over and her smooth creamy back was completely vulnerable to the riding crop Wendy carried in her hand.

"Why do we use different styles of glasses,

slave?" Wendy asked. She was wearing elbow-length leather gloves and occasionally she would slap the riding crop against her palm. The loud smack of leather on leather made Brenda cringe.

"Each style complements the wine it was intended for, Mistress," Brenda said. She stole a quick sideways glance to see if her answer was acceptable, and visibly relaxed when Wendy stepped away from her to prepare a new question. Brenda had studied very hard and was proud of how much she'd remembered, but she also knew that Wendy might twist a question to trap her.

"Was 1934 a good year for port, slave?" The question was rattled off in machine-gun fashion.

"A great vintage, Mistress," Wendy replied, "but not as good as 1931."

Wendy turned her back quickly lest her face reveal her surprise. She knew Brenda had studied hard, but she never dreamed that such information would be retained. She smiled; if Brenda was going to learn all her lessons this well, she was going to make a superb slave.

She turned, and her smile disappeared instantly. Brenda knew she had answered a very difficult question correctly, and her expression was one of pride and satisfaction. She didn't realize that Wendy had seen her or know how angry her mistress had become.

She found out quickly. "Don't be too sure of yourself, slave," Wendy said coldly. "How many bottles make up a rehoboam?"

"Four," Brenda said quickly, then gasped as she realized she had given the wrong answer. "Oh, no, Mistress, six! Six bottles! Forgive me, Mistress, it's six." There were tears in her eyes already.

"A slave who thinks she has outsmarted her mistress does not receive the chance for a second answer," Wendy said quietly. "If it was only the question, I would accept your second answer."

She walked around until she stood in front of Brenda, her stiletto-heeled boots tapping a warning on the polished floor. "But you were so proud of yourself, thinking you were so smart because you got the vintage question right. It was a good answer, slave. But pride is one thing you will never be allowed to have."

The first strike of the crop was so hard Brenda felt her stomach churn, and she swallowed rapidly and blinked back her tears. Wendy felt her pussy tighten as she looked down at the wide red welt she had made on the tender skin. Brenda's back was her canvas, to paint burning red with each stroke.

She brought the crop down twice more, then stood back to admire her work. The three stripes were blood red. "That was for the incorrect answer," she said. "Now there's the matter of your pride."

With her foot she pushed Brenda over. Her wrists and ankles shackled together, Brenda fell helplessly on her side. Through her tears she watched her mistress select a brand-new leather paddle. As Wendy walked back with it, Brenda could see that the paddle's wide face was covered with bright chrome studs.

"No, Mistress, please!" she cried, but of course it did no good. The paddle crashed down on her exposed buttock. With immense satisfaction, Wendy saw that every stud was mirrored in red on her slave's skin. She struck again, drinking in Brenda's cries and pleas for mercy, enjoying the sight of the creamy skin going bloodlessly white for a split second before welling up angry red. She could only strike one buttock, since Brenda was lying on her side, and she compared the untouched flesh with the red skin that she had paddled. Yes, the injured side was so much better!

She punished the slave's ass several more times, then threw the paddle into the corner. Brenda was sobbing, her back and her buttock burning bright red. "I hope this is one lesson you'll learn right away, slave," Wendy hissed. "I will not allow any slave of mine to be proud!"

"I'm sorry, Mistress," Brenda sniffled. "I won't forget, Mistress, I promise!" Her skin was so sore it felt as if it might slip away from her bruised flesh if she moved.

Grasping a think handful of blonde hair, Wendy hauled her helpless slave upright until she was once again sitting on the hard floor. Brenda's mouth opened in pain, but no sound came out.

"Now, slave, I have some news for you," Wendy said, walking about so that her heels tapped on the highly polished floor. Brenda kept her head down, her eyes straight ahead. Her scalp was burning, and her reddened ass and back stung.

"You're not going to be taking your training alone," Wendy continued. At this news, Brenda raised her tear-stained face.

"Mistress?" she asked.

"I'm opening a school for slaves," Wendy explained. "It seems that there are just too many of you out there who are poorly trained. I've decided to take on students and teach them the proper way to serve a mistress."

Brenda's heart sank. Sharing her beloved mistress with other slaves! A sob escaped her lips.

"What's wrong, slave?" Wendy demanded.

"Oh, Mistress," Brenda cried, "I love you so

much, and it hurts me to think of other slaves trying to get your attention!"

Wendy stood in front of her and leaned down, taking Brenda's chin between her well-manicured fingers and lifting it. "Very touching, slave," she murmured. "Very touching indeed."

Then, so swiftly that Brenda didn't even see it coming, she smacked the helpless slave's cheek with a ferocious backhand. Once again Brenda fell to her side on the hard floor. The blow, delivered from a gloved hand, burned brightly on Brenda's pale cheek.

"I told you what I was going to do," Wendy said coldly. "I didn't ask for your opinion on it."

"I'm so sorry, Mistress!" Brenda sobbed. There didn't seem to be a single part of her body that didn't hurt. She wanted desperately to wipe away her tears and put a comforting hand to her cheek, but her wrists were secured to her ankles by the heavy leather restraints.

Wendy continued as calmly as if nothing had happened. "My holding the classes here will mean some extra responsibility on your part," she said.

"Yes, Mistress," Brenda whispered.

"The mistresses who are sending their slaves to me are doing so because they believe I am the best person to train them," Wendy said. "Now, how would it look if my own slave wasn't obedient?"

When Brenda didn't answer right away, she felt the sharp toe of Wendy's boot connect with her thigh. "Not very good, Mistress!" she said.

"It wouldn't look good at all," Wendy concurred. "Now, these mistresses understand that you're still undergoing training as well. It will be understood if you are still ignorant about a few things that we haven't covered in class yet."

She picked up the riding crop and brushed

Brenda's spine with it. Shackled and helpless, Brenda held her breath, fearful that the whip would land. "What won't be understood is if you don't listen in class. If you misbehave. If you answer back rudely, or if you don't reply when you're spoken to. Is that understood?"

"Yes, Mistress," Brenda whispered.

"I will be relying on you to set an example for the other slaves in class," Wendy said. "Your manners will be beyond reproach. You will learn your lessons thoroughly, and we'll have none of this pride that you flaunted before me earlier. You will be a model student in every respect. Is this understood?"

"Yes, Mistress," Brenda said.

"Good. I'm glad we agree on that," Wendy said coldly. "Because your options are very plain. You can behave as you should, or I can find myself another personal slave. It doesn't matter to me."

Brenda felt numb. She knew that Wendy meant exactly what she said, and that she could very easily find herself without a mistress.

"Is it very plain to you?" Wendy demanded.

"Oh, yes, Mistress!" Brenda whispered.

"Very good," Wendy said, and turned on her heel. "The first official class begins tomorrow." She left the room, closing the door firmly behind her. Brenda remained on her side on the floor, her hands and feet shackled together, her whole body aching. She didn't know if she would be left like this for a few minutes or several hours. She began to concentrate on each individual pain, on her battered ass, her back crisscrossed by whip marks, her cheek bruised by her mistress' leather glove—and her pussy tightened and throbbed at the thought of each one.

FOUR

"Good morning, class," Wendy said, closing the door behind her.

"Good morning, Mistress," three voices chimed together.

Wendy smiled her approval. The three were kneeling on the floor in a row, their hands held behind them by the handcuffs she had snapped onto their wrists before ordering them into the classroom. They were naked, except for the collars she had decided upon for all of her students. These were heavy black leather dog collars, complete with chrome rings, which hung loosely around their throats. A leash could be applied easily or, if necessary, she could wrap her whole fist around the collar to drag a slave around by it.

First in the row was her own Brenda, her eyes

41

firmly on the floor, very unhappy about sharing her mistress, but too wise now to let it show.

Beside her was Diane's slave, Alicia, the youngest of the three. She was thin and fragile looking, and her beautiful hair was a heavy black crown. But Wendy had received a full description from Diane, and knew that Alicia could take whatever punishment was necessary to bring her in line.

The third slave was Leslie, who belonged to Diane's friend Anne. She was obviously uncomfortable on the hard floor, and was fidgeting with her shackled wrists; Wendy guessed that she hadn't been a slave for very long. Her brown hair was cut short and threads of silver were just starting to weave through it. She was slightly plump, with large delicious breasts and a dark triangle between her legs. Wendy had only met Anne once, when Diane brought her over to introduce them and enroll Leslie in the school. She knew nothing about this new slave and looked forward to the challenge.

Her "classroom" was done to her taste as well. The walls still smelled faintly of fresh paint, and the hardwood floor had been buffed to a high shine—by Brenda, nude and on her hands and knees. On one wall was a large, school-type chalkboard. It looked extremely out of place against the adjoining wall, which was dotted with hooks. The hooks were filled with the tools of the school's trade: whips, crops, masks, handcuffs, leather shackles, leashes, a straitjacket, paddles, and Wendy's prized cane.

The sling still hung from the ceiling, and the padded sawhorse was pushed against one wall. But there was another toy: a wooden X-frame, with rings at each end, its arms spread wide to stretch out a disobedient slave.

Leslie had obviously never seen so many devices

in one room before, and she kept looking around the room. Brenda and Alicia looked at the floor, but all three of them sprang to attention when Wendy announced that school was now in session.

Their teacher was certainly dressed for the occasion. Wendy was wearing a tight black lace corset, with fishnet stockings snapped into the garters. Her open-fingered gloves were made of matching black lace and reached to her elbows. The corset covered her beautiful breasts, but her dark cunt was exposed and she knew that the three slaves were eyeing it. Her feet were clad in her favorite stiletto-heeled leather boots.

"I am Mistress Wendy, your teacher," she announced. "Your class is now in session, and I will begin with some rules.

"My number-one rule is that you are to remember that I am training you on behalf of your mistress, who has given me permission to treat you as if you were my own. You cannot expect any leniency from me, none whatsoever. I am not the type of mistress who thinks about what she would like to do to a disobedient slave. I do it."

She walked over to Brenda, who kept her eyes on the floor. "Turn your head, slave," she said. The other two immediately noticed Brenda's bruised and swollen cheek, the result of Wendy's leather-gloved blow. "Now look at her back," Wendy ordered, and they noticed the puffiness that remained from the lashes with the riding crop and the leather paddle.

"This is what you can expect," Wendy said. "No slaps on the wrist here. You will learn, and if I have to beat your lessons into you, then that's the way I'll do it." Again she saw the confused look in the women's eyes; half fearful, half longing for the punishment.

"I will be teaching you everything you need to

know about being a slave," Wendy continued. "We will learn such things as how to pleasure a mistress properly, and how to serve her food and wine correctly. We will learn proper manners, and how to behave when her friends are around."

She paced in front of them slowly. Brenda and Alicia watched the ground, while Leslie still stole curious glances around her. "At the end of your training course, I will assess each one of you and decide if you are good enough to graduate. If you are not, you will continue your lessons until you are."

She stopped and smiled at them. "I think you will all want to graduate the first time. There is a very special surprise waiting for those slaves who do graduate from this school, and I don't think you'll want to miss it. It will be something that will differentiate you from ordinary slaves and will show that you have been specially trained to properly serve your mistress superbly. If I were you, I would make every effort to earn it."

She paced again, then stopped before Leslie, her delicious dark pussy right before the bound slave's face. "Service me," she said.

Leslie looked up at her, questioningly. "Mistress?"

Wendy cracked her hard across her cheek with the back of her hand; Leslie's head snapped sideways and her skin burned red. Wendy's voice was quiet and icy. "I know that you are new to this," she said, "so I will teach you your lesson now. When a mistress gives you an order, no matter what it is, you do not question it. Ever. You do what you are told the first time, right away. Is that understood?"

"Yes, Mistress," Leslie whispered. Both her cheeks were burning now, from the blow and from her shame.

Once again, Wendy positioned herself before Leslie's face. "Service me."

This time there were no questions. Leslie pushed the tip of her tongue into the folds of Wendy's dark pussy, at first timidly, then a little bolder. "You two may watch this," Wendy told Brenda and Alicia. "Then we can discuss it."

The room was silent except for the sound of Leslie's lapping tongue. She tried eagerly, but out of the corner of her eye, Wendy could see Brenda almost imperceptibly shake her head with disapproval. The young blonde submissive knew most of the motions that her mistress liked best, and it seemed that Leslie wasn't even coming close.

Wendy stood for fifteen minutes while Leslie licked and sucked at this most sensitive part of her body. Her expression never changed from a look of boredom. Leslie had never been called on to perform this duty for so long, and her tongue was sore and her jaw cramped. But the rich smell of Wendy's pussy, and the excitement of licking this cruel and unforgiving Mistress overshadowed her discomfort. She licked and sucked eagerly, and since she didn't dare look up into Wendy's eyes, she thought her clumsy movements were pleasing the woman whose cunt had been thrust before her mouth. Her own pussy was throbbing and she longed to touch her cunt lips for relief, but of course he hands were firmly held by the cold steel cuffs.

Finally, completely bored, Wendy stepped back. Leslie licked her glistening lips, savoring a last taste of the delicious pussy she had just enjoyed. But her eyes flew open in horror when she heard Wendy's quiet, steely voice.

"You are a most useless slut," she said. "I can see why your mistress sent you to me. I think I would rather go without than have you service me. You are sloppy and clumsy; I can see where a lot of your training will have to lie."

Tears appeared at the corners of Leslie's eyes. "You are fortunate that this is only an assessment," Wendy continued. "If any slave of mine performed like that, I would horsewhip her."

She walked behind Leslie and gently caressed the back of her neck. Her touch was like ice to the submissive, who shivered in fear. "We will work on it," Wendy said. "Right now you are worthless scum, but with time and lessons, I will make you superb. All of you will be, because no matter how long it takes, no slave will leave my school until she is perfect, and until she carries the proof that she has graduated. I will accept nothing less."

She walked around, her razor-sharp heels tapping on the floor, and stood before Alicia. "Let's see what you can do," she said, and thrust her dark triangle into the face of Diane's slave.

Alicia was determined to outshine Leslie. Unable to use her hands, she probed with her tongue between the folds of Wendy's pussy until she reached the clit. She played with it for a while, running her tongue along both sides of it, then she flicked her tongue straight across it. She grasped it gently between her teeth and tickled it with the tip of her tongue, then sucked it in between her lips. She was rewarded with Wendy's sweet nectar, which she hungrily lapped up. Wendy's expression still did not change. This slave was much better than the first, but still desperately in need of lessons.

Alicia was becoming more turned on each moment and, like Leslie, she longed to be able to touch herself for relief. Of course she knew that it would not have been allowed, even without the handcuffs, and her pussy throbbed uncontrollably all the time her tongue was buried in Mistress Wendy's sweet bush.

She wanted to push her tongue right into Wendy's tight hole, but could not lean forward far enough. Instead, she played her tongue across its opening as best she could before returning to Wendy's beautiful clit. It was heavenly to suck on it, and she was bitterly disappointed when Wendy finally stepped back from her.

"Your mistress described you very well," Wendy said. "She told me that your skills were barely adequate. She was right. You will need considerably more training before I decide that you are good enough to pass my test."

Now she stood before her own slave, who was waiting eagerly for her turn at Wendy's pussy. She was proud of herself, for she knew that her skills were so much better than those of the women bound beside her. She had learned her lesson thoroughly, though, and not a trace of it showed on her face, which was still bruised from her previous error.

Wordlessly, Wendy stood in front of Brenda with her legs apart. Brenda was on her clit in an instant. Wendy's face betrayed no emotion, but she thoroughly enjoyed the warm rush from her pussy as Brenda's tongue made its contact.

She knew full well that Brenda's performance was not only based on a desire to please her mistress, but to point out the difference between herself and the other two slaves. Wendy didn't particularly care. At that moment, the hot tongue on her cunt was of prime importance even if she didn't let it show.

Brenda worked her clit the way she knew her mistress liked. Wendy's hot juice was quickly lapped up as Brenda licked both sides of the hard nub, then concentrated on the very tip of it. First she teased it lightly, then pushed hard against it, her tongue flicking quickly back and forth. Wendy's whole pussy was hot and throbbing, and she could feel the sweet buildup beginning in her belly.

Brenda knew the effect her tongue was having, and she stepped up her efforts. Her tongue was now flashing over Wendy's clit and teasing the entrance to her velvety hole. As always, Wendy's expression never changed, but she shivered slightly as the sweet, delicious hot waves rushed all through her body when she came. She stepped away, her dark pussy hair glistening from Brenda's mouth and her own rich juice.

"As you can see, this slave is much better at servicing a mistress than you are," Wendy told the other two. "She still needs much fine-tuning, and will be learning her lessons the same way you will be. But I expect both of you, within the week, to be at the point where she is now. If you aren't, I shall be very disappointed, and I'm sure you don't want that to happen."

Wendy picked up the small key and walked behind her three charges, unsnapping their handcuffs. Each woman stretched her arms out, trying to work the muscles out of their cruel positions.

"Now that I have assessed you, it's time to start your training in this most vital area," she said, and left the room. When she returned, she carried three halves of green pepper, the central rib still intact.

"At this stage, these will be your workbooks," she said, handing each woman one of the pieces. "I expect that when you go home, you will use similar ones for your homework. I don't want to feel your tongues on me again until you are qualified enough to do so. I can't be bothered spending my time standing here, while you worthless scum attempt to lick my cunt. I'll wait until you're good enough to at least raise my interest a little bit."

The three slaves looked at the vegetable halves they had been given, a bit puzzled. Leslie ran her hand over the smooth green skin.

"Stupid slaves," Wendy muttered. She roughly took the pepper away from Leslie and handed it back to her with the cut side up, then shoved the woman's hand to her face. "Imagine that this pepper is my cunt," she said. "Now lick it like it's supposed to be licked. Like you'll be punished if you don't do it right. Which you will," she added threateningly.

Indeed, the hard green pepper shell surrounding the thick white central rib did like a lot like a pussy, once it was pointed out to them. Brenda, determined to show the other two up, ran her tongue lightly around the shell and teased the rib with the very tip of her tongue. The other two women pushed at the rib with the flat of their tongues.

Wendy had had enough. Picking up the riding crop, she slashed Leslie hard across her smooth back. None of them knew the blow was coming, and the sharp smack of leather on skin made them jump. Leslie cried out as a vicious red welt rose up on her skin. "Please, Mistress!" she cried out. Wendy responded with a second cruel blow. Leslie sobbed.

"You are to speak only when spoken to," Wendy hissed. "That was what the second blow was for. The first was for not learning your original lesson. When I assessed you, I informed you that your performance was worthless. I see that, given a second chance, you have done nothing to improve it. I do not expect perfection immediately, but I do expect that you will learn something with each criticism you are given and that you will do better each time. Do you understand?"

"Yes, Mistress," Leslie said, sniffling. Quickly she retrieved the pepper lest she be punished for dropping it. Her back was on fire and her face burned with shame. The other two women glanced at her, fearful that their mistress' rage wasn't completely vented and that they could be next.

"Brenda, lick your pepper," Wendy ordered, and Brenda quickly brought the vegetable to her mouth. She continued as before, slowly running up and down the shell as if she were probing the outer lips of her mistress' sweet pussy. She slipped her tongue inside it as she did when she parted Wendy's pussy lips with the very tip of her tongue. She played with the bottom of the pepper, pretending that it was the entrance to her mistress' tight hole, then slowly and teasingly worked her way up the central rib until she reached the spot where her mistress' clit would be waiting, eager to be flicked and sucked. She lavished attention on this spot as the other two women watched.

"You can see the obvious difference between what you did and what she is doing now," Wendy continued, pacing back and forth as Alicia and Leslie watched Brenda passionately licking the pepper. "You all have pussies, don't you? You know which areas are sensitive, don't you? So pay attention to those places where your tongue will do the most good!"

Brenda's tongue was now flicking madly across the top of the pepper. Her own pussy was hot, imagining that once again her tongue was buried in Wendy's crotch. She loved her mistress and especially loved it when she was given the privilege of licking her. She was determined that her work would ensure another session at her mistress' feet.

"Note how she moves her tongue across the

top," Wendy coached the other two. "That is how
you should be treating the clitoris. But she doesn't
stay there too long, because she wants to give equal
time to the other areas. Now she's going all around
the outside. That's how your tongues should be pressing against the pussy lips just before you move
inside." The two slaves watched as Brenda continued
to run her tongue over the pepper.

"Now, let's see you two do it," Wendy ordered.
The crop was still in her hand, and Leslie's eyes
stayed on it as she raised the pepper to her lips.

There was a marked improvement in both of
them. This time they paid special attention to the
shell before zeroing in on the rib that symbolized the
clit. "Much better," Wendy crooned as she watched
all three licking and sucking as eagerly as if their
mouths were pleasing her own pussy. "See, it isn't
difficult. You just have to pay attention and try harder."

She walked behind them and stood while they
licked the peppers. She knew that each one was on
edge, trying her best to please her, since they had no
idea if or when a blow was coming. She was thrilled
to see that their movements were becoming easier
and more fluid as she watched. Just that small
improvement let her know that her school was going
to be a success.

Ten minutes later she gave the order to relax.
She collected the peppers, then stood before them.
The three slaves had been kneeling on the hard floor
for some time, and Wendy noticed with growing disgust that Alicia and Leslie were not sitting up
straight.

Roughly, she grabbed hold of the leather collar
around Leslie's throat and yanked her upright with it.
"No slave will ever graduate if she doesn't learn

proper posture," Wendy hissed. Terrified, Leslie remained straight once the hand was off her collar.

Wendy moved so quickly that Alicia was still off guard when her collar was grasped. Wendy's hand grasped a large lock of hair along with the collar, and Alicia's head was roughly pulled back. "Mistress, that hurts!" she protested.

Scarcely believing her ears, Wendy let go and stepped back. "What did you say?" she demanded.

Realizing what she had done, Alicia clapped her hand over her mouth, but it was too late. "What did you say, scum?" Wendy insisted again.

"Nothing—nothing, Mistress," Alicia replied, her voice trembling with fear.

Brenda and Leslie looked straight ahead, not daring to glance over, as Wendy moved back to glare at Alicia. Her voice was low and icy. "This is not some freethinking college," she said. "This is a school for slaves. For students who do not comment on the things their teacher does. And especially, for students who do not lie to their teachers when they are asked a question."

She stood before Alicia, who was trembling. "Stand up," she ordered. Alicia did so immediately. "Over to the horse."

Teacher and student walked over to the padded sawhorse standing against the wall. Deftly, Wendy snapped a pair of handcuffs on each wrist, then bent Alicia over the horse and attached the cuffs to rings on the sawhorse legs. Alicia's bare ass was now at Wendy's mercy, and Wendy could see that her dark pussy was glistening with excitement even as she trembled with fear.

Wendy picked up one of the discarded pepper halves, and pulled Alicia's head up by her hair, then roughly shoved the pepper into her mouth as a gag.

"You two turn around and watch this," Wendy ordered Brenda and Leslie. "I want you to see exactly what will happen if I am not implicitly obeyed."

She went over to the wall containing her gruesome collection of toys, and deliberated for some time. Out of the corner of her eye, she could see Alicia watching her. She touched the studded leather paddle and noted with satisfaction how Alicia's eyes widened. She teased the bound slave several times like this, caressing a heavy plaited leather whip and a heavy leather belt. Finally she reached for her boarding-school cane.

She had never used it before, and she whipped it back and forth a few times in the air. It was supple and the end flexed back and forth. There was a low whistle of rushing air as she moved it around. She smiled; she had really been looking forward to trying it out.

Back at the sawhorse, she decided to make the most of this lesson. First she gently rubbed her fingers over Alicia's creamy, smooth ass. Then she ran the cane over her skin with whisper-light strokes. Alicia moaned, her cries muffled by the pepper in her mouth.

Then Wendy turned the cane around, and used the handle to rub on Alicia's glistening pussy. The black-haired slave groaned with delight, and pushed her pussy against the cane. Wendy knew it would feel so delicious on those starved cunt lips. She rubbed until Alicia's moans got louder, and then abruptly pulled the cane away. Alicia slumped in frustration.

She tensed up again, though, when she realized that Wendy was getting ready to strike. Wendy noticed the muscles in her asscheeks tighten as she raised the cruel thin cane.

The cane made a thin whistling sound as Wendy

brought it down. It landed with a loud, satisfying crack on Alicia's bare buttocks. She jumped, but the cold steel handcuffs held her firmly across the sawhorse. The pepper muffled her cry of pain.

Wendy stepped closer to see the effect of the cane. A red line, as delicate as a ruby pinstripe, rose up on the white skin. Wendy shivered with excitement and traced the line with one long fingernail. The welt matched the blood red enamel on her nail.

Again she raised the cane, and again the whistling, the sharp crack. This line overlapped the first. In quick succession, Wendy brought the cane down several more times, until Alicia's burning ass was bright red and covered with thin welts. Tears were streaming down her cheeks and only the pepper in her mouth prevented her from screaming in agony.

"Come over here," Wendy ordered, and Brenda and Leslie got up stiffly and walked over. "Look carefully." The two examined the thin red stripes on Alicia's bare ass, once again with that mixture of terror and longing. "I will not stand for any bad habits in my students. You cannot graduate with bad habits, and you will be punished for them. Let this be a lesson to you."

She ordered them back to their positions on the hard floor, then unlocked the handcuffs on Alicia's wrists. The black-haired slave stood up and removed the pepper from her mouth as ordered. Her face was flushed bright red and her eyes were rimmed with tears. To prolong the agony, Wendy forced her to sit on her ass while the other two knelt. The wooden floor was no comfort to her burning caned buttocks.

Wendy picked up a piece of chalk and stepped over to the blackboard. In her fine hand, she wrote the heading "Dinner Settings," then turned to the three naked women, their slave collars about their throats, and smiled.

"There's much more to being a slave than being able to lick peppers," she said. "Who can tell me which side the forks go on?"

Three hands shot up, and Wendy smiled again. They had come to her with bad habits, but Wendy was sure that they would graduate as superb examples of the dominatrix's art.

FIVE

The stunningly dressed dark-haired woman set her drink back down on the table and leaned forward. "I was just so thrilled when I heard that you were running this school, Wendy," she said. "I knew you were the answer to my prayers. I just hope you know what you're getting into by accepting this one."

Wendy took a sip of her own drink. "I think I can handle it, Leah," she smiled. "I'm determined that no one will ever drop out of my school. No matter how long it takes, every slave will graduate."

She sat back and looked around the room for the waiter. The two women were sitting in the lounge of an opulent downtown hotel, Wendy having informed the other managers in her office that she had an important meeting with a client.

That was true, but certainly not the way they would ever have dreamed. Leah was another one of

57

Wendy's occasional lovers. She had heard about the school and invited the teacher out to discuss putting two of her slaves through training.

"Ellen's been with me for a couple of months now, and she really isn't much of a problem," Leah continued. "She's rough, and I'd like you to smooth her out and teach her some of the finer arts."

"That's no problem," Wendy replied. She had seen Ellen a couple of times; she was a very small woman with beautiful full breasts and creamy skin that took a lash so well. Wendy had only seen her naked, wearing wrist cuffs. It was delicious to think of having the small, fine woman under her control.

"Margot's the problem one," Leah said. "I'm still very confused about her, and I'd like your opinion before I even bother enrolling her in your class. I've known her for only a few weeks, and I don't know if she's worth the trouble."

"Why not?" Wendy asked.

"Well, she's got the strangest attitude I've ever seen in a slave," Leah said. "At first, I wasn't even sure if she was one. She fights me all the way. She won't do what she's told no matter how she's threatened; sometimes it seems like she's the mistress!"

"She wants punishment," Wendy observed.

"I suspected that, but she fights the punishment too," Leah said. "I even sat down with her and asked if this was what she wanted, and she said yes. But no sooner had she said that, then she got that wicked look in her eye again and wouldn't obey me at all."

"What kind of punishment did you use?" Wendy asked.

"The standard type, I guess," Leah said. "I tried a riding crop and a whip, but nothing more exotic than that."

Wendy smiled, a cruel smile that Leah found

very enticing. Wendy could feel her pussy getting wet at the thought. "I think that with some real punishment, you could have one of the best slaves around," she said.

"Do you really think so?" Leah took another sip of her drink.

"I really do," Wendy said. "Think of a racehorse. It doesn't want that saddle on its back and it fights, but the trainer wins out and the horse has to wear it. That horse doesn't want to carry the jockey, and he doesn't want the bit in his mouth, but they're forced on him. Then they put him in the starting gate. He's furious because he doesn't want all these things on him. Then they open that gate and he runs faster than any other horse around, because he's got all that pent-up emotion in him."

She reached over and touched Leah's hand. "It sounds to me like you have a racehorse on your hands. It's going to be difficult to keep her in line, but once we do, she'll outperform any of the others because it's all inside her. She needs some serious humiliation and some drastic punishment. We need to get all of that emotion under control so we can put it to good use."

The sound of her own words was turning Wendy on. In her mind's eye, she was looking over her wall of instruments, deciding which ones were severe enough for a challenge such as this. She could picture Margot spread-eagled, firmly fastened to the X-frame, or at her mercy hanging from the leather sling on the ceiling. She looked over at Leah and smiled, and the sultry look that Leah returned made her clit throb with desire. Leah's lips were sweet and full, and Wendy longed to reach over the table and kiss them.

"So long as you don't think it's too much of a challenge, I'll send them both over to you," Leah said.

"I just know I'm right about this one," Wendy said. "In fact, I'll make a deal with you to prove how sure I am. You pay the tuition for the other one—Ellen, is it? You don't pay me anything for this tough one until she's graduated from school. If I can't make her toe the line, then you don't owe me anything for any of the lessons that I give her."

"Fair enough," Leah said. "I really do hope you can turn her into a real slave, though. I don't know why, but I find her really exciting even if she is difficult to control. Maybe it's like you said; maybe it's all that pent-up emotion in her. Perhaps it just needs to be harnessed."

"I'll harness it for sure," Wendy said, and she shivered just a little as a hot rush went through her from her pussy. She could almost feel the heavy braided whip in her hand, ready to land it on a smooth back. She had had many clumsy slaves and several novices, but never before an unwilling slave who still wanted to be a slave. Strangely enough, she found herself looking forward to having this new student in her class.

"I suppose you have a contract or something that you want me to sign," Leah said. "I'd like to get them enrolled right away."

"No, no contracts," Wendy said. "Just let me know when they can begin."

"Nothing to sign?" Leah asked. She feigned a look of disappointment. "I was hoping you'd have to come back to my apartment to have me fill out the forms."

Wendy smiled. She could feel her panties growing damp as she admired her friend. "Maybe in lieu of forms, we can just get together and discuss what I'll be putting your slaves through," she said. By the look in Leah's eyes, she could see that the dark-haired beauty was just as turned on as she was.

Leah paid the bill, and they left the hotel and flagged a taxi. Leah had a beautiful apartment in the heart of the city, elegantly furnished and monitored by a doorman who, like Diane's, often wondered about what went on behind the heavy oak door leading to this mysterious woman's apartment. Leah and Wendy, their faces flushed with anticipation, swept past him and hurried for the elevator.

Leah couldn't wait once the apartment door was closed behind them. She took Wendy into her arms and pressed her mouth with a long, sultry kiss. Wendy opened her lips and pushed her tongue hard into Leah's mouth. The tall, elegant woman pressed her own just as hard, mingling with Wendy's tongue and moaning softly. She moved her hands up and down Wendy's back, grabbing at her firm ass before moving up to caress her again.

Wendy's own hands were on Leah, teasing her buttons open. Leah wore a lacy black bra and Wendy's fingers moved over it and played with the fabric. She dipped a finger behind it and gently rubbed against the hard nipple inside. Leah groaned and kissed Wendy hard, deeply, pressing her body up against her and trapping Wendy's hand between them with her fingers on that firm nub of flesh.

"Oh, hon, you feel so good," Leah whispered, and planted a row of tiny kisses on Wendy's neck before she returned to her sensuous mouth. "I want my tongue in your cunt. I want to taste your pussy."

"Come here, then," Wendy said, and led Leah over to an armchair. She sat her down, then knelt before her on the thick carpet and opened the rest of Leah's buttons. The black bra looked delicious against Leah's creamy skin.

Wendy sucked at her nipples through the fabric. They were so swollen and hard they stuck out firmly, and Wendy played with one while she tongued the other. She slipped her tongue in between Leah's breasts, and finally opened the tiny clasp in front and pushed the fabric away.

"Oh, you've got such beautiful tits," Wendy said, and sucked one into her mouth. At the same time, she slipped her hand under Leah's skirt and realized that she was wearing stockings. Slowly and teasingly, she ran her fingernails over Leah's thighs just above the stocking tops. Leah groaned and slouched into the chair, trying to position her pussy closer to Wendy's hand, but Wendy smiled and pulled back. "No use hurrying this," she said. "I've got all afternoon."

She sucked on Leah's nipples again, moving her hand closer and closer to the dark pussy that she wanted so badly. She teased unmercifully, rubbing one finger across the top of the hairline, then over Leah's thighs and back down to the tops of her stockings. She knew that once she did put her hand within that delicious triangle, she would find it hot and wet, waiting impatiently for her.

She decided to make Leah wait a little longer. She stood up and as Leah watched, she slowly unbuttoned her shirt, running her fingers over her exposed skin as her blouse opened a bit more each time. She was not wearing a bra, and she rubbed her nipples through the silk fabric before she finally pulled the shirt away from them. Her own nipples were as hard as Leah's and she pinched and played with them while Leah watched, nodding her approval and longing to hold them herself.

"They're going to feel so good when you get your hands on them," Wendy whispered, and she lifted them and held them out, just beyond Leah's reach.

"You bitch," Leah smiled. "You always did love to tease, didn't you? You wait until I'm between your legs. You'll be sorry."

Wendy's shirt was off now, and she unzipped her skirt and let it fall to the floor. Like Leah, she wore stockings with no panties, and her own dark bush looked hot and luscious. With a wicked smile on her face, she ran her hands through it, and pushed her fingers up between her pussy lips. "It's so hot and wet," she whispered. "It's just waiting for your tongue to be there."

"At times like this I wish you were a slave," Leah smiled. "Then I could just order you to bring that pussy over here."

"So you could," Wendy agreed, and she rubbed herself hard, enjoying the longing on Leah's face. "But just think about how good this is going to feel when you finally get close to it."

She played with herself for a bit longer. Her clit was throbbing and it felt wonderful to have her fingers on it, but she forced herself to pull her hand away. She was saving it for Leah. She knew how good Leah's tongue could feel on her, and she was looking forward to it as much as Leah was anticipating having Wendy's tongue on her.

She reached for Leah's hand, and the two of them went into the bedroom where Leah shed the rest of her clothes. Like Wendy, her body was firm and gorgeous, and when she stretched out on the bed, Wendy couldn't help but admire her for a moment before she bent down and ran her tongue from her nipples down to the dark hair between her legs.

She was just as much of a tease here. She used her tongue the same way she had used her fingers, to trace a circle around Leah's pussy over her belly and down to her thighs. The hot, rich aroma of Leah's cunt made her own throb wildly, but she resisted the temptation to bury her face in it. Instead she moved back and forth around it, until Leah was gasping and moaning with desire.

Finally she used her fingers to spread the swollen lips apart, and pushed her tongue against the hot clit. Leah shivered and moaned loudly as Wendy's tongue slowly ran up and down the length of her clit and then moved to the entrance of her hole.

"Oh, stick it in, hon," Leah whispered, and Wendy poked her tongue as far as she could into the wet hole. She then replaced her tongue with her finger, and Leah groaned as she pushed inside. The walls of Leah's vagina were hot and soft as velvet, but the muscles held her finger firmly as she pushed in and out. As she did, she flicked her tongue over Leah's clit, which was now so large it pushed out between her pussy lips. Gently Wendy sucked it in between her lips and nibbled on it with her teeth.

"Fuck my cunt!" Leah said, and Wendy pushed two fingers inside the velvet hole, then moved them back and forth rapidly. Her mouth never left Leah's huge clit and her own pussy was soaked. She ran her tongue up both sides of Leah's button, then flicked rapidly across it, pushing it back and forth as hard as she could. Leah's hips were moving, bringing her clit in contact with Wendy's tongue, and she groaned loudly as the hot rush went through her each time her clit was licked.

"Oh, that feels so good!" Leah groaned, as Wendy sucked hard on her clit. As she held it between her lips, she also teased the tip of it with her tongue. Leah was grinding her pussy against Wendy's mouth, pushing her hips toward the tongue that was doing such wonderful things to her cunt. Wendy's face was wet with pussy juice and the rich smell filled her nose. She tried to get as deep into Leah's cunt as she possibly could.

She could feel Leah trembling, and she stepped up her efforts. Her fingers were buried in Leah's smooth, wet hole, and her tongue was moving as fast as possible over Leah's hard clit. Leah stiffened and then cried out loudly as she came. Wendy stayed on her clit the whole time, as Leah's hips bucked and ground against her. Finally, when it was over, she gently lapped Leah's pussy and pulled her fingers out of her hole, sucking the thick, sweet juice off of them.

"Oh, girl, come up here," Leah said, and Wendy moved up on the bed and straddled her pussy over Leah's full, sensuous lips. The first touch of Leah's tongue on her throbbing pussy was a fire-and-ice sensation, so hot and sweet that if it had been any harder Wendy might have come right then.

Leah reached up to hold Wendy's ass, and she used her grip to move Wendy's pussy on her tongue. She licked up and down the sides of Wendy's clit, then tickled the entrance to her tunnel and finally moved back to flick her tongue against the tight hollow of Wendy's asshole.

"Oh, that's not fair!" Wendy said, as she realized that Leah intended to tease her by moving all around her most sensitive areas, skirting them to build up the pressure in Wendy's clit.

"Sure it is," Leah replied. "Remember who teased me?" She went back to her slow circling, and Wendy gasped as she was allowed a light touch on her clit.

The touch flicked away, though, and Wendy again enjoyed the sweet buildup as Leah's tongue snaked its way around her hole, pushing her pussy lips aside and running up and down the groove around her clit. Then, finally, as Wendy had done to her, Leah began to concentrate on Wendy's clit.

The hot, delicious rush up Wendy's spine was glorious as Leah's tongue worked over her pussy. Wendy groaned and pressed her hips down until her pussy was right on top of Leah's mouth. Leah lapped up her hot juice eagerly, then pushed her tongue against Wendy's clit again.

"Lick it right there!" Wendy gasped, and Leah responded by lapping quickly at Wendy's clit. One finger was massaging the opening to Wendy's hole. Wendy herself was playing with her tits, pinching and rolling the nipples between her fingers as the heat in her cunt spread throughout her whole body. This had definitely been worth waiting for.

The pressure in her belly and her pussy was almost unbearable, and she squeezed her nipples hard as she ground her cunt on Leah's tongue. The wave broke over her, and she moaned as her orgasm rushed all through her. When it was finally finished, she collapsed into Leah's arms, and the two of them kissed and caressed each other's satisfied bodies.

"You certainly had a good teacher," Wendy teased, as she cupped Leah's breast in her hand and rubbed it gently.

"I must have been a good student," Leah agreed, smiling. "I can even make a teacher come."

"Very well, too," Wendy purred. Her pussy was still sensitive and she shivered when Leah's hand brushed against it. She loved the warm feeling she had after an orgasm, when her whole body felt alive and tender.

Leah kissed her and stood up; Wendy admired her body as she stretched. Her beautiful tits stood straight out, her belly was firm and flat and her mound rose gently, covered with thick, delicious hair. Wendy felt her own hot pussy stirring again.

Going to the closet, Leah selected a heavy, white satin robe, which she draped over her shoulders. She offered Wendy a gorgeously patterned silk one, which Wendy put on, enjoying the slippery cool feeling as the fabric touched her skin. She sat back on the bed and watched Leah. The dark-haired woman didn't bother to tie her robe closed, and it hung open in front, giving Wendy tantalizing glimpses of sweet, hard nipples and dark, inviting bush.

Leah left the room, and Wendy heard her in the kitchen. A little while later, she returned with two china cups of coffee on a small tray. Wendy sipped hers as Leah opened a bedside drawer and took out a small book.

"I'm going to get those two over here," she said. "You can meet them and then we'll make arrangements for their classes."

"Excellent idea," Wendy said, putting her thin china cup down. It really was a good idea. She always preferred seeing how slaves interacted with their mistresses on their own ground, in familiar settings. It would give her an idea as to how she should focus their training, and give her some insight as to how the mistress would like her slave to behave. It would be especially helpful with Margot, the difficult one. Wendy thought that if she could meet this problematic woman with Leah there to give her orders, she might begin to understand why she was so un-slave-like when she claimed that being a slave was really what she wanted.

Leah looked up the first number and dialled. "Ellen, please," she said, and covered the receiver with her hand. "This one works in a small office," she told Wendy. "Naturally she can't call me 'Mistress' when I call her there. Each time I see her after speaking to her at work, I punish her for not using the proper form of address." Wendy smiled, and made a mental note to use such a trick in the future on her own slaves. She loved cruel little schemes such as that.

"Ellen? I believe you know who this is," Leah said. "Good. Ellen, I need you to come over here right away. This is very important and I will not be kept waiting."

She paused for a long time, and Wendy guessed that the woman on the other end was struggling for something to say. Her theory was verified when Leah said, "Repeat after me, Ellen. Oh, Mother, I'm so sorry, I forgot that I was supposed to drive you to your doctor's appointment today."

She paused again, and when she spoke, her voice had the ice-cold, steel-hard inflection of a mistress who expects to be obeyed implicitly. "You may show your appreciation when you arrive. Now hurry up. I know exactly how long it takes you to get from your office to here, and I will be timing you. There will be a lash for every half-minute you are late."

She hung up the phone and turned to Wendy. "That one is a breeze," she said. "She's so eager to please, she's almost the perfect slave already. The only thing wrong with her is her rough edges. She isn't fully versed in serving techniques and things like that. But I can't fault her sincerity."

"No problem," Wendy smiled. "When I'm finished with them, you will have two perfect slaves, both of them fine and polished. You'll be proud of both of them."

Leah took a sip of her coffee, then looked up another number in her book. "I hope you're right, Wendy," she said. "But I wouldn't be too sure until you get a good look at this one."

"Do they know about each other?" Wendy asked. "Have they met?"

"Oh, yes," Leah said, dialling the number. "I've always had at least two at all times. Margot's the newcomer, so it wasn't like she was being cast aside or anything. And Ellen doesn't seem to mind at all. She was a replacement for that blonde slave, the one who got transferred to another city. Then I got Margot, and Ellen became even more submissive and fawning. I guess she wanted to prove to me that she was better than the rookie. Unfortunately, so far she is."

There was an answer on the other end, and Leah's warm voice again took on its steely quality. "This is your Mistress, slave," she said. There was a slight pause.

"I need you here right away. I have someone you have to meet, and she won't be kept waiting. Neither will I." There was another pause, and Leah's face flushed a little. "I don't care, scum. I don't give a shit if you're scheduled for major surgery in three minutes. Either you show up here, right away, or you don't bother coming back ever again. Is that understood? Good. Now hurry up. If you're not here within half an hour, my door will be locked and will remain locked to you forever." She slammed down the phone.

"Trouble?" Wendy asked.

"Claims a dental appointment," Leah said. "See what I mean? I've found that the only way I can make her obey implicitly is to threaten to get rid of her."

"I expected that," Wendy said. An idea was forming in her mind, an insight into Margot's troubling character. "I think I'm beginning to understand just what's going on."

"I hope you're on the right track," Leah said. "I don't know why, but I'd hate to lose this one."

Wendy glanced at her watch. "How long before they arrive?"

"Ellen needs about twenty minutes to get here," Leah said. "If she hurries, Margot can be here just a few minutes after that. Why, do you have something in mind?"

"I certainly do," Wendy said, and reached over to the opening in Leah's satin robe. She took one of Leah's large breasts into her hand and massaged it, then sucked on the nipple. Leah groaned and stretched out beside Wendy. She untied Wendy's sash and her hand strayed down to that hot, wet spot between her legs.

Wendy pushed her own fingers between Leah's sex-swollen pussy lips. Both of their clits were still sensitive from their explosive orgasms, and even the lightest touches sent delicate chills from those hot nubs right up their spines.

"Finger me!" Leah whispered, and Wendy took the hard clit between her finger and thumb and gently rocked it back and forth. Leah's hand was massaging Wendy's clit as well and the two kissed deeply as they felt each other's pussies. Wendy's free hand found its way to Leah's nipple and she stroked and squeezed it gently as she slipped two fingers inside Leah's soaked tunnel.

"Oh, that feels good," Leah moaned as Wendy pushed her fingers deep into Leah's cunt. Her own pussy was on fire as Leah's hand moved quickly but delicately over her clit. She pushed her tongue into Leah's mouth as hard as she could. She wished she could have pushed it right down her throat. Leah met her and their tongues mingled, snaking over each other and sliding back and forth. The kiss muffled their moans and their hips were moving rapidly, putting their clits in direct contact with probing fingers.

Wendy's fingers were so wet with Leah's juices, they slipped effortlessly between her pussy lips, and she ran them up and down the grooves beside Leah's clit. When she pressed on the hard button, Leah moaned again and stepped up her efforts on Wendy's pussy.

They kept each other on the edge for a long time. There was a knock at the door and Leah pulled her hand away, but Wendy took it and firmly put it back between her legs. "It's only a slave, silly," she said, running her fingers over Leah's clit. "Make her wait."

Leah did. Wendy tickled the entrance to Leah's hole, then pushed two fingers inside. At the same time, her thumb rubbed hard over Leah's clit. Leah, meanwhile, was flicking her fingers on Wendy's clit, pushing it back and forth and pressing down on it with each stroke.

Wendy came first. The hot wave broke over her and she gasped and cried out, her hand still in Leah's cunt. She kneaded Leah's nipple while her other hand fucked Leah's cunt and rubbed her clit hard. It didn't take long before Leah was moaning too, thrashing her hips and trembling as she came.

They kissed gently a few more times, then got up off the bed, adjusted their robes, and walked into the living room.

Leah opened the door. Ellen was waiting in the hallway; at Leah's command she came inside, then automatically dropped to her knees in front of her mistress.

The blow came swiftly, and Ellen's cheek burned brightly where Leah's hand had slapped her. "I'm so sorry, Mistress!" she cried. "I wanted so badly to address you properly!"

"I really don't care," Leah replied coldly. "You may thank me for the excuse I gave you." Her feet were bare and Ellen bent down and kissed them reverently, slipping her tongue deftly between the toes.

"Get up," Leah ordered, and Ellen did. "Mistress Wendy is here. You have met her before."

"Yes, Mistress," Ellen said. She rushed over to Wendy and curtsied before her. "Good afternoon, Mistress Wendy."

Wendy nodded. She was pleased to see that Ellen was respectful to another mistress and that the curtsy seemed to come naturally to her. However, she also noted that Ellen had not dipped as low as she would have liked, and that she got up far too quickly. Wendy decided that a proper greeting would be one of Ellen's first lessons.

"Our coffee is cold," Leah said, and Ellen immediately rushed into the kitchen. Shortly afterward, she returned with freshly filled cups, and cream and sugar on a silver tray. The two women had seated themselves on the sofa, and Ellen placed the tray on the table before them. She mixed in cream and sugar to their specifications and then handed them the cups, kneeling before them, her eyes on the floor.

"You've given me some good material to work with," Wendy said, as she took the cup.

"I told you this one was pretty good," Leah agreed, speaking about Ellen as if she was still at her office and not kneeling before them. "Oh, I almost forgot. Ellen, take your clothes off."

"Yes, Mistress," Ellen replied, but in a very unhappy voice. She stole a quick glance at Wendy before she stood up to unbutton her blouse and skirt.

Her cheeks were bright red; Wendy wondered why, since Ellen hadn't seemed to mind being naked in front of her before. Indeed, it was the first time Wendy had ever seen her with clothes on.

Ellen stripped off her blouse. She was a very small woman, but her breasts were full and tipped with lovely rosy nipples. When she slipped the skirt off, Leah smiled and Wendy understood the embarrassment. "You may stop there, slave," Leah said.

Ellen whispered, "Thank you, Mistress," and again knelt on the floor. She was wearing a most ridiculous getup: a small pair of men's boxer shorts patterned with small red hearts.

"Other than washing them and bathing, you haven't taken them off, have you?" Leah demanded.

"No, Mistress," Ellen replied.

"You slept in them as well?"

"Yes, Mistress," came the whispered answer.

"For the whole week, as I commanded?"

"The whole week, Mistress," Ellen said.

Wendy smiled. "The hearts match your cheeks right now, slave," she said, enjoying the humiliation Ellen was feeling.

"Thank you, Mistress," Ellen replied, her eyes on the floor. Wendy could hardly wait to get this one under her command.

There was another knock on the door. "Get that," Leah commanded, and Ellen jumped up and ran to open the door. Leah noticed that she stood behind it, so that the visitor would not be able to see her. "Out in front!" Leah snapped, and Ellen stood in front of the door as she opened it, her whole face and neck red.

The woman at the door was stunning. Tall and slim, with shoulder-length brown hair, she wore a low-cut shirt that showed off the tops of her heavy, creamy breasts and a short skirt that put her long, well-shaped legs on display. She stepped inside, and as Ellen closed the door, the tall woman looked down at her with a condescending grin that spoke volumes. Ellen rushed back to her mistress and knelt before her; tears of shame and fury coursed down her scarlet cheeks, but she did not say a word.

"That's enough, Margot!" Leah snapped. "Now come in here."

Margot did, and in that instant Wendy was amazed. Her expression was sullen, as if she was sulking at having been ordered to do something. At the same time, her eyes were warm and filled with love as she looked at her mistress sitting on the sofa.

Her eyes changed right away when she noticed Wendy. As she took in the sight of the loosely fastened robes and the satisfied expressions on their faces, it became obvious that she knew what Wendy and Leah had just shared. Her swift glance at Wendy was cold and jealous.

"Margot, this is Mistress Wendy," Leah said.

Margot hardly glanced in Wendy's direction as she nodded her head. "Mistress," she said, then turned her attention back to Leah.

"I didn't tell you to come here so that I could look at your clothes," Leah said pointedly.

"Yes, Mistress," Margot said, and opened the few remaining buttons on her shirt. She was so maddeningly slow that it was obvious she was testing her mistress. Frustrated, Wendy had to suppress the urge to leap up and strike her to the ground for her impudence. If she were mine, Wendy thought, she'd be black and blue right now. Then she realized that soon this woman *would* be hers to train and control, and the thought made her smile. It amazed her how much she was looking forward to making this woman knuckle under. She would lay that smooth back right open if necessary, but she was determined that she was going to win this one.

Slowly the bra came off. Margot's breasts were large, but very firm with hard nipples. She had a model's perfectly sculpted body, right down to her beautiful dark triangle which took forever to be uncovered. Wendy had to admit that she was one of the most admirable looking slaves she had ever seen. The thought of that body wearing a collar and shackles turned her on, and a picture of Margot strapped to the X-frame and feeling the cruel ends of a cat-o'-nine-tails had her hot all over again.

"On your knees," Leah ordered. Again, the order was carried out with an infuriating slowness. Wendy noticed that the slow actions were totally at odds with the look of love and devotion on the woman's face. She decided to test her theory.

"Don't you think," she said to Leah, "that those two commands were carried out a bit too slowly?"

"I think you're right," Leah said. She caught onto Wendy's plan right away. "Yes, you are right. I think we'll have to do something about that."

Wendy noticed that Margot's eyes lit up like candles. She drew her breath in and her eyes followed her mistress' every move as Leah got up and walked over to an antique writing desk across the room. Tucked into a drawer was a piece of rubber hose. Wendy saw Margot's eyes close in passion and a smile cross her lips.

"On your hands and knees!" Leah ordered. Wendy noticed that there was none of the insolent slowness this time; Margot was on all fours swiftly and it seemed that she arched her back to present her ass fully to her mistress.

The rubber hose landed with a loud thud, and

Margot gasped. Wendy could well imagine how much the blow must have hurt. Still kneeling on the floor, Ellen looked over fearfully, terrified that the hose might also land on her. But Margot's eyes were tightly closed and even though the hose had formed a large welt on her ass, her lips still held the hint of a smile.

Thwack! The hose found its target again. Margot was trembling and her eyes were screwed shut, but only a tiny moan escaped her. This time the hose hit her back, and her skin welled up a painful red. There was a bit of moisture in her eyes, but it was obvious she was enjoying herself.

Wendy was surprised at the punishment Margot could take. Her ass and back were crossed with welts so big and red that Wendy felt her excitement rising as she looked at them. Yet only a quiet groan escaped her when the hose struck.

Leah lifted her arm again and brought the hose down as hard as she could. This one must have really hurt, for two small tears moved down Margot's cheeks. Her face was as red as the welts, but still she held her ass out for Leah to punish. Leah brought the hose down three more times and finally a sob escaped the tall woman. Her back and her ass were so red they looked burned and blistered.

"Kneel," Leah ordered, and again Margot obeyed her swiftly. Leah put the hose back in its drawer, then stepped in front of Margot. The punished slave looked up at her devotedly.

"Leah, would you go into the kitchen for a moment?" Wendy asked. Leah did, and Wendy watched as Margot followed her every move until she was out of sight. Once she was gone, Margot's expression changed again, and Wendy thought she looked just like an abandoned puppy. When Leah came back out, Margot's face once again became radiant as she caught a glimpse of her mistress.

"You two into the bedroom," Leah ordered as she sat down. Ellen sprang up instantly, read to obey; back to her old habits, Margot got up slowly and shuffled toward the bedroom. It was obvious that she resented being forced to leave while Wendy was left behind with her mistress.

"So what's your opinion?" Leah asked.

"Well, I'm no psychologist, but I think I've found the answer," Wendy said. "You've never looked at her face while you're beating her, have you?"

"No," Leah replied.

"She's in ecstasy. She absolutely loves everything you give her. I think if she had a wish, she'd ask for a bigger hose," Wendy said. "I haven't seen a slave that fond of pain in a long time. Part of the problem is that she's just begging to be punished."

"So what's the rest of it?"

"She absolutely adores you," Wendy continued. "She was like a little lost soul when you went into the kitchen. I really think she does a lot of it to get your attention. When you're punishing her, it's obvious that you're paying attention to her. So she demands punishment by misbehaving."

"Well, that's fine that she likes punishment, but she's getting on my nerves," Leah said. "I like doling out punishment, too—when it's called for. But I don't think I have to wear my arm out every time I want a cup of coffee brought to me. She needs to be taught that I'm not going to put up with it."

"Well, she's still testing you," Wendy said. "You mentioned that threatening to get rid of her makes her obey instantly. Right now it's the one thing she's really afraid of. Whenever she misbehaves, you beat her right away, don't you?"

"Instantly," Leah said.

"Maybe we can try ignoring her completely when she does something wrong. It's the attention she craves. And I'm going to try to find a punishment that's beyond what she enjoys. Maybe then she will fear punishment as well as anticipate it. When you can get them looking forward to it and dreading it at the same time, you've got them around your little finger. She's not at that point yet. In that respect, she's as green as a slave that's only put on a collar for the first time."

Leah smiled. "It sounds so obvious, I'm surprised I never noticed it," she said. "I guess you need someone else to look at it from a different perspective. So, do you think she's worth it?"

"Oh, definitely," Wendy replied. "Actually, Leah, she's magnificent. I'm a little jealous that you found her before I did. I really think that once her spirit is tamed, she will be superb."

Leah called the two to come back, and they did, kneeling before the dominatrixs sitting on the sofa.

"Mistress Wendy is the teacher I was telling you about," Leah said. "You will be attending her classes regularly. There will be no excuse for absenteeism. The first time I hear that you are not in class, you will also not be stepping through my door again. Understood?"

"Yes, Mistress!" Ellen replied quickly. By her expression it was obvious that it never occurred to her to play hooky from Wendy's school. Her mistress had ordered her to attend, and attend she would.

Margot was a different story. It was just as obvious that she did not want to have anything to do with Wendy and her classes. But the threat of being dismissed entirely was too much for her. "Yes, Mistress," she replied.

"When you are with Mistress Wendy, it is the same as being with me," Leah continued. "You will obey her no matter what the command. She will punish you however she sees fit, and I don't care how severely she does so. How she treats you is none of my concern. The only thing I care about is that you do the very best you can. I will not be ashamed of my slaves at any time while they are students in Mistress Wendy's school."

Wendy stood up and walked behind the two who knelt before her on the floor. "Your mistress has instructed me that both of you will graduate as perfect slaves," she said. "That's obvious because only perfect slaves will ever leave my school. The question is how long it will take, and that is entirely up to you."

She walked behind Ellen and flicked a finger on her cheek. "I like your respect, slave," she said. "You have a lot of it. Unfortunately, you don't know how to use it. Your greeting to me was too quick. You carried the coffee sloppily. You will need a fair bit of fine-tuning."

She walked behind Margot. "You are another kettle of fish altogether," she said. "You think that this whole idea of going to school is a joke, don't you? My dear, I am going to prove you wrong."

She reached down and touched Margot's cheek just as she had touched Ellen's. Unlike the smaller slave, Margot shrank back to avoid Wendy's fingers.

Wendy was upon her instantly. She grabbed a huge handful of hair and yanked it back hard until Margot's head was forced backward, her eyes level with Wendy's. She gasped loudly; she hadn't imagined that Wendy could move so quickly that she could get the better of her. Wendy realized this and was thrilled by the knowledge.

When she spoke, her voice was so filled with restrained fury that even Leah was shocked.

"There are three things that can happen, worm," she hissed. "One is that the slave will get the better of the teacher, and the teacher will have to give in. That will never happen, and the faster you get that through your skull the better.

"Second is that the slave and the teacher are equal and that no one wins. You can get that one out of your head, too.

"Third is that the slave learns just who her superior is. Your superior happens to be any mistress who gives you a command, whether it's your Mistress Leah, or it's me, or it's any other mistress who stoops low enough to speak with you. You might like the sounds of the first two options, but let me give you a little reality, scum. The only thing that's going to happen is that you are going to learn some respect, and you are going to learn it in my classroom whether you like it or not. Your feelings don't mean anything to me. The only thing that matters is that you are going to learn your place." Using the handful of hair, Wendy threw Margot to the ground. Shocked by Wendy's speed and strength, Margot stayed there, looking at Wendy with a new expression: one of wonder and just a little excitement.

"Tomorrow evening, six o'clock," Wendy told them both. "Your mistress will give you the directions. She has warned you what will happen if you do not show up. Let me also warn you that there are dire consequences for being late." She sat down beside Leah on the sofa. Margot was still sprawled on the floor. "Get up, slave," she ordered. Although she did it slowly, Margot did rise up to a kneeling position, and both of them knew that the first battle had been won.

"Now both of you get out of here," Leah ordered. "Mistress Wendy and I have things to do." Ellen gratefully pulled her clothes up over the heart-patterned boxer shorts. Margot put her clothes on as well, sullen now that her session with her beloved mistress was over, a session that she had to share with both the small slave and the teacher who would be training her. If her clothes rubbed painfully on her bruised flesh, she showed no sign of it.

When the door closed behind the slaves, Wendy turned to Leah. "You know, you really are pretty good with that rubber hose," she said.

"You really think so?" Leah asked. Her hand was again straying over to the opening of the silk robe.

"I really do," Wendy said, and she stood up, offering her hand to Leah. "Come on in. We'll discuss it." She led Leah back to the bedroom, her pussy throbbing. She could hardly wait for her first full class to begin.

SIX

Wendy bunched up one of her black stockings, slipped her toes into it, and slowly pulled it up one long leg. When it was completely unrolled on her long leg, she bent and fastened it into her garter, then put on the other one and carefully attached it as well to the black leather garter strap.

Her whole outfit was supple, buttery-smooth leather. Her bra held her large breasts in place, and the nipples peeked through holes at the end. Black leather panties were visible under the leather garter belt, and a studded leather belt encircled her waist. She pulled on her favorite stiletto-heeled boots, then picked up her riding crop and walked down the hallway to the closed classroom door. She walked slowly, confidently. She knew the tapping of her heels on the hardwood floor would be heard through the closed door. She also knew that five women would be listening, waiting, anticipating, and dreading her entry all at the same time.

She opened the door. All five were kneeling on the hard floor in a row, as she had ordered. She smiled and closed the door behind her. "Good evening, class," she said, and walked to the front of the room.

"Good evening, Mistress," the voices chimed. Wendy looked at them approvingly as they knelt, their eyes on the floor.

All were naked, and wearing the leather collars that signified they were students. Brenda, Alicia and Leslie were completely submissive, kneeling motionless, their backs straight, their eyes down. Ellen shifted slightly, not used to the hard floor but trying desperately to please her teacher. She had been given permission by Leah to forsake the red-hearted boxer shorts and her sweet little body pleased Wendy very much.

She looked over at Margot. As she expected, the tall, stunning slave was glancing sideways, looking over her environment, adjusting her position on the floor, her expression sullen. As Wendy had imagined, the collar around her neck looked wonderful. It set off her perfect body, the unyielding leather circle harsh against the supple, smooth skin. Wendy wanted to grab it in her fist and drag her around by it. She smiled; she knew that soon enough, Margot would give her reason to do it.

"I'm glad to see everyone here and in their positions," Wendy said. She stepped over and gave Ellen a quick flick with the riding crop. It was just a reminder, a tap with the end, which stung and left a small reddish glow on the skin. "Don't squirm, Ellen," she said. "Slaves must sit perfectly still until they are told by their mistresses that they may move.

You look like a child that needs to go to the bathroom, not like a trained slave. I will not tolerate that."

"I'm sorry, Mistress," Ellen whispered, and kept as still as she could.

"As most of you are aware," Wendy continued, "none but perfect slaves will graduate from this school—or as perfect as you worthless things can become. And only graduates will have a special honor bestowed upon them to prove that they have graduated. Your mistresses will be thrilled when they see you with this honor. I don't believe I have to tell you what might happen if you fail my school and disgrace them."

She walked over to where a small wooden console was set up with a television set and a video player. "Some of you may be wondering just what I mean by a perfect slave. Since none of you are even close to that goal, I have some examples to show you. This is what you should be aiming for. This is the only type of behavior that will allow you to graduate and earn your honor."

She switched the television set on. The tape was one that had been given to her by Julie, the owner of the leather boutique. Wendy had already watched it once and had been so excited she had put her hand between her legs and rubbed her hot, wet pussy until she came.

The first portion of the tape had been shot at a dominatrixs' convention held in a large downtown hotel. Wendy was at first fascinated by all the different costumes worn by the mistresses. There were women in leather corsets, in tight leather dresses, in business suits, in wild outfits made of straps and chains, in romantic lacy dresses, in tight jeans and T-shirts.

The five slaves on the floor also watched the screen, captivated by what they saw. Each mistress had at least one slave, and many had two, three, or even four attending her. Like the mistresses, the slaves were in all types of uniforms and costumes, including a pair of delicious blonde twins who wore only leather cuffs on their wrists and sparkling jeweled collars around their throats, finished with gold chains held in their mistress' hand.

"Look at them carefully," Wendy said. "Watch how they behave."

The behavior of all of the slaves was beyond reproach. The camera focused on one slave wearing a leather mask, with holes for her eyes, nose, and mouth. The woman was fetching a glass of champagne for her leather-clad mistress; she carried it perfectly and bowed slightly, eyes down, as she offered it. Her mistress took it from her, and the slave bowed again, then immediately took her place behind her mistress.

"I have attended functions such as this in the past," Wendy told her captive audience. "I did not take any slave whose behavior I questioned even slightly. In a room filled with other mistresses with perfectly trained slaves, I would only take the very best slave I had.

"It is an honor for a slave to be allowed to attend such an event," she continued. "You will not even be considered unless you are as good as the slaves you see here. If I were you, I would make it my goal to become as well trained as the slaves in this film."

The camera moved through the crowd in the hotel. There was a slave, dressed in a coarse peasant's dress, who knelt at her mistress' heel while her mistress, beautifully dressed in an expensive suit, spoke with another mistress. Suddenly, the mistress turned around and gave a command. The slave leaped up and quickly walked away, returning moments later with a drink for her mistress. Once the drink was accepted, the slave once again knelt at her mistress' feet.

"You will notice that each mistress has her preference when it comes to specific behavior," Wendy said. "One mistress might like her slave to kneel at all times, another might like something else. That doesn't matter; what does matter is that no matter what the command, it is carried out swiftly and without question."

She turned the television off. "We'll save the rest for a little later," she said. "First we will have a lesson."

She indicated a small table against the far wall, where a champagne glass filled with water had been set. "I want each of you to go and get that glass and bring it back to me. Imagine that we are at the function you just watched. Imagine that the whole room is filled with other mistresses and other slaves."

She motioned for Ellen to go first. The small woman hurried over and picked up the glass by the bottom of the stem, then brought it to the leather-clad teacher, who was still carrying her riding crop. Wendy noticed that she quickly glanced at the crop as she bowed before her teacher, offering the glass.

To Ellen's relief, the crop stayed down. "Good," Wendy said. "Next time, though, place your free hand on your thigh when you bow. It makes a much neater presentation."

"Yes, Mistress," Ellen said. Wendy motioned for her to return the glass to the table. "Thank you, Mistress."

Leslie, Alicia, and Brenda all brought the glass over; Brenda earned an extra bit of praise for her quick bow before she went to get the glass. Her first lesson had not been forgotten, and she did not allow even a flicker of pride to cross her face.

"Your turn, Margot," Wendy said, bracing herself for the first confrontation. "Bring the glass over here."

Margot was in fine form. She glanced at the other slaves, kneeling on the floor in a straight line, then slowly got up. She stood before Wendy, but did not give the small bow that had earned Brenda praise. She then walked across the room, slowly, and picked up the glass.

Brenda, Alicia, and Leslie looked shocked at this new pupil's behavior. Ellen, who knew what to expect, simply looked disgusted. Margot carried the glass by the stem, but when she presented it to Wendy, there was no bow, no display of submission; she simply offered the glass the same way Wendy might have given a drink to another mistress.

"That will do, Margot," Wendy said coldly. "Now put it back."

As Margot turned to go, the riding crop struck her across the backs of her thighs. Wendy was thrilled to see her jump, and the hard blow left a thin red welt across both legs.

Margot stopped instantly and stood, waiting. But Wendy simply tucked the crop under her arm. "Put it back, slave," she said. "We don't have all night." Margot stood for a second longer, then walked back across the room and replaced the glass on the table. When she came back and took her place in line, Wendy could see disappointment on her face. Wendy congratulated herself for holding back and denying Margot the additional punishment she had expected. Margot glanced up and caught Wendy's eye for a moment. In that split second, she realized why she

had only received the one blow, and she put her eyes
back down.

First round goes to me, you worthless bitch,
Wendy thought to herself as she turned to the blackboard and began writing the names of different types
of wines. She drilled the five for a few minutes on
their knowledge, gave them a quick oral test, and
then ordered Brenda to go into the kitchen and bring
her a glass of wine. Brenda's eyes were almost moist
as she thanked her mistress for the honor and rushed
out of the room. While she waited for her drink to
arrive, Wendy arranged several different restraints at
the front of the room. She could see Margot's eyes
light up.

On a small table at the front, she had placed
lengths of rope, handcuffs, leather cuffs with snap
rings, some very evil-looking thumbscrews joined
together, and a canvas straitjacket.

"The type of restraint your mistress will use
determines the position you will take when you stand
before her," Wendy said. "Brenda, come up here."

The blonde-haired slave quickly stood up and
hurried to stand before her beloved mistress. Wendy
smiled. The competition in the room was helping to
ensure that Brenda would learn her lessons fully and
retain them completely. Wendy was sure that she
would be very pleased with her own property once
all had graduated.

Wendy picked up a length of rope. "For ropes, it
is easiest if the wrists are crossed," she said. She nodded, and Brenda held out her arms in the proper
fashion, a method she had learned from Wendy even
before the school had been set up. Swiftly, deftly,
Wendy lashed her slave's wrists together. "You see
how pleasing it is to the mistress if everything is
ready for her," Wendy said. "Now let me see all of

you take this position." Four sets of wrists went out, properly crossed; even Margot was swift to do it properly. "Good, good," Wendy said, and she untied Brenda's wrist and sent her back to kneel on the floor.

Alicia got the handcuffs, and the pupils were taught several ways to present their wrists both in front and behind themselves, and several hand positions. Once again, Wendy noticed that Margot was extremely attentive, and swift to hold her hands in each of the new positions.

Leslie was the model for the leather cuffs, while Ellen got the thumbscrews. Wendy was not easy with them, and by the end of the demonstration, tears were visible on Ellen's cheeks. The thumbscrews themselves held Ellen's hands together by attaching to each thumb with nasty screws that pressed painfully into her flesh. By the look on Margot's face, it was obvious that she was very disappointed that the screws were not biting into her own thumbs.

Finally it was Margot's turn, and the sullen slow movements were gone; she was on her feet and standing before Wendy in a flash to receive the straitjacket. Wendy surprised her by being very gentle as she positioned Margot's arms to show the rest of the class how to stand in preparation for receiving the jacket. When she slipped the jacket on, she did so carefully, and she was careful to position Margot's arms rather than yank them into place, as she so dearly longed to do. Once the jacket was in place, Wendy made a few comments to the rest of the class, then unstrapped it and removed it from the gorgeous slave as gently as she could. Once Margot was naked again, save for the chrome-ringed leather collar, Wendy indicated that she could join her place in the lineup.

Such a change! Wendy noted with satisfaction that Margot's cheeks were bright red, whether from shame or frustration Wendy didn't know. Her eyes looked dull and hurt, almost like she was going to cry. Her expression was one of confusion. The teacher she had expected to be so cruel had actually been nice to her! Wendy smiled. Round two, she thought to herself. Soon you will be groveling before my feet and you won't even know what hit you.

She took a sip of the wine Brenda had brought for her, and tried to come up with a plan for round three. It came to her as she was putting the restraints back in their spots on the wall.

"Now, slaves," she said, as she walked back up to the blackboard in front of them, "something that you should definitely know is how to treat your mistress when she comes home. There is a pattern you should follow, and I expect that by next class you will have it memorized."

She wrote each item down on the blackboard. "First you must greet your mistress properly, holding the door for her, taking her coat and her bag, making sure that her chair is ready," Wendy said. "When she sits down, you ask permission to remove her shoes. When that permission is granted, you do so. If they are dirty, you ask permission to clean them. If you are told to do so with your tongue, then you do it—and thank your mistress for the privilege of doing so." She could see Margot catch her breath at the thought of being forced to lick the city grime off of the soles of Leah's shoes.

"You put those shoes away carefully, and you ask your mistress for permission to bring her some refreshment. If she grants you permission, you bring her whatever she wants, carried properly and served with a bow. Then you ask permission to do anything else your mistress might want you to do to make her more comfortable. She might ask for a pillow, or for assistance in putting on her robe, or for you to run a hot bath for her, or even for you to put your tongue in her pussy. No matter what the request is, you fulfill it immediately, you thank her for the privilege of doing it, and you do it correctly. There is simply no other way."

She pulled a chair over and stood beside it. "We will have a demonstration," she said. "I am just coming home, and I wish to be greeted properly by my slave. Let's see—Margot, you will show us how it's done."

Margot looked very slowly at the other four slaves, then got to her feet. It was just what Wendy and Ellen had expected, but Brenda, Alicia and Leslie stared, open-mouthed, at her insolent manners. They could not believe that any slave would not snap to attention once a command had been given.

Wendy had not only expected it, but had hoped that Margot would pull her famous act. She smiled, but it was an icy, bitterly cruel smile. Brenda saw it and felt her skin grow cold. She knew full well the fury that her mistress was holding in, and also knew that there was a plan under way. There was no other explanation for her mistress' leniency, and Brenda shivered, thankful that she was not on the receiving end of Wendy's wrath. It would be swift and very brutal.

The stunningly gorgeous slave stood before Wendy, her weight on one foot, her spine bent, looking more like an arrogant teenager than a submissive slave. Wendy took it in, but said nothing. She sat in the chair.

"I will already assume that you have taken my coat and greeted me," Wendy said. "You may now ask permission to remove my shoes."

Margot paused for a second before she said, "Mistress, may I remove your shoes?"

"You may," Wendy said.

Margot slowly bent in front of Wendy and touched her hand to the top of the beautiful stiletto-heeled boots. Without warning, Wendy gave a massive kick, and Margot was knocked onto her back. Before she could even register what had happened, Wendy was upon her, one strong fist grabbing the stout leather collar.

Margot didn't even attempt to rise, and Wendy dragged her along the wooden floor by the collar. The other four slaves watched.

"You still think that you can get the better of me, don't you, scum?" Wendy hissed. "I thought we went over your options before. There is only one thing that is going to happen here, and that is that you are going to leave this school perfectly trained and nothing less. Well, dogshit, your training begins now."

Margot was a tall woman, but Wendy was much more powerful, and she hauled the recalcitrant slave across the room to the padded horse. Pulling her by the collar, Wendy lifted her up and threw her across the horse. "Move and you're dead," she said, and got leather cuffs for her wrists and ankles.

The cuffs were on in seconds, and Wendy had to stop for a moment and admire them. The black leather and chrome rings looked so good against the firm flesh. Then she snapped them in place on the horse, so that Margot was bent over, her ass in the air, her head facing the floor.

Wendy then walked back to the front of the class. "This demonstration is actually going much better than I had planned," she told the four remaining slaves, all of whom looked terrified of her, wondering if her rage would be vented on them as well. "Not only will we learn how to greet our mistress, but we will also learn what might happen if we don't do a good job."

She then went back to the lesson, this time selecting Leslie to demonstrate how to properly greet her mistress. To her delight, the novice slave performed adequately and only required a tap with the riding crop when her bow was not as deep as Wendy would have liked. From across the room, she could hear Margot's heavy, excited breathing, and the occasional click of the chrome snaps against the steel rings. She could imagine Margot's frustration at being lashed to the horse with no further punishment. She continued the lesson, determined that she was going to win all three rounds during the evening's class. Margot's face was already red and every so often she would pull back against her bonds, as if testing them. At one point, Alicia stole a glance back at her, and received a blow across her cheek that snapped her head sideways. Wendy was determined that everyone in the room would ignore Margot until she was almost beside herself with the desire to be whipped.

The captive slave was left alone for a half hour, while Wendy continued the regular lessons. By this time she could see that Margot's pussy was glistening and her nipples were as hard as rocks.

Wendy walked to her wall of devices and carefully selected a large nine-tailed leather whip. After discussing the problem with Leah, she had come to the conclusion that while Margot enjoyed being punished, she hadn't really received anything brutal. The cat, she thought, would go a long way in breaking this slave's spirit.

"Now, all of you are going to watch this," she

told the other four, and they obediently turned around. "I want you to know that naughty pupils don't just sit in the corner when they're bad in my class. I want you to see what will really happen."

She then lifted the whip and with all the strength in her arm, brought it down on Margot's back. It landed with a gut-wrenching slap of leather on skin. She was right; Margot had never experienced anything like this before. A loud cry escaped her lips, then a moan.

Wendy felt her own pussy throb as she looked at her handiwork. Nine perfect welts rose on the skin as the blood welled up under it. With the second cruel blow, several thin lines of blood appeared on Margot's back.

Whap! Again the bitter lash came down. The other four slaves winced when it fell, and Ellen looked so white that Wendy thought she might faint.

Indeed, the punishment had been more than even Margot had expected. Her face was streaming with tears and she was sobbing loudly. "Mistress!" she cried. "Please, Mistress, mercy!" The words were as sweet as honey to Wendy's ears, and she smiled as she brought the whip down again.

Margot could hardly speak now for her sobs, and Wendy heard only part of her request for leniency. Once more her arm went up, and the cat-o'-nine-tails came down a final time, drawing several more thin lines of blood. Then Wendy threw the whip aside and went back to the front of the classroom.

She spoke calmly over Margot's sobs and gasps for breath. "I believe you all get the point," she said. "There are very clear-cut lines in a mistress-slave relationship, and those lines become even clearer when the mistress decides that it's time for punishment. Any questions? No? Very good. Now Alicia, tell me, when your mistress asks for red wine, what type of glass do you use?"

Seemingly oblivious to Margot's discomfort, Wendy went on with the lesson. When it was over, she walked back to the horse and unsnapped the wrist cuffs that held the beaten slave to it. She hauled Margot up by her collar, over the horse and down on the floor. Still attached to the horse by her ankle cuffs, Margot sat up, facing it. Her face was covered with tears and mucus, and her back was striped with welts and thin lines of blood.

Wendy looked at her with disgust. "You make me sick," she said. She got a scrap of rag from a hook on the wall. "Clean yourself up. You look like a baby with a runny nose." Margot wiped her face off. Her eyes were red-rimmed from crying and her cheeks were swollen.

Wendy wasn't sure if the battle was completely over, but she knew she had made some major inroads with that lesson. She snatched the rag away from the slave; it was wet in the middle. She tied it over Margot's eyes where it made an effective, if somewhat disgusting blindfold.

She returned to the television set at the front of the classroom. "I promised you more of this," she said. "This part will be a little treat for you. Those of you who performed adequately this evening will be allowed to watch it. Those who didn't will have to miss it." Margot, facing the horse, her eyes blindfolded, hung her head. Wendy's words had not been wasted on her.

Wendy turned the tape on. They watched the last few moments of the dominatrix convention; then the tape switched to an elegantly furnished room. A young, slim, blonde woman was kneeling on the thick carpet. She wore a leather collar around her throat, and there were cruel steel clamps on each nipple. There were straps around her waist that reached down between her legs. As the camera moved around, the slaves instantly noted that it was a chastity belt. Wendy smiled as she watched the obedient line of pupils, all kneeling on the hardwood floor. Their eyes were glued to the screens, their attention riveted to the screen. In the corner Margot was quietly sobbing.

The camera moved all around the kneeling slave. The slaves noticed that a heavy steel chain was attached to her collar and it hung down along her spine. The black chastity belt was tight against her buttocks and they noticed that she had thin leather cuffs around her ankles. Wendy smiled; she loved the sight of a well-outfitted slave kneeling so motionless, so submissively. One day her whole class, Margot included, would be just as good.

The camera focused again, from the front, on the cruel clamps, on the tight collar. Then it pulled back for a wider shot, and a tall black mistress walked in and stood beside her slave.

The four slaves watching the camera all drew in their breath. The mistress was gorgeous with an icy expression and a confident manner. She wore the same cruel, razor-sharp stilettos that Wendy favored, and her suit was made entirely of straps and rings. Each nipple pressed out from inside a chrome ring, and the straps that held them in place crisscrossed her body and made her breasts stand out perfectly. Her delicious dark triangle was complemented by the dark straps and the bright rings: Each slave longed to be able to obey her commands and place their tongues there. Long leather gauntlets ran up each arm, leaving her fingers exposed, showing off her long, perfectly lacquered, blood red nails.

"My boots are dirty, slave," she said. Her voice was as cold and sharp as a shard of broken glass.

"Yes, Mistress," the slave replied, and instantly she was on the floor. The slaves winced, imagining the sharp stab of pain once those nipple clamps were pressed into the carpet by her weight. But the blonde woman didn't even seem to notice; she was too intent on the shiny, patent-leather boots.

Her tongue snaked out and licked all over one of her mistress' feet. The black woman lifted it up, and the blonde woman's eyes were closed in ecstasy as she lapped the grime off the sole. She sucked the thin heel into her mouth, trying to take in as much of it as she possibly could. Then she moved up the boot, as her mistress put her foot back on the floor. The boots reached up to her mistress' thigh and she sat up to clean the tops of them.

The excitement was obviously too much for her, and her tongue strayed off the leather and onto the rich, smooth skin of the black woman's leg. Instantly, the mistress' expression changed from one of satisfaction to one of displeasure. Again, Wendy heard the slaves gasp, knowing that there was something very wrong.

Indeed there was. Swiftly the mistress reached down and grabbed one of the cruel clamps that bit into her slave's nipple. The red-nailed hand turned and twisted the clamp hard. The blonde slave cried out in agony.

"That isn't my boot, slave!" the woman hissed. "You were told to lick my boots. Now do as you're told!"

"Yes, Mistress!" the slave sobbed. The mistress let go of the clamp, and the slave slumped for a moment, swallowing hard as the pain returned to a dull throb. Then once again her tongue was on the patent leather, licking every inch of the tall boots.

"You will notice," Wendy interjected, "how quickly the mistress was able to grab the nipple clamp and twist it." Her words were not meant for the four kneeling before her; for them it had been obvious. The object of her lesson was still strapped to the horse, blindfolded and unable to watch the scene that would have been such a treat. Wendy smiled when she saw Margot slump a little and draw in her breath. Knowing that she was missing such an exciting scene must have been almost as painful as the whipping; Wendy felt like she was rubbing salt into those bloody welts.

Slowly and carefully, the slave licked clean the second boot, lapping the sole when it was lifted and sucking on the sharp heel before moving up to wash the rest of it. This time her tongue stayed on the leather and did not venture onto her mistress' skin. The slaves could see that the twisted nipple was still bright red from its ordeal, although both breasts must have still been throbbing and aching from the steel clamps that had not yet been removed.

"Now stand up," the mistress ordered when her boots were completely cleaned and polished by her charge's hot tongue.

The slave did so. The mistress grabbed both nipple clamps and pulled on them. Wendy noticed that Leslie closed her eyes as the woman's breasts were stretched out by the horrible clamps. Immediately Wendy walked behind her and slapped her hard on the side of her head. "Open your eyes," she ordered. "This was given to you as a treat and you are going to enjoy it."

"I'm sorry, Mistress," Leslie cried, and watched the screen. As she watched the tall black woman torture her blonde slave, she had to admit to herself that it was more and more exciting all the time. The cruelty that she had closed her eyes to was slowly starting to make her pussy throb.

The mistress pulled on the clamps until tears ran from her slave's eyes. Then she snapped them off. The blonde woman shrieked and put her hands to her bruised nipples. Oblivious to her pain, the mistress reached behind and grabbed the steel chain that was snapped to the collar.

"How convenient," the mistress crooned. "You already have your collar and leash on. Now down on all fours like the dog that you are." Sobbing, the slave obeyed.

The camera following her movement, the mistress started to walk around the room. Her steps were long, and the blonde woman had to hurry to keep up with her, moving along on her hands and knees. At one point, she fell behind and was rewarded with a hard pull on the chain.

The camera moved behind them, and Wendy could clearly see how ingenious the chastity belt was. It was open to allow the slave her toilet functions, but there was no way that she could play with herself once the device was in place. It looked extremely interesting, and Wendy made a mental note to ask Julie to order a couple for her. They might come in handy some time.

There was much more on the tape, but Wendy walked up and snapped the television set off. The slaves were clearly disappointed, but they did not dare complain.

"I think that's enough for tonight," Wendy said. The four remained in place, watching the blank screen, while she went back to the horse. She pulled off the rag that had served as a blindfold, then unsnapped Margot's ankles from the horse.

"Stand up," Wendy ordered, and Margot did so

meekly. "Take your place." The tall woman walked back and knelt in the lineup—much slower than Wendy would have liked, but faster than she had done before. Wendy knew that there was still a lot of spirit in this slave, but this lesson had gone a long way toward vanquishing it.

"I will give you permission to leave now," Wendy said, "all except for Brenda. You stay behind."

"Thank you, Mistress," the other four said. Wendy noticed that Margot was a bit slower than the others, but she had still chimed in.

The four slaves rose and walked out the door. Wendy waited until they had dressed, then she saw them out of the house. "Good night, Mistress," all four of them said, even Margot. Wendy noticed that she walked carefully, in great pain, and before she put on her coat, Wendy saw a few drops of blood seep through her white shirt. Once again, Wendy could feel her excitement rising.

She closed the door, then went back to the classroom. Brenda was still kneeling obediently on the hard floor. "Come with me, slave," Wendy said, and the blonde submissive got up and followed her mistress into the living room.

Once there, Wendy pulled off the soft leather panties, and Brenda could hardly believe her good fortune as she watched her mistress stretch out on the sofa, her legs apart and her beautiful dark pussy exposed. "Your tongue, slave," Wendy ordered.

Brenda needed no further orders. Within seconds she was on her knees on the carpet in front of the couch, her head between Wendy's legs. Wendy shivered slightly at the first touch of Brenda's hot tongue on her throbbing clit.

As always, Brenda knew the right spots. Her probing tongue found its way between the sweet secrets of Wendy's pussy lips, and back to her hole. She pressed her tongue inside the velvet tunnel and moved it back and forth, fucking her mistress deeply with her mouth. Wendy put her head back on the pillow and closed her eyes. It was so enjoyable being able to control her pleasure and order her pussy eaten any time she felt like it!

For her part, too, Brenda was thrilled. It was obvious to her that she was still her mistress' personal slave and not just another student in the classroom. She lapped heartily at her mistress' pussy, her tongue coated with her mistress' thick, creamy, delicious juice. Inside the classroom, she had to act just as the other slaves did, those slaves whose mistresses had paid for the privilege of having their slaves at Wendy's feet; but outside, it was she who catered to her mistress' needs, who licked her mistress' pussy! Screw those other ones, she thought, that one who is still a rookie, and especially that one who needs her skin flayed off! Imagine acting that way toward the mistress! Brenda would have liked to whip that insolent bitch herself, for not treating Mistress Wendy with the proper respect. But then she laughed to herself. All those bitches had to put their clothes on and go home by themselves, while she was left behind in her mistress' house to serve and obey the teacher!

Wendy's thoughts were on the classroom as well. Her mind's eye saw Margot bent over the padded horse with her strong wrists and shapely ankles firmly fettered to the unforgiving steel rings. How deliciously creamy her skin looked! And how much better it was when it welled up red and bloody after the taste of the lash! Her clit throbbed, and when Brenda's tongue flicked over it, she shivered with the mad hot rush through her body. Again she could see the whip rise and fall on that vulnerable skin. She could see the thin lines of blood appear, mingled with sweat, along the sides of each hideous welt. And those words, rushing out between sobs: "Please, Mistress, mercy!" The cunt had begged for mercy! And Wendy had simply smiled and brought the lash down again. That face, that face that had been so sullen and so proud, now streaming with tears and swollen from crying, and that look in her eyes that told Wendy that they both knew who had been the victor. The whole scene made Wendy so hot, her skin seemed alive and pulsating. "Lick me, slave!" she ordered, and then stretched out to enjoy the results.

Brenda did as she was told. She ran her finger-nails up and down the insides of Wendy's thighs, then applied her tongue hard against the side of Wendy's clit before moving up and down the length of her pussy in slow, graceful sweeps. She circled Wendy's tight asshole and played over it with the very tip of her tongue, then moved back up to circle the hole to her hot tunnel before moving further up to tongue her clit.

Wendy's hands were on her nipples, which poked through the holes in her leather bra so invitingly. She kneaded and pulled at them, amazed at how hard and long they had become. It was a combination of Brenda's tongue in her cunt and the thought of how she had beaten Margot into a sniveling, pleading slave that made them hard, and she pinched them and dreamed up further punishments.

The hot wave crept up on her so quickly she could hardly believe it. Brenda teased her clit back and forth, then sucked on it, rubbing it with the tip of her tongue as she held it between her lips. Within moments, Wendy felt her cunt grow hot, and then her belly was on fire. The orgasm swept through her as

Brenda kept her mouth firmly on her mistress' pussy, sucking until every last thrill was spent.

"Enough, slave," Wendy said, and Brenda sat back on her heels, waiting for her next command. It came when Wendy rolled over onto her stomach. "Massage my back," she said.

Carefully Brenda unhooked the leather bra, then swiftly got up and rushed to the closet, returning with a bottle of expensive perfumed lotion. She squirted a wide squiggle of it on Wendy's back, then began to rub it in. Wendy relaxed under her hands. Since that first disastrous foot massage that had helped to bring about the whole idea of the slavery school, Wendy had given her slave books on the art of massage. She still wasn't an expert masseuse, but she had learned well enough that her movements on Wendy's back were enjoyable.

When the lotion had been worked in and Wendy felt no more tension in her muscles, she ordered Brenda to run her a hot bath. Again the blonde slave obeyed so quickly that Wendy had to secretly smile. Her fellow dominatrixs weren't the only ones benefitting from the classes!

The bath was ready shortly. As she had been taught, Brenda regulated the temperature with a bath thermometer, then added her mistress' favorite oils to the water before announcing that the tub was ready. To her extreme joy, she was allowed the privilege of helping her mistress out of her leather garter, boots, and stockings.

Wendy let out a little sigh of delight as she lowered herself into the steamy water. This was what being a mistress was all about! Her pussy eaten with a simple command, her back massaged, her bath drawn for her, and all she had to do was lie back and enjoy it.

She relaxed for a long time, until the water finally began to cool down. She was sleepy now, and called for Brenda to bring her a towel. Brenda appeared immediately, with a huge fluffy bath towel. As Brenda wrapped it around her, Wendy was pleased to note that it had been warmed for her. Her little slave, so rough and filled with bad habits, was rapidly turning into a submissive she could be proud to own.

Brenda held a satin robe open for her, then rushed to the kitchen to put on some boiling water for the tea her mistress had ordered. She served it to Wendy, who was lounging on the sofa reading a magazine, and sat quietly at her mistress' feet on the floor while Wendy finished both her reading and her hot drink.

"I'm going to bed now, slave," she said, and Brenda was disappointed, expecting to be told to leave. She perked up immediately when Wendy added, "I have an early appointment and I want my breakfast and coffee brought to me before I leave. You'll have to stay here tonight; I can't be bothered getting up to let you in that early."

Brenda's heart rose, and she whispered, "Thank you, Mistress!" quickly and sincerely. She knew it meant sleeping on the hardwood floor outside of Wendy's door, and she knew just how stiff and uncomfortable she was going to be in the morning. But she didn't care; she was staying with her mistress!

Wendy wasn't giving her slave a bit of thought, however. Her mind was on the morning. She had a couple of things to clear up at the office—might as well go in, she thought, I can leave when I have to—and then she planned on stopped by Julie's boutique and asking about a couple of chastity belts. They looked so interesting, and Wendy was sure she could find a use for them. Then, at noon, she had arranged lunch with Diane and Leah, to discuss how the school was going and how their slaves were behaving. She had also phoned Anne, who wanted to meet her and discuss how Leslie's schooling was progressing, but Wendy had been careful not to make any plans for the afternoon. A lunch with Diane and Leah could lead to just about anything, and Wendy wanted to keep her options open.

She went into the bedroom and slipped between the cool sheets. Brenda tucked in the blankets at the foot of the bed, then turned out the light and closed the door behind her. She went through the house and turned off all the lights, then returned to the door behind which her beloved mistress was sleeping.

She took a moment to finger the heavy leather collar still around her neck, then she kissed the fingers that had touched it, and curled up into a ball on the cold hardwood floor. It was the best bed she could have imagined and within moments she fell into a deep sleep filled with dreams of her tall, dark, leather-clad mistress.

SEVEN

"Chastity belts?" Julie said. "Wendy, you won't believe this. I think you are psychic." She disappeared into the back room.

Wendy spent her time looking over the marvelous collection that hung from the walls of Julie's store. It was erotic just being in here, surrounded by all the tools of her trade in all their diversity. She hoped that Julie would be gone for a while so that she could just stand there and enjoy. She closed her eyes and breathed deeply. The musky smell of leather was sweeter than the most expensive perfume.

She walked over and fingered a lovely thick braided whip. She could feel the muscles in her arm tighten as she imagined a lovely slave, desperately in need of punishment, bent over her padded horse, waiting for the first blow to land. The sound such a whip would make as it whistled through the air! And the snap it would make as it landed on that fair, untouched skin! She could see the welt rise, hear the slave sob. Her pussy was stirring deliciously as she walked over and looked at a mask.

This one was leather, made to cover a slave's head, with small holes so that she would be able to breathe and see. She had one at home that she had yet to use; she was waiting for the day when a slave would do something bad enough to deserve it. She didn't want to use it for some petty indiscretion; this was going to be a special treat, for slave and mistress both. She played with the heavy chrome zipper that closed the hole for the mouth. It was going to be a fantastic day when it finally arrived, she decided.

She spent some time examining several paddles, fashioned from leather and rubber, some with holes in their faces, some with studs. She liked paddles, liked the heavy, direct blows she could give with them. Unlike whips, she could feel the slaps of the paddle right through her arm, and they covered such a wide expanse of a naughty slave's skin. They were a treat to use and she could always reduce a haughty slave to tears with just a few well-placed strikes.

Julie came out of the back room carrying items wrapped in plastic bags. "I got them in just yesterday," she said. "I didn't even have time to unpack them, which is why I don't have any on display yet."

She opened one bag. The belt was an amazing thing, fashioned out of hard, cold chrome and warm, thick leather straps. Like the one Wendy had seen in the film, they were cleverly made so that a slave could wear them at all times, even when using the toilet, but there was no possibility of sexual contact. They closed with a small lock and tiny key, ensuring that only the person who placed it on the slave could remove it again. The slave would be helpless, trapped in the unyielding device until her mistress finally decided it could be removed. Wendy was amazed by their beauty and by the way they were exciting her. She would have complete sexual control over her slaves even when they were miles away from her.

"They are nice, aren't they?" Julie said. "My supplier brought them to my attention and, of course, I just had to order a few. I really think they're going to be hot sellers."

"They are now," Wendy said, fingering the leather straps. "I'll take two of them. That should do me for now. And by the way, what do you have in the way of nipple clamps?"

Julie showed her a selection, and when Wendy was finished, she once again had a large shopping bag filled with several different devices, all intended to keep her students in line.

"Did you give Elizabeth a call?" Julie asked, writing out the bill for Wendy's purchases. "You know, the woman I recommended?"

"That very day," Wendy said. "I went to see her, and you were right. She's exactly what I was looking for. Right now she's working on the items I asked her to make up. They'll be ready for the day that my students graduate."

"Your students are going to be the envy of everyone," Julie said. "Not only will they be perfectly trained, but they'll be wearing those! You're going to have mistresses banging your door down, begging you to take their slaves into your school."

"Well, I'm going to be limiting my classes to five slaves at a time," Wendy said. "That's the number I find best to work with. I do hope I have more to fill up my class when these are through. It really tears me apart! One side of me is looking forward to turning out perfectly trained slaves and being able to say that I taught them how to behave. The other side of me is dreading it, because it's so much fun commanding all five of them at once."

"Well, when your own slave graduates, you have to bring her here and let me have a look," Julie said. "I really want to see how those little goodies look."

"I will," Wendy said, and picked up her well-filled shopping bag. "I promise. I'm looking forward to seeing her with one myself."

Outside, she got into her Lincoln and drove to the restaurant where she was to meet Diane and Leah. Once again she was early, and she sat at a table and ordered a drink while she waited. The waiter brought her a glass, and Wendy was thrilled when she noticed how closely the actions of her students matched his graceful, fluid motions. In such a short time she had brought her charges so much closer to perfection.

Diane appeared shortly afterward, and Leah came in just a few minutes later. They greeted each other with quick kisses, then sat down and ordered cocktails. Leah's eyes were shining with excitement.

"Wendy!" she said. "You are a marvel! How on earth did you do it?"

"Do what?" Wendy asked, puzzled.

"Margot, my bitch!" she said. "I ordered her to come over last night after her class was finished. She came over right away, with no argument at all. She obeyed every command—just a little slowly, but nothing like before—and didn't question anything. I couldn't believe it was the same slave!"

Wendy smiled. "You looked at her back, didn't you?"

Leah closed her eyes. "It was magnificent." She turned to Diane. "You just wouldn't believe it, Diane.

Whip marks like railroad tracks all over her back. They'd been bleeding a bit, it was still on her shirt. They were just gorgeous. I got so excited I made her pleasure me, and she actually did an adequate job."

"With Margot, it's going to be quality of lessons, not so much quantity," Wendy said, basking in the glow of her success. "She's got to be outsmarted. I put her in positions where she expected to be punished, but she got nothing. That confused her. Then when she thought that was going to be my method, I bent her over my horse and beat the shit out of her."

"Brilliant," Diane said as she sipped her drink.

"Oh, the battle's not over yet," Wendy cautioned. "I'm not resting on my laurels, because I know I haven't completely won. She's still got a streak in her that she has to lose before I can even begin to think about graduating her. But I think she knows that ultimately I will win. It's just a question of how long it takes for me to do it."

"Well, your methods are fantastic," Leah raved. "Even her wrists and ankles were raw where you'd chained her up. It was beautiful."

"You are doing a fine job, Wendy," Diane agreed. "I can see the change in Alicia already. And even Anne was going on about how much you've taught her little novice." She smiled. "And you said it wouldn't work! You should have listened to me right from the very beginning. I knew you'd be the best possible person for the job."

Wendy smiled modestly. "Well, I think you're both going to be happy when your slaves graduate," she said. "They'll be trained to the very best of my ability. And they'll have their special graduation honors, which I'm sure you're going to love."

"Still won't give us a hint, will you?" Diane said.

"Not one," Wendy teased. "But believe me,

graduation day is going to be enjoyed by everyone."

The waiter came by and took their orders. Their lunch, when it arrived, was excellent; afterward they sat with cups of hot coffee and small snifters of fine brandy on the side.

It was obvious that Leah's mind was far away, and Diane teased her about her inattention.

"I'm really sorry," she said, flushed with embarrassment. "My mind was elsewhere, I guess."

"Worried about something?" Diane asked.

"Oh, no!" Leah said. "I was thinking about the way Margot looked when she came in last night. You could see submission in her eyes, and her wrists were all chafed and raw. Then I ordered her to strip, and she did it, right away. Then I saw her back—oh, Diane, you wouldn't believe what Wendy did whipping her. I'm getting hot and wet just seeing it all over again."

"I can understand that," Diane said, smiling seductively. "I've been looking at Wendy's beautiful new dress while we've been sitting here. It sure fits nice around those beautiful tits of yours, Wendy. I could lift them out and suck on them right here and now."

Wendy picked up her snifter and drained it. "That's enough out of both of you," she said. "I've been teased enough. Either you're both going to be quiet, or you're going to put your words into actions. In or out?"

"In, of course!" Diane laughed, and she and Leah quickly finished their coffee. Wendy called for the check and set down a credit card while the others gathered their belongings.

Outside, they got into Wendy's Lincoln and she drove them toward Leah's apartment. The sexual tension inside the car was almost strong enough to touch, and Wendy thought her panties would be soaked right through to her skirt before they arrived. Her nipples were hard and pressed against her shirt. She looked over at Diane, who sat in the front seat beside her; she could see that the tall, thin black woman was ever so carefully squirming in her seat, trying to appease her throbbing pussy.

The valet took the car and the doorman opened the doors for them at Leah's building. Once upstairs, Wendy got a surprise when Leah opened the door to her apartment: Ellen, naked except for the lather collar that identified her as Wendy's student, sat on the carpet. A chain snapped to the collar held her securely to the sofa. The little slave put her eyes down respectfully as the three mistresses entered the room.

"Good afternoon, Ellen," Leah said, as she threw her thin coat on the chair.

"Good afternoon, Mistress," Ellen said, then added, "Good afternoon, Mistress Wendy; good afternoon, Mistress Diane."

"Nice touch," Diane complemented Leah.

"She's been there since I ordered her over early this morning," Leah said. "Don't worry, Wendy, she'll be at your next class. I just felt like having her around today." She turned to the small woman shackled to the sofa. "Do you have to use the washroom, slave?" she asked.

"Yes, Mistress," Ellen replied. "Very badly, Mistress."

"Good," Leah said, and led the other two women into the bedroom. "You can wait until I'm ready, and be aware of what will happen if you stain the carpet." She closed the bedroom door, and Ellen hung her head, straining desperately for sounds through the bedroom door, wishing desperately that she could be permitted to serve all three mistresses at once.

Leah, of course, forgot Ellen completely once she closed the door. Her mind was focused entirely on the two beautiful women who were now hugging each other and kissing deeply. "Make room for one more," she laughed, and the three stood together, kissing back and forth, without regard to whose mouth they were kissing so long as they had lips to meet and a tongue to touch with their own.

It was Leah who first unbuttoned her blouse, and then suddenly they were all struck with a desire to undress. Within moments, their horrendously expensive designer clothes were simply piles on the floor, and their beautiful breasts and dark pussies turned them on even more. Now they were massaging nipples and slipping hands between legs, again without regard as to who they were touching so long as their hands were full.

Diane took the initiative, and pulled away toward the bed. "Come here, my honeys," she crooned. "I want to taste pussies, so don't take forever." Wendy and Leah were kissing deeply and holding each other's nipples, squeezing and pulling them gently, but they broke apart and moved toward the gorgeous black body that was now stretched out on the huge bed.

It was Wendy who got on her knees and put her pussy over Diane's probing tongue. Meanwhile, Leah got between her legs and gently pushed her thighs apart. "Such a gorgeous hot pussy!" she crooned, and within moments she was down on the bed, her mouth firmly on Diane's ruby red cunt lips. Diane moaned gently as Leah's hot tongue touched her clit, and she grabbed Wendy's asscheeks and pulled them down so that she could force her own tongue into the burning hot beauty of Wendy's pussy.

Within moments, the three of them were moaning as they licked and sucked each other. Wendy, with Diane's tongue lashing over her clit, reached down and stroked Diane's tits, then tweaked the hard nipples. Diane responded by pushing her tongue into Wendy's hole.

Leah, meanwhile, was taking her own sweet time on Diane's delicious cunt. She licked the smooth, dark thighs, then moved up to tickle the tightly curled hair over Diane's mound. Her fingers lightly touched Diane's pussy lips, followed by the very tip of her tongue. She moved all around the clit carefully, licking with long, slow strokes.

All the time her other hand was in her own cunt, moving over her clit with gently rocking motions that sent sweet shivers throughout her body. Her moans were whispery as she licked Diane's wet cunt and fingered her own juicy lips.

Outside the door, chained to the sofa, Ellen could hear the muffled moans of the three mistresses as they enjoyed each other. She held her breath, listening, imagining the wonderful scene inside. The throbbing heat in her pussy was tempered with the agony of a bladder filled to bursting and begging to be released. She could only sit, not daring to touch herself, and hope that when they were finished she would be ordered to bring them drinks, or help them to dress—anything for these gorgeous women who were her superiors!

Wendy, perched on Diane's tongue, her hands all over her dark magnificent breasts, looked down at Leah. "Oh, hon," she said, "you can't be getting yourself off! This is supposed to be treats for everyone."

Diane stooped for a moment. "All by herself?" she asked. "Oh, that won't do at all. Here, Wendy, move around so that we can all get a turn."

Wendy did, lying on the bed beside Diane, turned so that her hot pussy was close enough for Diane to lick. Leah moved up as well, and the three of them formed a chain. Within seconds they were licking each other again; Wendy's tongue was firmly in Leah's cunt, while Leah was once again eating Diane, and Diane lapped at Wendy.

"Much better," Wendy crooned, and gave her attention over to Leah's dark-haired pussy. Although she dearly loved lying back and ordering a slave to pleasure her, Wendy also loved having her tongue in another mistress' pussy, and she ate Leah with practiced strokes that soon had Leah moaning and bucking her hips.

All three of them were becoming more and more turned on as they licked and were licked in turn. Their moans were louder, and each woman was trying to grind her pussy hard against the tongue that was giving her so much pleasure. The sweet, thick smell of sex hung in the air and filled each woman's nose as the hot nectar filled their mouths. The only thing on Wendy's mind was the hot clit she was licking and the shivery rush that coursed through her body from Diane's tongue.

Not only their tongues were busy, but their hands were everywhere, caressing skin, squeezing asscheeks and pinching nipples. Ellen, listening to their wild moaning through the wall, savored the sounds, shivered at the unique sensation of her hot pussy and her painful bladder, and hooked two fingers through her heavy leather collar, rubbing it as gently and lovingly as if it were a mistress' body.

Diane stopped suddenly and lifted her head from Wendy's cunt. "Let's play switch," she suggested, and the other two stopped and turned around on the bed. The chain was reversed; Diane was now enjoying

Leah, Leah was licking Wendy, and Wendy's tongue found the ruby richness of Diane's hot cunt.

"Oh, right there," Wendy groaned, as Leah's tongue found its mark on Wendy's clit. She then applied herself fully to Diane, running up and down the familiar folds of skin and into the hot depths of her wet treasure.

Leah was enjoying some very intense sensations of her own, and Diane moaned enthusiastically as Leah pressed her cunt hard against the tongue that was doing its magic on her. She stiffened, then gasped and moved her hips frantically. Her tongue never left Wendy's pussy, but she cried out and trembled all over as she came.

"First one out!" Diane laughed, picking up on an old game they had often played. Like a loser in musical chairs, Leah moved aside on the bed while Wendy and Diane maneuvered into a sweet sixty-nine. There was no shame in losing at this game, however, and Leah was quick to join in on the other two, squeezing Wendy's firm, creamy asscheeks and reaching between the two to fondle Diane's delicious tits.

The two dominatrixs ate each other with a delicate fury, their tongues whipping over each other at a speed that seemed almost impossible to achieve. Turned on as they were, they seemed capable of licking each other for hours like that. Both were moaning as they lapped up pussy juice.

Diane softly whimpered as she could feel her pussy tighten and heat up. Wendy kept up the pressure on her hot nub, and very shortly Diane was also crying out and thrashing on the bed as her orgasm swept over her. Her skin was glistening with sweat and she hugged Wendy tightly as she came.

Wendy had been on the bottom, and she stretched out as Diane moved down on the bed. "I won this one!" she laughed, as Diane tried to catch her breath.

"It's not over yet," Diane said, as she and Leah moved on the bed. Leah pushed Wendy onto her side and then, before Wendy even realized what was happening, they were both licking her, Leah from the front and Diane from behind. Wendy gasped. To be licked by one beautiful woman was fantastic, but from both sides by two—heavenly!

Diane and Leah were both getting into their work, and their tongues mingled together over Wendy's pussy. This was a new experience for all three of them and they were enjoying it immensely. Wendy felt like her whole pussy was being covered by their probing tongues, and Leah's hands tweaking her nipples just added to her ecstasy.

"Oh, that's so good," Wendy crooned, and she arched her back and pushed her cunt hard against the two tongues that worked her over so expertly. Her whole body was tingling and she felt almost light-headed from the wild sensations that were rushing from her pussy. If there's a heaven, she thought, it has to be pretty close to this.

Leah was now sucking on her clit, and Diane's long tongue was probing deep inside her hot tunnel. Wendy could feel the hot pressure building up in her belly and she cried, "Harder! Please!" The two women pushed their tongues against her fiery wetness and flashed over her clit.

"Oh, keep that up!" she cried, as Leah's tongue pushed her clit back and forth and Diane probed at her hole. They did, and it wasn't long before the rich sensation swept over Wendy completely. She moaned and gasped, and the two women rode out her orgasm, their tongues flashing over her until she was completely spent.

"So, Wendy," Diane teased, as Wendy stretched out on the bed and enjoyed the afterglow of her orgasm, "is it true that two are better than one?"

"Well, that one really had a lot to recommend it," Wendy smiled. "Come here, both of you." They lay down on each side of her and Wendy kissed each of them as they hugged each other. She loved the taste of her own pussy on their mouths and she pressed her tongue in deeply to enjoy it.

They stayed locked in each other's arms for a long time. Wendy couldn't believe how much the explosive orgasm had relaxed her, and she closed her eyes and just basked in being held tightly by her two gorgeous colleagues. If this was what happened, she thought, she would have to schedule meetings to discuss the students more often.

Eventually they got up, and Leah suggested that they go into the living room for coffee. They left their clothes on the floor and walked out of the bedroom.

Ellen looked up quickly, then dropped her eyes as the three came into the living room. She desperately wanted to stare at the three women, all of them naked, but she had been trained well enough that she focused her attention on the carpet, even when Leah came up behind her and unsnapped the chain that held her to the sofa. "Thank you, Mistress," she said.

"We will have coffee, Ellen," Leah ordered.

"Yes, Mistress," Ellen replied, getting up slowly. "Mistress, may I ask something?"

"Go ahead," Leah said.

"Mistress, please may I have permission to use the washroom?" Ellen's discomfort was very evident.

Leah turned her back and walked toward her favorite chair. "When I say you may," she said. "A little self-control is a very good thing."

"Yes, Mistress," Ellen replied, and went into the

kitchen. There were tears in her eyes and she prayed that her strained muscles would be able to hold out a little longer. It did not cross her mind to disobey the order. She had been told to wait, and wait she would, even if it meant squeezing her thighs together and concentrating everything she had on holding her muscles tight.

She brewed coffee and set out the cream and sugar, then arranged cups on a silver tray. Linen napkins and spoons were placed as Wendy had taught her. She then carried it into the living room and set it on the table before the three mistresses, with as deep a bow as she could manage with the agony of her full bladder.

"Wendy, I swear you've done miracles with this one, too," Leah said, as she took her cup of coffee. "I wasn't being served like this two weeks ago. You really are doing a fantastic job."

"Well, Ellen is doing well in her schooling," Wendy said, and she saw the small woman flush at the compliment. "I told you before, Leah, none of them will leave my school until they're perfect, and until they wear their honors."

"Still won't let it slip, will you?" Diane smiled.

"Not once," Wendy countered. "Just make sure you're there for the graduation ceremony and you'll see what I have up my sleeve. I guarantee you'll love it."

Leah sipped her coffee. "Our clothes must be all wrinkled up by now, lying on the floor," she said. "Ellen, go in and get our clothes and hang them up. Press them if they need it. When you're done you may use the washroom, but if I find you've hurried and done a poor job, then you'll think the punishment that Margot got from Mistress Wendy was a backrub!"

They ignored her as she rushed out of the room. Tears of shame were on Ellen's cheeks as she picked up the expensive clothes off the bedroom floor. Even her trips to the bathroom were regulated by her mistress! But her beloved mistress had ordered it, and Ellen would never consider anything but complete obedience. She got out the iron and carefully pressed out some stubborn wrinkles in the rich fabrics, then hung up everything on the lightly scented hangers from Leah's closet.

She checked each article minutely, making sure that there were no wrinkles left, and finally decided that they were as perfect as when the women had come in. She then rushed into the bathroom and sobbed with relief as she was finally able to empty her bladder.

The three women finished their coffee, and Wendy checked her book for Anne's number. She called and made an appointment to meet this woman whose slave was her student; Diane, who had introduced them, agreed to come along.

"Ellen, our clothes!" Leah called, and instantly Ellen appeared with them. Leah checked them for wrinkles, reminding Ellen of her threat should she find any. The little slave then helped Diane and Wendy to dress, holding their shoes for them and fastening buttons.

Diane and Wendy kissed Leah good-bye and waited while the valet brought the Lincoln to the door. They ignored his stare and got in.

"So what is Anne really like?" Wendy asked, as she drove toward the address she had been given over the phone.

Diane smiled, a little slyly. "I think you'll really like her, once you get to know her," she said. "You'll find she's a lot like us."

Anne's house turned out to be a huge one, with well-tended gardens, just on the outskirts of the city. As Wendy parked the Lincoln in the driveway, she noticed a young woman weeding a flower bed at the side of the house. She wondered if this gardener was a paid employee or, more likely, a slave happy to kneel in the dirt and plant flowers as her mistress had commanded.

The door was opened by Wendy's novice student, Leslie. She was surprised to see her teacher on the doorstep, but quickly composed herself and greeted them properly as she had been taught in school. Once they stepped inside, Leslie took their coats and then led them into the house.

Anne was waiting for them in the living room. Wendy was used to luxury, but even she was amazed at how gorgeous the house was. It was almost completely furnished with antique furniture, the mahogany polished until it shone like glass.

"Please sit down," Anne said, and Wendy and Diane enjoyed the comfort of the overstuffed sofa. "Leslie, some refreshments, please."

"Yes, Mistress," Leslie replied, bowing slightly before she hurried off down the hall.

"Diane, I can only thank you for telling me about Wendy's school," Anne said. "I've always taken on slaves who were set in their ways and it was almost impossible to train them to do things the way I wanted. Now I've not only started off with a novice, but she's being taught exactly the way she should be."

Wendy, meanwhile, was also grateful to Diane, for bringing her to Anne's house. Anne was irresistible. She was tall and slim, and her flawless skin was the same dark, rich tone as Diane's. Her clothes were exquisite, and her skirt was short enough that Wendy could admire her long, beautiful legs and high shoes. She could imagine Anne in tight leather, with a whip in her hands, and the thought was enough to make her pussy start throbbing again.

Leslie returned shortly carrying a silver tray with three wineglasses on it. Wendy sipped at hers and discovered a rich Chardonnay. She sat back on the sofa to enjoy both the wine and the company.

"How is the school working out overall, Wendy?" Anne asked, and Wendy thought she detected a special fire in the deep brown eyes.

"Better than I expected," Wendy replied. "I have to thank Diane as much as you do. After all, it was her idea."

"Any problems with discipline?" Wendy noticed an unmistakable look this time, and she knew instantly that under the sophisticated exterior, there was a cold and cruel mistress who thoroughly enjoyed the sound of a whip on flesh and the cries of a slave begging for mercy.

"Well, there's the usual little problems," Wendy admitted. "Your own slave needed a couple of taps now and again. I do have one that's actually thinking she can get the better of me and I'm having a lot of fun with her."

"Really?" Anne asked. "Actually thinks she's better than the teacher?"

"Well, she did at first," Wendy smiled. "Once I put her over a horse and laid her back open with a cat she got some second thoughts pretty quickly." Anne's eyes opened and Wendy knew she was imagining such a scene. Then she looked over at Diane, and saw her eyes close for a moment, then open wide. Poor Margot's punishment was being savored by both of them!

"That was enough to do it?" Anne asked, taking a drink of her wine.

"Well, my job's not quite done yet," Wendy said. "I have a few more tricks up my sleeve that I know will get this stupid notion out of her head. I'm waiting for the right time to use them. Besides," she added, "it's fun playing with her like this. She hasn't got a clue when the bomb's going to fall."

"And when it does?" Anne prompted, sitting on the very edge of her chair.

"When it does," Wendy promised, "she's going to be the sorriest slave I've ever seen."

"I wish I could be there to see it," Anne said huskily, sitting back and sipping her wine. "It sounds like a good time will be had by all."

"Anne has quite a few slaves here," Diane explained to Wendy.

"They're better than hired help!" Anne laughed. "They look after the yard and do the housework quite well and never ask for a raise. If they don't do everything just as they're supposed to, I have the pleasure of beating them. I had a slave specifically to attend to me, bring me meals, and run my bath, but she moved away and I replaced her with Leslie. I like the little slut, but she didn't know the first thing about serving me properly. That was why I was so glad to hear about your school, Wendy. You saved me the trouble of doing all that training myself, and now I just sit back and enjoy the results."

"I'm sure you will enjoy them," Wendy smiled. "Your slave is coming along very well. I have no doubt that she will graduate with honors soon."

"That reminds me," Anne said. "What is this graduation honor that I've heard so much about? Leslie mentioned it when I grilled her about the school, but she didn't seem to know much."

"No one does," Wendy said, "not even Diane. It's my little surprise for all of you, and I'm sure that you're going to be thrilled with it once your slave achieves it."

"Then she'd better learn her lessons and earn this surprise honor," Anne said. "If it's as interesting as your school, I'm sure I'll love it."

"Wendy's always full of surprises," Diane said. "I'm looking forward to this one too."

They finished their wine, and Wendy commented on how beautifully decorated the living room was.

"I really like antique furniture," Anne explained. "I've been collecting it for a number of years now. Would you like to see the rest of the house?"

"I certainly would," Wendy said, setting down her wineglass and standing up. As Anne stood up, Wendy admired her all over again. She had large, gorgeous breasts that were barely concealed under her low-cut blouse, and Wendy suddenly longed to put her tongue on that chocolately-smooth skin and reach for the nipples that she could glimpse as hard nubs under the silk fabric.

Anne took them on a tour of the house. As Wendy had suspected, the rest of the rooms were decorated in the same rich, luxurious style, the furniture hand-polished to a mirror finish, the rugs thick and comforting. The dining room could easily seat twelve, although Anne admitted that she lived alone, with regular visits from her slaves, who not only kept the house in perfect condition but also attended to their mistress whenever she required.

They went upstairs; Anne's bedroom contained a huge mahogany bed and matching antique furniture. Wendy noticed a leather paddle, its face studded with chrome nubs, on the bedside table. Her pussy grew warm as she looked at it, imagining Anne ordering a slave to lick her, and using the paddle hard on the slave's ass with each lap of the willing tongue.

"You keep your tools handy," she commented, as she walked around the bed and lightly brushed her fingers over the paddle.

"There are items in every room in the house," Anne said, smiling at her. "You just never know when you'll need something." She looked at Wendy, and the gleam in her eyes was obvious. "The slaves worry most when I'm in my library. That's where I keep my belts. I have a lovely one with sharp studs on it, which leaves a most beautiful impression on misbehaved slaves."

They left the bedroom and walked down the long hall, stopping before a door with an old-fashioned keyhole. "This is my special retreat," Anne said, fishing in her pocket for the key.

It turned out to be a special torture room. Smaller than Wendy's, but just as well stocked, it was a glorious tribute to the mistress' art. One wall was covered with steel rings for chaining slaves; another wall was covered with shelves and chests of drawers. The shelves were piled high with all manner of shackles, whips, handcuffs, collars, masks, and other goodies.

Wendy was examining the collection when she heard a sound behind her. She turned and was startled to find that a black shape in the corner was moving. She walked over and found that it was a slave, clad in a head-to-toe black rubber suit, complete with a mask with three holes for the victim's eyes and nose. The eyes that looked out at her contained that intoxicating mixture of fear and delight. Around the rubber-clad throat was a stiff rubber collar, attached to the wall by a short, thick metal chain.

"What happened here?" Wendy asked. The other two turned around; Diane was also startled, then intrigued by the rubber-clad slave who sat, curled into a ball, on the hard floor.

"My kitchen wench," Anne explained. "Just a little while before you came, we had an episode with the dish washing. It seems that one of the crystal wineglasses slipped, or so the story goes, and smashed on the floor. This is her reward for that so-called slip."

"It looks terribly uncomfortable," Wendy observed.

"I would imagine that it is," Anne said. "I have to be carefully, since I've had a few pass out after a while. The rubber really is effective, though. I don't think I've ever had to use it twice for the same indiscretion."

She reached forward and grabbed the rubber mask at the back of the neck, then roughly tore it forward off the woman's face. The slave gasped and shook her head. Her short hair was plastered to her head with sweat, and her skin was mottled with a horrible reddish rash. She dared not speak a word.

"I've only used leather," Wendy said. "Maybe I should invest in one of these suits as well. It looks marvelous." It felt marvelous too, and her pussy was growing hotter and wetter the longer she looked at the slave, who had crumpled into a heap on the floor. Only the short length of chain at her throat kept her from falling over.

"We'll leave her for now," Anne said, as Diane and Wendy followed her out of the room and watched as she locked the door again. Wendy could imagine the slave's horror at once again hearing the key turn in the lock. "That one can take a lot of punishment, and after all, it *was* one of the nicer glasses."

They glanced into the huge bathroom, with its sunken tub, gold fixtures, and marble sinks. They were about to move on when Wendy noticed a glass door inside. "Where does that go to?" she asked.

"I'll show you," Anne said, and led them over to it. It opened into a large room, its walls lined with cedar; in the center was a whirlpool.

"Very nice," Diane said.

"You know, that's something I've often thought about getting in my own house," Wendy said. "I've only used the one at the health club. Are they really all that nice?"

"Well, don't take my word for it," Anne smiled. "We can try it out if you like."

"I didn't bring a bathing suit," Wendy said, not quite sure of her hostess' intentions.

"I was sort of hoping you didn't," Anne said.

Diane smiled at Wendy over Anne's shoulder, commenting, "See, I told you she was just like us."

Wendy was so eager she could hardly believe herself. Anne pushed a small button on the wall by the whirlpool; within moments, Leslie was at the door. "Some towels and refreshments," Anne ordered, and Leslie disappeared to fulfill her mistress' command.

Anne began to undress, and Diane and Wendy unbuttoned their clothes as well. To Wendy's delight, Anne was just as lovely as she had imagined. Her breasts were soft and full and her nipples were huge; Wendy could see herself sucking on them.

Anne reached for Diane, and within moments the two were in each other's arms. Wendy watched them as they kissed slowly, their tongues in each other's mouths, their hands caressing smooth skin and hard nipples. Then Diane broke off the kiss.

"Wendy, come here," she said. "Don't let us have all the fun." Wendy stepped over to them and within seconds she was into her second threesome of the day, her hands reaching for breasts and pussies as the soft dark hands reached for her own.

The three were still kissing when Leslie tiptoed in with their towels and drinks. Setting them quietly beside the whirlpool tub, she wondered whether or not to disturb them and announce that she had brought everything. She decided against it and stepped back out of the room.

She was intrigued by the three dominatrixs, embracing, kissing and fondling each other, and she stopped for a second. Perhaps if she stood just outside the door they wouldn't realize she was there. She thought about it for a moment, and then remembered Lisa, the kitchen slave, who had been punished for dropping a wineglass. Anne had taken Leslie upstairs and shown her the poor slave, who had been clad in the fearsome rubber suit and left chained to the wall. The example was branded on Leslie's mind, and she knew that similar punishments would be selected for her if she were caught spying on the three. She turned and rushed from the bathroom.

"Let's get into the tub," Anne suggested, as she turned a dial on the wall. Instantly the water in the pool swirled into motion as the underwater jets, set into the pool's walls, shot the water out. The steaming, bubbling pool looked inviting, and Wendy stepped in and sat down.

What bliss! The hot water swirled all around her, and a jet right behind her back shot a massaging stream against her spine. She accepted the glass of wine that Anne offered her, taking a sip before putting her head back and closing her eyes. "Definitely," she said. "They can come in tomorrow and measure for one of these. I don't know how I ever got along without one."

"You won't be sorry," Anne promised, handing Diane a glass and then stepping into the bubbling waters herself. "Especially when I show you my little secret."

"What secret is that?" Diane asked, as she sipped at her wine and enjoyed the hot bubbling water.

"Watch," Anne said. She put down her wineglass and sat deep in the tub, facing the side of it. "Now you two do the same thing."

Wendy set down her drink, mystified, and assumed a similar position. As soon as she faced the tub wall she understood. What a secret! The jet that had been forcing hot water on her back was now shooting a deliciously hard stream of water right at her pussy.

Diane had found the right position as well. "Oh, Anne, you sly devil!" she said as the water rushed over her sensitive cunt. "No wonder you spend so much time in this thing!"

"Play with it like it's a vibrator," Anne suggested.

Wendy did. By raising herself off the bottom of the tub, she could control how the torrent of water pressed against her. She sat right up against the jet, letting the water play over the entrance to her hole and push against the tight bud of her ass. Then she moved down, and the cascade sent shivers through her as the water pushed her clit.

Anne turned a chrome knob on the side of the tub, and instantly the bubbles in the water increased so that they gently tickled the women's nipples when they broke against them. Wendy moaned softly at this combination of a gentle caress on her tits and the firm spurt of water on her cunt, and she closed her eyes and enjoyed the hot rushes that went through her whole body. She felt almost weightless in the water; her pussy seemed to float up to meet the spray as it coursed out of the underwater jet.

"Anne, this is positively divine," Wendy said, feeling her body tighten up in response to the spurt of water on her clit.

"Let me make it even better for you then," Anne said. She slipped over beside Wendy and put her hand down between Wendy's legs. Her fingers found Wendy's pussy. Gently she pulled the pussy lips wide open so that Wendy's clit was completely exposed to the jet of water.

"Ooooh!" Wendy moaned as the water rushed directly onto her. With her other hand, Anne found Diane's pussy and held it open as well to the relentless surge.

"That's as good as a tongue on it!" Wendy moaned, moving her hips and working her pussy all around the jet. "Hold it open, Anne! Wider!"

Her fingers were now on her nipples, squeezing and tweaking them. Her whole body was alive to the sensations from her tits and her pussy. She leaned back and met Anne's mouth in a rich, deep kiss. The feeling of Anne's hot tongue against her own only added to her delight. They broke off and Anne turned to kiss Diane the same way, then she returned to Wendy. Back and forth their kisses went as Anne held both their pussies open, and Diane and Wendy played with their nipples in the steamy whirlpool.

Wendy played the jet like a lover, moving closer to it, then back, up and down, experiencing the full range of sensations on her pussy. Anne's hand followed every movement. Wendy's heart was racing and she could feel the buildup all through her body when she finally concentrated the stream right on her rock-hard clit. She gasped as her body, already hot from the steamy water, burned with a special fire all its own.

"Kiss me!" Wendy demanded, and Anne turned to press hard against her lips. Wendy's tongue lashed as the hot rush from her pussy grew in intensity, spreading throughout her belly and up through her whole body. She thrashed against the torrent of water as she came, moaning, her mouth locked on Anne's, her body trembling, her fingers grabbing her rock-hard nipples.

She was just about to relax when Anne, with a smile, pressed her fingers against Wendy's clit, holding her pussy lips open again to the jet. Within seconds, her clit responded and she groaned as her whole pussy throbbed and burned. A second orgasm, even stronger than the first, ripped through her and she cried out.

"Now you can sit back," Anne laughed, and Wendy collapsed against the side of the tub, gasping, while Anne worked her magic on Diane. Within a few moments, Diane was also gasping and crying out as she came.

Not to be outdone, Anne finally concentrated on her own pleasure, and sat as the jets played their familiar dance on her clit. She moaned and trembled as her orgasm rocked her, and finally she too relaxed and sat back with the others.

Once again, they hugged and traded kisses as the swirling hot water bubbled up around them. Wendy enjoyed a drink of her cold wine and sat back to enjoy the massage.

"That's some secret, Anne," she said, as her breathing gradually returned to normal. "That was one of the best ones I've ever had."

"It does create some pretty intense ones," Anne agreed, sipping her drink. "A lot of people say a whirlpool really relaxes you. I don't think they realize just how true that is."

Diane smiled mischievously. "Any more little secrets, Anne?"

"I've got a whole bag of tricks," Anne smiled. She rang the buzzer beside the pool; in a moment, Leslie appeared at the door.

"Slave, tell the kitchen that there will be two guests for dinner," Anne said. "Then come back here and prepare robes and towels for us. We will have cocktails in the living room before dinner."

"Yes, Mistress," Leslie said, and turned to go.

"One more thing, slave!" Anne said.

"Mistress?" Leslie asked.

"When you return," Anne said, "be sure you are naked, with just a collar around your throat." She smiled at Diane and Wendy. "We might like a little after-dinner entertainment."

EIGHT

"Mistress, please!" Alicia begged. "No, Mistress! Please have mercy!"

"I am merciful, worm," Wendy replied. "I could have chained you upside down."

Alicia sobbed. She stood spread-eagled, chained by her wrists and ankles to the X-frame against the wall. Her bare back was exposed to her teacher, who stepped behind her with a varnished wooden paddle in her hand.

The other four students were kneeling on the floor, watching; Margot's eyes were bright with anticipation. Alicia had committed the grievous error of being one minute late for class.

"This will be a lesson to all of you," Wendy said. She walked back and forth between the students on the floor and the black-haired woman chained to the frame, her shoes tapping a warning on the hard wood. Her costume this day was a body-hugging cat-suit made of supple black leather. "Punctuality is one of the most important things a slave must learn. If she is not punctual, she is not obedient. If she is not obedient, then she will never be a perfect slave."

She reached over and ran the wooden paddle down Alicia's spine and into the crack of her delicate ass. Alicia held her breath. When the paddle was removed, she let out a sob.

"Imagine this picture," Wendy said. "Your mistress tells you to meet her outside a restaurant at five o'clock. You don't arrive until a quarter past. Your mistress stands outside for fifteen minutes waiting for you. She looks foolish hanging around outside a restaurant waiting. People wait for her, she doesn't wait for them! Would you put your mistress in such a situation?"

She waited; the slaves were silent. Wendy whacked the paddle against her palm with a loud crack. "Would you?" she demanded.

"No, Mistress!" the class chimed.

"Late is late," Wendy said. "Whether it's one minute or fifteen, it's still disobedience. And it will not be tolerated!"

Thwack! The wooden paddle landed on Alicia's buttocks. She cried out, and the other slaves winced. The long, thin paddle left a stunning welt across both asscheeks. Wendy smiled with satisfaction.

"If your mistress tells you to arrive at five, you arrive at five o'clock," Wendy continued. "You are not early, you are not late. You are precisely punctual."

Thwack! Another welt joined the first on Alicia's creamy asscheeks. Her face was wet with tears and she slumped against the frame, held up by the shackles on her wrists.

"You do not try to outthink your mistress, and you do not try to anticipate her," Wendy continued. "You do exactly what you are told. If she says five o'clock, you are there at exactly five o'clock. If you know she is going to be late, you are there at five o'clock, and you wait for her. There is no other way to behave."

Thwack! Thwack! The blows came quickly together, and Alicia gritted her teeth and squeezed her eyes shut to keep from screaming out. Her ass was burning and blood red.

"That looks so nice," Wendy said, standing back and admiring her handiwork. "I hope this is an effective lesson for all of you. If anyone is late for any other class, she will not graduate. Period." Thwack! "She will not participate in the graduation ceremony, and she will not receive her graduation honor." Thwack! "She will have to repeat her lessons, and be chamed before all of her classmates and her mistress." Wendy held the paddle with both hands now, and delivered a final, terrifyingly hard blow to Alicia's ass. Alicia screamed, then sobbed loudly as her poor bruised ass welled up an angry red in response.

Wendy put the paddle down and went back to the front of the classroom. "Does everyone understand?" she asked.

"Yes, Mistress," the class replied.

"I would suggest that before you leave today, you ensure that your watches are synchronized with the clock here," she said, ignoring Alicia's loud sobs. "It might help you avoid the situation your poor sister has gotten herself into."

Wendy then went on with her regular lesson, teaching the slaves how to make and serve coffee. She noticed that every now and again, Margot stole a quick glance over at Alicia as she hung on the X-frame, her buttocks raw and burning. Wendy couldn't mistake the look in Margot's eyes, and she knew that the tall gorgeous slave longed to be paddled herself.

"Margot," Wendy said, "perhaps you'd like to demonstrate to the rest of the class how to set the tray for coffee."

Margot paused just a moment before she replied, "Yes, Mistress," and Wendy knew that she was eager for her share of punishment. She was definitely jealous that Alicia had received such cruel fare and when she got up, she walked slowly. From the corner of her eye, she watched Wendy to see if her tardiness was having any effect.

If it was, Wendy didn't let it show. She played Margot as she had before, teasing her with a promise of pain and then holding back. She picked up a riding crop and used it to gently tap Margot's hand, explaining that she should pick up the cup by the handle. Margot left her hand on the cup for a moment longer, then realized that there would be no further blows from the crop. Disappointed, she handled the cup properly and put it on the tray.

"The napkin must be folded properly," Wendy said, and the class watched as Margot folded it. The spoon was placed incorrectly, but again to her disappointment, Margot received only a slight tap with the riding crop as a warning.

The rest of the class looked on, wondering why Wendy wasn't beating this slave senseless. A sharp glance from their mistress immediately let them know that such behavior would be tolerated from no one else. Kneeling on her heels, Brenda got the impression that the only person in the room who didn't realize a plan was brewing was Margot herself. The tall slave seemed oblivious to the fact that she was being set up for a terrible and final punishment. Brenda shivered involuntarily as she thought about what was going through her mistress' mind, and she was only grateful that her mistress' wrath would not be aimed at her.

The class watched as Margot poured the coffee into the cup and set it on the tray, then carried it over to Wendy and presented it.

"I trust everyone watched carefully," Wendy said, ignoring Margot who stood before her. Wendy then walked to the front of the class, leaving Margot standing foolishly in the middle of the room with the tray in her hands. Wendy watched from the corner of her eye.

Margot stood for a moment, almost in disbelief. She looked over at Wendy, who was now explaining the finer points of cappuccino to Brenda, Leslie and Ellen. She completely ignored Margot, whose face turned red. For a moment, Wendy thought that she might fling the tray to the floor. Instead, she stood for a long moment, then humbly brought the tray back to the front of the class. Still ignored by her mistress, she returned the tray to the table and then took her place beside the other three.

Another victory! Wendy thought triumphantly. Her plan was working, and the other slaves knew it too. It would only be a matter of time, and a few more events, before Margot would become the magnificent, perfectly trained slave that Wendy knew she could be. Leah was right; the slut was worth the trouble. Besides, Wendy was rather enjoying the cat-and-mouse game she was playing. The best part was that Margot seemed to be completely oblivious to it. The final showdown, Wendy knew, would be terrifying and also immensely satisfying. She was actually looking forward to it, even though an exact plan was still in the future.

Once they had gone over espresso and iced coffee, Wendy walked over to the wall and released the shackles on Alicia's wrists.

The young slave gasped in agony as the feeling came back into her numb hands as a prickly fire. She did not forget her training, however, and managed to sob, "Thank you, Mistress!" as she rubbed her chafed wrists. Her poor ass was still throbbing, colored a rich burgundy from the wooden paddle. Wendy noted that it would probably be a few days before she would be able to sit comfortably.

Wendy opened the cuffs that held her legs apart, then ordered Alicia over with the rest of the class. "Thank you, Mistress," Alicia repeated, as she hurried over to her place in line and knelt on the floor. Wendy noticed that while all the others sat on their heels, Alicia was careful to keep her asscheeks up so that the burnished skin would not be touched.

Wendy also noticed that Margot kept glancing over at Alicia. The fact that Alicia could not put her ass down was not lost on the tall, cold slave. Wendy decided that it was time to put Margot's longing for pain to good use. Although she hadn't planned on using this particular lesson just yet, it seemed like perfect timing. Not only would the other slaves benefit, but she would have an opportunity to win yet another victory over Leah's belligerent slave.

"You may recall," Wendy said, stepping to the front of the class, "that a little while ago, you were taught how to properly present yourselves when your mistress wanted to secure you. I believe we used such items as thumbscrews and handcuffs, did we not?"

"Yes, Mistress," the class chimed, and Wendy noticed that there was no hesitation on Margot's part when she answered.

"It's very important that your education be complete," Wendy continued. "The restraints we learned about the last time were very basic ones. It's time to move on to other things."

Margot's eyes went as bright as Christmas candles. As Wendy left the room, she saw that the tall slave followed her every move. When she returned, carrying a large bag, Margot looked like a child who had been promised candy. Keep falling, little one, Wendy thought. The trap is set and you're walking straight into it.

The first item Wendy pulled out of the bag was a bridle, her most recent acquisition from Julie's store. At the center was a cold steel snaffle bit, the same type that a horse would wear. The difference was that the leather bridle attached to it was shaped to go over a woman's head. There were long reins attached to the bit rings.

"Margot, come up here." Wendy ordered, and she marveled at how quickly Margot got up and rushed to the front of the classroom. Very soon, she thought, you'll be doing that for every command I give.

"The bridle is an important toy for a mistress," Wendy explained, holding it up. Margot's eyes never left it. "It can be used for riding a slave or for guiding her. It also makes a very good gag. Leslie, come up here."

Leslie did; Margot looked confused. Wendy turned to her. "Margot, put the bridle on Leslie," she said. "I think it's fairly obvious how it goes on."

Margot's face fell. She stood for a second, then replied, "Yes, Mistress," and unbuckled the straps to the bridle.

Leslie was totally unaware of Margot's disappointment; she was too excited by the bridle. As a novice, she had never seen such a thing, and she loved it. All the glasses of wine served, all the taps with the riding crop she had endured—now this was a reward! She could not believe how wet the device was making her pussy. She wanted to wear it for Mistress Wendy, and she longed to be buckled into it by her own beloved Mistress Anne.

She opened her mouth wide; Margot roughly shoved the bit in. The steel was cold on Leslie's tongue and it pinched painfully where the rings came out at the sides of her mouth, but, to her delight, she found that she loved it! Margot buckled the straps around her head and the bridle was firmly in place.

"On your knees," Wendy ordered, and Leslie did so eagerly. Wendy picked up a riding crop and grabbed the long reins, standing behind Leslie. She tapped Leslie's ass with the crop as she would a horse in harness. "Forward," she ordered. Leslie moved ahead on her hands and knees.

"You will notice how your mistress will use the bridle to control you," Wendy told the class. They were learning about this new form of control. But their lessons were nothing compared to the revelation that Leslie herself was going through.

She moved forward on her hands and knees in front of Mistress Wendy. As she did, her face flushed and her heart began beating wildly. She was so excited, she thought she might come just from Wendy pulling her head to the side with the bit. The smell of the leather, the steely taste of the bit in her mouth, even the coppery sting of the drop of blood that appeared at the corner of her lip—all excited her even more. So this was what being a slave was all about!

She had been controlled by her mistress through commands and through the occasional punishment she had received. But nothing compared to this! Mistress Wendy had total control over her. She slowed for just a moment, and received a sharp crack of the riding crop across her ass. She moved just slightly in the wrong direction, and had her head pulled back immediately by the reins. She could go nowhere on her own, do nothing that she wanted to do. She was completely in Mistress Wendy's control, at Mistress Wendy's mercy. And she loved it!

Wendy led her back to the front of the class. "Your mistress will undoubtedly come up with many more uses for this kind of device," she said. "A slave can also be ridden, in addition to being driven." To illustrate, she sat on Leslie's naked back.

Leslie gasped with pleasure. The weight on her back, the feel of Wendy's supple leather catsuit on her skin, the way Wendy gathered up the reins and used the ends to whip her across the shoulders—she shuddered and tightened the muscles in her pussy in an effort to stop it from throbbing so much.

Wendy ordered her forward, and Leslie immediately obeyed. It was much more difficult with the extra weight on her back, and at one point a tiny piece of gravel tracked in on Wendy's shoes cut painfully into her knee. She didn't care. She would have carried Wendy on her back out on the street if her teacher had ordered it. The only thing that could have made her happier at this point was if Mistress Anne had been there. But she was confident that her beautiful mistress would use this kind of treatment in the future. She would beg on her belly if necessary, but she would find a way to be controlled!

For her part, Wendy didn't miss any of Leslie's revelation. She had noticed the look in Leslie's eyes, heard her gasp and, most importantly, had seen the glint of moisture around Leslie's exposed pussy.

Wendy herself was so excited she could hardly believe it. She had succeeded! She knew exactly what Leslie was feeling at this point, and she knew why.

Wendy was so excited she could feel the crotch of her leather suit becoming hot and damp. She had taken an untrained, novice slave, who was so green she hardly even knew what slavery was all about, and had cultivated her from a tiny seed into a beautiful blossom.

Wendy rode Leslie around the room, and as ordered, the other slaves watched every move. One of them needed no orders to do so. Margot's mouth was positively watering as she watched. She glanced quickly into the large bag and saw a jumble of leather, chrome rings, and chains. She wondered what device she would be strapped into! Whatever it was, she would love it! She listened carefully as Wendy described how a slave should behave once she was strapped into the bridle. "Quite often you will be given a saddle to wear as well," she said, and both Margot and Leslie closed their eyes, letting a rush of sexual energy pass through them as they imagined the slap of the leather saddle as it was dropped on their backs and the heft of the metal stirrups slapping against their sides. Leslie longed for the feeling of the girth being tightened around her stomach, and she decided that as soon as she saw her Mistress Anne again, she would plead and beg for such treatment.

"Sometimes your mistress will even strap spurs on her boots," Wendy said, and Margot thought she might faint with the joy. Imagine the tips of blunt spurs against her ribs or, even better, a razor-sharp rowel! She could almost hear the jingle of the spurs and the ringing of their chains on the floor, how they would look against the black leather of a riding boot.

Her mind wandered to Mistress Leah, dressed in chaps and pointed-toe boots, spurs on them, fringed leather gloves on her hands, a riding whip between her fingers, carrying the saddle and bridle. How she would obey her commands then! How quickly she would drop to the floor when ordered! How she would carry her mistress around, speed up at the tap of a whip or the touch of a spur, change course when her head was cruelly pulled around by the bit! Her thighs were wet with juice as she imagined the scene, and both she and Leslie were disappointed when horse and rider returned to the front of the class and that portion of the lesson was finished.

Swiftly, Wendy unbuckled the bridle and pulled the bit out from between Leslie's teeth. "Face the class," she ordered, and Leslie did so. "Sit down there," she told Margot, indicating her spot in the lineup. Slowly, Margot left her spot beside the bag of leather devices and reluctantly knelt on the floor.

"Class, I believe that something very important has happened here right now," Wendy told the class. She looked down at Leslie. "Am I correct, slave?"

Leslie smiled, and tears of joy appeared at the corners of her eyes. "Oh, mistress, you know!" she beamed. "I was hoping you would, Mistress!"

Wendy smiled at her. "Perhaps you will tell the class what we're talking about," she said.

Leslie faced her classmates. "Mistress Wendy is correct," she said. "Something did happen just now. When my own mistress enrolled me in this school, I didn't really know a lot about being a slave. I thought it just meant that I would bring my mistress her wine when she asked for it, and rub her back when she ordered it, and carry out her duties. I'm ashamed to admit it," she said, lowering her head a little, "for a while I wasn't really sure if it was what I wanted. It seemed pretty menial to me. I didn't really understand why the other slaves my mistress kept always looked so happy and were so eager to serve my mistress. I knew I had to be missing the point of it all, but I didn't know exactly what the point was."

"Go on," Wendy coaxed. "Tell them what happened."

"It all became clear to me when Mistress Wendy put the bridle on me, and forced me to obey her," Leslie continued. "I'd never been controlled so physically before. I haven't been with my mistress very long and she hasn't had the time to restrain me and force me the way Mistress Wendy just did. Now I know what being a slave is all about. I don't have any will at all of my own. I am my mistress' property, and I must do my mistress' bidding, whether it's a spoken command or a physical force. I am happy to say that I am a slave! And I am proud to be one!"

The other slaves on the floor broke into spontaneous applause. After a moment, they stopped and looked at Wendy, remembering their place. But Wendy smiled and nodded, and the applause continued—with the exception of Margot, who looked sullenly at the woman who had just found her calling.

"I think you should welcome Leslie into the fold," Wendy said, and as Wendy took her place, the others hugged and kissed her, congratulating her on her discovery. Then Leslie turned to her teacher, smiling. "Thank you, Mistress Wendy, thank you!" she cried. "I am forever in your debt, Mistress Wendy!"

"That will be enough," Wendy said, returning instantly to her role as teacher. The classroom instantly became quiet, all eyes on her. Their moment of gaiety, allowed by their teacher, was over. They were once again slaves.

"We will get on with our lesson," Wendy said, picking up her riding crop and using it to point at Brenda. "Up here, right now. And Margot, you come here as well."

Once again Margot was ordered to put a restraint on her fellow slave; this time, it was a cruel leather cone that was slipped over Brenda's head. It was big enough that it completely covered her torso, with only her head sticking out through the hole in the top. A strap was passed between her legs and buckled so that she was unable to move her arms at all. A second strap was tightened around the cone to hold her firmly.

"In this device," Wendy said, "your mistress can control you completely." She used her stiletto-heeled boot to push the kneeling slave over. Brenda could do nothing but fall on her side, unable to put out her hands to break her fall. Margot sucked in her breath quickly as she saw how helpless Brenda was. Why couldn't she be the one in the leather cone!

Wendy demonstrated a few more features of the cone, and showed how a mistress might open the straps to allow a bit of a movement, or tighten them completely so that a slave would not even be able to wiggle her fingers. Then, on Wendy's orders, Margot slowly unbuckled the straps and pulled the cone roughly over Brenda's head. Both of them returned to their places and knelt on the floor.

Wendy decided it was time for Margot to receive a little extra training. Since mild punishment was the reward that Margot so badly craved, Wendy thought that she would prove to the gorgeous slave that here no rewards were given out unless orders were obeyed, and obeyed immediately without question or hesitation. Since she was still hot and wet from riding Leslie around the room, Wendy thought that she might combine a little lesson with a bit of pleasure. She opened the metal snaps that held the crotch of her leather catsuit closed and pulled the flaps back. Her beautiful dark pussy was exposed, shiny with juice and throbbing with excitement.

She walked over to Margot, who knelt on the floor before her, and stood so that her pussy was right over the slave. "Pleasure me," she ordered.

Margot looked at her for a moment, then turned her head and said, "You're not my mistress."

The room was deathly silent, and then a loud collective gasp went up from the other four slaves. None of them could believe it. Their shock immediately turned to dread as they looked at Wendy's face.

Margot, too, was silent as she met Wendy's eyes. Her words, so carelessly thrown out, had doomed her and she knew it. Instantly she was on the floor, crying out, "Mistress, I'm sorry! Please forgive me, Mistress! I didn't know what I was saying! Please, Mistress, mercy!"

Wendy's controlled fury made her voice so cold that Alicia closed her eyes and tried to shrink away. "Too late for that, you stupid, worthless fuck," Wendy told Margot, who was on her belly on the floor. "I don't really think you understand just what kind of a predicament your mouth has gotten you into. I don't want to hear another word out of you until I order you to speak. By that time you will be grateful to obey every command any mistress ever gives you."

She reached down and wrapped her fist around Margot's heavy collar, then dragged her on the floor over to the wall. Although she struggled, Margot was no match for the powerful mistress and she could only sob as her spine bumped on the hard floor.

At the wall, Wendy selected the gruesome

leather mask. Roughly she pulled it down over Margot's face and snapped it closed around her neck. Then once again she pulled the tall slave over the floor to the front of the class. Margot's sobs were muffled by the black leather as Wendy swiftly handcuffed her wrists together behind her back.

"I will never give a command that will not be obeyed!" Wendy hissed. The other four slaves cringed, but Wendy ignored them completely. This was the turning point and they all knew it. Wendy would not stop this lesson now until Margot was completely, entirely broken.

"Stick your tongue out!" Wendy ordered, but Margot was sobbing too hard to obey. Ruthlessly Wendy picked up the riding crop and stuck the handle inside Margot's mouth. She pushed down on her tongue and forced her to stick it out. Then she pulled the zipper across. Margot's tongue stuck out of the side of the leather mouth. She couldn't pull it back in because the edges of the zipper bit into the tender side of her tongue; she had to leave it right where it was, stuck grotesquely out of the corner of the leather opening.

"I gave you an order, and you are going to carry it out!" Wendy said. She dragged Margot upright on her knees by the heavy leather collar. Then, with a hand on either side of the leather-clad head, Wendy pulled Margot against her pussy. Margot's tongue, pulled out and held tight by the mask's zipper, rubbed against her clit.

While the rest of the class watched, horrified and yet fascinated, Wendy used Margot's tongue like a dildo. Margot gasped and cried but was helpless as her tongue was rubbed against Wendy's hot, wet clit.

Wendy pleasured herself with the slave's tongue. To her delight she found it exciting. The domineering slave was now totally under her control! The thought made her pussy burn even more, and she cooled it with the tip of Margot's tongue. She pressed back and forth, pushing against her clit, ignoring Margot's sobs and concentrating on how good her pussy felt to have the unwilling tongue rubbed against it.

Her clit was throbbing with a life of its own. "Suck my pussy, scum!" she whispered, and roughly maneuvered Margot's head. Spreading her legs wide apart, she moved forward until Margot's tongue was on the entrance to her tunnel, then she pushed back so that the tip was pressing her clit. Hot rushes went through her body, born both of sex and dominance. It was the ultimate reward for a mistress—to humiliate completely, to dominate absolutely! It was Wendy's finest hour and she gloried in it.

"Never again will you deny a mistress!" she told Margot, as she pushed and pulled at the masked woman. "Never again will you disobey a command!"

She rubbed hard against her clit. The mask was now soaked with her pussy juice. Margot, in agony, was unable to do anything but submit to her mistress' whims. At one point she fell back on her heels, but Wendy grabbed her by the heavy collar and roughly pulled her back upright so that her tongue would once again reach Wendy's wet cunt.

She pushed Margot away for a moment and cried, "Will you disobey me again?" Unable to answer, Margot shook her head no. Immediately her swollen tongue, cramped in its position and cut by the cruel metal zipper, was pushed back against Wendy's clit. After a moment, she was pushed back again. "Will you obey your commands when they're given?" The leather mask nodded assent, and was again forced back to Wendy's cunt. "Have you learned your lesson?" More nodding, and again the rough push back to the swollen clit.

Wendy was now using Margot's tongue not to punish her, but to please herself. The most delicious sensations were running through her whole body as she rubbed her clit on Margot's tongue. A heady rush went though her and she trembled just a bit. Then her clit exploded and she ground Margot's head against her cunt as she went over the edge and came.

Once the last swell had died down, there was no basking in the afterglow. Immediately she grabbed Margot's collar and dragged her across the floor. The leather mask was shiny with a mixture of saliva, pussy juice and a bit of thin, watery blood from the cut on Margot's tongue. Still unable to pull her tongue back in because of the zipper's teeth, Margot was limp, her tongue sticking out foolishly from the side of the mouth. There was no fight left in her at all.

She was dragged to her feet before she even realized what was going on; then, roughly, Wendy shoved her into the leather sling that hung from the ceiling. Face down in the sling, Margot could only whimper and lie still. Her hands were still cuffed behind her back and she was completely at Wendy's mercy.

Wendy was anything but merciful. "There's something to be said for you, worm," Wendy said scornfully. "At least I'm getting a chance to try out all my new purchases.". She went through the large bag and then walked back to the sling where Margot was held.

The first item was a pair of nipple clamps, but these were especially nasty ones. Attached to each clamp was a small, thin chain, and at the end of the chain was a small lead weight. Reaching under the sling, Wendy pulled Margot's nipples between the straps of the sling. Margot cried out as a clamp was snapped onto each nipple. The weights pulled them down, and the other four slaves winced as they saw Margot's breasts stretched out, the nipples held by the metal clasps.

The second object was even worse. It was a large purple dildo, long and thick, with a huge knobby head. Without any ceremony, Wendy spread Margot's asscheeks and jammed the dildo inside. Margot screamed, muffled by the leather mask.

Then, calmly, Wendy looked over her handiwork, smiled, and returned to the front of the class. The four slaves were as attentive as they could possibly be when, to their shock, Wendy casually went right back to the lesson she had been giving before Margot had given her such trouble. When ordered, Ellen stood at the front of the class, and Wendy demonstrated the proper way to stand when a slave was required to wear a leather device that chained her ankles to a collar around her throat.

All of them ignored the slave in the corner, Wendy because it was part of her plan, and the other students because they dared not turn around and look. It was difficult for them not to. Margot was anything but quiet about her agony. Occasionally she would sob hysterically, and then calm down to a whimper. Once she tried to squirm in the sling, but screamed when the nipple weights and the dildo in her ass moved. Wendy smiled to herself. Everyone has a breaking point, she thought. I finally found this one's.

The lesson went on for half an hour, then Wendy walked to the back of the room where Margot hung helpless. Because the leather mask covered her ears, Margot wasn't aware that Wendy was beside her. Wendy reached under the sling, grabbed the nipple weights, and yanked them off by their chains. Margot almost blacked out, and her muffled scream was so loud that the other slaves were chilled through. Alicia's hands went to her own nipples in sympathy. Wendy laughed. "I knew they must hurt as much coming off as they do on," she told the helpless slave. "Enjoy it while you can, scum." Then she walked back to the front of the room and continued with a new lesson on proper grooming.

Two more hours passed before the evening's class was finally over. Wendy had the four slaves turn around to face the sling. It was a good lesson for them as well, she said to herself. She didn't expect to have any trouble from any of them again.

First, she roughly pulled the dildo out of Margot's ass. Margot was too exhausted to do anything but whimper. "You're lucky I'm feeling very nice tonight," Wendy told her. "Any other time I would have ordered you to clean it off with your tongue."

The handcuffs came off next. Margot's arms were so swollen and stiff she could not move them. Roughly Wendy pushed them down beside her body and, again, Margot could only whimper. When she was shoved out of the sling, her knees gave out and she feel to the floor. Wendy left her there and pulled off the mask.

Margot didn't even look human. Her hair was plastered to her head with sweat and her skin was a horrible mottled red. Her eyes were swollen and red-rimmed from crying. Her face was smeared with tears and mucous and there was blood on her chin from the cut on her tongue. Her lips were swollen and she moved her jaw painfully.

"I hope we've learned something here tonight," Wendy said.

"Yes, Mistress." It was a whisper through painful lips.

"Go clean yourself up," Wendy ordered. "You make me sick looking at you." She held out the horrible leather mask. "Clean this up as well, and hurry back."

"Yes, Mistress," Margot said, and immediately struggled to her feet and took the mask. Walking stiffly, she hurried out the door. They could hear water running down the hall and shortly afterward, Margot hurried back. Her face was washed but still mottled red, her lips and tongue swollen. Immediately she dropped to her knees before Wendy, put her head down, and offered the cleaned leather mask.

"Thank you, slave," Wendy said, taking it and hanging it back up on its peg on the wall.

"May I have permission to speak, Mistress?" Margot asked.

Wendy thrilled to hear her. "Yes, slave," she said.

"Mistress, I'm sorry." It was difficult for her to form the words with her tongue so badly swollen. "I'm sorry I acted the way I did. I have learned my lesson. I am a slave. You are my Mistress. I will not forget that."

Wendy didn't think she'd ever heard sweeter words. "Don't ever forget, slave," she said. "Now, class, you are dismissed."

She watched as they chimed, "Thank you, Mistress," then stood up to leave. It had been a very important night for all of them. Brenda, Alicia, and Ellen had learned an essential lesson about how ruthless their teacher could be if provoked. Leslie had discovered her true identity. And Margot, who had been such a worthless waste of time, had started to blossom into the truly magnificent slave that both

Leah and Wendy had known she had the potential to become. Once again Wendy felt the leather catsuit grow warm and wet between her legs.

"All but you," Wendy indicated to Brenda as the slaves passed out the door in front of her.

"Thank you, Mistress," Brenda replied gratefully, and immediately knelt on the floor, ready for a command. With all her heart, she hoped that the spot before her mistress' door would be hers again this night.

Wendy watched as the slaves dressed, carefully fastening the top buttons of their shirts so that the leather collars would not be visible. She then stood at the top of the stairs as they filed out of the house into the cool, black night.

She turned and walked back to the classroom, taking off the skin-hugging catsuit as she went. Her nipples were hard and she tweaked them with her fingers, then went inside. Brenda, she knew, would be only too eager to take care of the rest.

NINE

As silent as a whisper, the Cadillac limousine turned the corner. Comfortable in the luxurious back seat, Wendy took a sip of the champagne she held, and looked through the darkened windows. The city streets were ablaze with lights and crowded with people rushing off to their evening engagements. Wendy just smiled to herself and sipped again.

She stretched out her legs, clad in black fishnet stockings. Her shoes were impossibly high and the buckles were finished off with tiny silver padlocks. Her suit was made of the same rich, shiny black leather, a sexy one-piece affair that dipped low between her breasts and gave onlookers just a teasing glance at their magnificence. Cut high in the crotch and as tight as a second skin, it showed off her beautiful body to its fullest advantage. It was the first time she had worn it; nothing but a new suit would do for this most special occasion.

She had told the class to think of it as a "school field trip," but, of course, it was much more than that. It was a special one-night event for mistresses and their slaves at a lavish hotel and she was going to use it both as a special lesson and as a coming-out party for her students.

She was finally confident enough in them to make the arrangements. All of them were doing exceptionally in her class, especially Margot. The night spent in the sling had been the turning point. Now it seemed that she couldn't do enough for her teacher, and, at times, the other slaves were jealous of how well she performed.

Just as the limousine pulled up at the front of the hotel, Wendy noticed that her five students were getting out of a taxi parked a respectable distance from the front door. As they noticed the Cadillac, they hurried and waited by the side of the building. It wouldn't have done for them to make a grand entrance in the hotel's driveway, but they also didn't want to be a second late for their mistress' arrival. Wendy looked at her watch and smiled. They were precisely on time.

The car pulled up in front of the hotel, and the driver got out and opened the back door for her. Her costume was covered by a long coat, but the driver was still intrigued by the stiletto-heeled shoes with their silver ornaments. Wendy, of course, ignored him, except to tell him that he was to wait for her no matter how long she was. Likewise, she ignored the doorman who held the door while the regal mistress and her five students walked inside.

At the entrance to the ballroom, Wendy gave them permission to remove their coats. She checked them over. They all had matching outfits, made of red leather straps and chrome rings, which concealed their pussies but fitted around their exposed breasts so that they stood out beautifully. Their everyday leather collars had been replaced by matching red ones, accented with chrome studs and rings for leashes.

Wendy checked her own coat, then ordered them into the position she had taught them earlier. She had arrived late to make an entrance and was determined to do so. Her own slave, Brenda, was behind her. Margot was at the end of the line. Nodding to the woman at the door, Wendy walked into the party.

Everyone nearby stopped and stared as the class and their teacher entered. Wendy never looked better, and the five slaves in their matching outfits made a magnificent entourage. As she had expected, Wendy heard the crowd gasp as the final slaves walked into the room. Margot was gorgeous enough to be on the cover of every fashion magazine in the country. Instead, she was here, clad in a leather suit that showed off her perfect breasts, walking behind a mistress whose every desire was her command.

Through the grapevine, almost every mistress at the party had heard about Wendy and her school, and they flocked to talk to her. The slaves stood as they had been taught while Wendy shook hands, and hugged and kissed and greeted the women who came forward.

When everyone nearby had been greeted, Wendy turned to Brenda. "Drink," she said abruptly, and Brenda rushed to get one for her mistress. She presented it, kneeling, then immediately went back to her place behind her beloved mistress. It was a very special night for her as well. Of the entire class, she was the one chosen to serve her mistress, the one who walked directly behind her. She couldn't have been happier.

"Wendy! Good to see you!" Wendy turned to greet a friend who was looking over the five slaves carefully.

"Susan! I haven't seen you for so long," Wendy said, kissing her. The woman was tall and blonde, clad in a leather bra and garter; the small slave who stood behind her wore nothing but a collar. The leash attached to it was in Susan's hand. The little slave's eyes were glued to her mistress and the devotion in them was beautiful to see.

"So this is your class, is it?" Susan said. "Wendy, it looks like you've been really busy with them. And this one—this isn't the one that Leah was telling me about, is it?"

"Certainly is," Wendy said, indicating the beautiful slave who kept her eyes deferentially on the floor. "Margot, come here." Margot obeyed immediately.

"Oh, it can't be," Susan laughed. "The one Leah told me about wouldn't have obeyed you like that."

"Oh, it is," Wendy said. "This slave and I came to a little understanding not long ago. She was just as bad as Leah described. You'll notice there's been a bit of a change. Slave, tell Mistress Susan what happened."

"Mistress Wendy taught me about being a slave, Mistress," Margot said. "I owe it to her."

Susan looked the tall slave over. "I am so jealous of Leah!" she said. "She really is as beautiful as Leah said she was. Wendy, she's a credit to your school. That reminds me," she added, taking a sip of her drink, "Will you be holding more classes once this one graduates?"

"Definitely," Wendy said. "It's too much fun to quit now!"

"Then I'm getting my order in right now," Susan said. "I have another one at home. I couldn't bring her here tonight—too rough. She really tries hard, but she doesn't quite come up to my standards. I want to put her into your next class.

"I couldn't help overhearing!" another mistress said, leading over a pair of slaves who were hand-cuffed together and held by a leash. "Are you taking on more students, Wendy? Save me two spots. After seeing what you've done with those five, I won't let you leave here until you agree to sign me up in the next class!"

The requests turned into a deluge. Suddenly everyone was around Wendy, examining the slaves that stood so quietly behind her, demanding a spot in her classroom. Wendy could hardly believe it, and she congratulated herself on bringing the students to the party. Within half an hour, she had her next class filled and was taking names for the class following that one. Never had she dreamed that there would be such a demand for her services.

Her slaves, as well, were having a special night of their own. While they were all very careful to keep their pride well hidden, Wendy didn't miss a few of their glances at other slaves, or the looks that her charges got from other women in chains and collars. It was obvious to other slaves that these were different, having been honed to their maximum potential. Their rigorous training was evident in the way they carried themselves and the way they served Wendy instantly whenever she ordered them to do anything. While the other slaves were attentive to their mistresses and obeyed them completely, it was easy to see that a few of them were jealous that they had not been schooled in their tasks as these privileged five had been.

Wendy made her way through the party, greeting

old friends and making introductions with new ones. The entire time, her class's behavior was beyond reproach. A few times Wendy glanced back, just to make sure that the tall slave at the end of the line was in form. She needn't have worried. Margot was indeed the perfect submissive that Leah had known all along she could become. Wendy smiled. When they got back to class, she just might snap on some nipple clamps as a reward. Margot still craved pain and Wendy now used it as an incentive rather than a punishment.

"Wendy!" She turned and saw a tall, beautiful Japanese woman walking toward her. She was dressed in a skin-tight miniskirt and a short motorcycle jacket, hung with chrome rings and bright chains, with nothing under it. A tantalizing glimpse of her breasts was visible, and Wendy noticed a tiny tattoo on the side of one.

"Elizabeth! Good to see you," Wendy said, and even though she didn't know the lovely woman all that well, Elizabeth brushed her cheek with a kiss before stepping forward to glimpse Wendy's leather-clad students.

"So these are the ones, are they?" Elizabeth looked them over carefully. She put one well-manicured hand under Ellen's chin to lift it, and Ellen kept her eyes down properly. "It looks like you've done a good job, Wendy."

"I think I have," Wendy said proudly. "The school worked out even better than I expected."

Elizabeth went down the line of slaves, who kept very still, their eyes on the ground. When she came to Margot, she let out a low whistle. "My heavens, they weren't kidding, were they?" she said. "Wendy, she's magnificent."

"She is now," Wendy said, and she noticed just

the lightest flush on Margot's cheeks. "It took a lot of work, but I think it was worth it."

"I heard all about that, too," Elizabeth said. "Your reputation's perfect just on this one alone." Addressed Margot directly, she said, "You're a very lucky slut. Most mistresses would have just thrown you out. You owe Mistress Wendy a great deal."

"Yes, Mistress," Margot replied, bowing her head just the proper degree. "I'm very grateful to my teacher, Mistress."

Elizabeth walked back up the line. "Well, it should be fun to do this group, Wendy," she said. "Everything that you ordered is finished. Whenever you're ready to have it done, you just give me a call."

"It will be very soon now," Wendy promised. "Their final examinations are this week, and then we'll be ready for graduation."

She and Elizabeth accepted fresh drinks from a slave carrying a tray through the party, and walked over to greet another group of friends. Still in their perfect row, their eyes afire with devotion for their teacher, her slaves followed every step she took.

Alicia looked at the cork carefully, and then inserted the tip of the corkscrew into it. She prayed that it wouldn't crumble and deposit even a single shred of cork into the wine below. As she slid it out of the bottle, she held her breath. A light film of sweat was on her upper lip, and she breathed a quiet sigh of relief when the cork slid out whole.

After wrapping a clean white cloth around the neck of the bottle, she poured a small splash into the glass, and presented it to Wendy. Once her teacher had sampled the wine, she filled the glass to its proper level and once again presented it in the manner she hoped would be most pleasing to her mistress.

Wendy took the wine, sipped it, and then set it down beside her on the table. "You may sit down," she said, and then wrote on the piece of paper attached to her clipboard. Alicia had no way of knowing what was written, but once again she prayed, this time for favorable marks on this, her final exam.

One by one, the students went up to the table and showed their expertise in opening and serving wine. Each time, Wendy offered no comments on their performance, but simply wrote on her clipboard, and by the end of the exercise, all looked exhausted with worry. The notes would decide whether they would pass or fail!

The tests were done randomly to catch them off guard. Sometimes all five would be ordered to perform the same task; sometimes just one or two. They did not know what order the tasks would come in, or even if the subjects they had painstakingly studied would be tested. The only thing they knew for certain was that they had to perform everything flawlessly.

They quickly learned that anything could happen. In the middle of pouring coffee, Leslie was ordered to lick her mistress' shoes. Wendy was glad to notice that there was not even a moment's hesitation when the command was given. Leslie immediately put down the coffeepot and rushed to fall on her belly and apply her tongue to Wendy's shiny patent-leather shoes. When Wendy indicated that the job was done, Leslie begged permission to empty the half-filled cup so as to pour her mistress a fresh, hot one. Wendy nodded, and made a notation on her clipboard.

Every aspect of their submission was tested, as they discovered one day when Wendy walked into the class wearing only stockings, garter, and gloves. She stood before Margot. "Pleasure me," she ordered.

Not too long before, that order had set off a dis-astrous chain of events for the tall, gorgeous slave. This time there was nothing but complete submission. Murmuring, "Yes, Mistress! Thank you, Mistress," the slave applied her tongue to her teacher's delicious dark pussy.

How delicious it was indeed! Margot was pleased to find Wendy's cunt was already wet, and she eager-ly lapped up the juice with her tongue. She had learned an amazingly wide range of techniques in this school and she put several of them to use.

First her tongue circled Wendy's lips, teasing just to the point that Wendy would allow. Then she pushed her tongue out fully and slid it between the tips, pushing against the point of Wendy's clit. Wendy was careful not to let her expression give her away, but inside, she was reveling in the sweet, icy-hot chills that ran from her clit right out to her fingers and toes.

Margot's face was soon wet with Wendy's juice. She licked at the entrance to Wendy's hole and pushed her tongue in as far as she possibly could. As the other students watched, jealous that it was Margot and not them pleasing the teacher, she moved back and forth between the sensitive points of Wendy's pussy. Her tongue flashed quickly over the clit; she took a few slow, full laps, and then went back to the rapid thrusts that she knew her teacher so enjoyed.

The room was silent but for the lapping and sucking. The students, having been given permission to watch, saw Margot arch her back and press her mouth against Wendy's pussy to take the clit between her lips and tickle it with the tip of her tongue.

Without warning, Wendy stepped back, then moved over to Leslie. "Finish the job," she ordered, and watched Margot out of the corner of her eye. Margot's expression did not change even though she was disappointed that she had to stop. A mistress had decided that another slave should take over and because Margot was only a slave herself, she had to accept that without question. She noticed that even in her disappointment, she was thrilled. She had to do exactly what her mistress ordered because she was nothing but a slave!

Leslie took over eagerly, after thanking her mistress for the opportunity. Like Margot she had a wide repertoire of styles, and she started by working her tongue in a circle around Wendy's clit before pressing it back and forth with her lips. Also like Margot she happily lapped up the thick, creamy nectar from her teacher's pussy and longed for more.

The other slaves watched as Leslie pushed her tongue against Wendy's clit and shook her head back and forth to flash over it. Wendy was on fire with the heat from her pussy and the slave's tongue felt so good! The novice had blossomed so beautifully. Wendy closed her eyes for a moment as Leslie's tongue worked like a finger on her cunt. Anne would be so pleased with her slave, now trained to perfection!

Leslie licked and sucked, both from obedience and from love of licking her mistress. Wendy felt her belly tighten. Then within seconds, all in a rush, the orgasm overcame her. She was so strong that no one in the room realized what had happened. But as she stepped back from Leslie without a word, her skin was so sensitive it felt as if it was on fire, and her pussy throbbed and quivered with a mind of its own. It was the ultimate glory of being a mistress, of giving commands that filled her with such delicious feelings.

The examinations went on for a week, until the five slaves were a mass of nerves, fearful that one tiny slip might ruin their chances for graduation. Each movement of Wendy's pen on the clipboard kept them wondering. A smile from her was enough to raise their spirits for the day; the slightest frown could make them worry all night, tossing and turning because they were too upset to sleep.

They needn't have worried. At the end of the week, Wendy stood before the five naked slaves, all of them still in their heavy leather classroom collars.

"Your week of examinations has gone quite well," she informed them. "I believe I have taken you through almost every type of service you will ever be required to perform for a mistress. Many people don't realized it, but the things they consider to be trivial are often the most important, and they are the things that you must always strive to complete with perfection. A slave who can impart pleasure with her tongue is absolutely worthless if she can't properly serve a glass of wine.

"That is why we spent so much time on what may have seemed to you to be minor items, and why you were so well tested in them. Any slave can lick a mistress' boots or kneel before her for punishment. You are beyond that. You can serve your mistresses, accompany them, serve their guests, all because you have received training that ordinary slaves have not."

She allowed herself the faintest smile at them. "I am pleased to inform you," she said, "that all of you have passed with honors."

There was a collective sigh, many smiles, and a chorus of, "Thank you, Mistress! Oh, thank you!" If they had been given permission they would have danced around the room. But Wendy was pleased to see that no matter how excited they were, all of them kept to their positions and did nothing more than they were allowed.

"In four days, there will be a graduation ceremony," Wendy continued. "At that point you will receive your honors. I will not tell you what they will be except to inform you that undoubtedly your mistresses will command you to wear them at all times. They will mark you as graduates of my school, as slaves who were trained as such for the sole purpose of serving their mistresses."

She walked back to the head of the classroom. "You will not wear them with pride, of course, because you are nothing but slaves and you are not permitted to be proud," she continued. "You will wear them as a reminder of what you are, lowly slaves whose only mission in life is obeying commands, no matter which mistress gives them to you."

She looked at them, all kneeling on the hard wooden floor, all of them with their eyes on the floor, all of them thrilled as could be with their accomplishment. "Now go," she said. "In four days I will see you all again, and you will never be quite the same."

TEN

Leah knocked at the door of Wendy's house. In seconds, it was opened by Brenda, who as Wendy's personal slave had been given the privilege of serving guests before and after the graduation ceremonies. Brenda led her to the living room, politely asked if she may serve a drink, and then hurried off to prepare a glass while Leah joined the others.

The mistresses were all present, having sent their slaves over earlier to prepare for the ceremonies. Dressed in their very best, holding glasses of fine champagne between well-manicured fingers, Diane, Anne, and Wendy each kissed Leah and congratulated her on her slave's graduation with honors.

"Where are they, Wendy?" Leah asked. "I only saw your own wench."

"They're getting ready for the ceremony," Wendy explained. "I put them in the spare rooms for now. At the moment it's best. I don't want them getting too excited."

The mistresses chatted among themselves, and Leah took the glass of champagne offered by Brenda. She lifted it in a toast. "To Wendy!" she said. "To the teacher who took our rough, unpolished sluts and turned them into slaves we can be proud to own."

"To Wendy!" the others repeated, and Wendy beamed as the three mistresses sipped their champagne. She was so proud of her school and of the job she had done on the five slaves.

There was a knock at the door and Brenda rushed to open it. Waiting on the step was the beautiful, tall Japanese woman from the party.

"Come in, please, Mistress," Brenda said, and closed the door behind the woman before taking her thin jacket. She also offered to take Elizabeth's bag, but the woman kept it with her.

"Your mistress is expecting me," Elizabeth said, and followed Brenda to the living room. As soon as she saw her guest, Wendy rushed over to greet her. Brenda, meanwhile, disappeared into the kitchen for another drink.

"Elizabeth! So glad to see you," Wendy said, kissing her cheek. "Ladies, I would like you to meet Elizabeth." she made the introductions. "Elizabeth will be a very important part of our ceremony today," she said mysteriously. "I'm sure you will very much appreciate her handiwork."

"Pleased to meet you all," Elizabeth said, and shook hands with the three women before accepting a glass of champagne from Brenda. "I saw your slaves at the party Wendy attended. I'm sure you're all very happy with the job Wendy has done."

Wendy motioned for Brenda to come to her; the blonde slave did so immediately. "Yes, Mistress?"

"Inform the other slaves that we will be calling for them in about an hour," Wendy said. "They should be ready the moment we require them."

"Yes, Mistress," she said, and hurried away down the hall.

The slaves had been sequestered into two spare bedrooms, in pairs so that they could help each other to get ready. Brenda opened the first door, and gave the message to Leslie and Margot, then informed Alicia and Ellen, who were waiting in the second bedroom, sitting on the large bed.

The door closed again behind Brenda, and Alicia looked over at Ellen. Their heavy, every-day classroom collars were gone and both were completely naked. On the dresser sat their combs and brushes, along with the beautiful new velvet collars they would wear for the ceremony. There were also two mortarboards for them to put on their heads in recognition of their graduation.

"Another hour," Alicia lamented. "I can hardly wait! Why do we have to sit here another hour?"

"Hush your mouth!" Ellen said sharply. "Mistress Wendy has ordered us to wait for an hour and we will do it! I would wait ten hours if Mistress Wendy ordered me," she added.

"Well, I would wait ten hours, too," Alicia said. "It's just that I'm so excited about the ceremony, I'm hardly able to sit still. I'm so horny you couldn't possibly imagine it. My poor pussy is just begging for some attention." Slowly, gently, she reached over and stroked Ellen's arm.

"Stop that!" Ellen jerked her arm away as if it had been burned. "We're not allowed to do that! We're slaves!"

"I know that," Alicia said slowly, leaning across

the bed to touch Ellen again. "But I'm such a horny slave. And who would ever know?"

"Mistress Wendy might find out!" Ellen warned.

"How?" Alicia asked. "You heard Brenda. They won't be back for us for another hour. There's a lot you can do in an hour, when no one's going to disturb you."

"Well, it's just not right," Ellen said.

"I know it's not right," Alicia agreed. "But my poor pussy doesn't seem to realize it. Aren't you horny too?"

"Well, yes," Ellen reluctantly admitted. "But I can't do something like that. Mistress Wendy wouldn't allow it."

Alicia put her hand on Ellen's leg and noticed, to her joy, that while Ellen trembled slightly she did not pull away. Encouraged, she caressed Ellen's skin. This time there was no resistance at all, and Alicia knew that she was winning.

"Mistress Wendy will never know," Alicia whispered, and drew herself up so that she was kneeling behind Ellen. Her hot breath tickled the back of Ellen's neck when she pulled the hair away, and she kissed softly, working her way around to Ellen's face.

"It's not right," Ellen said, but her words were stopped by Alicia's kiss. Her pussy was throbbing too much and she could not resist any longer. She met Alicia's mouth, hungry as a starving woman, and they breathed deeply and searched each other's mouths with their probing tongues. Finally meeting the touch she so desperately craved, Alicia's hands moved all over her sister slave.

Both knew it was wrong, but the love-famished slaves had gone too far to stop. They were careful to keep their moans quiet, but Ellen couldn't suppress a gasp when she felt Alicia's hands on her breasts. Then, suddenly, Alicia's tongue was on her nipples.

She turned around on the bed so that they could suck on each other's tits at the same time.

"They're so good," Alicia whispered, and sucked Ellen's nipple in between her lips. Ellen groaned softly and ran her tongue all around Alicia's breast before flicking back and forth over the nipple, which became rock-hard. Alicia's hand moved down slowly and found its spot between Ellen's legs. It was no surprise to her when her fingers came away soaking wet.

"You want this as badly as I do," she said, probing the depths of Ellen's pussy with her fingers.

Ellen did. "I want to taste your pussy!" she whispered. "Please let me lick it. Please lick mine!"

"Move down, then," the young, black-haired slave said. They positioned themselves so that they could suck each other's pussies.

It was the hottest sixty-nine Alicia could remember. She had to bite her tongue to keep from crying out when Ellen's tongue touched her swollen, needful clit. Ellen's clit was just as wanting, and Alicia lost no time in putting her mouth to it and sucking.

They lashed over each other's pussies like crazy women. Each was grinding her cunt into the other's tongue in a hot sexual frenzy, gasping at the sensations that flowed through them as they did.

"Harder!" Alicia gasped, and Ellen pushed her tongue against her partner's clit as firmly as she could. There was no grace, no teasing, just raw movements from women who had been denied them for so long. All of their careful training was forgotten in their quest to simply come. Alicia's mouth was glued to Ellen's clit, and she sucked it as hard as she could. Ellen lapped Alicia's clit with an intensity that surprised her.

Soaked with sweat, the two slaves writhed on the bed, Alicia on top, Ellen below, their fingers pushed

into wet, velvety cunts. "Fuck me with your hand!"
Alicia begged, and Ellen pushed and pulled at
Alicia's hole while her tongue never stopped its
relentless flicking on her clit.

They were so close to coming! Their pussies were
tight, throbbing, filling their whole bodies with hot
waves. Only a few more seconds, Ellen thought, and
my cunt will explode! How good that would feel....

They were so involved that they never heard the
footsteps in the hall, never noticed the door handle
turning, never even realized that Wendy was in the
room until they heard her shriek, *"What the fuck do
you think you're doing?"*

Their blood went cold with the shock. Their sexual appetite was completely forgotten as they
glimpsed their teacher, her face filled with rage,
standing in the doorway. Instantly Ellen was on the
floor, groveling before her mistress.

"Please, Mistress Wendy!" she pleaded. "I didn't
want to do it!" Tears began to stream from her eyes
and she sobbed. "I didn't want to, she forced me!
Please Mistress Wendy, please believe me!"

A savage kick shut her up and sent her sprawling
to the floor. "Not another word out of either of you!"
Wendy hissed.

Alicia was still on the bed. Wendy grabbed a fistful of her long black hair and pulled her onto the
floor. Alicia screamed in fear and pain. With her
other hand, Wendy grabbed Ellen by the hair. She
dragged them from the room, and they struggled to
keep on their feet, sobbing. When they fell, Wendy's
strong arms dragged them up again by their hair.

They found themselves being dragged into the
classroom, which had been festively decorated for
the graduation ceremonies. The three mistresses and
Elizabeth were relaxing in comfortable chairs in the

room, but all rose to their feet when Wendy dragged the two into the room and threw them harshly on the hard floor.

"Wendy! What's wrong?" Diane asked.

"These two," Wendy said, indicating the slaves sobbing at her feet, "were in their room having sex together!"

The mistresses gasped with shock; then, instantly, Diane and Leah looked as furious as Wendy had as they glared at their slaves.

Still trying to escape punishment, Ellen threw herself on the floor before Leah. "Please, Mistress!" she sobbed. "Alicia forced me to do it! Mistress Wendy didn't realize! I didn't—" but she was silenced again, this time by a fierce backhanded blow that knocked her against the wall. Dazed, she stayed on the floor, sobbing, too frightening to look into her mistress' face.

"I might have expected this from Margot," Leah said. "But not from you, Ellen! I thought you would be so good! And now you have shamed me and shamed yourself. This will not be forgotten."

"No, Mistress," Ellen moaned, and tried to blend into the wall. It struck her that her best plan at that moment would simply be to remain silent, and she did.

Alicia, meanwhile, was cowering under Diane's infuriated glare. "I had such hopes for you," Diane said, slowly and coldly. "We will discuss this further when we get home." Alicia curled into a ball and trembled, trying, like Ellen, to just disappear.

"I'm very sorry," Wendy told Leah and Diane, "but you understand that I can't let these two graduate after such an episode."

"I understand, Wendy," Diane said, and Leah nodded. "There's really nothing you could have done to prevent it. Who would have thought they would have done such a thing?"

"Well, they will receive further lessons, and I will test them again," Wendy continued. "There are no failures in this school. They will graduate, and they will earn their honors; it will just take a little more time. Of course, there will be no charge for the necessary extra schooling."

She looked at the two cowering on the floor, their faces bloodlessly white, and she thought of something. "They have shamed themselves tonight," she said. "With your permission, I would like them to receive their first lesson. I would like to teach them what it's like for someone else to really shame them."

"Go ahead, Wendy," Diane said.

Leah added, "She's all yours. Do your worst."

Wendy left the room, and came back a little while later. She stood at the front of the classroom, while Elizabeth and the three mistresses returned to their chairs.

"As you know," she began, "a very embarrassing incident took place here this evening." She indicated the two disgraced slaves, who wisely had not moved from their spots against the wall.

"These two thought they might enjoy a little bit of sex. They knew it was wrong of them to do so, but they went ahead and carried out their plan anyway. It was a very bad judgement call. They will not graduate tonight and will be held back for extra lessons. That first lesson will take place tonight, right here, in front of all of us."

Alicia and Ellen looked at each other, their faces masks of fear. There was also fury in Ellen's eyes, for the slave that had persuaded her into the situation in the first place.

"When I was a child," Wendy continued, "it was

very common to take a disobedient child and give her exactly what it was she craved. If a child thought she might like to smoke, the parents would often give her a big cigar and stand by while they made her smoke the whole thing. It was usually enough to persuade her that perhaps she really didn't want whatever it was she thought she desired."

She turned to the two slaves, who shrank back from her stare. "You two wanted sex," she said. "And so you shall have it."

She went to the doorway and indicated that the slaves standing in the hallway should come in. They did. Brenda, Leslie, and Margot entered the room, and the eyes of the shamed slaves widened with horror. All three of them were wearing huge dildos strapped to them.

"Both of you sank low enough to turn to another slave for your sexual pleasures," Wendy said. "For a mistress to command pleasure from a slave is one thing. But to beg your pleasure from another submissive as you have done—well, I'm only glad that I shall never have to do such a disgraceful thing."

She walked over to Alicia and once again grabbed her by a fistful of her long black hair. Dragging her to the front of the room, she forced the young slave to her hands and knees so that her ass was up in the air. She then motioned for Leslie to come over.

"Now," Wendy said, coldly, "you will beg for this slave's dick in your cunt."

Alicia hesitated, puzzled by the strange command. Her instant reward was a slice from the riding crop that Wendy grabbed. The welt rose on her skin and was joined by a second. The lesson was clear.

"Please," Alicia said woodenly to the slave who stood before her, "put your dick in my cunt."

Furious, Wendy came down twice again, hard, with the riding crop. The eyes of the mistresses in their chairs lit up. "This is not a high school play!" she said. "You are begging for your very life here, slave, even if you're not aware of it! Now beg, and mean it, or you will feel my whip!"

Tears ran down Alicia's face as she cried, "Oh, please, please, slave, I want your dick in my cunt!" She sobbed loudly. "I want it so badly! Please, slave, give me your dick!"

At a command from Wendy, Leslie obeyed. Standing behind Alicia, she pushed the head of the dildo in; all too late, Alicia realized that the dildo was going into her ass. She screamed with pain as Leslie thrust with her hips and stuck the huge dildo inside.

Oblivious to Alicia's cries, Leslie kept up the rhythm that her teacher had ordered her to do. Tears ran down Alicia's face and she cried out each time the dildo was pushed into her ass. Wendy commanded Leslie to continue, and stepped over to where Ellen watched, horrified. Calmly, Wendy grabbed her by the hair and dragged her to the front of the room.

"I recall seeing you at your mistress' house," Wendy told her. "At that time you really didn't like the other slave your mistress had. You thought that you were better than she. For a while it looked as if it might be true. But in one careless move, you proved yourself wrong."

She motioned for Margot to come over. "Now we will see who is the more obedient slave," she said. "You heard what your partner over there had to say in order to receive the fucking she is now getting. I want to hear the same thing from you."

Ellen was already sobbing ad shaking her head, and the words came out broken but loud enough for Wendy's approval. "Please, slave," she cried, "I want your dick in me! Please stick your dick in me, please, slave!"

Margot had to kneel behind the small slave, but the huge dildo finally found its way into Ellen's poor tight ass. The mistresses in their chairs laughed and jeered at the two slaves who first had to beg their torture from another slave and then endure the huge plastic shafts in their assholes.

Wendy indicated that Brenda should come over, and when she did, she was ordered to stand in front of Alicia, who was still being roughly fucked with the dildo by Leslie.

"Now, Wendy said, "you will beg this particular slave to allow you to suck her cock."

Like Ellen, Alicia could hardly speak for crying, and her words were punctuated by each thrust of the cruel dildo. "Please—slave!" she cried. "Let me—suck—your cock!"

"That was hardly erotic," Wendy said sarcastically, and she lifted the riding crop as a warning.

"Please, slave!" Alicia sobbed. "Please, please, let me suck your cock! Let me take it in my mouth, please!" The mistresses jeered at her and laughed as she strained her neck to reach the tip of the dildo.

"Much better," Wendy smiled, and indicated that Brenda should push the head of the cock within her reach. Once Alicia's lips were around the head of it; however, Brenda was ordered to thrust forward, and Alicia gagged as the whole dildo was stuffed into her mouth. She swallowed hard to regain her composure, but Wendy would not allow the dildo out of her mouth again. Choked with tears, she endured the huge dick in her ass while she licked and sucked obediently at the one strapped to Brenda. What a punishment for a few moments of pleasure! She vowed that never again would she do anything to displease any mistress, no matter how sure she might be of concealing it.

"Now the other one," Wendy said, and Brenda went over to Ellen. The poor little slave, rammed from behind so hard by her slavemate, was also forced to take the huge dildo into her mouth and suck on it lovingly. She too made a vow, to always follow her own slave nature and never be led astray by anyone, no matter how tempting the reward. The punishment was just too severe.

"That will be sufficient," Wendy told Ellen after she had sucked the huge cock for several minutes. Brenda stepped back. Wendy also indicated to Margot and Leslie that they could stop their thrusting. Alicia and Ellen sobbed with pain and relief when the huge dildos were finally taken out of them, and Ellen collapsed on the floor.

"Now go take those off, and prepare yourselves as I told you," Wendy said. The three murmured, "Yes, Mistress," and left the room.

Wendy walked over to her supply wall, while the other mistresses congratulated her on how well she had humiliated the two disobedient slaves.

"It's no wonder you run such a wonderful school, Wendy," Leah said. "You're an expert in putting them in their place."

"You certainly are, Wendy," Anne agreed. "That little scene was just delicious. I'm going to remember that one for a long time."

"I'm glad you enjoyed it," Wendy said, as she found two of the regular, heavy leather classroom collars. "But the best is yet to come."

"We've figured that out," Diane laughed. "We tried to coax it out of Elizabeth when you were gone, but she's as tight-lipped as you are! We can hardly wait."

The regular collars were buckled around Ellen's and Alicia's throats, indicating that once again they were only regular students who had not finished the course. More than the ass-fucking, more than the dildo-sucking, the familiar heavy collars around their throats shamed the two. Their classmates were graduating; they had failed and would be left behind. Wendy then led them to the wall and snapped chains on the collars, fastening the other ends to the steel rings in the wall. Separated from the ceremony, they were forced to watch as another reminder of their momentary indiscretion that would cost them so dearly.

The three slaves returned. Cleaned up, their hair combed, they wore the special velvet collars about their throats and carried their mortarboards in their hands. They stood by the doorway, their eyes down deferentially, awaiting further instructions from the mistress who would not be their teacher much longer.

"You may put those on," Wendy said, and the three obediently adjusted the flat boards on their heads. From their spot chained to the wall, Alicia and Ellen watched with envy. Their physical pain was nothing compared to the shame they now felt.

"I will give these in alphabetical order," Wendy said. "Mistress Anne, will you come up here?" Anne did.

Wendy then called Leslie over, who immediately knelt at her mistress' feet, naked but for the mortarboard and the velvet collar.

"Your slave is a credit to our school," Wendy said. "In her lessons, in her examinations, and in every aspect of her training, she has shown herself to be a slave capable of tending to any need you might have. For this reason I would like to present this proof of her graduation." She shook Anne's hand,

and gave her a parchment diploma rolled and tied with a bright red ribbon. Anne thanked her, then returned to her chair, while Leslie walked over and knelt on the floor at the far side of the room.

"Mistress Leah," Wendy called. Leah came up, and at her teacher's orders, Margot came over and knelt respectfully beside her mistress, a position Leah had believed she would never see.

"This night is one of joy and also disappointment for you, I'm sure," Wendy said. "On the one hand, it is truly a shame that your other slave committed her little indiscretion, for she has the potential to become a superb slave. However, I am confident that with a few more lessons, you will be accepting her diploma as well very shortly. I know that tonight's lesson has made quite an impression on her." Ellen hung her head and sobbed quietly for shaming her mistress before the whole school.

"But you have a great joy here as well," Wendy continued. "I know that when you first brought this slave to me, you were doubtful that she would ever work out.

"Not only did she work out, but she has proven herself to one of the best slaves I have seen in a long time. I know that you will have nothing but satisfaction with this one, and I would like to present you with this proof of graduation."

Again a beribboned scroll was handed over, and Leah shook Wendy's hand, then returned to her chair, while Margot walked over and knelt next to Leslie.

At a hand signal, Brenda came over and knelt before her mistress.

"It seems rather strange that I should be handing out one of these to myself," Wendy said. "But if it hadn't been for this particular slave, there might never have been a school.

"This slave came to me with several bad habits, and I was determined that I wasn't going to put up with them. When I discussed it with Mistress Diane, she mentioned that she had noticed slaves with bad habits as well, and we thought that someone should do something about it. Well, one thing led to another, and that someone turned out to be me."

She picked up the diploma and held it between her hands as if it were her riding crop. "This slave was the first student of the school, and I am proud to say that she completed the course perfectly and has also graduated with honors."

She put the diploma in a drawer of the table, and Brenda walked across the room and knelt beside the other two. There was a round of applause from the floor, and the slaves blushed even though they knew it was not for them, but for their mistresses and for their teacher.

For Alicia and Ellen, there was nothing but misery. They looked at the two diplomas left on the table, beautifully tied with ribbon, that should rightfully have been theirs. They would have been up there, accepting their awards with honor, had they not fallen! Their faces were scarlet with shame and they hung their heads.

"Now," Wendy said, "it's my pleasure to unveil the special honors that you have heard so much about. They will be given to all slaves who graduate from this school!" The two chained to the wall received a swift admonishing look from Wendy before she continued, "And only to those who graduate. If you see a slave with one of there, it means that she has been trained in every aspect of the art of service to a mistress. Almost like a guarantee of quality," she added, and the mistresses laughed at her joke.

Elizabeth handed her a small box, and Wendy stepped over to where the three mistresses sat and opened it. They craned their heads for a look.

"Oh, Wendy, it's marvelous!" Diane said.

"Just gorgeous," Anne agreed.

"You're a genius, Wendy," Leah said. "Only you could have thought up something so beautiful and so special."

Nestled in the box was a gold nipple ring. Although it would have been beautiful on its own, this one was decorated with a tiny gold "W" nestled between two tiny diamonds.

"The 'W' indicates that they have graduated from Mistress Wendy's school," Wendy said. "I hope it will be a continuing reminder of the lessons they have learned and the way they must always serve their mistress—perfection only, nothing less."

"I can assure you that Margot will wear it constantly," Leah said. "Ellen, too—when she graduates." Ellen shrank at her mistress' cold words.

The mistresses discovered that an object pushed into the corner with a cloth thrown over it was actually a folding cot. At Wendy's command, Brenda brought it to the front of the class and unfolded it.

"Again, we will go in alphabetical order," Wendy said. "Mistress Anne, your slave may prepare for her graduation honor."

"On the cot," Anne ordered, and Leslie obediently got on it instantly. Although she was not looking forward to the needle itself, she hoped that it wouldn't be long before one of the gold nipple rings was inserted into her flesh.

Elizabeth opened her bag and laid the tools of her art on the table. She sat beside Leslie, stretched out on the cot, and prepared her by rubbing the area carefully with disinfectant. A regular customer would have had the operation explained to her, and would have been guided through it, but Elizabeth showed no more emotion than a veterinarian preparing to give a dog an injection. The woman on the cot was only a slave, simply property to be pierced, and that was what she was there to do.

Wendy took a moment and glanced at the other two slaves waiting their turn on the floor. Brenda's face was filled with anticipation; she wanted desperately to wear her mistress' nipple ring. Margot's eyes were alive with joy and craving. She wanted the nipple ring too, but she was also longing for the long silver needle that would unhesitatingly slide through her flesh.

Elizabeth checked her equipment and then selected a fine, long-handled pair of forceps with tiny loops at the end. She used these to grasp Leslie's nipple and pull it up. Leslie held her breath and watched, fascinated, as Elizabeth worked.

The long, thin needle was lined up against one of the forceps loops holding the nipple in place. Then, in a graceful, fluid motion, Elizabeth pushed it into the nipple to line up with the loop on the other side.

Leslie flinched for just a moment, but Elizabeth held her nipple firmly. The needle passed smoothly through the flesh, and the whole room—mistresses and slaves alike—watched, fascinated, as Elizabeth pulled it through. Once it was done, she pushed up one of the nipple rings and quickly pushed it through the hole and fastened it. The job was done.

Leslie let out her breath and looked down. The ring was firmly in place, her proof to the world that she had passed her examinations with honor. She didn't think she'd ever seen a more beautiful piece of jewelry.

"Just gorgeous," Anne repeated, and the others nodded.

"Wendy, the first thing I'm doing is going out and showing this to everyone," she continued. Leslie got up off the cot, slightly shaky after her experience, but she quickly regained her composure and walked back to take her place beside Brenda and Margot. "I want everyone to be envious of this. They'll be putting their slaves through your school just so they can get one of these."

"Mistress Leah, your slave next," Wendy said. Leah did not have to give any command to Margot; within seconds she was on her feet, eager to lie down and have her soft nipple pierced by the cold steel.

Everything was switched as the new slave stretched out for her ring; Elizabeth put on fresh gloves, and clean forceps and needle were opened. Once again the nipple was sterilized, but there was no holding of breath this time. Elizabeth squeezed the nipple tightly, and Margot smiled as the cold forceps loops held her flesh firmly.

The sharp tip of the needle pricked her nipple, and Margot almost groaned with pleasure. Then came the strong, sure, fluid movement that drove the needle completely through her. She closed her eyes and sighed ever so quietly, savoring the moment. She wished the piercing could take an hour.

It was over very quickly, however, as Elizabeth inserted the special gold ring and fastened it. Margot walked back over to her spot and knelt. Her nipple was burning and she sat contentedly, enjoying every twinge and discomfort. She only hoped that one day her mistress might decide that a chain on it, perhaps with a small weight on the end, would make a nice decoration occasionally. In her mind's eye, she could see the small ring weighted down, pulling her nipple down with it, and she smiled.

It was Brenda's turn next, and there was a special surprise for her. Since she was not only a student but also the mistress' personal slave, her nipple ring had four diamonds surrounding the "W." Her eyes lit up when Wendy pointed out the difference to the other women, and she thanked her mistress for it profusely.

She longed to wear it, and stretched out eagerly on the cot. Once again the gloves were changed and fresh instruments opened, and Brenda felt the cold forceps grasp her nipple and squeeze.

The needle found its mark and slipped through the warm flesh easily. Once the ring was in place, Brenda admired it, the way the rich gold looked against her skin and the sparkle of the tiny diamonds. She got up and went back to the wall to kneel with the other two.

The mistresses admired them as they knelt, all of them with the gold rings in their right nipples.

"They look lovely on their own, but there's so much you can do with them," Wendy said, as Elizabeth packed the piercing equipment back into her bag. "You can hang chains off them or other jewelry. And if your slave gives you any kind of problem, you can always twist it to get your point across. Except," she added, "I don't expect much problem with this group. If they've graduated, then they're superb slaves."

The two misguided slaves still chained to the wall had completely learned their lesson. To miss the diploma was bad enough, but this! Ellen knew that Margot would wear the ring like a badge in front of her. They were both bitterly disappointed that their breasts were not adorned like the others, and both resolved that they would quickly learn their extra lessons and hopefully win back Mistress Wendy's approval and pass their final examinations again. How they wanted to wear the rings!

The graduation ceremony over, the mistresses retired to the living room, where the three slaves, their nipple rings shining, served them champagne and finally brought out the trays of delicious hors d'oeuvres that had been delivered by the caterer earlier in the day. The women discussed the ceremony while the three slaves stayed nearby, ready to refill an empty glass, take a plate, or bring a clean napkin.

Naturally no one discussed Ellen and Alicia, who remained in the classroom with the lights out, chained to the wall, nursing both their sore asses and their badly wounded pride. They also knew that their lesson had just been a taste of things to come, for both of them had yet to go home and face the wrath of their mistresses for what they had done.

They could hear the party faintly in the living room. Out there, mistresses were smiling and congratulating Wendy and mentioning other mistresses who had already expressed interest in enrolling their slaves as students.

"I filled my next class already," Wendy said. "I may have to have two going at the same time to keep up with the demand. I never dreamed this would be so successful."

"I told you it would," Diane said, smiling over the rim of her champagne glass.

"Well, in a way it is comforting to know that there are so many slaves out there filled with bad habits," Wendy said.

"Why is that?" Leah asked, puzzled. "I thought the whole idea behind setting up your school was because you were tired of slaves with bad habits."

"Oh, they're certainly no fun when they're your

own," Wendy laughed. "But when you get the opportunity to beat those bad habits right out of them—now that's more fun than you can imagine."

"Oh, of course!" Anne said. "And back in that classroom you certainly showed us how well you can do that. Wendy, I'm still all hot and bothered over that little episode."

"Then I have just the thing for you," Wendy said. "We can all check out my new toy. The slaves can clean up in here while we're gone."

"A new toy?" Diane asked, as she put down her glass and got up, following Wendy.

"An inspiration from Anne," Wendy said. "I had a whirlpool installed. I thought it might be interesting whenever we wanted some … hmm … good clean fun."

The three mistresses, along with Elizabeth, followed Wendy down the hall to the room where the huge whirlpool was. Ignoring the two slaves who were picking up glasses in the living room, Brenda stood in the hallway.

She knew that very shortly her mistress would call her to bring clean towels and fresh glasses of champagne; her training told her that she would, and her love of her mistress ensured that she would wait patiently until the call came and the order was given.

She touched the gold nipple ring with her finger, and shivered at the burning that went through her from the tender, newly pierced flesh. Then she brought the tip of her finger to her lips and kissed it.

Her mistress would need her, and her mistress would command her. Touching her nipple ring, fingering her velvet collar, Brenda stood in the hallway and waited. The call would come and without fail, at any time, at any place, she would be ready. There simply was no other way.

Order These Selected Blue Moon Titles

My Secret Life $15.95
The Altar of Venus.....................$7.95
Caning Able $7.95
The Blue Moon Erotic Reader IV $15.95
The Best of the Erotic Reader..........$15.95
Confessions D'Amour $14.95
A Maid for All Seasons I, II $15.95
Color of Pain, Shade of Pleasure $14.95
The Governess $7.95
Claire's Uptown Girls $7.95
The Intimate Memoirs of an
Edwardian Dandy I, II, III............. $15.95
Jennifer and Nikki $7.95
Burn $7.95
Don Winslow's Victorian Erotica $14.95
The Garden of Love $14.95
The ABZ of Pain and Pleasure $7.95
"Frank" and I........................$7.95
Hot Sheets $7.95
Tea and Spices $7.95
Naughty Message $7.95
The Sleeping Palace...................$7.95
Venus in Paris $7.95
The Lawyer $7.95
Tropic of Lust $7.95
Folies D'Amour $7.95
The Best of Ironwood $14.95

The Uninhibited $7.95
Disciplining Jane $7.95
66 Chapters About 33 Women $7.95
The Man of Her Dream $7.95
S-M: The Last Taboo..................$14.95
Cybersex $14.95
Depravicus $7.95
Sacred Exchange $14.95
The Rooms..........................$7.95
The Memoirs of Josephine $7.95
The Pearl $14.95
Mistress of Instruction $7.95
Neptune and Surf $7.95
House of Dreams: Aurochs & Angels ...$7.95
Dark Star $7.95
The Intimate Memoir of Dame Jenny Everleigh:
Erotic Adventures $7.95
Shadow Lane VI $7.95
Shadow Lane VII $7.95
Shadow Lane VIII $7.95
Best of Shadow Lane $14.95
The Captive I, II $14.95
The Captive III, IV, V $15.95
The Captive's Journey $7.95
Road Babe $7.95
The Story of O $7.95
The New Story of O $7.95

ORDER FORM
Attach a separate sheet for additional titles.

Title   Quantity   Price

_____ ___ _____

_____ ___ _____

_____ ___ _____

_____ ___ _____

Shipping and Handling (see charges below)   _____

Sales tax (in CA and NY)   _____

Total   _____

Name _____

Address _____

City _____ State _____ Zip _____

Daytime telephone number _____

❏ Check   ❏ Money Order   (US dollars only. No COD orders accepted.)

Credit Card # _____ Exp. Date _____

❏ MC   ❏ VISA   ❏ AMEX

Signature _____

(if paying with a credit card you must sign this form.)

Shipping and Handling charges:*

Domestic: $4 for 1st book, $.75 each additional book. International: $5 for 1st book, $1 each additional book
*rates in effect at time of publication. Subject to Change.

Mail order to Publishers Group West, Attention: Order Dept., 1700 Fourth St., Berkeley, CA 94710, or fax to (510) 528-3444.

PLEASE ALLOW 4-6 WEEKS FOR DELIVERY. ALL ORDERS SHIP VIA 4TH CLASS MAIL.

**Look for Blue Moon Books at your favorite local bookseller
or from your favorite online bookseller.**